HOLLYWOOD HILLS

HOLLYWOOD HILLS

A NOVEL

JOSEPH WAMBAUGH

Little, Brown and Company

New York   Boston   London

Little, Brown and Company
Hachette Book Group
237 Park Avenue, New York, NY 10017
www.hachettebookgroup.com

First Edition: November 2010

Little, Brown and Company is a division of Hachette Book Group, Inc.
The Little, Brown name and logo are trademarks of Hachette Book Group, Inc.

The characters and events in this book are fictitious. Any similarity to real persons, living or dead, is coincidental and not intended by the author.

Library of Congress Cataloging-in-Publication Data
Wambaugh, Joseph.
    Hollywood Hills : a novel / Joseph Wambaugh. — 1st ed.
        p. cm.
    ISBN 978-0-316-12950-3 — ISBN 978-0-316-13058-5 (large print)
    1. Art dealers — Fiction.   2. Art thefts — Fiction.   3. Rich people — California — Los Angeles — Fiction.   4. Police — California — Los Angeles — Fiction.
    5. Hollywood (Los Angeles, Calif.) — Fiction.   I. Title.
    PS3573.A475H6485 2010
    813'.54 — dc22   2010026155

10 9 8 7 6 5 4 3 2 1

RRD-IN

Printed in the United States of America

ACKNOWLEDGMENTS

As ever, special thanks for the terrific anecdotes and great cop talk goes to officers of the Los Angeles Police Department:

Art Arguirre, Randy Barr, Kevan Beard, Charles Bennett, Vicki Bynum, Don Deming (ret.), Nicole Garner, Brett Goodkin, Mike Gray, Richard Guzman, Tracy Hauter, Craig Herron, Jack Herron (ret.), Don Hrycyk, Oscar Ibanez, Bart Landsman (ret.), Al Lopez, Kathy McAnany, Alfred Morales, Dan Myers, Bruce Nelson, Jeff Nolte, Thomas Onyshko, Al Pesanti (ret.), John Robertson (ret.), Sunny Sasajima, Tom Small, Mark Stainbrook, John Thacker, Geraldine Thomson, Obie Vaughn, Jeff Von Lutzow, Carl Worrell

And to officers of the San Diego Police Department:

Brigitta Belz, Meryl Bernstein, Cindy Brady, Sarah Creighton, Jessie Holt, Ron Ladd (ret.), Joe Lehr, Lynda Oberlies, Mo Parga, Jesus Puente, Tony Puente (ret.), Donna Williams

And to officers of the Lompoc Police Department:

Jon Bailey, Jason Flint, Ron Hutchins, Joe Rapozo (jailer/dispatcher)

And to officers of the Chula Vista Police Department:

Greg Puente, Brian Treuel

HOLLYWOOD HILLS

★ ★ ONE ★

THE BUTT-FLOSS BUNNY'S busted, bro," said the alliteration-loving, sunbaked blond surfer. He was already in his black wet suit, lying on the sand and ogling the photo shoot thirty yards farther south on Malibu Beach on a late summer day that made Southern California's kahunas wonder why the rest of the world lived anywhere else.

"They can't jam her, dude," his taller surfing partner said, hair darker blond and also streaked with highlights, as he squirmed into his own black wet suit. "The ordinance says no nude sunbathing. Well, she ain't sunbathing and she's wearing a gold eye patch over her cookie and a pair of Dr. Scholl's corn pads over her nibs. So she ain't technically unclothed, even though she is, like, hormonally speaking, as naked as Minnie the mermaid who haunts my dreams."

"Anyways, everybody can see she ain't no surf bunny," said the shorter surfer. "Even her toenails are way jeweled up and all perfectamundo. So if chocka chicks wanna go denuded for a professional photo op, they deserve a pass."

"She deserves more than that for putting up with that met-sex woffie, for sure," the tall surfer said, referring to the skeletal metrosexual photographer in a tight pink T-shirt, with a fall of *so* casual highlighted hair draped over his non-camera eye. The photographer

3

was yapping orders to his perspiring young male assistant, whose gelled hair was combed up from the sides in a faux-hawk 'do, almost as fast as he clicked photos of the redhead.

"If she gets a ticket, it should be for littering a public beach with those two hodads in rainbow rubber, not for displaying her fabuloso physique," the shorter surfer replied, alluding to the two male models sharing the photo session as mere backdrop.

One was wearing a cherry-red wet suit with a white stripe up one leg, and the other a lemon-yellow wet suit equally offensive to the observing ring of sneering water enforcers who claimed this part of Malibu as kahuna turf. They viewed anyone wearing anything but a solid black or navy wet suit as dissing surfing traditions, and as a legitimate target to be surfboard-speared if they dared enter the water to claim a wave.

That lip-curling judgment was further confirmed by the leashes attached to the spanking-new longboards being used as props, surfboard leashes being almost as objectionable as colored wet suits to the gathering group of surfing purists watching the goings-on. The longboards, one turquoise, one violet, were positioned directly behind the magnificent redhead, who kept changing poses for the photographer. He was carefully framing provocative body shots fore and aft, unfazed by the L.A. Sheriff's Department black-and-white pulling into a parking space reserved for emergency vehicles.

"Here comes five-oh," said the taller surfer to his partner when two uniformed deputies, a young man and an older woman, got out and strode across the sand toward the photo shoot.

"Never a cop when you need one, bro," the shorter surfer noted. "And we don't need one now. The last time the little scallywag jiggled, one of her corn pads popped loose, which was like, too cool for school."

The taller surfer said, "Roger that. She is fully hot. Fully! But personally, right now I'm all dialed in to see what happens if the pair of rainbow donks actually hit the briny on their unwaxed logs.

The surf Nazis're gonna go all return-of-*Jaws* berserk when they smell that kooker blood in the water."

"Get your happy on, bro," his partner said. "Forget the two squids. Just wax up and enjoy the gymnosophical gyrations of that slammin' spanker."

"Gymno . . . ?" said the tall surfer. Then, "Dude, I hate it when you take community college classes and go all vocabu-lyrical instead of speaking everyday American English."

Just then, the woman deputy, a tall Asian veteran with her black hair pulled into a tight bun, moved ahead of her burly young Latino partner to confront the photographer, who reluctantly stopped shooting and faced her.

"This is attracting an unruly crowd," she said. "It's not the time or place for a photo session of this nature on Malibu Beach. I'd like you to shut it down and take it to a more private location."

As the deputy said this, the redhead was performing splits on the yellow surfboard that one of the male models had placed flat on the sand as a pedestal for the next flurry of shots. But when the red-head got into the splits position, she lost control of her eye patch thong, attached by a string that rode over her hips and disappeared between the cheeks of her liquid-tanned buttocks. When the eye patch got crumpled against her upper thigh, her shaved genitalia were exposed, and a cheer went up from the raucous ring of twenty young men, most of them in wet suits, now completely surrounding the photo shoot. A salvo of lascivious commentary followed as the young men pushed in closer.

"See what I mean?" said the woman deputy to the photographer. "Shut this down now."

"About her thong," the photographer said. "If she puts one on that's made of wider material, will we be all right? I mean, I've been told that if there's a patch over her tulips and enough material in back so that her cheeks don't touch each other, it cannot be considered nudity on a public beach."

The giggling redhead, seemingly aroused by the male effluvium enveloping her like funky smoke, said to her boss, "You mean it'll make my costume legal if my cheeks don't touch?"

And with that, she arched her back, grabbed a buttock in each hand, and spread them slightly, all the while winking at her play-surfer colleagues in rainbow suits. Both of them had declined her offer to whiff a few lines just before the photo shoot and now looked unnerved by her coke-driven behavior.

The one in the lemon-yellow wet suit whispered in her ear, "Gloria, this is not risqué, this is fucking risky. We're surrounded by testosterone-crazed animals."

"That's it," said the woman deputy as the model rearranged her thong. "You're in violation of the law. Get off this beach and stand by our car. Do it now."

The photographer sighed in disgust, hands on his narrow hips, and gazed up, muttering to the vast cloudless sky over Malibu and the Pacific Ocean before reluctantly saying, "Okay, kids, it's a fucking wrap."

"I was just getting into it!" the redhead cried, snatching a towel from a folding chair.

And though alcohol consumption was prohibited on the beach, the grungiest of the nonsurfers were hammered, and an open can of beer was thrown from the back of the crowd. It soared over the heads of the nearest surfers, striking the deputy on the back of the head just above her bun of hair, splashing beer onto her tan uniform shirt.

"Owwww!" she yelped, whirling toward the mob.

"I saw which one did it!" her partner said, barging through the ring of wet suits, running down the beach after a fleeing teen in a torn T-shirt. As a result of having sloshed down two 40s of Olde English and a six-pack of Corona, the teen tripped over an obese, snoring tourist in plaid golf pants who was tits up and turning bubblegum-pink under the late afternoon sun.

The deputy wrestled the kid to the sand, looking as though he were trying to decide whether to grab handcuffs or pepper spray, when his partner, blood droplets wetting the collar of her uniform shirt, ran up and pounced on the thrashing teen, who yelled, "I didn't mean to hit nobody! It was just a lucky shot!"

"Unlucky for you, asshole," the Latino deputy said.

"I can hook him up," the woman deputy said to her partner as they grappled, "if you'll get his goddamn arm twisted back."

"I'm suing you!" the kid hollered. Then to the milling crowd of onlookers, "You people are witnessing police brutality! Give me your names and phone numbers!"

After their prisoner was handcuffed, they jerked him upright and started dragging him toward the parking lot.

Then another of the grungier beach creatures, in board shorts, inked-out from his neck to his knees with full-sleeve tatts on both arms and missing an incisor and two bicuspids in his upper grille, yelled, "Let him go. He didn't do nothing. Some nigger threw the beer and ran off."

He drunkenly slouched toward the deputies, full of booze and bravado, holding the neck of an empty beer bottle like a hammer, and the young deputy drew his Taser and pointed it at him. The female deputy immediately talked into her rover and requested backup while she kept her eyes on the increasingly rowdy mob, at the same time trying to decide which of the half dozen nonsurfing sand maggots could be a real threat.

She didn't realize that backup was much closer than she thought, and it arrived in a violent explosion of energy that stunned everybody. The tall blond surfer and his shorter partner issued no warnings, but running full speed, the taller one surged in low like a blitzing linebacker and slammed his shoulder into the lower spine of the guy with the beer bottle, who sailed forward, back bowed, and crashed hard against two surfers, knocking both of them flat on the sand. One of the other sleazed-out beach lice in ragged jeans instantly leaped on the back of the tall surfer as he was getting to his feet and tried for a stranglehold. He let go when the shorter surfer grabbed his hair, jerked his head back, and dug three piston punches into the guy's kidneys, which made him drop to the sand, howling louder than his wounded mate.

"Get him to your car fast!" the tall surfer yelled to the deputies.

He picked up and brandished the beer bottle, standing shoulder to shoulder with his partner, facing off the jeering gaggle of now-hesitant surfers as the deputies continued dragging their hand-cuffed prisoner across the warm white sand of Malibu Beach.

The remainder of the surfing crowd suddenly had to rethink the whole business after seeing the two beach rats get cranked by the dynamic duo, whoever the fuck they were. And besides, since the wicked wahini and her crew were scampering to their SUV, the sexy rush was over. They figured that pretty soon there'd be more cops.

And anyway, they'd been out of the water too long. Adrenaline started gushing and synapses snapping when they saw half a dozen other surfers digging through the breakers. The surf was peaky and a young ripper came slicing in on a hugangus juicy while other surfers hooted him on. So what the fuck were they doing on dry land dicking around with these cops anyway?

Suddenly, as though on command, they all turned and began scrambling toward the ocean like a raft of clumsy sea lions, but once in the water and on their boards, they were transformed, and they darted, sleek as otters, through the shore break, with cops and even the redhead utterly forgotten. Their only concern was not get-ting cut off as they paddled from break to break in waves punchy and raw, waiting for a big one because this . . . *this* was what it was all about. They had discovered the meaning of life.

After the deputies got their handcuffed prisoner strapped into the backseat of the caged patrol unit, the tall surfer and his shorter partner heard the yelp of sirens as the LASD black-and-white units came roaring into the parking lot.

"Dude, I mighta rearranged a few disks in that sand maggot's back," the tall surfer said to his partner. "If we don't wanna get bogged to the ass in paperwork and lawsuits and shit, I think we should, like, fade out at this point and maybe frequent Bolsa Chica Beach for the next few weeks."

"I hear ya, bro," his partner said. "The sleazed-out surf rat that I nailed is gonna be pissing blood for a few days, so I ain't ready to answer a bunch of questions about why we didn't ID ourselves and advise them of their rights and give them all a chance to kick the shit outta the deputies and us, too. I say, let's bounce."

The younger, Latino deputy was busy corralling the photo crew as witnesses for his reports, and the older, female deputy was gingerly touching her injured head and scanning the growing crowd of looky-loos, but she couldn't find the surfing pair who'd decked the beach rats. She definitely needed them for the arrest and crime reports now that they were going to book their prisoner for the felony assault on a peace officer, but the arriving backup units caused a traffic snarl and she had to direct cars out of their way. This allowed the tall blond surfer and his shorter blond partner, hiding behind the throngs of beachgoers, to slip away, collect their boards, and scurry unobserved to their pickup truck in the parking lot.

They drove off and headed for the closest In-N Out Burger, where they each devoured two cheeseburgers and fries. They arrived at work in time for a shower, a shave, an allowable application of hair gel, and a quick change into uniforms, ready for the 5:15 P.M. midwatch roll call.

All of the other police officers at Hollywood Station referred to this team of surfer cops as Flotsam and Jetsam.

★ TWO ★

FOR YEARS, HE had been dubbed "Hollywood Nate" because he carried a Screen Actors Guild card and was forever seeking stardom, as were thousands of Los Angeles bartenders, waiters, parking attendants, receptionists, window washers, dog walkers, and even people with vocations and professions, all nurturing similar hopes and dreams. Hollywood Nate's mother and older sister had always maintained that if only he had not been cast in a couple of TV movies early in his police career—back when Hollywood still made TV movies—the bug might not have bitten him so hard. Lots of cops from Hollywood and other police divisions worked the red carpet events or were hired as off-duty technical advisers on feature movies or TV shows, and that was the end of their emotional involvement with show business. But Nate was different.

Hollywood Nate's handsome hawkish profile and wavy dark hair, now going gray at the temples, along with his penetrating liquid brown eyes and iron-pumping build, had gotten him more than just sleepovers from below-the-line female employees on nearly every production he'd worked. Nate had also been given lots of paying jobs as an on-camera extra, and he'd even gotten those few speaking parts in TV productions, soon gathering enough credits to get a SAG card, which he proudly kept in his badge wallet beneath his police ID card. The "Hollywood" moniker would be his for the rest of his police days because the LAPD had always loved having a "Hollywood Lou" or a "Hollywood Bill" among its ranks, and since the seventeen-year LAPD veteran "Hollywood Nate" even had a SAG card, that made it better.

The thirty-eight-year-old cop had been somewhat indulged for a few months by his fellow coppers on the midwatch during a time of deep sadness for all of them. It came after Nate's partner, Dana Vaughn, had been shot dead by a thief whom Nate then killed with return fire. Nate had grieved intensely for Dana Vaughn and had needed to surmount overwhelming feelings of survivor guilt and deep regret for never having told her certain intimate things, like how she had touched his heart and what she had meant to him in the short time they had worked together as patrol partners. Now he had recurring dreams of telling her those things, and in the dreams, she never answered him but would smile and chuckle in that special way of hers that always made him think of wind chimes.

It was during that mournful and restless period that Hollywood Nate had been offered an audition that came from working the red carpet on a warm summer night at the Kodak Theatre on Hollywood Boulevard. There were thirty cops there that night, all happily drawing overtime pay. Rudy Ressler, a second-rate director and producer who once had coproduced an Oscar-nominated movie, attended that affair with an up-and-coming pair of young beauties known only to people who spent their lives watching nighttime TV designed for Gen X-ers. Ressler's personal escort that evening was a UCLA theater major skinnier than Victoria Beckham and younger than his own daughter. When the event ended and the Kodak was disgorging the multitudes, Nate had occasion to apply some muscle to the stampeding paparazzi that had crowded in on the foursome as they walked to the director's rented limo.

It wasn't that the aggressive paparazzi were interested in shooting photos of the director, but Brangelina, moving fast, had emerged from the crowd right behind the Ressler foursome. Things got very unruly very quickly, and the frightened UCLA coed began whimpering when an obese paparazzo with a camera hanging from a strap around his neck and a Styrofoam cup in his hand backed against her, mashing her into Ressler's hired limousine.

Nate had stepped in then with pap pressing on all sides and hooked a low elbow very hard into the belly of the fat guy, causing him to let out a *woooo*, double over, and spew Jamba Juice all over other paparazzi. Nobody in that crush of nighttime fans, including other pap, had seen the surreptitious elbow chop, and even the groaning paparazzo didn't know what had hit him. But Rudy Ressler saw it, as did one of the security aides of the LAPD chief of police. The aide waited by the chief's ominous-looking SUV with its dark-tinted windows.

When the Ressler party got into their limo, the director turned and said to Nate, "Thank you for helping us, Officer. If there's anything I can ever do for you..." And he handed Nate a business card.

Hollywood Nate said, "You may regret that rash remark, sir." And he took the badge wallet from his pocket to show Rudy Ressler his SAG card, and said, "At the station they call me Hollywood Nate because of this."

"I'll be damned," the director said. He laughed out loud, turning to his companions and saying, "This officer is a SAG member. Only in Hollywood!"

"Have a good evening, sir," Nate said with a hopeful smile.

"Call me when you get a chance, Officer. I'm serious," the director replied, looking at Hollywood Nate appraisingly this time.

Before the limousine pulled away, Nate heard Rudy Ressler say to the driver, "We're dropping Ms. Franchon at her sorority house and then you can take the rest of us to Mrs. Brueger's home in the Hollywood Hills. Do you remember where it is from last time?"

"Yes, sir, Mr. Ressler," the driver said.

The limousine drove off, leaving the other cars blowing horns and flashing their high beams at the inevitable traffic jam, and the paparazzi still snapping pictures. Hollywood Nate decided to take a better look at the chief's SUV and at the LAPD security aide standing beside it, who looked familiar. When he got closer, he recognized the wide-bodied, balding, mustachioed Latino cop in the dark three-piece business suit. It was Lorenzo "Snuffy" Salcedo, an old friend and classmate who had served with Nate in 77th Street Division when they were boots fresh out of the police academy, as well as later, when Snuffy had worked patrol at Hollywood Station for two years.

Snuffy had served nine years in the navy before becoming a cop and was ten years older than Nate. But he wasn't showing the effects of his forty-eight years. He had competed in power lifting in the Police Olympics and had a chest like a buffalo. Snuffy had acquired his nickname from his habit of tucking a pinch of Red Man chewing tobacco inside his lower lip and spitting tobacco juice into a Styrofoam cup. Some cops mistakenly thought that he was dipping snuff. Nate remembered that their training officers at 77th had threatened to make Snuffy drink the contents of his cup if they caught him, but at Hollywood Station, once he was off probation, he'd kept his lip loaded most of the time. He was always the division champ when it came to chatter and gossip, in a profession where gossip was coin of the realm.

Back then, their late sergeant, whom they'd called the Oracle, was often tasked by the watch commander to deal with Snuffy's droopy 'stash. But the Oracle would simply say to him, "Zapata is dead, Snuffy. Trim the tips off that feather duster next time you're clipping your nails."

Snuffy seldom did and the Oracle didn't really care. Then Nate thought of how much he missed the Oracle, who'd died of a massive heart attack on the Walk of Fame in front of Hollywood Station. The stars in marble and brass on that part of Wilcox Avenue were not there to commemorate movie stars but as memorials to the Hollywood Division coppers who had been killed in the line of duty.

Nate's reminiscing stopped when Snuffy Salcedo left the LAPD chief's SUV at the curb and jogged toward the red carpet parking area, arms outstretched. Under the mustache his toothy grin was glinting arctic white from all the lights on Hollywood Boulevard.

Nate said, "Snuffy Salcedo, I presume?"

Snuffy said, "Hollywood Nate Weiss! Where the fuck you been and how are you? *Abrazos, 'mano!*"

He gave Nate a rib-crushing embrace, and up close Nate saw that bulge under Snuffy's lower lip.

Snuffy said, "I saw you spear that chubby pap, you rascal. Glad to see you still got the chops you learned back in the day with me." Then he did an Elvis impression and sang, "Down in the ghet-to!"

Nate said, "I see you still got that revolting wad of manure inside your lip. Does the big boss let you drive with a cup of tobacco juice in the cup holder?"

"It disappears when Mister shows up," Snuffy said.

Many of the veteran LAPD cops had never accepted this chief of police, the second one to be imported from the East Coast since the Rodney King riots. This chief had come seven years ago, and when the coppers referred to him privately, it was not with "Chief" before his surname but with "Mister," the ultimate invective, meaning that he was just another imported civilian politician and could never be a real LAPD copper.

"So how do you like driving for this one?" Nate asked.

"Have you ever had a colonoscopy?" Snuffy said.

"Why've you stayed in Metro all these years, Snuffy?" Nate asked. "Aren't you sick of it yet?"

"The overtime money driving for this one has been keeping me where I am," Snuffy said. "Mister is the first LAPD chief to need security aides everywhere but in his bathtub. You'd think a guy that's been married as many times as he has woulda picked a babe that cooks this time around, but there's no food in their house and they go out every night to eat. On his weekend days off, he even needs us with him. We're a full-service detail with this one. There's five of us security aides and we're all getting richer than Bruce Springsteen and the E Street Band."

"I had a feeling his Irish twinkle might mask a gloomy Celtic interior," said Nate.

Snuffy Salcedo said, "In addition to an ego that makes him think the MetLife blimp should have his face on it instead of Snoopy's, I think Mister's got something like OCD. He has a thing about stoplights and he counts them. I might get yelled at if I take a route with too many of them. And he's obsessed with wiping his face with Kleenex. If there was even half the oil coming out of Mister's pores that he thinks there is, we wouldn't need any more imports from Saudi Arabia. Since I don't have a degree in abnormal psychology, I just concentrate on the overtime money when he's like that. By the way, did you get married again?"

"Not a chance," Nate said. "And no kids."

"You were so lucky her casabas never got to producing dairy products. Me, I'll be paying for our kids till Jesus returns."

"Even without kids I know what divorce costs," Nate said, nodding. "Twelve months of eating Hungry-Man nukeable food until I could afford an occasional lamb chop."

"I used to call mine RK," Snuffy said, "because during sex she was about as active as roadkill. Yet she talked me into paying for a boob job for both her and her sister, and she went wild after that. Four new mammaries and I had no access to any of them. I was the boob."

Nate said, "Me, I'm not gonna marry another Jewish woman

no matter what my mother wants. My ex turned scary mean the minute her blood sugar rose with morning orange juice. It took a while after the divorce till she stopped breaking eggs on my car."

"Guys like you and me should mix 'n' match," Snuffy said. "And always marry outside our tribes."

"I'd sure like to see you transfer back to Watch Five at Hollywood Station," Nate said sincerely. "It'd be like old times. We could partner up. I'd even let you keep your spittoon in the cup holder and try not to puke all over myself when you used it."

"What!" Snuffy said incredulously. "You haven't heard?"

"Heard?"

"I've finally had enough of this driving gig. I'm transferring back to Hollywood in time for the next deployment period. I thought there'd be notices on the bulletin boards by now, and pictures of me in the roll call room right next to the Oracle's."

"Fantastic!" Nate said. "Wait'll I spread the word. Snuffy Salcedo's turning in his chauffeur's cap and coming home to roost."

"Long overdue," Snuffy said. "I've driven for three chiefs. The only one I liked was the first one that City Hall imported from the East Coast. I wish the mayor hadn't gotten rid of him when he found out the dude wouldn't trade his Las Vegas jaunts for eternal youth. I grew fond of him. Basically he was just a harmless old porch Negro."

Nate was about to ask Snuffy if he'd heard from any of their classmates lately, when the burly Latino cop stopped chattering long enough to turn toward the herd of people emerging onto the red carpet, and said, "Holy shit! He's already out!"

Hollywood Nate turned and saw the chief of police, his wife, and another elegantly dressed couple standing on the curb in front of the Kodak Theatre, and the chief wasn't twinkling. All of the bonhomie that he'd shown to the paparazzi was gone.

Snuffy Salcedo scampered to the SUV, jumped in, and zoomed

to the pickup area, where he leaped out and ran around to open the rear door for Mrs. Chief. Nate saw the chief jawing at Snuffy and neither looked very happy.

On the next transfer list, P2 Snuffy Salcedo did return to Hollywood Station, where he could no longer get as rich as the E Street Band.

★ THREE ★

Leona Brueger had always referred to her home located high in the Hollywood Hills, almost to Woodrow Wilson Drive, as a mini-estate. Three residential lots had been bought and cleared of aging houses and tied together to make it the largest parcel in that part of the Hills, with a splendid view almost to the ocean. Her late husband, Sammy Brueger, had made most of his early money by buying into three wholesale meat distributors at a time when people said you couldn't make real money in that business.

Sammy Brueger proved them wrong and did it with a slogan that his first wife dreamed up: "You can't beat Sammy's meat." And then, early in the presidency of Richard Nixon, Sammy started following the New York Stock Exchange and became interested in a stock for no other reason than that its NASDAQ symbol, POND, was the maiden name of his wife. He was a born gambler, and when he learned that POND stood for Ponderosa Steak House in Dayton, Ohio, he thought that Lady Luck was calling him. The stock symbol bore his wife's name, and the product was something that he bought and sold every day—meat! So Sammy plowed everything he had into that stock and it zoomed upward an astounding 10,000 percent and he became very rich. He divorced the wife named Pond and married a failed actress whose surname never helped him, and neither did she. Because of the prenuptial, the second one wasn't so expensive to unload.

His third and final wife, Leona, thirty-two years younger than Sammy, told other trophy wives at her Pilates class that the meat slogan had certainly been true in the last ten years of the old man's life, and she thanked God for it. She still shuddered when she thought of him in his old age crawling over her at night like a centipede.

Leona Brueger was still a size two, and was trainer-firm, with expressive brown eyes, delicate facial bones, and a Mediterranean skin tone that bore no evidence of the considerable work she had bought in order to stay looking so good at the age of sixty. Her last birthday had been devastating, no matter how much she had tried to prepare for it psychologically. Leona Brueger's natural hair color had been milk chocolate brown at one time, and she hated to think what color it would be now if she ever stopped the monthly color and highlights.

On a summer afternoon while sitting by the pool skimming *Elle* and *Vogue* and reading *Wine Spectator* cover to cover, she happened to see a mention of a Beverly Hills art gallery where Sammy had bought three very expensive pieces of Impressionist art, two by French artists and one by a Swede. Leona couldn't remember much about the artists and hardly noticed the paintings back when Sammy was alive, opining to girlfriends that trees and flowers should look as though they were living things distinct from the land that nourished them. And the nearly nude body of a peasant woman feeding a kitten in one of the paintings depressed her. She feared that she would look like that when, despite Pilates and a weekly game of tennis on the Brueger tennis court with her Pilates partners, her ass finally gave up and collapsed from boredom and fatigue.

But the article she was reading made her wonder why it had taken her so long to have the paintings appraised after Sammy died, trusting him that they were of "museum quality." He'd always said that the very pricey pieces should hang exactly where he'd placed them: in their great room, the dining room, and along the main corridor of "Casa Brueger."

She strolled inside from the pool, sipping an iced tea, wishing it were late enough for a nice glass of cool Fumé Blanc, and studied the three oldest pieces to try to see why anyone would think they were so valuable. She stood before the largest, the one of a woman squatting beside what looked to Leona like a pond or a lagoon. She decided to call the Wickland Gallery on Wilshire Boulevard to ask Nigel Wickland when he'd be coming back for the appraisal. The art dealer had stopped by a week earlier at her request and taken a preliminary look, but he'd said he needed to "research the provenance" before he could give her accurate information. It was hard for her to think about appraisals or any other business when she was about to embark on one of the great adventures of her life.

She'd leased a villa in Tuscany for three months and was going there with Rudy Ressler, the movie director/producer she'd been dating off and on for more than a year. Rudy was amusing and had lots of show-business anecdotes that he could relate by mimicking the voices of the players involved. He wasn't as young as she would like if she decided to marry again, but he was controllable and an amazingly unselfish lover, even though that didn't matter as much as it used to. And he still knew enough people very active in show business to ensure that they'd always have interesting dining partners. His one Oscar-nominated film had kept him on the A-list for the past twenty years. If they ever married, she figured she'd end up supporting him, but what the hell, she was bucks-up rich. Sammy had left her more than she could ever spend in her lifetime. And that reminded her again that she was now sixty years old. How much of a life *did* she have left?

For a moment Leona couldn't remember what she was about to do, but then she remembered: call the Wickland Gallery. She got Nigel Wickland on the phone and made an appointment for the following afternoon, when he would have a closer look at the thirteen pieces of art. She'd have to make a note to ask the gallery owner if he thought her security system was adequate to protect the artwork while she was in Tuscany. But then she thought, screw it. Sammy had the art so heavily insured that she almost hoped someone would steal all of it. Then she could buy some paintings that were vibrant and alive. It was time for Leona Brueger to get out and *really* live, away from her palatial cocoon in the Hollywood Hills. She might finally take the risk and buy a vineyard and winery up in Napa Valley.

Raleigh L. Dibble was in his third-floor apartment in east Hollywood, getting ready for the part-time job he was doing that evening on the only day off from his regular work. It paid chump change, but it helped with the rent and the car payment on his nine-year-old Toyota Corolla, which needed tires and a tune-up. He stood before the mirror and adjusted his black bow tie, a real one, not one of those crappy clip-ons that everyone wore nowadays. He fastened the black cummerbund over his starched dress shirt and slipped into his tuxedo jacket for a big dinner party in the Hollywood Hills celebrating the release of a third-rate movie by some hack he had never heard of.

All Raleigh knew about the homeowner tonight was that the guy was a junior partner in a Century City law firm who needed an experienced man like Raleigh to augment his hired caterers and make sure that things ran smoothly. Raleigh's past life as the owner of a West Los Angeles catering business had qualified him for these quasi-butler jobs where nouveaus could pretend they knew their ass from corned beef. Raleigh had met a lot of wealthy people and earned a good reputation, which brought him a small but steady income and had kept him from drinking the Kool-Aid after his business had gone belly-up.

He thought he didn't look too bad in the tux. Mother Nature, the pitiless cunt, had put macaroni-and-cheese handles around his middle, and it was getting scary. At only five foot seven he wasn't tall enough to carry the blubber overload. Though he didn't have much hair left, what he had was nutmeg brown with the help of Grecian Formula. And his jawline was holding up, but only because the extra fat had puffed his cheeks like a goddamn woodchuck. Now he had a double chin—no, make it a triple. If he could ever earn enough money, he hoped to get a quarter of his body siphoned into the garbage can by one of the zillion cosmetic surgeons plying their trade on the west side of Los Angeles. Then maybe a hair transplant and even an eye lift to complete the overhaul, because his eyes, the color of faded denim, were shrinking from the encroachment of the upper lids. Enough money could rectify all of that.

Before he left the apartment for that night's gig, he figured he'd better call Julius Hampton, his full-time boss for the past six months. The old man had just turned eighty-nine years of age when he'd hired Raleigh, who was thirty-one years younger almost to the day. Raleigh had been hired the month after Barack Obama took office, and it was an okay job being a live-in butler/chef and all-around caretaker six days a week for the old coot. He was being paid by a downtown lawyer who administered the Hampton trust fund, but the lawyer was a tight ass who acted like it was his money, and Raleigh had had to practically beg for a wage increase in early summer.

Julius Hampton had been an indefatigable and flamboyant cruiser of Santa Monica Boulevard in his day, but he'd never made any kind of pass at Raleigh even before learning that his new employee was straight. Raleigh figured that gay or straight, it wouldn't matter to the old man anyway, since Raleigh was no George Clooney, and the geezer was through with sex. Julius Hampton was left only with fantasies stoked by their weekly visits to west Hollywood gay bars, more out of nostalgia than anything else.

This boss had been a longtime friend of a lot of other rich old men on the west side, not all of them gay by any means. Raleigh had driven Julius Hampton to many dinner parties where Raleigh would hang around the kitchen with the other help until the party was over or his boss got tired. On nights when the old man's phlebitis was bothering him, Raleigh would bring the collapsible wheelchair from the car and wheel him out to the old Cadillac sedan that his boss loved and Raleigh hated. Raleigh figured that in his day, Julius Hampton probably had a lot of boy sex in that Cadillac, back when his plumbing still worked. Maybe sitting on those beat-up leather seats brought him delicious memories. In any case, his boss had dismissed the suggestion every time Raleigh urged him to junk the Cadillac and buy a new car.

Raleigh L. Dibble had been in the catering business almost continually since his high school days in San Pedro, the third child and only son of a longshoreman and a hairdresser. As a young man he'd begun concentrating on using good diction while he was on a job, any job. He'd read a self-improvement book stressing that good diction could trump a poor education, and Raleigh had never gone to college. All he'd ever known was working for inadequate wages in food service until he went into business as a working partner with Nellie Foster of Culver City, who made the best hors d'oeuvres and gave the best blow jobs he'd ever known. They'd done pretty well in the catering business when times were good, working out of a storefront on Pico Boulevard. But they'd gotten into some "difficulties," as he always described his fall from grace.

Raleigh had been forced by circumstance to write several NSF checks, and after that was straightened out, the IRS got on them like a swarm of leeches, sucking their blood and tormenting them for over a year until a criminal case for fraud and tax evasion was filed in federal court. Raleigh had done the manly thing at that time and taken the bullet for both himself and Nellie, claiming to authorities that she knew nothing about the "edgy paperwork" that had helped to keep them afloat temporarily.

He'd been sentenced to one year in prison to be served at the Federal Correctional Complex in Lompoc, California, and the night before he had to report to federal marshals, Nellie gave him a tearful good-bye and thanked him for saving her ass. She promised to write and to visit him often. But she'd seldom written and never visited, and she married a house painter two months after Raleigh was behind bars. And he didn't even get a farewell blow job.

Raleigh had served eight months of his sentence, gotten paroled, rented a cheap apartment in a risky gang neighborhood in east Hollywood, and lived by hiring out as a waiter to various caterers he'd known when he was in the business. Then he'd stumbled into the position with Julius Hampton as what the old man called his "gentleman's gentleman." Julius had seen too many English movies, Raleigh figured, but he made sure his diction was always up to par when he was in his boss's presence.

The dinner party in the Hollywood Hills that night turned out to be disastrous because the lawyer homeowner had hired a Mexican caterer to serve what was supposed to be Asian fusion. As far as Raleigh was concerned, there was nothing more dangerous than a Mexican with a saltshaker, and everything tasted of sea salt. Raleigh played his role to the hilt, but Stephen Fry as Jeeves the butler couldn't have saved this one. His feet and knees were killing him when the night finally ended and he could get home to bed.

The next morning Raleigh was up early and on his way to pick up Julius Hampton to take him to Cedars-Sinai for a checkup with his cardiologist. After that, they went back to the Hampton house, where the old man had his afternoon nap, and he was raring to go again when he woke up and remembered that it was the night for his weekly lobster dinner at the Palm. Raleigh had never been crazy about lobster but he could have a rib eye and a couple of Jack Daniel's to get him through the rest of the evening at one of the west Hollywood gay bars that the old man still liked to frequent at least one night a week.

By the time they'd finished dining and arrived at the gay bar, it was filling up with other customers also arriving after dinner, and they were lucky to get a small table. The sweating waiters couldn't deliver drinks to the customers fast enough. Raleigh and his elderly boss were sipping martinis close enough to the three-deep bar patrons for the old letch to gawk at all the muscular buns in tight pants, some of which Raleigh figured were butt-pad inserts. Many of the younger hustlers wore tight Ralph Lauren jerseys with jeans or shorts, and the old boy gazed at them with melancholy. Raleigh was certain that their crotch mounds were from stuffing socks in their Calvins. He figured the youthful hustlers must buy socks by the gross at Costco.

Julius Hampton recognized Nigel Wickland before the Beverly Hills art dealer recognized him. "Nigel!" he said as the art dealer was passing their table on his way back from the restroom.

At first Raleigh thought that Nigel Wickland was about sixty years old, but up close, he looked more like sixty-five. He was tall and fashionably thin, with a prominent chin, heavy dark eyebrows, and a full head of hair so white that it looked mauve under the mood lighting. He wore a tailor-made, double-breasted navy blazer, a pale blue Oxford cotton shirt, and an honest-to-god blue ascot impeccably folded against his throat. Raleigh wondered if the blazer was Hugo Boss or maybe Valentino, or was it a Men's Wearhouse copy? And how about the shoes? Were they O.J. Simpson Bruno Maglis or knockoffs? Nigel Wickland wore his clothes so well that you couldn't tell if they were the real things.

Then Raleigh's attention was drawn to the man's exquisite hands. The fingers were long and tapered, the nails beautifully manicured, and there were no prominent veins to be seen, which there should have been on a man his age. Raleigh wondered if guys even had cosmetic surgeons do their hands around here, and if so, whether they called it a hand job.

The art dealer stroked his chin and seemed nonplussed for a

moment, probably thinking that Julius was just another dotty old queen who frequented the west Hollywood clubs, until the octogenarian said, "It's me, Julius Hampton. Remember? We played bridge at the Bruegers' a couple of times before Sammy passed away."

"Julius!" Nigel Wickland said. "Of course I remember. How *are* you?"

As they shook hands, Julius Hampton said, "Still upright, more or less, with the help of my man here. I'd like you to meet Raleigh Dibble. I don't know what I'd do without him. Sit down and join us."

The art dealer extended his graceful hand to Raleigh and said, "Nigel Wickland. Pleased to meet you."

"Same here, Mr. Wickland," Raleigh said.

"Nigel, please," the art dealer said to him. "And may I call you Raleigh?"

"Of course," Raleigh said.

Raleigh wondered if the toffee-nosed accent was legit or something the art dealer affected for L.A.'s west-side nouveau. Raleigh had spent nearly six months bumming around Europe as a young man and had lived in London for a summer, waiting tables at a bistro. He'd even considered affecting an Oxbridge accent like Nigel Wickland's when he'd been in the catering business but decided that it could backfire if his customers found him out. They liked their phonies to be less obvious phonies around these parts.

"What'll you have?" Julius Hampton said to the art dealer, and Raleigh noticed that the old man's bony hands were trembling most of the time. It was hard for him to hold a martini glass anymore without spilling it.

Nigel Wickland ordered a banana daiquiri and chatted with Julius Hampton about the bargains now available at the Wickland Gallery. Raleigh Dibble figured he knew the Nigel Wickland type well enough. The west side of L.A. was full of them. Given the art dealer's obvious ego, the gallery would of course bear his name. And even though a man as old as Julius Hampton would be an unlikely prospect for a sale, Nigel Wickland seemed compelled to chat him up about the treasures to be had just a few blocks away on Wilshire Boulevard. Raleigh figured that the art dealer was constantly chumming the waters in case any of Julius Hampton's less grizzled friends or neighbors was ever tempted to take the bait.

"The bloody recession is forcing people to sell for indecently low prices," Nigel told them, and signaled to the waiter for another round when his glass was still half full.

Boozer, Raleigh thought, but then reminded himself that in the gay bars everyone seemed to drink more to bolster their courage for encounters that were often risky.

It was then that Nigel Wickland said, "Have you been to the Brueger house since Sammy passed? I sometimes wonder how Leona is really holding up."

Old Julius Hampton cackled and said, "The merriest of widows is dear Leona. I understand she sometimes dates a filmaker named Rudy Ressler when he's not molesting children at UCLA, where he lectures at the film school. He's one of those people who make cheap indie films that probably go straight to DVD."

Raleigh had been impressed many times by his employer's knowledge of the movie business as well as any other business that was peculiarly relevant to Angelenos. Like his father before him, Julius Hampton had made his fortune as a real-estate developer, and the Hampton brokers bought and sold to real Hollywood names on a regular basis, not to second-raters like Rudy Ressler. As Julius Hampton and Nigel Wickland chatted about people they knew in common, Raleigh excused himself and went the restroom.

While Raleigh was gone, Nigel Wickland said, "Nice chap. Seems competent."

"Very," Julius Hampton said, with just enough drink in him to gossip. "His catering business failed some time ago and he's eking out a living now. He's basically very honest but he got in some tax trouble with Uncle Sam back then. Had to spend some time locked up in federal prison. I have a PI do a background on everyone I hire. I've never questioned Raleigh about his past even though I know a lot about it. I can tell you that he cooks like Julia Child."

"The poor fellow," Nigel Wickland said. "That is certainly a spot of bother to live down, isn't it? Still, many people around here have had similar problems with the IRS. That doesn't make him a criminal."

When Raleigh returned from the restroom, Nigel Wickland started paying more attention to him than to Julius Hampton. Raleigh didn't sense that it was a gay thing. It just seemed that Nigel Wickland wanted to learn about his work history. Nigel asked if this was his first job as a butler/chef. And he seemed very interested in Raleigh's former catering business, saying he thought he remembered Raleigh's employees catering some soirees at the Wickland Gallery. Raleigh thought that was just bullshit until he remembered that Nellie *had* catered a fancy gig at a Beverly Hills art gallery. They'd lost money on it when she'd failed to anticipate the amount of champagne needed, and she'd had to quickly run to the nearest liquor store and buy cases at retail. Was that the Wickland Gallery? He couldn't remember.

Then Nigel Wickland started to wheeze. He took a few short deep breaths that didn't seem to help him. He muttered, "Please forgive me," and took an inhaler from his trousers pocket, turning away from Raleigh and Julius Hampton. He put the inhaler in his mouth and pressed the canister, simultaneously inhaling deeply, holding the steroid in his lungs as long as possible.

When he exhaled, he turned back to them and said, "I'm sorry. Adult-onset asthma. It started three years ago. Part of the indignities of advancing age."

Julius Hampton said, "You think you're old? Like Willie Nelson said, I've outlived my dick. I wouldn't want to outlive my liver. Without a decent martini, what's the point in any of it?"

Nigel Wickland then said to Raleigh, "Did you ever think about starting up your catering business again? I don't mean in the middle of this recession but later."

"It takes starter money to get a business like that going," Raleigh said. "I'd have to win the lottery or something."

"Still, there's nothing like the feeling of independence that being one's own boss can give. Especially with men of a certain age, like you and me."

Julius Hampton said, "What it all boils down to is relevancy. All the elderly understand that. You will, too, sooner than you think. Marty Brueger always talks about it. He says when he started feeling irrelevant, he knew he was through with living. That's what he's doing in Leona's guesthouse — waiting to die."

"Well, you're not irrelevant, Mr. Hampton," Raleigh said quickly.

Nigel Wickland said, "Hear me, god. Save us all from irrelevance."

As Nigel returned to pumping the chubby butler about his work history, Julius Hampton began getting restless at being left out of the conversation. After the second martini, the old man said, "Well, Raleigh, is it time to go home and see what's on TV tonight?"

Then Nigel Wickland said quickly, "Raleigh, here's my card. Give me a ring and I'll show you around the gallery. Any time at all. I think you'd enjoy it."

When they were driving home, Julius Hampton said, "Well, well, Nigel Wickland seemed smitten with you, Raleigh. What's the secret of your attraction?"

"Unless he likes Pillsbury Doughboys, it couldn't be physical," Raleigh said, patting his belly. "I've got so much flab spilling over my belt that my hips look like a muffin top. I think he was just being friendly, Mr. Hampton."

"Nigel doesn't strike me as the overly friendly type," Julius

Hampton said, looking at Raleigh as though he certainly couldn't figure out Nigel's interest.

The next afternoon before taking his nap, Ralcigh's cmploycr told him he could take the afternoon off. Raleigh couldn't decide whether or not to visit Sharon, his older sister in San Pedro. His other sister had died of lung cancer when he was in prison, and both parents were gone, so Sharon was the only close relative he had left. But she was an Evangelical Christian who always spent at least half of every visit trying to bring him to Jesus. He decided he didn't feel up to it today.

He thought about going to a movie in Westwood, or maybe visiting an old friend who used to work for him and Nellie in the catering business. She was a busty Brazilian in her midforties. Alma was hopelessly clumsy and had broken more glasses than the Sylmar earthquake, but she'd sleep with him if she was in the mood, and he loved to kid her that she had tits from here to paternity. Raleigh couldn't remember the last time he got laid and was almost horny enough to buy a knobber from one of those Asian masseuses on Hollywood Boulevard. He phoned Alma but the number was no longer in service, so on a whim he drove his Toyota to the Wickland Gallery and popped in unannounced.

A prim young woman in a jacket and skirt and very sensible heels said, "Good afternoon, my name's Ruth Langley. Is there anything I can help you with today or would you just care to have a look around?"

"Mr. Wickland's invited me to stop in for a personal tour of the gallery," he said. "The name's Raleigh Dibble."

When she escorted him to Nigel Wickland's office, the art dealer stood up, came around his massive mahogany desk, and shook hands energetically.

"So glad you came. You're just in time to come and have a drink with me," Nigel Wickland said, donning his linen blazer, the color of a martini olive.

Raleigh figured the ascot must be for evenings in gay bars, because the art dealer was wearing a white shirt with a forest-green silk necktie. He made Raleigh feel shabby in his off-the-rack rusty brown sport jacket worn over chinos, with black leather loafers that needed the heels replaced.

They went to the bar at the Ivy and took a table. Just as before, Nigel Wickland ordered a banana daiquiri, and a second one before he'd finished the first. In the light of day Raleigh could see that the art dealer's eyes were watery and there were broken veins on the sides of his nose. A juicehead for sure, he figured. Still, he was buying the drinks and Raleigh's curiosity was killing him, so he ordered a Jack on the rocks.

After he was half finished with the second drink, Nigel Wickland said, "If you don't mind my asking, Raleigh, did you actually sell your catering business or . . ."

"It tanked," Raleigh said with a wry grin, starting to feel the Jack Daniel's already. "I got nothing out of it. So here I am, a domestic servant."

"Hardly that," Nigel Wickland said. "I'm sure you're a valued employee to Julius. But I can't imagine that the pay is very good."

"A living," Raleigh said. "Sort of. But the food's great because I buy and cook it for both of us. Mr. Hampton still has a young man's appetite." Raleigh drained the glass, and Nigel Wickland immediately signaled for another.

"I'd like to rely on you to be discreet, Raleigh," the art dealer said. "I know you've been with Julius a relatively short time, but I might be able to offer you a better position."

"With you?" Raleigh said. "I'm an art Neanderthal."

"I don't mean in my gallery," Nigel Wickland said. "After meeting you the other night I realized that you have exactly the qualifications that a client of mine needs at this time. You heard Julius and me mention her name. Leona Brueger?"

"I vaguely remember that," Raleigh said, getting into the second

Jack, a delicious golden burn sliding down his throat and making him feel the glow coming on.

"I've recently learned that Leona Brueger is deeply involved with Rudy Ressler, the filmmaker that Julius mentioned."

"The child molester?" Raleigh said. "That's what Mr. Hampton called him."

Nigel Wickland smiled and said, " He doesn't try to entice children with a kitten and chocolate bars, believe me. College coeds, his targets of choice, are not exactly children, even if they do behave that way. But Rudy's changing his ways and has been getting increasingly serious about mature women, especially the widow Brueger."

"It sounds like you know them pretty well," Raleigh said.

Nigel said, "I've come to know more than a little about Leona Brueger after having been contacted to appraise the late Sammy Brueger's formidable art collection. I've been led by her to believe that she's going to sell it all, along with the house, perhaps to marry Ressler and move to Napa, where she'll grow grapes or whatever people do when they have more money than good sense."

"Nigel," Raleigh said finally, "this is all very interesting, but I don't see how I could possibly fit in here."

Nigel said, "Leona Brueger has been saddled with Sammy's brother Marty, who is eighty-seven years old and ailing. Marty spends most of his time in Leona's guesthouse, but occasionally he likes to get out and about. She needs the services of a butler/driver/companion who can cook three meals a day for him. Just as you do for Julius. Leona Brueger also likes an occasional little dinner party at home, but the people she's hired have been unsatisfactory. It's not so easy for her to find a man who can cook and manage a dinner party as well as do the rest of it for her brother-in-law. After we met, I realized that with your background and experience, you're just what she's been looking for. You're a perfect fit, Raleigh."

"But I've got a job," Raleigh said. "And it's permanent, not temporary."

"If you're happy where you are, forget I mentioned it," Nigel Wickland said. "But Leona told me she'd pay seven thousand dollars a month to the right man, and of course you'd have luxury quarters to live in and meals you'd prepared yourself. You can buy anything you'd like from the markets and bill it to your employer's account. You'd have no living expenses. The job would probably end around the first of next year. After that, she's going to arrange for a luxurious retirement home for Marty Brueger when she sells the house. She'd do it now, but he refuses to go, and his lifetime care and contentment are prominently mentioned in Sammy's will, so she must accommodate him. But by year's end, his growing dementia will probably take care of things. The urgency here and now is that she wants to leave for a long holiday in Tuscany and she's in need of the right man ASAP."

Raleigh was quiet for a moment and then said, "Of course that's a whole lot more than I make, but my job's permanent. I don't know about quitting Mr. Hampton for a temporary job."

"How permanent is any job with a boss who's eighty-nine years old?" Nigel Wickland asked. "Do think about it and let me know if you're interested. I'm just doing this as a favor to my client Leona Brueger. It's nothing to me one way or the other."

Raleigh thought there was something not quite right, and he said, "I remember that when you and Mr. Hampton talked about Leona Brueger, you wondered if she was holding up well since her husband's death. It seemed like you didn't know all that much about her."

Then it was Nigel Wickland's turn to pause. He finally said, "Frankly, since I've been involved in the appraisal of her artwork, I've come to know her well enough that I've learned about her plans. Naturally I couldn't mention to Julius that I thought you'd be so much better off working for my client. If it weren't that you're just so perfect for this job, I wouldn't be bringing it up to you at all. So whatever you decide, mum's the word, Raleigh."

"I've got to think about this," Raleigh said.

"Yes, do have a think," Nigel said.

When Raleigh left Nigel Wickland, he decided that the prospect of earning that kind of easy money was tempting, but after the job ended, what would he do? He'd successfully completed his parole, but memories of prison had kept him superstraight. He'd even been afraid to tell lies on job résumés, and it was no cinch for an ex-con to get decent employment after mentioning a prison record. Yet it was true that with an eighty-nine-year-old boss, how permanent could his current job be? And he was sick of having to plead with the shyster who managed the Hampton trust fund to give him the pay he deserved.

Raleigh Dibble hardly slept that night. The next morning he phoned Nigel Wickland, and when he reached the art dealer, he said, "Nigel, it's Raleigh Dibble here. When can I have an interview with Mrs. Brueger?"

★ FOUR ★

AN EXTRAORDINARY NUMBER of celebrity names turned up in crime stories during the first full year of the Great Recession. Many of them ended up on reports passing across the desks of Hollywood Division detectives. The police station in which the detectives were housed was an unusual place, perhaps the world's only police facility where framed one-sheet movie posters decorated the walls. In the geographic territory of the station the bizarre was commonplace, and if something eerie or outlandish could not be explained or even understood, more often than not, the cops would just shrug and say, "This is fucking Hollywood." After that, nothing more needed to be said.

During that last year of the eight-year federal consent decree, which finally ended in July, only about a dozen detectives remained at Hollywood Station, when there should have been three times that many. The LAPD had labored under the oversight of federally mandated watchdogs since the Rodney King riots, as well as the so-called Rampart Division scandal, an ignominy that turned out to involve exactly two felonious cops. But it was enough for the critics who had been lying in wait to bring down the proud, some would say arrogant, police department.

After charter amendment F stripped the LAPD chiefs of civil service protection, politicians began calling the shots, and hundreds of LAPD investigators were diverted to serve the monitors of that consent decree in "reforming" a police department that no LAPD police officer thought needed to be reformed. For years the plaintive refrain heard all around the Department was, "Charter amendment F changed our world." And what with budget shortfalls and the fact that the state of California was itself on the brink of bankruptcy, all the street cops and detectives who were still doing actual crime suppression were overwhelmed.

There had been a rash of burglaries in Los Angeles that targeted young celebrities. Two of the main suspects among a group of seven were a young man and young woman in their late teens from Calabasas, a rather affluent suburb in the San Fernando Valley. They'd met in a remedial school, a kind of last-chance high school. Another of the young women involved in the burglary and fencing ring would boost celebrity magazines from newsstands and supermarkets, and pick out targets that would be researched on the Internet. Celebrity homesites were Googled and satellite maps of their homes were obtained, and their schedules could be followed online in celebrity blogs. Another one of the young women in the group of burglars had been part of a TV reality show that at first purported to show an ex-Playmate raising three wild kids.

The burglary victims included actors Orlando Bloom, Lindsay Lohan, Audrina Patridge, Rachel Bilson, Megan Fox, and famous person Paris Hilton. Some of the homes had security cameras, and on one video, a youthful man and woman were photographed during the crime. On the video from another of the celebrity homes, four of the young burglars could be seen parking their car on Outpost Drive and walking about a hundred yards, arm in arm *backward* until they were safely past the surveillance camera, at which point they turned around and tended to business.

They made several stops at residences they were casing before being satisfied, and they did not wear hoodies, trying not to look like the public's conception of a typical burglar. They entered through unlocked doors, open windows, and doggie doors. Only occasionally would they have to pry open a window. There were even a few hot-prowl burglaries, committed with people at home, in the county area policed by the Los Angeles Sheriff's Department.

The burglary ring stole clothing, jewelry, purses, some electronics, and cash. They burglarized Paris Hilton's home a few times, but she knew about only one. When the police cracked the case, they called her at 3 A.M. and she came in to identify her stolen property, seeming delighted to have the loot returned. She claimed that its value was well into seven figures, but detectives, who lived in a more mundane world, had their doubts. Orlando Bloom, whom detectives referred to as "a gentleman," was always helpful when called upon, and had there been such a thing, would have gotten the detectives' favorite victim award.

Search warrants were served as far away as Las Vegas on one of the teenage females and on their fence, a twenty-eight-year-old who called himself a nightclub promoter. He handled the stolen goods and was charged with receiving stolen property and other related crimes. LAPD and LASD detectives believed that perhaps two dozen burglaries were committed during a two-year period.

Defense lawyers negotiated, offering to discuss the return of missing property if new felony counts were not filed, but it all ended in what detectives said was akin to "a failed hostage negotiation" after one of the attorneys walked out, saying, "I'm not in the property business."

Another defense attorney, whose young client claimed to be working for a Christian organization that assisted people in need of housing, seemed to believe every word that his sobbing client told him. A detective said of the lawyer, "He's the kind of guy who goes to a strip club and believes that the lap dancer really loves him."

None of the young people were hard-core junkies but some of them smoked OxyContin, the equivalent of synthetic heroin, the drug du jour of countless young Americans and a powerhouse opioid that had even addicted America's leading conservative talkshow host, Rush Limbaugh. The news photos of the pretty, female suspects in their low-rise jeans, hiding their faces but not their firm bare bellies, provided weeks of entertainment for TV and tabloids. They were dubbed "The Burglar Bunch" and "The Hollywood Hills Burglars" and, even more provocatively, "The Bling Ring."

Local and national media described their antics as cautionary tales of the dangers to young people posed by the Hollywood celebrity lifestyle. The rationale was that it was constantly in their faces thanks to websites that detailed the shenanigans of celebutantes, along with reality shows that portrayed people their age living the life in Hollywood nightclubs. According to celebrity commentators who never eschewed a cliché, an abundance of danger to young people was out there on those "boulevards of dreams."

There were a number of boulevard dreamers who couldn't get enough of the Bling Ring, one of whom was twenty-two-year-old Jonas Claymore. He was a dropout from Hollywood High School who'd smoked way too much crystal meth during his final year of school and had never gone on to community college or done much of anything that his working-class parents had expected of him. The meth eventually led to terrifying attacks of paranoia where he became convinced that he was under twenty-four-hour surveillance by LAPD narks, and on one unforgettable evening, two of his former schoolmates decided to wean him off methamphetamines by introducing him to the wonders of 80 mg green tablets of OxyContin and other oxycodone drugs like Percocet, Percodan, and Tylox.

His current housemate, Megan Burke, was a twenty-year-old high school graduate from Bend, Oregon, who had been a good student, popular, and college-bound, before she'd developed a yen to "experience Hollywood," as had so many thousands before her. She could not have specifically defined what that meant. Of course, she would have been embarrassed to admit that there were vague fantasies involving the movie business, and even then, she was too mature to think that she would be "discovered." Yet it was always there at age eighteen, the notion that where life moves at twenty-four frames per second, anything is possible.

She had persuaded her mother to let her come to Los Angeles for the summer before college with a list of places in Southern California that she wanted to visit. She had explained to her mother that this was her "odyssey," the journey of self-discovery that she and many of her classmates believed was essential for self-fulfillment. The original plan was to stay for two months working at the Gap for a former Bend neighbor who had moved to Los Angeles and managed the store. The woman had even arranged for Megan to share an apartment with two other girls, and the money she earned selling clothing had allowed Megan to support herself. She had hoped to send part of her earnings to her mother, who had raised Megan and her younger brother, Terry, after their father had deserted the family when the children were still in elementary school.

Experiencing Hollywood wasn't anything like Megan thought it would be, especially after she learned how expensive everything was in L.A., but things went well enough until she was persuaded by her roommates to experiment with some of their trendy pharmaceuticals, like Xanax and Percocet. Those drugs led her to Vicodin and finally to OxyContin, by far the most addictive and powerful of the prescription drugs available to her, and OxyContin led her to Jonas Claymore, whom she met through a girlfriend at work.

Jonas was a valet parking attendant at upscale restaurants and he made good tips. He was tall, rail-thin, cute, and goofy, with a bush of cinnamon hair and a gap-toothed grin. He made her laugh easily and sold her OxyContin twice a week when he'd come by her apartment.

When they got high together for the first time, he said, "You won't be offended if I drop trou and show you something, will ya?"

"Show me what?" she said uneasily.

"This," he said, turning away from her and lowering his jeans and underwear. On one buttock was tattooed *what*. On the other buttock was tattooed *ever*. When he pulled his pants up he said, "Most of the girls I know think it's kinda funny."

After several drug experiences they became sexually involved, but it was never satisfactory for either of them because of Jonas's drug-induced ED problems. Megan liked the other oxycodone products, like Vicodin, referred to as "norcos" or "watsons," and she liked the Percocet, aka "perks," but nothing could beat the 80 mg OxyContin, called "OC" or "ox" or "80s" or "beans." Soon, Megan Burke fell passionately in love, not with Jonas Claymore, but with smoking ox. He loved it even more than she did and always seemed to have it in abundance. Then her life quickly fell apart. She lost her job at the Gap and got a part-time job at Denny's as a waitress, but she lost that, too, and came to dread the desperate phone calls from her mother when the college plans were abandoned.

Megan finally sold her old Hyundai when money ran out, after she had been living with Jonas for nearly a year in a cheap apartment in Thai Town, but not with the knowledge of his landlord or her despairing mother in Oregon. By then, Megan had begun avoiding most of her mother's phone calls and would not reveal her address or anything about Jonas Claymore, not wanting her worried parent to know how far she had fallen and how fast had been the descent.

After reading and seeing TV reports that members of the Bling Ring smoked ox, it had made Jonas Claymore proud that it was also his drug of choice. Ox was far more expensive than the crystal meth he'd formerly adored, and more than other pharmaceuticals that he'd use when he didn't have enough money for the OCs. He was barely hanging on to his current job of parking cars at two of the newest Melrose Avenue restaurants.

It wasn't often that Jonas actually read the *L.A. Times* or anything else, but when he thought there might be something in the paper about the Bling Ring, he'd run to the supermarket and buy or steal one. He adored reading about the designer wardrobes that the Bling Ring coveted and plundered, and especially the Chanel merchandise, Louis Vuitton purses, and Rolex watches they'd looted during their crime spree. They'd even stolen underwear that they could wear themselves while they dreamed. Jonas couldn't get enough of the stories and searched for more on television and especially in the tabloids.

One summer evening, Jonas was sitting in the front seat of a BMW 535i that he'd parked, engrossed in juicy Bling Ring coverage. At the same time, his boss, a chesty and bossy Russian lesbian who ran the valet parking concession for both restaurants, was looking for her young employee in the parking lot. The lanky lad was disappointed that there was no photo of Paris Hilton in this particular story, and he was only halfway through the article when his boss came up from behind and jerked open the door of the Beemer.

"What the fock you do-ink, Jonas?" she demanded in that Russki accent that he had come to hate.

"Sorry, Ludmila," he said, folding the paper and jumping out of the car. "Just taking a two-minute break."

"That is shit!" she said. "I am look-ink everywhere for you. I am all ate up with you."

"Fed," Jonas Claymore said.

"What?"

"Fed. You're all *fed* up."

She stood glaring up at the gangly young man and said, "Do not laugh at me, Jonas."

"I'm not laughing, Ludmila," he said. "How about letting me get back to work, okay?"

"You do not know how to work. You do not know shit," she said, and gave him an impulsive shove with her open hand.

"Hey!" Jonas yelled. "You just put your fucking hand on me. There's a law about employers harassing employees."

Two young women paused on their way to the nearest of the restaurants when they heard the raised voices in the parking lot. In what was left of twilight they saw a skinny, long-necked valet parking guy with a wiry thatch of cinnamon hair that was wind-tunnel wild from parking the cars with windows down. He wore a long-sleeved white shirt, black bow tie, and black pants, and was shouting at a burly woman identically clad, whose dark hair was cut as short as the guy's.

"Do not do threats with me!" Ludmila yelled. "You no good, worth-noth-ink shit!"

"You can shove your job up your fat ass, you lesbo freakazoid!" Jonas Claymore yelled back, his bobbing Adam's apple the size of a hen's egg. He ripped off his clip-on tie and flipped it at her, catching her right in the eye.

She responded with a blow. Not a bitch slap. A real punch. A straight right-handed corker with a lot of hefty shoulder behind it, and Jonas Claymore's upturned nose exploded in a blood spray and he fell back against the BMW, dropping to his knee for a second.

Then he leaped up, screaming, "I'm gonna tear your throat out, you commie cunt!"

One of the two women watching from the sidewalk took her cell phone from her purse and dialed 9-1-1.

By the time 6-X-32 of the midwatch showed up, both combatants were down on the pavement exhausted from having wrestled and punched and bitten and clawed for several minutes. Jonas Claymore clearly had gotten the worst of it. His face bore scratches and contusions, and his buttonless shirt was hanging out and blood-spattered. His breath came in short rasps and his hairless concave chest heaved as he pawed at his right ear where a tiny snippet of the lobe had been bitten off. His former boss had a purple mouse under one eye and a bruised lower lip and her left shirtsleeve was completely ripped away.

The black-and-white squealed into the parking lot and two blue-uniformed cops got out, the shorter one carrying a side-handle baton.

Jetsam said to his partner, "I'll take the female, bro."

"Roger that," Flotsam said, walking toward Jonas Claymore, who was standing, hands on his knees, bent over and trying to catch his breath.

Before the tall cop could speak, Jonas said, "That Russki douche bag started it! She pushed me and then she slugged me. I was just defending myself."

"You didn't do too good a job of it," Flotsam noted.

"She suckered me!" Jonas hollered, loud enough for gawking passersby to hear.

"Keep your voice down," Flotsam said. "And tell me what happened."

Meanwhile Ludmila was trying to tie her white shirt together in order to cover her size 46 E cup bra, and she said to Jetsam, "He is no-good bum. I hire him. I pay him good. He never share tip with nobody. He is worth-noth-ink shit!"

"How did the fight start?" Jetsam asked.

"He is say-ink rude things to me. He use his dirty mouth and make me fight."

"Are you saying that you got physical before he did?"

"What?"

"Did you hit him first?"

"Well...," Ludmila said, as though she were contemplating an exceedingly difficult question. "Is depend-ink how you see si-too-ation."

"Uh-huh," Jetsam said. "I had to be there, right?"

Flotsam suggested that Jonas tip his head back and press the remnants of his shirt to his nose and hold it there.

"Are you really interested in making a battery report?" Flotsam asked. "And a private person's arrest?"

"Wouldn't you?" Jonas pulled the balled-up shirt away from his face for a moment.

"I'd have to think about it," Flotsam said. "She's a woman."

Jonas said, "She's a slit-licking lizzy warthog! She ain't no woman."

"According to the law she is," Flotsam said. "We'll do what you want. You could make a private person's arrest and we'll be glad to transport, but then we'll expect you to follow through all the way. Think about going to court and telling in public how that babe clocked you. It could be way embarrassing, dude. Up to you, though."

That stopped Jonas cold. He thought about it a moment, about the humiliation and all the hassle, and he said, "Well, what if we forget about it, the both of us? Can we do that?"

"Okay with us," Flotsam said. "But I don't wanna get another call about you two duking it out again."

"You won't. I'm going home," Jonas said. Then he yelled to Ludmila, "You can't fire me! I quit, you goddamn commie carpet muncher!"

"Fock you, stupid head!" his former employer said and flipped him the bird.

That afternoon when Jonas Claymore got back to his apartment that he shared with Megan Burke in Thai Town, she was lying on the couch watching an old TCM movie in a Percocet fog.

She was shocked when she saw him, and said, "Jonas! What happened to you?"

"I got in a fight at work," he said, "with some fucking Russian. Hollywood's full of commie trash. There ain't no Americans in charge of anything these days."

Megan said. "You're hurt."

She was wearing a baggy T-shirt and cutoffs and her legs looked even knobbier and paler than the last time Jonas paid any attention to them. When he'd met her, she had healthy dark brown hair in a stylish bob that ended a couple of inches below her ears and looked like a dark hoodie. She liked to wear those cute tights from Target then, but now the tights and most of her clothes were gone, and her hair was longer, dull, and frizzy. He figured that pretty soon it would be bleached out and falling to her shoulders with bangs reaching to her eyes like Lady Gaga's. A lot of the girls he knew did that to themselves, trying to look like the singer, but they ended up looking like shot-out skeezers, all sunken-eyed, pruned, and shriveled. There were dark circles under Megan's nervous violet eyes and altogether he thought she looked like shit.

"Just get me a damp washcloth and a towel," he said. "I gotta lay down."

When he was lying on the couch, she returned and started dabbing at his wounds, causing him to yelp when she touched his damaged earlobe.

"Jonas," she said. "You've lost a chunk of meat from your ear! How did that happen?"

"A bite," he said.

"He bit you?" she said, shocked.

"Fucking Russians shoulda been nuked to the Stone Age," he said to the ceiling.

She said, "He hurt you pretty bad."

Then Jonas said, "You shoulda seen the damage I did. It wasn't one-way."

She dabbed at his ear with a soiled dishtowel, saying, "I'm sure you kicked his butt."

"I knocked the shit outta that Russian pus bucket," Jonas said to the wall. "Then I almost get busted by the cops for defending myself. Me, the victimized American."

Megan said, "Just rest now and don't think about it."

"This is why my grandpa killed communists in Vietnam?" Jonas said to the coffee table littered with fan magazines, candy wrappers, and pizza boxes, as well as OC paraphernalia, including a 6 × 10 inch piece of tinfoil creased in half, a cigarette lighter, and a ballpoint pen with the ink tube removed lying beside it.

"Try to calm yourself," Megan said.

"So a commie dirtbag could come to Hollywood and sucker me when I wasn't looking?"

Megan said, "Your nose'll start bleeding again. We've got half an eighty left. Do you want to chase the dragon?"

"A half of one bean?" Jonas said. "But I gave you a Ben Franklin yesterday!"

"It was three days ago, and Wilbur's charging us eighty-five per ox. And we smoked a piece of it when we did those watsons and perks. You're having a brownout. Don't you remember any of it?"

He vaguely recalled the Vicodins and Perocets, but he couldn't recall smoking half of an 80 mg OxyContin tablet. "It's that goddamn screw-top wine," he said. "It fucks up my memory. Can't you go boost a better bottle somewhere? I'd even settle for a couple forties of OE."

"I'm not a thief," Megan said.

Jonas was getting heart palpitations and was sweating cold. His knee joints and right shoulder were aching, which he blamed on the fight. But when he looked more closely at Megan he saw that she had broken into a sweat as well, and she couldn't stop yawning and scratching herself. That is, when she wasn't coughing.

"Goddamnit, Megan, look at us," he said. "We're jonesing. I gotta chase the dragon and I mean right now!"

She jumped up, ran to the bedroom, and got the last piece of the OC tablet, bringing it to the coffee table and placing it in the crease of the foil.

"This ain't a complete half," Jonas accused. "You smoked a bite off it, didn't you?"

Megan didn't reply and he was too desperate to press her.

"Just hurry up," he said.

Megan placed the flame of the lighter underneath the foil and heated the OxyContin tablet. Jonas picked up the empty ink tube, which, unlike a drinking straw, would not burn easily, and put it in his mouth. Megan tilted the foil, and as the heated fragment slid down the crease propelled by gravity and heated from beneath the foil, Jonas hungrily inhaled, and even swallowed as much rising smoke as he could, chasing that smoking ox down the crease before it burned up completely.

"You're not worried about me, are you, Jonas?" Megan said. "Don't you think I need a taste, too?"

Jonas said to her, "You call this chasing the dragon? All you left me was a crumb. There ain't enough ox here to chase a fucking lizard."

He waited for the rush, but all he got was an anemic feeling of lethargy. They were developing such a tolerance that for weeks neither of them had felt the warm flush of the skin or the wonderful drowsy euphoria that they used to get when there was enough for them both. When they weren't so addicted.

"Wilbur only deals in cash, no credit," Megan said between coughs. "I tried hard to talk a couple of OCs out of him when he came on to me, but he smells awful. I wouldn't ever let him so much as touch me for anything, Jonas. There're some things I won't do." She gulped back a sob and said, "I don't want to ever come to that!" She threw herself facedown on the sofa then and wept.

He looked at her, thinking, yeah, pretty soon she'd have the Lady Gaga hair and a tramp stamp or two, like the last woman he'd let live with him. She'd probably end up peddling her ass on Sunset Boulevard. Then he tried to remember the girl he'd met when she was selling clothes at the Gap. Why was it that every girl he met turned into a degenerate?

"Goddamnit," Jonas said, "we need enough bank for that

fucking quack over in Echo Park. He'll write us scrips for anything we want if the money's right."

Then Jonas felt a deep depression envelop him and he stopped looking at Megan and said, "I got fired," to Cuddles, her calico cat, who was squatting on a kitchen chair sleepily watching all the human drama unfolding.

The calico cat just yawned, lifted a back leg, and licked her ass, but Megan sat up and said, "You what? Oh, Jonas, what're we going to do?"

"Don't worry," Jonas said. "For quite a while I been thinking a lot about the Bling Ring. They only fucked up and got caught 'cause they didn't stay focused. I think they had a cool idea, though. You and me, we could do it right."

"Do what right?"

"Walk into the houses of celebrities and other rich people and take what we want. And make enough to live decent and stop slaving for all the foreign shitbags that're taking over the whole town."

"You're not making sense," Megan said. Then she started coughing again and her sweating increased.

"I'm making sense for the first time in a long time," Jonas insisted.

"Let's talk about it tomorrow," Megan said, wiping her face on her T-shirt. "It's stressful to talk like this when you're all beat-up and not thinking."

"Baby, it's easy," he said, "and the Bling Ring had a blast doing it."

"It's not like running out and boosting from department stores," Megan said. "Breaking into houses? That's very different and very scary."

"Whadda you mean 'breaking'?" Jonas said. "Those rich morons up in the Hollywood Hills, they leave their houses wide open. Know where Paris Hilton kept her house key? Under the fucking doormat. And they leave their windows unlocked. And you're getting so skinny these days, you could crawl through a doggie door too small for a fucking Chihuahua. Nothing could stop us from getting into any house we want."

Megan Burke suddenly flashed on how it had been in the beginning with Jonas Claymore, back when she was someone else and so was he. At first, they'd smoked pot on dates before doing zannies and benzos. It was carefree and it was fun at first. Then came the perks and norcos. And then they'd started smoking OxyContin, and after riding the ox for all these months, they had become unrecognizable people. Megan didn't know this Jonas, and in fact, she didn't even know this Megan that she had become.

"Can we please talk tomorrow, Jonas?" Megan pleaded. "This is nerve-racking and it's making me burbly."

"Jesus fucking Christ," Jonas moaned, eyes rolling back, not wanting to be reminded that he, too, was experiencing bouts of diarrhea since the jonesing episodes started. "I ain't got enough tribulations in life, I gotta hook up with a chick with irritable bowel syndrome? Why can't I catch a break just for once?"

"Sorry. Gotta do number two," Megan said, getting up and running to the bathroom.

"Go ahead, jingle bowels," he said. "Drop a deuce for me while you're at it."

FIVE

Two weeks after the red carpet event at the Kodak Theatre, Hollywood Nate Weiss was lying on the sofa in his North Hollywood apartment, where he lived alone, considering the business card he'd received from the director Rudy Ressler. For years, while working red carpet events and taking every opportunity to chat up the rich and famous, he'd been given plenty of business cards by virtue of being an LAPD cop from people who hoped he could fix a ticket or do other things for them that were equally impossible. He'd tried and mostly failed to meet the kind of people who could get him real work. No one was more aware than Nate that the clock was not on his side.

The last job where he'd had a speaking role was three years ago in an indie production that had vanished and not even gone to DVD. He'd been a day player on that one and of course had been typecast as an LAPD cop. His scripted line was "Put your hands on your head and grab the wall."

When he'd tried to tell the director, a no-talent bully ten years younger, that it was impossible to grab a wall or anything else when your hands were on your head, the director said, "And what're your qualifications in such matters?"

The assistant director then whispered to the director that Nate was an LAPD police officer in his other life, and the director grumbled something and then said to Nate, "Just go, 'Up against the wall.' And try to act excited because you've collared a perp you've been looking for." Then he turned to the assistant director and said, "Or maybe we should have the lieutenant say that?"

"Say what?" the AD asked.

"We just collared a perp we've been looking for," the annoyed director said.

"Excuse me," Nate interrupted. "The words *perp* and *collar* are terms used in the East, and though they're very popular on TV shows, we don't use either of them at LAPD. Would you like me to give you some substitute words that we use out here in the West?"

The director had dead-stared him for a moment and said, "Just say 'Up against the wall' and let it go at that. So okay, Officer... whatever your name is, let's try to get it right in one take and move the fuck on!"

Nate figured he must've gotten it right in one take. Either that or the little putz simply had had enough of him, because he growled, "Cut," two seconds after Nate delivered the line. Then he said, "Print it."

Nate was out of costume and on his way within the hour. If he could do it over again, he'd do or say whatever was asked of him without comment. It had been so hard to get work even as a day player that he hadn't done anything lately except take jobs as an extra a few times a year. And at age thirty-eight, time was surely of the essence.

Remembering his humiliation at the hands of that director caused him to get up and find the business card of Rudy Ressler. He opened his cell and dialed the number.

A young man answered, saying, "Rudy Ressler's office."

"This is Officer Nate Weiss, LAPD," he said. "Mr. Ressler asked me to call."

The young man said, "Just a moment," and put Nate on hold.

Nate almost gave up, but after nearly five minutes, the director came on the line and said, "Officer Weiss. I'm glad to hear from you!"

"You asked me to call you, Mr. Ressler," Nate said.

"I certainly did," Rudy Ressler said. "I owe you. Let's do lunch today. How about two o'clock?"

"You don't owe me anything," Nate said, disappointed. He'd hoped for more than lunch from this man.

"I certainly do," the director said. "And I'd like to discuss the possibility of you reading for me. I'll be starting a movie for cable a few months after I get back from Europe."

A job! That perked him up, and Nate said, "I'd love to have— do lunch with you. I don't have to go on duty till five fifteen. Where and what time?"

After they finished talking, Nate got dressed. He started to put on a Tommy Hilfiger jersey but decided instead to wear a red tapered Polo shirt to reveal his biceps in case the part was for a buff-looking guy. And then he had to settle on gray cargo pants from Banana Republic because they were the only pair he had that was clean other than jeans. He figured the cargos would be okay because he wanted to look younger. He wondered if he should tell Rudy Ressler that gray temples were *very* premature in his family and offer to dye them dark if the director preferred. He hated to think about the fortieth birthday about to befall him in just eighteen months.

Nate showered and got to feeling upbeat because this was the first night he'd be working with Hollywood Station's new arrival, Snuffy Salcedo. Of course, all cops were notorious gossips, and a police station secret was as hard to keep as a first marriage, but Snuffy was surely in a class of his own. Hollywood Nate figured he'd get an earful about the chief and Snuffy's life among all the police brass and the drones at City Hall. But for now, Nate had big game to hunt.

✳　　✳　　✳

At 1:50 P.M., Hollywood Nate pulled into the parking lot of a hot restaurant in west Hollywood. It was one of the new Italian places he'd read about that charged exorbitant prices to paint the food on the plate. They featured bite-size morsels of "imaginative" pasta and unrecognizable tidbits of sea creatures that wouldn't fill the belly of the baby opossums that raided the trash cans near Nate's apartment in North Hollywood. But he wasn't there for the food.

He spotted Rudy Ressler sitting at a patio table shaded by potted palms with an attractive woman who Nate figured was probably Ressler's age, though she looked younger. Nate understood the magic that was performed every day in the offices of plastic surgeons and dermatologists who almost outnumbered Realtors on the west side of Los Angeles. She was dressed for summer in a champagne-colored button-front sleeveless linen dress, and her highlighted chestnut hair was cupped just below her tiny ears.

Next to her was a younger man about Nate's age in a Calvin Klein multistripe gray suit, a crisp white shirt, and a necktie that cost more than everything on Nate's body. He had been around Hollywood types long enough to recognize the uniform of the day for agents from ICM and CAA.

Rudy Ressler was dressed supercool in a wrinkled cotton shirt, a black T-shirt beneath it, loose-fitting, acid-washed jeans, and retro black tennis shoes. In short, he took pains to dress as he had when he was in middle school, as did most of the above-the-line people on any shoot that Nate had ever worked. In the light of day the director looked older than he had on the red carpet. His rusty thinning hair was growing out at the roots, and his skin was getting blotchy. The director's eye job wasn't great either, and when Nate got close he could see the surgical scars by Ressler's ear. Nate thought the director ought to sue the quack who remodeled him.

At first Rudy Ressler didn't recognize Nate, but when he did, he jumped to his feet. "Officer Weiss!" he said, loudly enough for others at nearby tables to hear, obviously thinking it exotic and cool to be doing lunch with a cop.

Nate smiled and they shook hands. Rudy Ressler said, "I'd like you to meet my fiancée, Leona Brueger. And this is my agent, Todd Bachman."

Leona Brueger gave Nate a dazzling smile, held out her hand palm down, so that he didn't know whether to shake it or kiss it, and said, "Well, this is a treat. A real cop. Or should I say police officer?"

"Cop's fine," Nate said. "In fact, it's my favorite word."

He shook her hand, and it was quite cool for such a hot afternoon. The agent gave him a vigorous sweaty handshake and said, "Rudy tells me they call you Hollywood Nate, but I'm not sure why."

"He works at Hollywood Station," Rudy Ressler said. "And get this. He has a SAG card!"

"You're an actor as well as a cop?" Todd Bachman said.

"When I can get work," Nate said.

Rudy Ressler said to Nate, "Todd's with CAA."

"Would I have seen you in anything?" the agent asked Nate.

"I'm not sure," Nate said self-consciously. "But I'm always available if you need my type in a production you may be packaging."

Nate thought that everyone laughed too hard at that. He was trying to be amusing but he was also being very serious here.

"Are you represented?" Rudy Ressler asked.

"Well, not exactly," Nate said, getting stoked over the possibility of being represented by CAA.

Leona Brueger chuckled and said, "He's got a great look for anyone casting a cop character, doesn't he, Todd? The camera would love him."

When she said it, her lashes fluttered subtly, and Nate thought, An older chick batting her eyes at me? But then he noticed that her eyes were a bit heavy-lidded and there was an empty wine bottle in an ice bucket beside her, but neither the agent nor Rudy Ressler had a wineglass in front of him. So then he realized that Ms. Brueger liked to get her drink on.

The agent looked at his watch, and Nate saw that it was a Swiss Army watch like the one he wore. The absence of at least a Rolex made Nate conclude that the guy's client list probably included a lot of B-listers like Rudy Ressler.

The agent said, "Rudy, Leona, must go. More tomorrow. Will loop you in as soon as I hear more from A&E. Good to meet you, Officer."

He kissed the air in Leona's direction, rose, and departed. And Nate was disheartened that the agent hadn't even offered him a business card.

When he was gone, Leona Brueger stood wobbling for an instant and said to Rudy, "Damn these new Jimmy Choos. Too sky-high for me."

Nate looked down and thought that the double ankle straps looked very smart around her shapely ankles, but the leather resembled snakeskin, and he was not fond of reptiles. She took a little step sideways before righting herself and heading for the ladies' room. Sure, Nate thought, it's just the shoes.

When she was gone, Rudy Ressler said, "Leona and me, we're going to Tuscany for three months. At least that's the idea, but I don't think I can stay away that long. We plan to get married before the end of the year and move up to Napa. Leona's got a yen to own a vineyard and make wine." He pulled a sour expression and said sotto, "I don't know how long her fantasy will last, but you know how women are."

Nate said, "And, uh, how about the cable movie you mentioned? When do you think you might start prepping it?"

"Right after the first of the year," Rudy Ressler said. "I'd like you to read for the part of a police detective. It's not a big part but it does involve a couple of pages of dialogue and a big action sequence. Would you be interested?"

Nate's breath caught and he said, "Absolutely."

"Of course, I can't promise you the part right now. First you'll have to read for us. But if you do an acceptable job, it would be fun to have you in the role. The r-e-a-l cop playing the r-e-e-l cop. The publicists could have fun with it, too."

Nate took an LAPD business card from his wallet with his cell number on the back and said, "I'll be honored to read for you, Mr. Ressler."

"That's fine, Nate," Ressler said. "Just fine."

When Leona Brueger returned, she said, "Ready to go, Rudy?"

"I'll get the car," he said and headed toward the entrance.

Leona Brueger put her arm through Nate's and he walked her to the door, where a stunning young hostess who Nate figured for another aspiring thespian said, "Good day, Mrs. Brueger. Hope to see you soon."

Before Nate pushed open the door, Leona Brueger reached up with her free hand and squeezed his biceps, saying, "You've got impressive arms, young man."

"I have to work extra hard in the gym to keep them," Nate said. "It's hell getting older."

"You don't know older," Leona said wistfully, looking up at him. "Sometime you should drive up to my house and I'll pour you a drink and tell you sad stories about older."

When they got outside, Rudy Ressler's Aston Martin was waiting and he was standing beside it with a cell phone to his ear. He said to Leona Bruger, "Damn! Leona, I'm terribly sorry. I just got a call from our editor, who's practically in a fistfight with the director over the final cut. Can you possibly catch a cab?"

Nate said, "I can take Mrs. Brueger home."

"Could you, Nate? That's great," Ressler said. "Okay with you, Leona?"

"Go referee the fight," she said. "See you this evening."

Before he got in his car, Rudy Ressler said, "I just had a thought,

Leona. While we're in Europe, maybe Nate here could drive by in his patrol car once in a while and check in on the house and the new man. What's his name?"

"Raleigh Dibble," she said.

Ressler said, "Yeah, Raleigh. Would you mind, Nate? There's some valuable art in that house and that's a lotta responsibility for a new guy."

"Be glad to," Nate said, realizing that he did not get to do lunch.

When Rudy Ressler had pulled away and Nate was waiting for the parking attendant to retrieve his car, he smiled apologetically and said to Leona Brueger, "When was the last time you rode in a seven-year-old Corvette?"

"At one time in my life I drove an eighteen-year-old bathtub Nash," she said. "I was only slightly older than my mode of transportation but I loved that beast. I was driving it when I met my first husband, who I came to love a lot less than my old car, but through him I eventually came to meet Sammy Brueger. Now how about the story of *your* life, Nathan? Do they call you Nathan?"

"My mother and father do," he said. "But everybody else calls me Nate."

"Nathan Weiss." When she said his name, she gave his biceps another squeeze and hung on to him unsteadily. "How is it that a nice Irish-Italian girl like me ends up being attracted to gorgeous Jewish men?"

He smiled self-consciously and said, "Must be the circles you travel in. I haven't run into all that many gorgeous Jewish men. But I'm not much of a Jew anyway. Haven't even gone to temple since I was a kid." Then he paused and said, "Except a couple of times when somebody died."

"Relatives?"

"Cops."

"Jewish cops?"

"No, but I still felt compelled to go and pray for them, even though I know it's all mumbo jumbo."

She looked up at him and said, "Revealing that personal information to me just made you even more attractive. But I'll bet you're used to compliments from women, aren't you, Nathan?"

Nate was relieved when the parking kid arrived, and he drew the Vette up beside a Ferrari 599 that he'd read in *Motor Trend* was selling for more than $300,000. Another kid delivered an Audi R8 that Nate had read sold for a paltry $150,000.

The kid held the door open for Leona Brueger, and Nate tipped him $10, the most he had ever tipped for car service.

After he got behind the wheel, Nate said, "I do apologize for my car."

She smiled and said, "You really are too cute for words, Nathan." Then she took off her right shoe and said, "These goddamn things're killing me."

She removed the left shoe and held it in her hand while Nate drove north in heavy traffic. He looked over and touched the shoe, saying, "Is it really snakeskin?"

"Damned if I know," she said. "I'm not a shoe whore. I'm one of those broads that just buys the brand and hopes for the best." She yawned and leaned back, slurring her words slightly and said, "Go ahead and ask me."

"Ask you what?"

"How much I paid for them."

"I wasn't thinking that," Nate said, but he was.

"Come on, Nathan," she said. "I've had lots of cops in my extended family. The price of things was always on their minds. I understand you. I grew up poorer than you can imagine. I was a regular little Scarlett O'Hara when I came to this town, vowing never to be poor again. It didn't take me long to learn that everything in Hollywood is for sale if you know how to shop."

"Okay, how much do those shoes cost?" Nate asked.

Leona yawned again and said, "I think they were thirteen hundred and change."

That impressed him for sure. He looked down at the shoes again but didn't touch them this time.

Trying to make conversation to keep her awake, he said, "It sounds like you and Mr. Ressler have a wonderful vacation coming up. Two months in Tuscany sounds great."

Her eyes were closed when she spoke. "Tuscany again. A different villa this time. Rudy's never been there. Rudy's never been many places outside of Hollywood, Beverly Hills, Malibu, and the San Fernando Valley, where he can run his production company on the cheap."

"And you're getting married when you get back? Congratulations."

She opened her eyes and said, "My, my. Rudy shared a lot when I went to the ladies' room. It must be the badge you carry. He's very impressed with authority figures. When he has dinner with the chief of police he almost wets his pants." Then she told him her address in the Hollywood Hills and closed her eyes.

Nate wondered if a bottle of wine always made her so chatty. And he wondered if an innocent flirtation with Leona Brueger might give him more juice with Rudy Ressler. Then he remembered what an assistant director had said to him on one of the last jobs he'd worked. The AD had observed the producer's wife, a woman twenty years older than Nate, flirting with him. It made him say to Nate, "Officer, if you want to get work in this business, don't pet the cougars. Not when they belong to the boss."

She actually began dozing by the time they reached the foot of the Hollywood Hills and the Corvette began climbing up Outpost Drive to Mulholland. Nate had always enjoyed driving in the Hills in a black-and-white, admiring the view homes, fantasizing about that one break that could make it all possible for him, too.

When he got to the address she'd given him, he pulled up to the gate and stopped. It was easily the largest residential property in this part of the Hollywood Hills and Nate had to admit he'd love to be shown around.

He said gently, "Uh, Mrs. Brueger, we're here."

She opened her eyes and rummaged in her purse until she found a key ring that had a small remote device on it. She pressed it and the gate swung open. He drove in on a long, curving, faux-cobblestone driveway. He made the circle around a bubbling fountain so that the front of his car was facing the gate and she was on the side in front of the huge tiled arch over the main door.

He jumped out and ran around to open the door for her but she was already out, holding her $1,300 shoes in one hand and her purse in the other.

"Come in for a minute, Nathan," she said.

"Okay, Mrs. Brueger," he said.

This was a first. He'd been inside many homes in the Hollywood Hills over the years but as a cop, almost never as a guest.

She unlocked the door and pushed it open, walking to a nearby computer panel on the wall to punch in her code and deactivate the high-pitched alarm warning.

"Follow me," she said.

He did that, crossing a foyer of Mexican tile until he was looking down two steps into the great room. It was very large and it seemed that almost every square foot of the white plaster walls contained paintings: oils, watercolors, and numbered lithographs.

Leona Brueger tossed her shoes on a massive glass coffee table, knocking over some pricey-looking knickknacks.

She said, "Have a seat. I'll be right back. What're you drinking?"

The entire interior was done in cream and custard colors: the walls, the drapes, the carpet, the side tables, and even the twin sofas, with accent pillows in subtle pastels. It all spelled comfort to Hollywood Nate. There was none of that minimalist crap he was constantly seeing in magazines and in the *L.A. Times* home section.

This all looked stuffed and overstuffed. He had the impression of being enveloped by a giant voluptuous marshmallow.

And then there was the view. It was Hollywood, but not his Hollywood down there at asphalt level. This was Hollywood as seen by God, if there was one. The smog from this elevation was not ugly, not a dingy gray blanket of dangerous gases settling over the L.A. basin in late summer. No, this was a blaze of vivid primary colors propelled by offshore breezes and later would be lit by a last solar gasp before the sun fell into the Pacific. It was astonishing how beautiful and even delicious the L.A. smog could look from a $15 million home in the Hollywood Hills.

She paused on the top step and said, "Do you like the view?"

Nate said, "Up here the smog is the color of a cabernet and overripe plums and purple grapes with a spray of peach juice flowing through it. But somehow I don't think this is what they mean when they say that Hollywood is just a big fruit bowl."

Leona Brueger said, "Why, Officer Weiss, you do surprise me. Not only do you carry a SAG card but you have a touch of the poet in you. I wonder what other surprises you might be keeping hidden."

Nate looked at his watch and said, "I have to be at work and in uniform by seventeen fifteen—I mean, five fifteen. I better not have a drink."

She turned and said, "How about diet soda? You look like the healthy diet soda type."

"Fine," he said. "Thanks."

The coffee table between the two sofas was piled with art books that looked as though they'd never been opened, and women's magazines that looked well perused. When she returned with his diet soda in a crystal goblet, she had a goblet of white wine for herself. She held her glass up to his and said, "Chin-chin," which a makeup artist that Nate used to date said was "the cry of the Hills birds," meaning the women of the Hollywood Hills.

She sat down two feet away from him on the sofa and said, "I gave the butler the afternoon off. He won't be back until seventeen hundred—I mean, five o'clock."

That made Nate chuckle, and then he said, "Would he be Raleigh, the guy I'm supposed to see when I check on your property after you're gone?"

"That's him," Leona Brueger said. "Some of my friends say I shouldn't leave all this"—she waved in the general direction of the paintings—"with a man who's only worked here such a short time, but he's also worked for a friend of ours and comes highly recommended. Besides, I don't give a rat's eyeball for all this. It was my late husband's passion, not mine. It's well insured anyway, so que será, será."

"I don't know very much about art," Nate said, sipping his soda and thinking, Yes, this lady really does like to get her drink on.

"Neither do I," she said. "And I'm too old to learn. And speaking of old, how old did you say you are?"

"I'm thirty-eight," he said. "I know I'm getting a bit long in the tooth to make it in the movie business. I've been a cop since I was a baby of twenty-one."

"Hah!" she said. "Old. Thirty-eight is old, is it?"

She took a long pull from the wineglass and put it down on the coffee table. She scooted close to him and said, "I'll bet I could help your career a little bit. As far as the part in whatever the thing is that Rudy's doing, you've got it. I'll see to that. But it's only a couple of days' work. I know other people in the business. People with real topspin. I could introduce you around. Some evening when you're off duty, would you like to come here to a dinner party and meet a few of my friends?"

"You bet I would," Nate said, wondering if a chemical peel gave her that buttery skin.

"I have to warn you, though," she said, "all they talk about is diets, drugs that facilitate diets, and box-office grosses."

"Fine with me," he said.

"Can you really act?"

"Well, I'm not one of those who go through life imagining how everything would look through the lens of a Steadicam, but I've taken some classes," he said. "And I've had a couple of speaking parts, but not in a feature film yet. And I can't count the number of times I've been an extra." He stopped when he saw her lips curve up in a little smile, and he felt like a kid bragging to a wealthy aunt. Then he said, "So, yes, I think I can act. But so can thousands—no, make it tens of thousands—of other people trying for the same breaks. I know what I'm up against."

"Rudy Ressler is no Martin Scorcese," she said, "but I'm sure you're aware of that. Is that how you see yourself? In a crime movie directed by Scorcese or maybe by Clint Eastwood?"

"In my fantasies?"

"Yeah, let's hear your fantasies."

"To be honest, in my fantasies I'm not playing a cop. I see myself in a Woody Allen movie."

He watched her burst into laughter, and he wasn't sure how to interpret it until she stopped and said, "You are adorable, Nathan Weiss. I think I could like you a lot."

"I like you, too," he said, not knowing what else to say. And then it occurred to him that what was making him feel so uncomfortable and awkward was not just the fact that she was Rudy Ressler's fiancée and he wanted the job. And it wasn't just her age. She was a fit, hot-looking woman, even if she was as old as his mother. It was that she was *rich*. This was the first time in his life that Nate Weiss was playing a flirtation scene with a seriously wealthy woman.

"Meanwhile, you do have a job that you like, yes?" Leona said.

Nate said, "At Hollywood Station we used to have a sergeant we called the Oracle. He said that doing good police work was the most fun we'd ever have in our entire lives. And I've found that to be true." Then he thought of his former partner, Dana Vaughn, of her lying dead in his arms, and he said, "For the most part it's been fun."

"Where does acting come into it, then?" she asked.

Nate said, "I thought acting would be what I could do full-time after my pension is vested. I'll reach that in three more years, but if I retire at that time, I still won't be able to draw the pension until I'm fifty years old. I figure I could be a full-time actor in the interim. But I need a break. Don't we all?"

"So that's your dream, is it?" she said.

Nate said, "My dreams aren't complicated. Any one of the Kardashians could interpret them."

She said, "I'm surprised that when you serve twenty years as a cop you aren't able to receive any pension money yet."

"I'll still be too young then," Nate said.

"Too young," she said with a look of melancholy. Then her eyes narrowed and she said, "Me, I'm old enough to have my cop and eat him, too."

Talk about a cougar! This man-eater looked like she truly could come at him, fang and claw. While he was contemplating that troubling catamount image, she said, "I'm old enough for anything. *Any* damn thing at all."

With that she leaned over abruptly and kissed him on the cheek and then on the mouth. Her kiss was open-mouthed and warm, with lots of tongue.

When she pulled away, she looked at him, sloe-eyed, and he figured there was no way out, not if he wanted to be in Ressler's movie. This menopausal momma was about to debauch him right here in this goddamn marshmallow palace!

Leona stood up and unbuttoned her dress and let it hang open. He saw a lace-trimmed white bra that held breasts he guessed were helped by silicone, and a flat belly that she'd earned, and shapely thighs the color of burnished copper, compliments of a tanning bed, he supposed.

As though reading his thoughts, she said, "The tawny color is mostly mine even without tanning, compliments of my Italian old man. But my ma was Irish, so I can hold a grudge with the best of them. Don't ever cross me, gorgeous."

Nate watched her let the dress fall to the floor and he thought that she might be his mother's age but that's all they had in common. Then it occurred to him that he had actually flashed on a flittering image of his mother, and he thought, What the hell's this, Oedipus time? Was Hollywood Nate Weiss just another Jewish momma's boy? But no, that cliché was just too ridiculous.

Leona said, "We should behave like grown-ups and go to my bedroom for this first-timer, shouldn't we? Yet somehow, being with a lovely lad like you I don't want to behave like a grown-up. Do you?"

She unhooked her bra and let it fall to the floor with the linen dress, and he thought, Silicone for sure, but understated and very acceptable. Then it was his turn to give a command performance, so he put his glass on the table beside the sofa and stood. Just then another image flared, as hot and blinding as a red carpet spotlight. His mother still used those same words on him at least once a month: "Behave like a grown-up and find a nice woman, Nathan." Goddamnit! If he couldn't sweep away the terrifiying notion that he was about to shtup his own mother, he'd never even get it up!

Nate started feeling feverish and not in a good way. If ever he needed the tips he'd learned in that UCLA film class . . . Maybe if he were a method actor, he could go all Tom Jones sensuous and imagine something decadent, like a bathtub full of cherries jubilee or something. He had a sudden sensation of flop sweat, and he hadn't even flopped yet. Then he heard the sound of a car clattering down the axle-cracking, fake-cobblestone driveway, and it didn't sound like Rudy Ressler's purring Aston Martin.

"Shit!" she said. "That's Raleigh's car. What the hell's he doing back here after I gave him the fucking afternoon off? Jesus Christ!"

"I'd better get going," Nate said with more than a small measure of relief. "Does he come in through the main door?"

"No, the kitchen door, damn him. But you don't have to slink away, Nathan." She picked up her clothes hastily and said, "Let me run to the bedroom and change. We can still sit and chat."

"I'd better go," Nate said, moving quickly to the front door, thinking that he definitely didn't want the butler to gossip about him to Rudy Ressler. "You can tell him that I dropped you off and came in to use the bathroom for a minute so he doesn't wonder about my Vette in the driveway, okay?"

She stood with her crumpled dress in her arms and said, "When we get back from Europe, I want you here for dinner parties, yes? And other things?"

"Yes, ma'am," Nate said with a grin, handing her a business card bearing his private cell number.

"Yes, Leona," she prompted.

"Yes, Leona," he said.

"Don't ever call me ma'am or Mrs. Brueger," she said. "Never again."

"Never again, Leona," he said, with an even bigger grin that required more acting skill.

When Nate was in his Corvette and driving out through her gate, he thought once more of the assistant director who'd said, "Don't pet the cougar." It wasn't until he was motoring down Mulholland Drive that he began to understand his conflicted feelings in that house. Sure, it was her money, and her age, that triggered those childish thoughts of his mother, but there was something else. It was the first time in his entire life that he'd been put in the position of actually living the ultimate Hollywood cliché. She had challenged him to man-up and sell his ass for a movie role, and he had waffled like a teenage ingenue on a casting couch. She had been every inch a man-eating cougar, and Hollywood Nate Weiss had been nothing but a twitchy fucking rabbit.

★ SIX ★

As THAT SUMMER was winding down, most of the dozen working detectives at Hollywood Station had to wonder what else could happen. It wasn't just the antics of the Bling Ring by any means. Another crime spree involved the "BMW Bandits," who had attacked more than fifty BMWs, mostly on the west side and Wilshire district. They were discriminating thieves who often ignored personal articles such as laptops and other pricey items that owners left in their cars. What they were after were replaceable air bags and high-tech headlights, costing nearly $3,000 to replace in BMW 3 and 5 series cars. Other traditionally valuable and vulnerable car parts, like wheel rims, were being ignored, and the thieves were able to access and remove the air bags very quickly. Hollywood was expected to be next on their list of favorite areas of attack.

But the wave of home and auto burglaries was nothing compared with the strange and disturbing serial murders that occupied some of the detectives at Hollywood Station. One of the most bizarre involved the stabbing of homeless people. The first murder took place midday on a lovely Hollywood afternoon near Sunset Boulevard and Western Avenue. A homeless man managed to put in a call to police, saying, "I think I've been shot," before falling over dead. He had not been shot but stabbed, and he died of a lethal puncture wound to the chest.

Another murder occurred on Hollywood Boulevard by the Music Box Theater. A homeless man was found dead on the ground, where he'd been lying for hours. The initial patrol officers to arrive saw no blood trail and at first did not think he'd been stabbed. After detectives arrived, they learned that one of the nearby commercial buildings had a security camera on which their suspect, another homeless man, was recorded watching his intended victim. The killer would approach the sleeping man, and whenever a pedestrian passed by, he would walk away. At one point he even seemed to spot the video camera watching him, but he was undeterred.

He'd taped a steak knife to his forearm inside two pieces of cardboard that acted as a sheath. When he felt it was safe, he simply walked over to the sleeping man and seemed to poke him. There was no slashing, no overkill. Just the chest puncture, and it was enough.

A third attack occurred at Yucca and Wilcox Avenues. A homeless man awoke with pain in his chest. When he got up, blood gushed from a chest wound and he found that he could not walk. He was rushed to the hospital in time to save his life.

The killer turned out to be a former inmate of a state mental facility. Random beatings and even the senseless killing of vulnerable homeless people were certainly not rare, but this was Hollywood's first serial attacker of homeless people who was himself a homeless person. The detectives referred to him as "the ultimate self-hating bum."

Clearly, the most heinous case in the Hollywood detectives' murder books in the first year of the Obama presidency involved Michael Thomas Gargiulo, who was awaiting trial for serial murder. Gargiulo, a thirty-two-year-old air conditioner and furnace repairman, originally from the Chicago suburb of Glenview, Illinois, was initially linked in a peripheral way to a Hollywood actor.

Long before coming to Los Angeles from Illinois, Michael Gargiulo had been questioned as a teenager in the murder of his high school classmate Tricia Pacaccio. She was stabbed to death in what detectives called a "blitz attack" on her doorstep in August 1993, a week before the eighteen-year-old was to report to Purdue University as a freshman with an interest in environmental issues. In her high school yearbook, the bright and popular girl said she "wanted to save the world," but as it turned out, she couldn't save herself. Her murder went unsolved, although DNA material was found under the fingernails of the victim. Years later, Hollywood detectives became intimately acquainted with that case, following a terrible murder in the Hollywood Hills.

On February 22, 2001, actor Ashton Kutcher had driven to the Hollywood Hills bungalow of his girlfriend, Ashley Ellerin, to take her to a Grammy Awards party. She was a stunning twenty-two-year-old fashion student, a model, and an occasional Las Vegas dancer. The young actor knocked and rang the bell but got no answer. He looked through a rear window and saw what he thought were wine stains on the carpet. He left the bungalow, and Ashley Ellerin's body was found the next day by her housemate. The first detective to arrive called the crime scene "a massacre."

Every window in the bungalow had bars on it, and there was even a steel door. The doors were in good repair, all freshly painted with no sign of forced entry. Inside, from the front entry down a long passage, were spatter and drops of blood. Beyond that, there was a lot more blood all the way to the body lying on the top landing, described by detectives as "a bloody pulp." Her hair looked as though she'd just washed it and was fresh from a shower at the time of attack. She wore a terry-cloth robe and pajamas. Her throat had been sawed and ripped open and her head was knocked off the brain stem. Only mangled ribbons of tissue connected her head to her body. The medical examiner stopped counting stab wounds at forty-eight.

Criminalists tried to get latent prints and DNA evidence, but all of the fingerprints in the bungalow belonged to the victim or her housemate. Later, after searching his memory for any possible suspect whom she might have let into their home, the housemate of Ashley Ellerin mentioned "Mike the furnace guy" to police. He said that Ashley and a friend had met Mike when he'd walked out of the nearby dog park one day. Mike was described as being six two, 180 pounds, and having a "dark demeanor. " He had stopped by the bungalow one afternoon when Ashley was not at home, telling the housemate that he wanted to work on her furnace, and he had been spotted driving his truck slowly past the bungalow on another occasion.

That crime resulted in a seven-year investigation that eventually led Hollywood Division detectives to Illinois and the Pacaccio murder, as well as to other blitz attacks in the Los Angeles area in 2005 and 2007. A detective with the L.A. Sheriff's Homicide Bureau described one of them as "the most violent murder I ever saw, bar none." The attacker had done horrible "staging" with body parts on that one, and it looked as though the victim had been ravaged by a pack of sharks.

And finally, in 2008, a Santa Monica woman was attacked in her home but managed to fight off her assailant and survive, despite serious stab wounds. DNA evidence was collected and coordinated and it brought everything together. Michael Gargiulo was at last in custody, awaiting trial in 2010. And Hollywood paparazzi would be ready for Ashton Kutcher if he should be required to testify, drooling over the possibility that his wife, Demi Moore, might accompany him to court.

So there was no dearth of violence and other serial crimes for the dozen overworked detectives at Hollywood Station to deal with, and the detectives at the Major Assault Crimes table got their share of domestic violence cases in that first year of the recession. The MAC detectives who responded late on a blistering hot afternoon to an unusual domestic violence call from a woman in an apartment building in Little Armenia were both cops with more than twenty years on the Job. Gina Villegas, a forty-three-year-old energetic Mexican American, and Carl Cheng, a forty-two-year-old laconic Taiwanese American, were both children of immigrants who got to use their language skills frequently in the polyglot community that was Hollywood.

They hadn't needed their foreign-language skills when they got ordered to Little Armenia. They were responding to a telephonic plea made to their D3 supervisor by a terrified woman who said that she had been stalked and threatened by an ex-lover who was father to the baby she had given birth to only five weeks prior. Thelma Barker, their detective supervisor, was a bootstraps-up black veteran with thirty-one years on the Job. She was born and raised in Compton and had been a victim of domestic violence herself during a brief marriage at the age of nineteen.

The old three-story building in Little Armenia, consisting of twenty-eight rental units, was a rectangular block of gray stucco, and was possibly the most protected apartment building in that part of east Hollywood. Because of episodes of tagging by street gangs in the area, the owner had taken the extraordinary step of hiring local pensioners as watchmen. The geezers took turns sitting in a tiny office off the lobby from 9 P.M. to 6 A.M. seven days a week, when vandalism was a threat. There were no fire escapes or any exterior balconies that could be easily accessed.

The detectives rang the manager and were buzzed inside by a retired plumber who also did handyman jobs in the building. When he learned who the detectives were looking for, he said, "Confidentially, I don't like it when the owner of this property gets so charitable. The girl in three-ten is his niece, or so he claims. She's behind two months in the rent and still he lets her stay. Don't tell her I told you, but she leaves her two babies alone sometimes. I've felt like calling you when she does it, but she's the boss's special tenant, if you know what I mean, and I don't wanna lose this job."

Gina Villegas thanked him, and when they got to the one-bedroom apartment on the third floor, a dangerously thin woman met them at the door. She was a twenty-five-year-old strawberry blonde with frightened, darting eyes, trembling hands, and suspiciously stained teeth.

Carl Cheng's glance toward his partner said, Tweaker.

Before either cop could say anything to her, the woman said, "I'm the one who called your office. My name's Cindy Kroll. My ex-boyfriend is threatening me. I think he wants to kill me."

"And why would you think that?" Gina Villegas asked while Carl Cheng glanced around the little apartment.

There were two chairs at the small Formica table in the kitchen. And in the living room, if you could call it that, was a sofa, a shabby overstuffed chair, an infant's crib, and a playpen, all crowded together around a big-screen Sony TV.

Carl Cheng smirked subtly in his partner's direction as if to say, No matter how crappy they live, they always have a better TV than I do.

Cindy Kroll said, "Sorry there's no place to sit down." She pointed to a thirteen-month-old in the playpen. Then she said, "My five-week-old baby boy's asleep in my bedroom. We don't have much room here."

Gina Villegas said, "A thirteen-month-old and a five-week-old? You're not wasting time starting a family, are you?"

"My baby boy was an accident, and that's what's causing the problem," Cindy Kroll said. "His father wants me dead for demanding child support."

"Are you married to him?" the detective asked.

"No," she said. "After my first baby was born, my husband, Ralphie, took off and left us. I had a tough time and could only make a few bucks cleaning houses. I had a job cleaning the apartment of Louis Dryden every week for four months. He lives up on Franklin Avenue and has a pretty good job at a real-estate company in Santa Monica, selling vacation rentals. He's maybe ten years older than me, and, well, we started getting intimate while I was working for him and pretty soon I got pregnant."

"Pregnant by *him?*" Gina Villegas said.

"Of course by *him.*" Cindy Kroll's darting eyes flashed. "I'm no slut."

"No, I didn't mean that you were. But you also have a husband, right?"

"He's outta my life. I got pregnant by Louis and nobody else."

"Go on," Gina Villegas said.

"He gave me some cash to get an abortion but I didn't do it. I decided to have the baby and hire a lawyer. For the past couple of months my lawyer's been calling him, but Louis says the baby isn't his. He says he's engaged to a terrific woman now and I'm ruining his life with my lies."

"How about a paternity test?" Gina Villegas said. "That should settle the matter."

"That's what my lawyer's working on now. We're gonna take him to court."

Carl Cheng spoke for the first time and said, "Why're we here, ma'am?"

"He stalked me today," Cindy Kroll said. "He caught me at the Seven-Eleven store I always go to and told me this is my last chance. He said he'd give me five thousand dollars to leave me alone and quit saying the baby's his."

"And what'd you say?" Carl Cheng asked.

"I told him to talk to my lawyer."

"And when you were at the store, where were your babies?" Gina Villegas asked.

After a long pause, Cindy Kroll said, "I was only gone for a few minutes."

"You can't leave babies alone like that. It's child endangering and it's against the law," Gina Villegas said.

Cindy Kroll said, "I asked the woman in the next apartment to look in on them every few minutes. Don't you wanna hear what I got to say? This man threatened me!"

This time Gina Villegas glanced at her partner. A woman next door? Sure.

"Of course we want to hear," Carl Cheng said. "What did he say exactly?"

Cindy Kroll now addressed all answers to the male detective and said, "He told me his entire life and career were on the line. He said his fiancée was not like me. When I asked him what he meant, he goes, 'She's a lady, not a whore like you.' And then he threatened me."

"Use his exact words if you can remember," Carl Cheng said.

"Okay, he said to me, 'Whatever happens is on your head, not mine. You're forcing me to do whatever I gotta do to stop your blackmail from wrecking my whole life.' That's exactly what he said."

Carl Cheng said, "Did you ask him what he meant by that?"

"I knew what he meant," Cindy Kroll said. "I'm not stupid!"

Gina Villegas said, "What you know or think you know about the implication of his words will not satisfy the District Attorney's Office. Did he say more than that? Anything specific by way of a violent threat?"

Cindy Kroll directed her answer to Carl Cheng and said, "Then he goes, 'I'll make it ten thousand dollars but no more. Take the extortion money and get outta my life.' That's exactly what he said."

"What did you say?" Gina Villegas asked.

Cindy Kroll looked at her this time and said, "The same thing. That he should talk to my lawyer."

"It doesn't constitute a threat of violence," Carl Cheng said.

"Look, Detective," she said to him, "I had sex with that man lotsa times. All I want is a reasonable amount of child support to raise his baby boy." Then she paused and said, "*Our* baby boy."

"There're limits to what we can do," Gina Villegas said.

"You gotta do something now!" Cindy Kroll said. "The man's been smoking a lotta crystal meth. Way more since our troubles started, and it makes him totally paranoid. He had an insane look in his eyes today when he threatened me. Do you know what it's like to get all paranoid from smoking crystal?"

Carl Cheng's look said, No, but I'll bet you do.

"Do you know if he has a police record?" Gina Villegas asked.

"Not that I know of."

"Have you done crystal meth with him?" Gina Villegas asked.

"Oh, fuck!" Cindy Kroll said, and stifled a sob. "You don't care if he kills me! I need protection. Tonight is when he likes to go out and score enough crystal for the weekend. I'm in danger tonight."

Gina Villegas sat down at the kitchen table, pushed some baby debris aside, and opened her notebook and said, "Okay, give us his address and phone number. We'll try to have a talk with him."

"What if he's not home?" Cindy Kroll said. "I need protection at least for tonight."

"There are domestic violence shelters," Gina Villegas said. "And restraining orders. Have you talked to your lawyer about all that?"

"I don't wanna go to a fucking shelter!" Cindy Kroll said. "I want police protection here in my home."

Carl Cheng said, "We can't camp out here based on what you've told us. But we'll ask the radio car in this area to drive by tonight and keep an eye on the place. I gotta tell you, though, this building's like a fortress. I noticed that the rear fire door is steel-reinforced with no handle on the outside. And you have a watchman in the lobby, right? Does Louis Dryden have a key, either to the main door or to your apartment?"

"No," she admitted. "He only came in here a few times after he drove me home."

"Well, there you go," Carl Cheng said. "You're safe here. But just to put your mind at rest, a black-and-white will do drive-bys tonight. Okay?"

After returning to the station, the MAC team tried to reach Louis Dryden by phone but got no answer, and no answering machine picked up. They ran a record check using the description supplied to them by Cindy Kroll but came back with nothing that fit Louis Dryden on Franklin Avenue. They were already into overtime by then and so were five other detectives, busy in their tiny cubicles, making phone calls and working computers.

The MAC team told D3 Thelma Barker about the vague implied threat that Louis Dryden had allegedly made. They said that Cindy Kroll's boyfriend was a tweaker and they were sure she was, too.

"The mother of the year, she ain't," Carl Cheng finally told his D3. "Our read is that she gave birth to a baby she doesn't want just to trap the guy into marriage or blackmail him into a nice cash settlement, or maybe both."

"Tell you what," their D3 said. "I know it's getting late and you'd like to get started on your weekend, but just to be on the safe side, let's ask a patrol unit to drop one of your business cards with a phone-me message on Louis Dryden's doorstep. That'll put the fear of God in him if he's thinking of doing something stupid." She looked at her watch and said, "The midwatch is about finished with roll call. Why don't you tell the sergeant what this is all about and also ask that a radio car drive by the place a few times tonight for a quick look-see. You never know with tweakers when they're amped up."

"If she's a tweaker, too, maybe she's the one that's paranoid," Carl Cheng said. "That's what tweakers do, get all paranoid."

"It'll make me feel better if you do it my way," his D3 said with a look that ended the discussion.

"Okay, boss," Carl Cheng said with a sigh of fatigue. "Anything you say."

★ SEVEN ★

THE NEW WATCH commander, Lieutenant O'Reilly, conducted roll call that afternoon for Watch 5, the midwatch. He was a thirty-year-old lieutenant who so far the troops didn't much like. He'd tested well on promotion exams and was recently appointed to his rank with only nine years on the Department and sent to Hollywood Division for his probation. He gave them a condescending lecture that was so boring it couldn't have been enlivened with hand puppets. It was all about treating the citizens of Hollywood with the utmost respect, even those who were as crazy as rabid squirrels. And in Hollywood that included a lot of folks.

On the wall behind the long tables where his captive audience sat were framed movie posters, including ones for *Sunset Boulevard* and *L.A. Confidential,* an indication that the officers of Hollywood Station were very aware of their unique geography. Finally, the lieutenant ran out of things to lecture them about and said, "Let's go to work." The cops gathered their gear, but before leaving the room, each of them touched for luck the framed photo of their late sergeant whom they'd called the Oracle. They had loved their old supervisor, and he had thought of them as his children.

The framed photo, which was affixed to the wall beside the doorway, bore a brass plate that said:

THE ORACLE
APPOINTED: FEB 1960
END-OF-WATCH: AUG 2006
SEMPER COP

The assistant watch commander, Sergeant Lee Murillo, a calm and bookish Mexican American with hair the color of stainless steel and the knotty rawboned body of a long-distance runner, had fifteen years of LAPD experience and was a supervisor they did happen to like. He was downstairs in the detective squad room talking to the MAC team about Cindy Kroll and Louis Dryden, and he gave the Little Armenia drive-by job to 6-X-76 when Lieutenant O'Reilly was finished with them.

All five patrol units, including 6-X-32, manned by Flotsam and Jetsam, and 6-X-66, with Hollywood Nate driving and Snuffy Salcedo riding shotgun, left the kit room with their gear and headed for the parking lot at 6 P.M. They toted black nylon war bags full of gear, as well as Remington shotguns, Ithaca beanbag shotguns, helmets, Tasers, pepper spray, and rovers. During the prior several years that the LAPD had suffered under the federal consent decree, they had also been required to draw from the kit room devices to record superfluous data about people they stopped or arrested. None of that data collecting had ever provided police critics with information that they'd hoped would prove claims of racial profiling. As hard as they tried, the disgruntled critics of the LAPD were not able to wave the race flag when it came to traffic and pedestrian stops.

P2 Vivien Daley, one of three female officers working the midwatch that evening, was the driver of the shop belonging to 6-X-76, so called because of the shop numbers on the roof and doors of their Crown Vics. Those numbers allowed a unit to be easily identified by citizens and by the LAPD helicopters, called airships by the troops.

The late summer sun was still high enough that Viv Daley put on her sunglasses when she got behind the wheel. The thirty-year-old cop was born and raised in Long Beach and had played varsity basketball at Long Beach State, but she had disappointed her parents, who wanted her to become a teacher. She always said she'd applied at the LAPD "on a whim" but had never regretted it in the eight years that she'd served. Viv loved to quote the Oracle to her parents, especially his often-repeated mantra: "Doing good police work is the most fun you'll ever have in your entire lives." She found that to be true.

Viv Daley had scrubbed good looks, and the only makeup she carried was a pencil to darken her sandy eyebrows and a subtle pale lipstick, a shade approved by the Department. She kept her auburn hair pinned up above the collar of her uniform shirt, as was required of all female patrol officers. At end-of-watch, when she'd changed into her jersey and jeans and three-inch wedges, she stood taller than almost every male officer on the watch, but Flotsam could still look down at her, wedges or not.

Her passenger partner "keeping books," or "taking paper," which simply meant being the report writer, was twenty-nine-year-old Georgie Adams, who had seven years on the Job. He wore his raven hair slicked back, and with his black irises and chiseled features, he was as dark and exotic-looking as Viv Daley was fair and freckled. The dissimilarity extended to their stature as well. At a wiry five foot eight, he was the shortest male officer on the midwatch, a full five inches shorter than his gym-fit partner, and though he was well muscled, he didn't outweigh her by much due to her large-boned frame. He referred to Viv as "tall sister" and often called her "sis."

Because of his Anglo-Saxon surname but swarthy appearance, questions about his ethnicity came up immediately with new partners, and when it did, Georgie Adams was quick to display his sinister smile and say, "I'm a Gypsy boy. A distant cousin to the late George Adams, California's 'King of the Gypsies.'"

Nobody ever knew if Georgie's claim was true, and nobody had been able to pry much more of his history from him. He'd served in Iraq with the Marines and had been wounded by a roadside bomb, that much was known for sure. He was born and raised in San Bernardino, California, and sometimes he told what everyone figured was a preposterous story of having been bought from a Gypsy clan passing through town by a Syrian carpet importer and his wife, who raised him and let him keep his noble Gypsy surname. Yet whenever he was called to the home of an Arabic-speaking crime victim in Hollywood, it was clear that he could not speak the language of the Syrians. The next guess was that he was of Latino descent, but he could not speak Spanish either. All bets were off at Hollywood Station as to Georgie Adams's true ethnicity.

His personnel package downtown didn't reveal much, as one of the curious Hollywood Division supervisors who had taken a look at it learned. The supervisor even contacted the civilian employee who had conducted Georgie's background check. He was told that the applicant's parents, Jean and Theodore Adams, were third-generation San Bernardino residents whose forebears were Okies from the great migration of the 1930s. And further, the background investigator said, Georgie had come to them through a county adoption with almost nothing known about his birth mother, a teenage drifter, and nothing at all about his biological father.

The only certainties were that, immediately after graduating from high school in San Bernardino, Georgie Adams had joined the Marines and after his discharge had enrolled at a community college, which he left to join the LAPD. And that was it. The other cops referred to him as "the Gypsy," and he seemed to like the handle.

Georgie's partner, Viv Daley, never questioned him about his ethnicity or asked anything about his shadowy past. She simply said, "It's none of my business. And anyway, I love a mystery."

The surfer cops were attracted to Viv Daley and had tried many times to take her surfing, saying they'd turn her into a "quantum quebee," which she learned from Jetsam was a compliment, meaning a hot surfer chick. But so far Viv had resisted their many invitations to attend the nighttime ragers on the sand, including one that was scheduled for Sunday night at Bolsa Chica Beach, where many firefighters and cops liked to surf.

When she told her partner about the invitation, and her concern that a bunch of boozy surfers might get a bit too aggressive and handsy with any women present, Georgie offered to go with her as chaperone.

He said, "Sis, if any drunken surfer trash put their paws on my bosom buddy, I'll cut out their fucking hearts and feed them to the seagulls."

"'Bosom buddy,'" Viv said. "That's charming, but I don't think I'll be needing a Gypsy assassin as a chaperone."

When Jetsam heard from Viv about Georgie's offer, he informed Flotsam, who said, "Dude, maybe we oughtta like, rethink our rager invite to Viv. The Gypsy might spoil the party if he goes all aggro and starts carving up kahunas."

There'd been persistent rumors ever since he arrived at Hollywood Station that Georgie Adams carried a buck knife on duty in an ankle rig. There had been two known cases in LAPD history of unarmed undercover officers killing assailants with a knife when they were trapped in a deadly situation. The Gypsy was known for his mordant sense of humor, but when he showed his baleful smile and let it be known that he was looking for a chance to be the first *uniformed* LAPD copper to do it, the others tended to believe he might be serious.

The first time the rumor about the buck knife reached young Lieutenant O'Reilly, he ordered Sergeant Murillo to check it out, and if it was true, to put a stop to it immediately.

"Tell Adams he isn't playing a role in a spaghetti western here," Lieutenant O'Reilly said to his sergeant.

But the desk officer overheard the watch commander's order, and LAPD's jungle wireless went to work immediately. By the time Sergeant Murillo got around to asking Georgie Adams to accompany him to the locker room, the young cop didn't look at all surprised, nor did he question his supervisor about his reason.

"I'm sorry, Adams," Sergeant Murillo said when they were alone in the locker room, "but I've been tasked to find out if you carry a buck knife in an ankle rig, and if you do, to order you to stop doing it."

Silently, Georgie reached down and pulled up both pant legs all the way to his knees. Sergeant Murillo saw no buck knife. What he did see was mottled scar tissue from third-degree burns, and grafts that looked like scorched lumpy egg white, wrapped around Georgie's shins and calves from the top of his six-inch zip-up boots to just below his knees.

"Okay, thanks," Sergeant Murillo said, and left him in the locker room.

When he returned to the watch commander's office, Sergeant Murillo said, "I've spoken with Adams and checked for a buck knife."

"What did you find out?" asked Lieutenant O'Reilley.

"That he *earned* his Purple Heart," said Sergeant Murillo. "And I'm gonna invite him and his partner to meet me at Hamburger Hamlet for code seven tonight. Where I'll buy them any goddamn thing they want."

Lieutenant O'Reilley never asked Sergeant Murillo about the buck knife again.

Back when Viv Daley and Georgie Adams had first been partnered, Sergeant Murillo had taken her aside in the sergeants' room and said, "I know that Adams is an acquired taste. I was wondering if you're happy working with him?"

Viv Daley said, "Sarge, I wouldn't trade him for anybody at Hollywood Station. When the Gypsy's got your back, a girl couldn't be more safe at a sleepover in the Lincoln Bedroom." Then she added, "Except for when Bill Clinton lived there."

Viv and Georgie drove to Louis Dryden's apartment building on Franklin Avenue and slid the detective's business card in the jamb of Dryden's front door where he couldn't miss it, then began patrol and cleared for calls. While driving eastbound on Hollywood Boulevard on the way to their area, they saw that the Street Characters were out in force in front of Grauman's Chinese Theatre. The recession had brought hard times to even some of the costumed performers, who posed for photos with tourists and received voluntary tips for it. They were not allowed by law to panhandle or make demands of the tourists.

Newscasters gleefully reported to their audiences whenever tensions arose around the Grauman's forecourt, where the handprints and footprints of famous movie stars were set in the cement pavement. On a recent occasion, Elmo the Muppet had been arrested for aggressive panhandling, and so had the dark-hooded character from *Scream*. Street Character Freddy Krueger was also busted for taking his role too seriously and allegedly stabbing someone. Mr. Incredible had been jailed, as had Batman and Chewbacca from *Star Wars*. So far, the several Darth Vaders had behaved themselves, but Spider-Man, or rather one of several using that costume, got popped by Hollywood cops for slugging somebody.

As 6-X-76 passed Grauman's, Georgie Adams said, "I'm gonna be real disappointed if SpongeBob SquarePants ever gets busted for something. I always liked him on TV."

"I never much liked Spider-Man," Viv said. "Too creepy. Crawling around like an insect and all that."

"Let's make a pass by that apartment house we're supposed to check," Georgie said. "Then I can log it and get it over with. Sounds like it's just a PR job the detectives are foisting off on us poor overworked bluesuits."

In the last of the daylight, when the summer sun was settling down behind the Pacific Ocean, giving Hollywood its special rosy glow, the old apartment building in Little Armenia looked impregnable to the officers of 6-X-76.

"This is bullshit," Georgie Adams said. "Real-estate guys like Dryden don't kill their squeezes themselves. They hire it done. He'd just find an Eighteenth Streeter or some other local crusier and put a ticket on her."

"The detectives said he's supposed to be into crystal meth," Viv reminded him. "A desperate guy on ice might do anything when he gets all spun out."

"Anyways," Georgie said, "even Spider-Man himself couldn't get in there."

"Spider-Man," Viv said, mulling it over. She then drove around to the alley behind the building and parked by the attached carport.

"What're you looking for, sis?" Georgie wanted to know.

"Any sign of a trail from his web-shooter," Viv said with a sly smile. "I think old sticky foot *could* get into her apartment."

"How?"

"There," she said, pointing to the neighboring apartment building.

The building was in the process of being renovated and reroofed before the winter rains came. An eight-foot temporary chain-link fence was all that secured the construction site. Rolls of tar paper and shingles were visible inside the fence where workers had left them, along with two aluminum extension ladders.

"So?" Georgie said.

Viv said, "He could climb over the fence and borrow one of those extension ladders."

"So?" Georgie said. "She's on the third floor. Most ladders don't go that high unless you're a firefighter on a truck."

Viv said, "He could use the ladder to get onto the carport roof and then pull it up and extend it high enough to do the job."

"You got some imagination, sis," Georgie said. "But there's no accessible window over the carports."

"But from that point he could get clear to the roof of the building."

"Then what?" Georgie said. "He goes down her chimney? News flash, sis. There ain't no chimneys."

"I noticed the small window on the south side," Viv said. "She keeps it wide open. I'll bet there's no AC in that little place and she needs ventilation. He could scoot to the edge of that flat roof on his belly, lower his legs down in front of the open window, and swing right into her apartment."

"Like a spider?" Georgie said mischievously.

"Like a meth-crazed, desperate tweaker," Viv said. "With all those paranoid tweaker thoughts spinning through his head."

"That's probably the kitchen window there on the south side," Georgie said. "I'll bet it's over the sink. If he went in there, he'd land in her garbage disposal and she could just turn it on and flush that fucking spider right down the drain."

"You are *such* an asshole, Gypsy," Viv said, poking him in the shoulder when her partner showed her his wicked little grin.

Despite Georgie's protests, Viv managed to find time to drive by the apartment building and check out the alley two more times.

On their last check of the evening, Georgie Adams shined the spotlight on the graffiti sprayed on the stucco wall of the building on the alley side. There were gang slogans and the letters *AP* for "Armenian Power" written large.

Georgie said, "At least the Armenian cruisers respect education. All their graffiti is spelled right."

At 9:15 P.M. on that moonless night, when the smog and overcast blowing in from the ocean hung low over the Los Angeles basin, there was a ruckus on Hollywood Boulevard that brought four of the midwatch units responding. Catwoman, who had tried in vain to look like Halle Berry, head-butted Superman for muscling in on her tourist tips and knocked him right on his ass in Grauman's forecourt. The boozy superhero ended up dazed on John Wayne's boot prints and yelled to everyone that he was going to murder Catwoman.

This Superman was not one of the younger Street Characters and didn't much resemble the movie version's. He had a nose full of broken veins, and a double chin, and was starting to get a middle-aged paunch that his costume with all the built-in muscles couldn't hide. When he got to his feet, he lurched at the plucky Catwoman, who held her ground with claws extended. But then Marilyn Monroe, who was actually a forty-year-old transvestite named Melvin Pickett, came to Catwoman's aid.

Superman grabbed Catwoman, who fought back and tried to kick him in the groin. When Superman drew back a fist, Marilyn Monroe stepped in and belted Superman across the mouth with her leather purse, which was heavy with rolls of quarters she'd collected for the Sunset Strip Beautification Project. There was a major donnybrook going on by the time the first black-and-whites arrived.

Six-A-Fifteen from Watch 3 showed up before any of the mid-watch units, and that turned out to be unfortunate for Superman. The cop driving 6-A-15 was Preston Lilly, who'd served thirty-five years with the LAPD, twenty-two of them at Hollywood Station. He was a large, square-shouldered man with a massive shaved skull the color of old ivory. His eyes were gray and spaced too far apart, making them seem out of sync when aimed in your direction. Some people said that looking into the face of Preston Lilly was like looking at an enormous pale eel. He had already decided to retire before the end of the year, and he was sick of working 6-A-15 because he was always getting bullshit calls to the rich whiners in the Hollywood Hills.

"You can never make them Hills dwellers happy," Preston Lilly complained to his partner, a Cuban immigrant named Mario Delgado. "A bunch of guys with too much money and a bunch of trophy wives with too much time on their hands. They like to bitch just for the sake of bitching."

The phlegmatic Cuban just shrugged and said, "Better than working down in Watts, *'mano*." He had recently transferred to Hollywood Division from Southeast Division. Then he added, "We got to take some shit from the *jotos* in the Hills. They might be friends of the chief. Or maybe the mayor. That's the way life is."

"I own my own pink slip," Preston Lilly said. "My pension's vested. I could commit murder and they'd still have to send my pension checks to me at San Quentin. And I already filed my retirement papers, so nobody better fuck with me, in the Hills or in the flats. I got nothing to lose, *compadre*."

Superman found that out when Preston Lilly stepped in to break up the tussle. Because Marilyn Monroe was sober, she'd been able to get a good choke hold on the larger Street Character, and Superman was sitting on Grauman's forecourt with his back to Marilyn, who had him in not only a choke hold but also a scissors grip, with her shaved legs around his waist. The Incredible Hulk, a gentle soul who hated violence of any kind, had picked up Marilyn Monroe's purse and was guarding it and pleading in vain for the combatants to stop fighting.

Marilyn Monroe's platinum blond wig got twisted askew at the start of the fight and the hair was hanging in her face like a sheepdog's. Her white dress was ripped open all the way down the side and had been torn off one shoulder. A large falsie had popped up out of her bra and was resting on Superman's shoulder like an inverted cereal bowl. The panty hose on both of Marilyn's legs was shredded, and her open-toed three-inch spikes were now without heels. And while Superman sat helpless, Catwoman pounded his face with relatively ineffectual blows that nevertheless made him howl in drunken rage.

"You're dead!" he screamed. "When I get up, I'm killing you, you nigger cunt!"

"You gotta get up first, peckerwood!" she yelled back, and socked him in the eye with her little fist.

The first thing that Officer Preston Lilly did was grab Catwoman by the arm and flick her away from the brawlers. Then he said, "Cease and desist, Ms. Monroe! And you, too, Man of Steel!"

Meanwhile, there were hundreds of tourists watching, whistling, howling like coyotes, and it seemed like every single one of them was snapping photos.

Marilyn Monroe released her scissors hold as well as the choke hold and she stumbled to her feet with one shoe missing now. When Preston Lilly took Superman by the arm to drag him to his feet, the still boozy Street Character said, "Take your hands off me, you bald-headed pig fucker!"

"I don't like your mouth," Preston Lilly said. "You better lock it up."

Superman answered that by spitting on Preston Lilly.

The big cop looked down and saw the spittle dripping from his LAPD badge onto the blue uniform shirt pocket and running down to the pewter pocket button.

Mario Delgado saw Preston Lilly instinctively ball his huge right fist, but the little Cuban stepped in fast and said, "Whoa, partner! You're being watched by three hundred witnesses and about a hundred of them might be hostile."

That made the Cuban cop take charge of things and grab one of Superman's arms, and then both cops got Superman's hands cuffed behind his back.

Marilyn Monroe held up a heel-less shoe and yelled to Superman in her natural baritone voice, "I paid three hundred bucks for my Louis Vuitton's and that was a sale price, you sleazy turd! I'm suing your sorry ass!"

The arriving midwatch units got things under control, and after making the milling throngs move along, they began interviewing the other Street Characters who had witnessed the fracas. Preston

Lilly walked Superman to their shop and strapped him in the backseat, then got behind the wheel to await his partner.

Mario Delgado was busy talking to Flotsam and Jetsam, who were trying to help Marilyn Monroe get what was left of her white dress pinned up enough to cover her pantie girdle. It was then that Superman, bitching that he was the real victim and that Preston Lilly was a fascist swine, hacked up a big loogie and spit it through the caged partition of the police car right onto the shaved skull of Officer Preston Lilly.

Mario Delgado was shocked when he turned and saw Preston Lilly suddenly start up the engine of the black-and-white and heard him yell, "Catch a ride back to the station, partner! I gotta get Superman outta here!"

The black-and-white squealed away from the curb and was gone. Just like that.

"What the hell?" the baffled Cuban cop said to Flotsam, who replied, "Dude, I think Preston don't want any witnesses."

Nearly forty minutes later, Mario Delgado paced anxiously in the parking lot of Hollywood Station, but still his partner and Superman had not appeared. He went inside and up to the lunchroom, where he bought a soda from the machine and then joined Hollywood Nate and Snuffy Salcedo in the report room.

The Cuban cop was not finished with his soda when they all heard yammering coming from the passageway leading from the parking lot door. Mario Delgado and Nate and Snuffy all ran out of the report room and found Preston Lilly walking the handcuffed superhero to the holding tank, where he put him inside, removed the handcuffs, and pushed him down onto the bench. He closed the door, but everyone could still see Superman through the shatterproof window, and he kept hollering. They could also see that there wasn't a mark on his very flushed face other than the small abrasions he'd received in the fight.

Sergeant Murillo left the sergeants' room to come and see what the yelling was all about, and when Superman saw the chevrons on his sleeves, he hollered, "Sergeant, I demand to make a citizen's complaint! I've been tortured! It was worse than waterboarding!"

Preston Lilly looked at Sergeant Murillo and said, "That's preposterous."

Superman jumped up from the bench and ran to the glass window, yelling, "That skinhead Nazi took me to the Hollywood Freeway on-ramp and got out and grabbed my hair and pulled my head through the open window. And he rolled it up until I was trapped by the neck. There I was with my hands cuffed behind my back and my head hanging out, and he drove a hundred goddamn miles an hour for I don't know how long and I was screaming the whole time for him to stop! It woulda been better if he'd just tied me to the hood like a fucking road-killed deer!"

Sergeant Murillo looked at Preston Lilly, who said, "Go ahead and cut paper, Sarge. I'm at the end of my career, where I can take the safety off and tell the captain what I think. Or the bureau commander. Or the fucking chief of police, for that matter. I'm bulletproof now. But as far as what Superman says? It's preposterous."

Superman said, "Sergeant, I swear to you. When I begged for mercy, all he did was drive faster. I could hardly breathe. And do you know what he said? He floored it all the way and he yells to me, 'Nobody's whupping on you, Superman. I'm just letting your own lips beat you to death.' That's what he said."

Preston Lilly looked at Superman and at Sergeant Murillo and said, "That's preposterous."

Sergeant Murillo said to the big cop, "Preston, do what you can to move up your retirement date. And until you go, please leave the safety on."

★ EIGHT ★

JUST AFTER MIDNIGHT Cindy Kroll heard a scraping sound on the roof. Her first thought was that some crows were up there pecking at the composite material that was designed to look like wood. She had fed her baby daughter some applesauce and bottle-fed her infant son before lying down on the bed in her T-shirt and underpants. It was so hot, she was just trying to catch some breeze from the open windows, and she had not intended to go to sleep yet, but she had dozed. The wine she'd had earlier while watching TV had done it.

She reminded herself that she had to cut down on the wine and she was dying to smoke some crystal, but she knew she had to kick it. Then she remembered that her daughter had fallen asleep in the playpen and that she had to get up and put her in her crib. Her son was lying beside her asleep, and she looked at him. She thought he resembled his father, Louis Dryden. She didn't mind that. Louis was a good-looking man even if he—

Her thoughts were interrupted when she heard more scraping on the roof above her apartment. And then a cup fell from the sink in her kitchen and broke on the floor. And then all the dishes from the drainboard crashed to the floor, and her first thought was, Earthquake! Then she heard footsteps coming toward her bedroom.

*　　*　　*

The code 3 call came after the three warning beeps over the police radio. Then the RTO at Communications Division said, "All units in the vicinity and Six-A-Forty-nine, a woman screaming."

When they heard the address of the call that was given to a Watch 3 unit, Viv Daley said, "That's the Kroll address!"

Six-X-Seventy-six was very close to the location and jumped the call, arriving in less than three minutes. Georgie was out before Viv even brought the Crown Vic to a stop, and they both ran to the front door, standing in a wash of illumination from the security lights overhead.

The front entrance was well secured by a set of heavy wooden doors that opened out, and there was a small panel of double-glazed window in each door. The lobby inside was lit but there was no sign of the watchman that they were told would be there. They could see a door inside the lobby with a sign that said "Manager," but it was closed.

And then they saw Cindy Kroll. She was staggering down the staircase toward the lobby, wearing only the T-shirt and cotton underwear. The T-shirt was blood-drenched and ripped open, and her chest bones glistened in the light. She reached the lobby floor, lurched from side to side, and dropped to her knees. A man wearing a black hoodie sweatshirt and black jeans ran down the stairs, a knife raised high over his head, yelling something unintelligible at the fallen woman as he tried to stab her again.

He may never have seen the orange fireballs coming at him or heard the explosions, but Viv Daley and Georgie Adams fired a total of thirteen rounds from their .40 caliber Glocks through the glass panels in the doors. Two of Georgie's rounds hit Louis Dryden, one in the hip and one under the left eye. Three of Viv's rounds got him in the shoulder and chest.

Lights went on all over the apartment building and in the building next door, as well as in a private residence across the street.

Viv Daley yelled through the broken glass, "Open this door! Somebody come open this door!"

"Police!" Georgie Adams yelled, kicking the double doors twice. Open it!"

Then through the broken window panels they saw an elderly man emerge in terror from the manager's office. He stepped over the body of Cindy Kroll and yelled to the police, "Don't shoot! I'm the watchman!"

He opened the door and began babbling. When he became intelligible, he said, "I heard her scream once and I called you right away! But you got here so fast, somebody on the third floor must've called first! And a few minutes later I heard her screaming again but this time it sounded like she was coming down the stairs and a man was also screaming curses and he was coming down and I got scared and locked my door!"

Georgie Adams shined his streamlight onto Louis Dryden's face and saw the entry wound clearly. He holstered his pistol and grabbed his rover, calling for a rescue ambulance for Cindy Kroll. He also reported the officer-involved shooting that would bring dozens of people to the apartment building before the night ended.

Viv Daley turned Cindy Kroll onto her back in case CPR was possible. But the young woman's chest was slashed wide open, exposing her breastbone. When Viv saw that Cindy Kroll's eyes were open and her mouth was twisted into a rictus of violent death, she didn't bother to feel for a pulse.

Viv looked at her partner, who averted his eyes from hers, and he said to her, "You better check on the babies. I'll secure the scene here."

Viv's heart was hammering when she got to the landing of the third floor. She felt dry-mouthed and light-headed, and she could hardly believe that she had just fired her weapon outside the police pistol range. Though it was her first time, it had happened so fast and there had been such an adrenaline surge that she hadn't had time to feel much fright. But she was feeling it now.

She held up her hand, and in the light from the third-floor hallway the hand looked palsied. She had a streamlight in her other hand, and when she got to the door, she found it wide open. There was no sound from within and she was suddenly more afraid than she'd ever been in her life.

Viv put her hand on her pistol grip, but it wasn't for personal safety. The hand was acting reflexively, doing what a cop's hand does in moments of fear. Any personal threat to her was past, yet she was weak and feeling nausea from the overwhelming fright sweeping over her, from dread of what she might find in there.

Viv Daley crept into the apartment. She stepped gingerly into the cluttered living room and was so instantly relieved that her legs almost buckled. The thirteen-month-old was safe in her playpen, her face tear-streaked but she wasn't crying now. She wore a white jersey with a pink duck on the front, and a diaper, and she was sitting and staring at a brown teddy bear on the floor of the playpen as though in a daze.

"Hello, sweetie," Viv said to the little girl, who turned and looked at her in confusion.

Then Viv rushed hopefully into the bedroom and found the baby boy. He was wearing only a diaper and was dangling from the upper rail of the crib from a cord to a cell phone charger that had been tied around his neck. His face was purple and his eyes were shut tight.

"No!" Viv shouted, not even aware that she'd spoken.

She jerked the cord from the crib and her fingers slipped twice before she untied it from where it was digging into the soft flesh of the infant's neck, and she said, "I knew it! I knew it!"

And then she thought, This baby's dead. What am I doing? This is a crime scene and this baby's dead!

Still, she lifted the infant, thinking, He's so light. He's so small. She put the baby into the crib, and for no reason she could later fathom, she covered him to his wounded neck with his cotton blanket.

Viv stared at the dead baby and thought, All evening I imagined this. I knew Dryden could get in from the roof. I knew it. Why didn't I act on it? Why didn't I push the boss for a stakeout? What kind of cop am I?

The baby girl in the next room started crying then and was standing, holding on to the playpen rail. Viv went to her and picked her up, and she looked at Viv in shock and confusion and said, "Mommy."

The toddler wrapped her arms around Viv's neck, and Viv felt the silky blond hair against her cheek, and the child said it again: "Mommy."

Viv said, "Hush, baby, hush." And she began rocking her back and forth and didn't hear Sergeant Murillo, who appeared behind her along with Snuffy Salcedo and Hollywood Nate, who remained in the hallway, looking in through the open door.

Viv was a lot calmer now and she said in a monotone to her sergeant, "In there. I found the baby hanging by the neck from the crib rail. I hoped he might still be alive so I took him down. But of course he wasn't. I put him to bed."

Sergeant Murillo looked at her and entered the bedroom for only a moment before he returned.

He said quietly to Viv, "Don't touch anything else. A homicide team and SID will be here very soon to process the scene, and FID's also on the way. They'll separate you and Adams and it'll be a very long night of questions, from FID especially, but this is obviously an in-policy shooting, so I don't want you to stress over it. Just tell them exactly how it went down."

"I knew this might happen," Viv said quietly to Sergeant Murillo. "It's almost like I could see him coming in from the roof."

After hesitating, Sergeant Murillo looked at his officer and said in an even quieter voice, "Adams told me all about that, and yes, the ladder's still in place on the carport roof where the dead man left it. But you didn't know this would happen. It was just what-if speculation on your part. The place looked perfectly secure. You don't have a crystal ball. Nobody could've anticipated this, Viv. You can't blame yourself. The dead guy's to blame. Nobody else."

Viv Daley put the tot in the playpen and she immediately began crying and held her arms out to Viv saying, "Mommy, Mommy."

"She thinks you're her mommy," Sergeant Murillo said. "Dear lord."

Snuffy Salcedo, still in the common hallway with Hollywood Nate, said, "Jesus Christ. This is too awful."

Nate said nothing and Snuffy turned and went downstairs.

"I gotta get outta here," Viv said to Sergeant Murillo.

"Viv," he said. "You and your partner will have to be separated while you wait for FID. We're gonna see a lot of people around here in a little while. We'll transport the little girl."

When Viv got to the doorway, Hollywood Nate stood aside for her. She turned once to look back at the child in the playpen who held out her arms to Viv and between sobs said more urgently, "Mommy!"

Viv descended the stairwell to the lobby floor and found four cops from Watch 3 keeping neighbors away from the crime scene tape. Snuffy Salcedo was talking to Flotsam and Jetsam, who were in the street directing traffic and waving the criminalists' van from SID into a parking space. Several of the uniformed cops whispered to one another, an indication that word had spread quickly about what Viv Daley had found in the third-floor apartment.

Flotsam said somberly to Jetsam, "Dude, remember how the Oracle always told us that doing good police work was the most fun we'd ever have in our entire lives?"

Jetsam said, "Yeah, and Viv and Georgie did *real* good police work when they lit up that fucking maniac."

"True," Flotsam said, "but I don't think this night's going on their desktop in the category of fun."

Georgie was standing on the sidewalk outside the tape with the watch commander, Lieutenant O'Reilly, who was awaiting the imminent arrival of homicide detectives and the administrative team from Force Investigation Division, as well as the coroner's body snatchers. But when he saw Viv emerge from the building, he left the lieutenant and approached her.

She looked at her partner, at the anxiety in his eyes, and Georgie said to her, "I never thought it could happen, sis. Honest to god, I never thought for a second that anything like this could happen."

"Please, Gypsy, shut the fuck up," Viv Daley said.

★ NINE ★

RALEIGH DIBBLE WENT to work for the Bruegers two weeks after his employment interview, and Leona Brueger was so pleased with him that she decided to leave with Rudy Ressler for Tuscany the following week. Julius Hampton did not attempt to sabotage the job for his employee despite his disappointment and irritation at losing Raleigh on such short notice. When Leona's attorney phoned Julius Hampton for a reference, the old man truthfully said that Raleigh had been a splendid butler, cook, driver, and companion. He added that he hated to lose Raleigh but he could not compete with the money that Leona was offering.

The thing that clinched it with Leona Brueger was Raleigh's work in the kitchen. He demonstrated what he could do during an impromptu luncheon for Leona and a few friends, including Rudy Ressler. Raleigh prepared a simple coq au vin, minus the diced pork in case anyone had religious dietary issues. Leona Brueger's Guatemalan housekeeper and cook, Marta Sandoval, was sixty-six years old and planning to retire anyway, since the house was going to be put on the market. She told Leona Brueger that she was not jealous of the new man and was delighted to receive three months' severance pay. She planned on moving to the home of her eldest daughter in East Los Angeles.

Raleigh decided during that impromptu luncheon that Julius

Hampton had been right about Rudy Ressler. The schmuck actually complained that Raleigh's quiche appetizer had a "pinch" too much salt in it.

Pinch this, you phony, Raleigh thought, but replied, "I'm so sorry, sir. Can I get you anything else? A fruit and cheese plate, perhaps? A few sips of delicate Chablis with a hint of strawberry will cleanse any salt from your palate. May I get you a glass?"

Raleigh went to the butler's pantry and poured the director a glass of screw-top Chardonnay that he used for cooking and placed it before the director, saying, "It's an amusing little Chablis, sir. The hint of strawberry is balanced by an essence of mint, I believe."

Rudy Ressler passed the glass under his nose, sampled a tiny sip, and said, "Yes, I can taste the strawberry and the mint, but it's not overpowering." He sipped again and said, "That's a fine choice, Raleigh. Thank you."

Raleigh Dibble was willing to put up with just about anything in that house, especially after Leona Breuger promised him an unspecified bonus when she returned from Tuscany. She told him that she would then begin preparing the house for what she called "the big fall sale of Casa Brueger." Nigel Wickland told Raleigh that when she felt the urge, Leona Brueger could be "crazily generous" and that the bonus might be substantial.

Raleigh didn't even mind Leona Brueger's eighty-seven-year-old brother-in-law, Marty Brueger, who stayed in the guest cottage almost all of the time, watching the E! network with his dentures in a glass beside his chair grinning at him. The wizened old coot never so much as entered the main house unless he was looking for whiskey, so Raleigh tried to make sure that the liquor cabinet in the cottage was well stocked.

Marty Brueger was shrunken from age and spinal stenosis, and he spent most of his time in his chair with his legs elevated on a pillow. Marty had a nest of wiry hair with some surprising sprouts of black growing among the dull gray strands. He wore thick glasses that made his brown eyes appear enormous and he looked like an ancient frazzled parrot. Leona Brueger told Raleigh that her brother-in-law had been an energetic skirt chaser until recent years, and his uncontrolled libido had been the cause of expensive paternity lawsuits when he was a young man, and sexual harassment lawsuits when he got old.

She said to Raleigh, "Just make sure Marty has some T and A videos to look at and good whiskey to drink, and he'll be no trouble."

One of the first things the old man said to Raleigh was "Can you make good chili? Since Chasen's closed down, nobody in this goddamn town can make a decent bowl of chili. I miss Dave and Maud Chasen like I miss my prostate."

"Mr. Brueger," Raleigh said, "you're in luck. Back when I was in college, I worked one summer as a busboy at Chasen's. I kept my eyes open and my palate on high alert. My chili won't disappoint you."

Of course it was a complete lie, but Raleigh had made enough chili in his day that he figured he could please the geezer, and he did.

Raleigh had everything well under control by the time Leona Brueger and Rudy Ressler actually left for Italy. Marta Sandoval stayed on for only two days after her employer was gone, which was just long enough to tidy up the house and change all the towels and bed linens. With the help of two grandsons, she moved all of her clothes and belongings from the housekeeper's quarters to a rented van, and she was gone. And then, with Marty Brueger tucked away in the cottage most of the time, Raleigh Dibble had the entire Brueger estate to himself, and it was sweet.

The security system was sophisticated but Raleigh learned it easily enough. The outside lights and video cameras were elaborate and took a bit of practice. He only had to take Marty Brueger to dinner two times in the first two weeks, once to Musso and Frank, of course, and then to the Formosa Café. The elderly Hollywood rich still loved the few old hangouts remaining. Raleigh was sure that the Polo Lounge at the Beverly Hills Hotel would be on the itinerary as soon as the old boy remembered clearly that he'd once loved their Neil McCarthy salad.

Marty bored Raleigh with personal anecdotes about all the celebrities in the caricature drawings on the walls of the Formosa Café, but Raleigh figured they were lies. He deduced that Marty Brueger was just the slacker sibling of an older brother who had made sure his kid brother was taken care of in old age. Still, Marty Brueger was even less trouble to care for than Julius Hampton had been, so Raleigh had no complaints, and he indulged the old man as much as possible.

Raleigh lived contentedly for nearly a month, and then one evening he got a call from Nigel Wickland. Nigel asked if Raleigh could meet him in Beverly Hills at Nic's on North Canon Drive for some "filet mignon with blueberries."

When Raleigh responded, "Puh-leeeze, Nigel, are you serious?" the art dealer said, "All right, never mind the trendy food. We'll just have a martini or two and a plate of their crispy onions. Meet me there at five thirty."

The guy was a mystery, Raleigh thought, and just about impossible to predict. Nigel had gotten him this great gig with the Bruegers, yet he hadn't wanted any thanks or favors in return. Now there was clearly a sense of urgency in the art dealer's latest invitation. Before he left for the meeting, Raleigh walked out of the main house to the cottage and made sure that Marty Brueger was contentedly watching his big-screen TV.

"I'm going grocery shopping," he said to the old man. "I'll make you a nice supper when I get back."

"Before you go, take the video out and put in the one on the shelf," Marty Brueger croaked. "I think I like *Keeping Up With the Kardashians* even more than *The Girls Next Door,* don't you? And stop at the liquor store and pick up a bottle of Jameson's Irish whiskey. Get me the rare stuff that costs two hundred bucks a bottle. Just tell them to bill it to Leona."

"Certainly, Mr. Brueger," Raleigh said. "I won't be long."

Raleigh made sure that every door in the main house was locked and then set the alarm and video cameras. He had permission to drive the Mercedes SL550, which Leona Brueger called her "run-around town" car, so he decided to take it instead of his old Toyota. He liked the way the car hugged the road as he drove down from the Hollywood Hills on his way to Nic's on North Canon Drive.

Raleigh found Nigel Wickland waiting in the Martini Lounge and he looked agitated. There was a busy late-afternoon crowd, and Nigel was sitting at a table sipping a vodka martini instead of his usual daiquiri. The art dealer's bonhomie wasn't on display this time when he motioned Raleigh to sit.

"Did you get caught in traffic?" Nigel asked, as though annoyed.

"No, but I had to lock up and see that Mr. Brueger was okay," Raleigh said. "I'm only twenty minutes late."

"Perfectly all right, "Nigel said quickly.

For once, he wasn't sartorially turned out like the Savile Row snobs that Raleigh had despised during his London days. Nigel was wearing a gray seersucker jacket that needed cleaning and a slightly wrinkled white dress shirt open at the throat.

After Raleigh's drink arrived Nigel said, "How old are you, Raleigh?"

Raleigh sipped and said, "What's this all about?"

"I'm older than I look," Nigel Wickland said. "I'm sixty-four years old."

No, you look it, Raleigh thought. The art dealer had a faint scar running behind his ear that Raleigh hadn't noticed before. He's had work done, but he still looks his age, Raleigh thought. Then he said to Nigel, "I'm fifty-eight."

"It's hell when you know you're growing old and can't afford it," Nigel said. "It's frightening, isn't it?"

"What do you mean, 'can't afford it'?"

Nigel said, "You're making a good wage with the Bruegers, but, Raleigh, it's going to end in a few months. They're not taking you with them when they move to their vineyard in Napa. You'll be out of work again."

"No, I didn't see myself as a grape picker in Napa," Raleigh said, a bit insulted. "I expect I'll get by in life without sitting at a stoplight with a sign saying, 'Will Butler for Food.' I'll find another position. I'll get by."

"Aren't you tired of just getting by?" Nigel Wickland was so intense that Raleigh hesitated.

Then Raleigh said, "Maybe I'll find me a Leona Brueger and marry her like that weasel Rudy Ressler is doing. Or maybe I'll win a big lottery."

Nigel Wickland showed Raleigh a patronizing smile, ran his fingers nervously through his mane of white hair, and said, "Be realistic, Raleigh."

Raleigh drained his glass and said, "You be realistic, Nigel. Or more to the point, be straightforward. What're you getting at?"

Nigel Wickland picked up his cocktail napkin and dabbed at his mouth, at the bead of sweat that had popped out above his upper lip. In fact, Raleigh saw, there was sweat forming on his brow as well. Then he said, "I'm in financial trouble, Raleigh. This fucking recession is killing my business. I may have to let Ruth go and I don't know how long I can keep the bloody doors open."

"Sorry to hear that," Raleigh said as Nigel signaled for a round of fresh drinks.

"You and I," Nigel said, "we could help each other. We could form a . . . partnership and help each other."

"What kind of partnership?"

"You could make more money than you've ever imagined," Nigel Wickland said.

"I tried that," Raleigh said. "And did eight months at Lompoc in a room with lots of guys you wouldn't care for at all."

Then, with a burst of words spoken so fast that it took Raleigh a moment to comprehend, Nigel Wickland said, "I just want you to let me into the house some afternoon for an hour or two. I'll need you to turn off the video cameras and let me in unseen. And you can help me for a few minutes and then go tend to Marty Brueger in his cottage until I'm ready to go."

After digesting the import of the art dealer's words, Raleigh said, "For this I'm going to make more money than I've ever dreamed of? And what do I tell the police when you steal her jewelry or whatever it is that you have in mind, Nigel? Do I tell them that a home invader came in with guns blazing, or what?"

Nigel Wickland said, "I just want to photograph two of her paintings."

"Photograph her paintings?"

"Yes, I've had some experience with photography and I think I can do it. All I'll have to do is return one more time two weeks later for about another hour, and that's it."

"I think you've been drinking too many of those martinis, Nigel," Raleigh said. "You're not making sense."

"It's about a painting switch," Nigel said. "I know of a custom lab owned by a sweet young man with whom I once had an understanding. He has mild Asperger's syndrome and can hardly manage to shake hands whenever we meet, but he's a marvel at what he does in a photo laboratory. I can shoot two of the Brueger paintings with a digital camera and get the proportions exactly correct. Then I can take the disc to him, and I guarantee you that he will produce an enlargement on poster board to the precise measurement of the paintings in Leona Brueger's house. It will cost me three thousand dollars but he's already promised that if he gets his money up front, he can get the work done in a fortnight, no questions asked." Then Nigel added, "That's two weeks."

"I know what a fortnight is, Nigel," Raleigh said. "I had the misfortune of working one summer in London at a bistro near the King's Cross tube station, and it was a misery. But I still don't know what you're talking about."

"We must have a chin-wag about dear old London town sometime," Nigel said. "Anyway, I shall have to return to the Brueger house another time after that."

"I don't like that next part," Raleigh said. "The part I now see coming."

"I'll need access again to replace the paintings with my photocopies on poster board, fitting them into the existing frames. And then I'll be on my way with the originals. No harm, no foul, as your basketball fans love to say."

"You're talking like a wack job," Raleigh said. "Whadda you mean, no harm?" Realizing that his diction was slipping, Raleigh lowered his voice and said, "You're talking about entering her house and stealing her paintings!"

"She's an ignorant arriviste, like most of my clients," Nigel retorted. "She cares nothing about Sammy Brueger's art or *any* art. She told me that she wouldn't mind if the house burned to the ground with all the paintings in it. Everything is insured to the hilt."

"And what the hell happens to me when she figures it all out and calls the police?"

"She won't figure it out, Raleigh," Nigel Wickland said. "She's culturally ignorant. She barely looks at any of her art, and I can promise you that only a close inspection by an expert could detect the switch. That may happen a few years from now when she bothers to take the paintings from the storage facility where they're going. She's told me they'll all be stored when she moves away from the house, and I guarantee you that's where they'll stay for a very long time because she doesn't care about any of them. In fact, she's commissioning me to box each piece and personally supervise the trucking transfer to her preferred storage facility."

"Hellooo!" Raleigh said. "So what happens when she does get around to collecting them and maybe putting them up for auction with some art dealer like you? Somebody'll spot the switch for sure!"

"That's the beauty of my idea," Nigel Wickland said. "After they're crated and ready to leave Casa Brueger, I'm going to make sure that the crate containing the switched paintings is a different manufacture from all the other crates, and that the crate shows subtle signs of having been tampered with. The people who transfer these things are just ordinary truckers who will notice nothing. When the switch is finally discovered years from now, the theft will be blamed on someone who works at, or has access to, the storage facility. Leona will collect from the insurance policy and nobody will be harmed except for the insurer, and when has anyone felt sorry for insurance carriers? It's foolproof, Raleigh."

Raleigh was silent for a moment and then said, "How much money could the paintings bring? Realistically."

"They could be sold easily in Copenhagen, Stockholm, Bern, or even Berlin. I've personally contacted a discreet European auctioneer who believes he can get at least six hundred thousand U.S. dollars for *The Woman by the Water.* The other piece of Impressionist art that I have my eye on is called *Flowers on the Hillside,* and he assured me that it should bring an equal amount. Raleigh, you and I will be dividing at least a million dollars after expenses. Tax-free! No more tending to dotty old men for you. And enough money for me that I can perhaps keep my gallery open until this goddamn recession ends. Plus there's a special bonus for me in that these two wonderful pieces of art will end up with someone who truly appreciates them and not with some vulgarians in the Hollywood Hills."

"Half a million," Raleigh said, and the sound of it brought a catch in his throat. When he spoke again he said, "When did you find out about me, Nigel?"

"Find out what?"

"That I'm an ex-convict. Someone who might seriously listen to your 'foolproof plan'?"

"The first night we met," Nigel Wickland admitted. "When you were gone to the gents, Julius Hampton talked about you. He said that you'd had a bit of difficulty with the law and had been in prison. You see, Raleigh, he had a background investigation done by a private investigator when he hired you. Perhaps you didn't know that."

Raleigh was quiet for a long moment, and then he said, "Nobody accepts an ex-con at face value. They all have to dig, and distrust you, and pay you less than they'd pay somebody who's ten times worse but never got caught. Someone who's done lots worse things than not paying enough of the taxes that the government gouges you with."

"I know how ex-convicts get shat on," Nigel Wickland said, putting his manicured fingers on the back of Raleigh's hand and patting sympathetically. "So yes, I confess that I did think you might be more amenable to my idea than the average person would be. But I could also see immediately that you were a man with imagination and ambition."

"Now you're going too far, Nigel," Raleigh said. "Quit while you're ahead."

"You look a bit peaky," Nigel Wickland said, eyes widening. "Are you in, then?"

"If this goes sideways and I get busted, I'm ratting you out to the police and making the best deal I can for myself," Raleigh Dibble warned. "You better understand that up front."

"Fair enough," said Nigel Wickland. "I'm not worried, Raleigh. Not at all."

"You will be if you end up inside with lots of other guys who had foolproof plans," Raleigh said. "And state prison, where we'll go, is a lot worse than Club Fed, where I did my time. In a state lockup you'll learn to sleep on your back with one eye open." Looking at Nigel Wickland, he added, "But maybe you're not so scared of that part."

"That was unnecessary, Raleigh," Nigel Wickland said. "Homophobic humor is beneath you."

TEN

"Up, up. get the fuck up!" Jonas Claymore said to Megan Burke, who had been awake most of the night, vomiting.

It was 10:30 A.M. and she was exhausted, and still suffering from withdrawal aches even though Jonas had taken the last $100 from his checking account and bought them half an ox. They divided and smoked it late in the evening after dining on a Fatburger that neither of them really wanted.

"I don't feel well," Megan said, lying on the double bed they shared, her makeup from last night smeared all over her face.

She looked like a blow-up doll that somebody had let the air out of, he thought. She looked like the corpse in one of those slasher movies, where the guy with the knife likes to paint their dead faces. Jesus! How did he get himself into this relationship?

"We gotta do some work today," he said. "We're dead broke."

Megan dragged herself into a sitting position, feet on the floor, and said, "I'll get another waitress job as soon as I feel better."

"Don't try to clown me," he said. "You ain't gonna feel better till you stop jonesing. And you ain't gonna stop jonesing till you give up the beans and norcos and perks. Because you can't handle any of it."

She yawned twice and said, "And you can, I suppose."

"I'm a recreational user," Jonas said. "I know my limits. But you? You're all smoked out."

"Sure," Megan said, shuffling across the bedroom to the bathroom. She sat down and continued, "You're always in control, aren't you?"

"That's disgusting," Jonas said. "Can't you close the door when you piss?"

She answered by slamming the door without getting off the toilet. Then she said, "You're the one that got fired. Get mad at yourself, not at me."

"I didn't get fired. I quit."

Megan didn't answer. She was nauseous and started dry heaving.

"Why can't I catch a break?" Jonas said to her impassive calico cat.

Then he dressed in a Warner Bros. sweatshirt that he thought made him look like a studio employee, along with relatively clean jeans and tennis shoes.

When Megan started to dress in another T-shirt and shorts, he said, "Why can't you call one of your old cock-blocking roommates and borrow some share wear? And for chrissake, brush the moss off your teeth. Any more, it'll look like you invented a tooth sweater."

By noon on a hot Los Angeles day, they were cruising in Jonas's fifteen-year-old VW bug in the Birds, those streets on the western side of the Hollywood Hills named for feathered friends, like Nightingale, Robin, and Oriole.

"Do you know that Harrison Ford don't even know how many airplanes he owns?" Jonas said as they drove up into the Hills. "I read this interview where he said he owns six or eight. He don't even know for sure how many."

Megan, who was wearing a passably clean yellow jersey, jeans, and flip-flops, slouched in her seat and stared out at the multimillion-dollar homes. "How long do we have to do this?" she said. "I'm getting carsick."

Ignoring her complaints as usual, he said, "And then there's Nicolas Cage. He's in financial trouble because it takes mega-millions for him to survive each year. Do you know he has a collection of comic books that's probably worth more than a few of Harrison Ford's airplanes?"

"Uh-huh," Megan said. "That's intriguing."

Any response at all from her these days encouraged him, and he said, "He had an Action One Superman comic book worth who knows how much. One like it sold recently for three hundred grand. And he didn't even know the comic books were stolen until months passed. Think of it, Meg, three hundred thou for one comic book. And they don't even miss them till somebody gooses them and says, 'Where's the fucking comic book?' That's the kind of stuff you find laying around celebrity cribs all the time. And the best thing is, you're not hurting anyone when you take it. Half the time they don't even know it's gone."

Megan said, "The way I feel today, I don't give a shit what they know. I need some ox. I'm sick."

"It's nice to hear you say something," Jonas said, "even if it's bitching at me. Usually I talk in an echo chamber."

She didn't respond and he said, "See that house on the left, the one two houses from the corner? See the security camera on the roof? I could just climb up on that garage and throw a bag over it. But first I'd have to know if the house belongs to a careless celebrity. We gotta stop at the library or the computer café and get on the Internet and find out who lives there. It's a promising target."

Jonas drove aimlessly until they were on one of the top streets, looking down at a midsize residential property on a corner lot, where an elderly woman in a bathrobe and sun hat was sitting on a chaise longue beside a swimming pool. She was drinking what looked like a glass of iced tea and watching a small TV that sat on a table next to her.

Jonas parked, continuing to look down at her, and said, "If we happened to be really desperate I could go to the door of that house and say I'm looking for the Lohan residence or something. And you could open the pool gate and go in there and grab that TV. We could easy trade it for at least an ox or two down at Pablo's Taco Shop."

"I'm really feeling awful, Jonas," Megan said.

"You down for it?"

She paused and said, "I guess so."

"You really down?" he asked. "Don't wuss out on me."

"I'm almost desperate enough to do Wilbur for a couple of OCs," Megan said, tears in her eyes. "That's what I've come to."

He looked at her closely. She really was all smoked out. She was jonesing way worse than he thought. He couldn't believe she'd even think about fucking that disease-ridden drug dealer. If she ever did something like that, he was dumping her ass for sure.

Jonas said, "Okay, we're gonna do this thing just for you. Just to score you an emergency bean or two."

He didn't want Megan to know how nervous he was when he stopped the car two houses from the corner and said, "Walk to the swimming pool gate. When you hear her go into the house, open the gate, run in and jack the TV, and meet me right here. If she's home alone, we're cool. If she's got a maid or if somebody else answers the door, we pass. Okay?"

Her chin quivered when she said, "Okay."

He drove down the hill and stopped thirty yards past the pool gate. The plaster-white wall around the pool was six feet high, and the pool gate was on the side street for the pool cleaner's easy access. He figured it might be locked but Megan could climb the wall with no trouble.

Jonas grinned at Megan with feigned insouciance when she got out and closed the car door. He drove around to the front of the house and parked at the curb by the driveway, where his license plates were not facing the residence.

It was one of the ubiquitous "Spanish-style" homes with red-tile roofs that dot the upscale hillsides all over Southern California, the kind that wouldn't look too crazy within five hundred miles of the Mediterranean Sea. He walked boldly to the front door of the house and was about to use the black metal knocker when he saw the doorbell and pressed it. He was expecting an intercom voice and he had a story ready about a neighbor he was looking for.

There was a wait of over a minute, which was a good sign, and then the door opened and the elderly woman in the sun hat, her face tanned and creased like old leather, said in annoyance, "Are you from Manny the Plumber? I've been waiting all morning for you."

Jonas said, "Uh, no, Manny couldn't make it but he wanted me to come and set up another appointment if that's okay."

"Can't you even fix a clogged toilet?" the woman asked, doubly annoyed now. And she opened the door as though thinking that any fool from a plumbing company could unclog a toilet if he'd just come in and look at it.

"No, ma'am," Jonas said. "I just work in the office and—"

He didn't get to finish it. An eighty-five-pound golden retriever barking deliriously leaped past the woman and slammed Jonas in the chest with both front paws and all his weight behind it.

"Sigmund!" the woman yelled. "Down! Down, Sigmund!"

Jonas was knocked flat on his back, and the dog began wagging and squirming, and for a moment Jonas thought his spine was broken. He felt a spasm when he tried to get up, but the dog was sitting on Jonas's head and drooling on his crotch.

The woman grabbed the beast by his collar and tried to pull him away, saying, "Bad boy! Bad Sigmund!"

But Sigmund didn't give a shit what she said, and he gave Jonas a big lick on the mouth before he decided to surrender to his mistress.

Jonas struggled to his feet in agony, his right hand pressing his lower back, and said, "I could sue you for this, lady!"

"Oh, please!" the woman said. "Sigmund didn't mean to hurt you. He loves people too much."

"He's a menace," Jonas said, moaning as she managed to get Sigmund inside and close the door.

"Let me take down your name and address," the woman said. "I'll call my insurance company immediately. Please believe me, he's an adorable dog. I'm so sorry."

When she opened the door and went inside to get a pen and paper, Jonas carefully descended the two steps, each one causing pain to shoot down his leg. He limped to his car, started it up, and made a U-turn just as the woman opened the door again, notepad in hand.

Jonas made a quick left and drove halfway down the block, where Megan came running to his car with the TV set.

"I did it," she said, opening the Volkswagen's door and putting the TV on the rear seat.

"You drive," he said. "Drop me at home and then go trade for the ox. A mad dog just attacked me. Oooooooh, my fucking back!"

Raleigh Dibble liked his job of overseeing the Brueger estate so much that he could go almost an entire day without thinking about Nigel Wickland. The art dealer was spending a great deal of time at the custom photo lab of his associate, learning enough photographic tricks to be able to do what he had to do. He phoned Raleigh every day on Raleigh's cell to report his progress. And every time that Raleigh considered Nigel's plan, he vowed to call it off. He'd lie beside the Brueger pool on hot afternoons and think of the dozen ways that this could go sideways.

And then Raleigh would wonder when Nigel was going to call and tell him that this was the day. He wished that Nigel wasn't a homo. In prison the more flamboyant butt pirates were always snitching on the straight guys to make points with the COs. Of course, that didn't mean that Nigel would go all fluttery if something did go wrong, and drop a dime on him. Nigel might turn out to be a stand-up guy. Maybe.

And then he'd remember how awful the federal prison had been, and he'd imagine how much more horrible state prison would be. He wouldn't be serving time with tax cheats and white-collar criminals and organized-crime guys, as he had at Club Fed. No, this time he'd be in with the vilest of psychopaths: rapists and serial killers and thugs and cutthroats of every stripe. His life would be in danger when he was just walking across the yard. He could be murdered by gang members just for talking to the wrong guy, or even to the right guy at the wrong time.

His fear would make Raleigh appreciate how this Brueger job was the sweetest setup he'd ever had. In some ways it was even better than when he'd had his own catering business, when he had always had to worry about finding decent meat and fish and produce for a price. And hiring people who actually gave a shit. And paying taxes. All that made him think of $500,000, tax-free. Tax-free! He'd get a safe-deposit box, and that's where it would stay until he could see what was what. He'd go to the bank from time to time just to visit his money. He'd take it out and run his fingers over it.

Or if the recession got worse and property values went in the toilet, maybe he'd use the money to buy the little condo he'd always dreamed of owning. Cash would be king if real estate really tanked. And he'd have cash, more than he'd ever had in his life. A condo that was worth a million nowadays could probably be had for half a mill when California eventually went bankrupt and Arnold Schwarzenegger went back to making dumb movies.

Raleigh grabbed his cell impulsively and dialed the Wickland Gallery, and when Ruth Langley transferred him to Nigel, he said, "Do you have a minute?"

"Only a minute," Nigel said.

"Is it okay to talk on your office phone, or do you want to call me back?"

"Ruth's with a customer," Nigel said. "Go ahead."

"When are you coming?"

"Are you getting eager?"

Nigel's tone was annoying, and Raleigh said, "No, I'm not that eager. But I want this thing to move along at a faster pace."

"I'm just about ready," Nigel said. "I've practiced at my friend's place of business, and after a couple of unsatisfactory attempts, I was successful the last time. Very successful. The work was perfect. You'd be amazed."

"So when're you coming?"

"Try to contain your emotions, dear boy," Nigel said. "It will happen at the right time, and that time is nearly at hand. Be prepared for a call this week. All right?"

When Raleigh closed his cell, he thought that's what he'd hated most about working in London, having to deal with supercilious condescending snobs. Just the sound of their flutey voices could be unbearable, especially the patronizing bitchier teabags like Nigel Wickland.

ELEVEN

BY THE END of the week, the surfer cops were unlucky enough to be on duty when there was a Hollywood moon, that is, a full moon over Hollywood, when anything could happen. Sergeant Murillo conducted the midwatch roll call, and after warning everyone that there would be a Hollywood moon in the sky that night, the last thing he did was search his Darwin list for something that might be a morale booster for the troops.

"And now it's time for the Darwin list," he said, turning to a recent bulletin. "That means people we're better off without. Last night in West L.A. a burglar who'd entered a commercial building through an A/C duct with a flashlight in his mouth fell twenty feet onto his face and the flashlight jammed in his throat and suffocated him. It looks like a clear case of death by Ever Ready."

The troops all cheered and whistled, and then he said, "Tonight we have a full moon. A Hollywood moon, and as you know, that makes citizens do all kinds of strange things. For you new people, that also means that I buy a large pizza with the works for the team that brings in the weirdest story at end-of-watch. Okay, let's hit the bricks."

Everyone gathered their gear and each cop touched the Oracle's picture for luck before heading for the kit room and then the parking lot.

*　　*　　*

The sizzle of the Santa Anas on the boulevards generated rays of heat rising from the blacktop and left people scratching their bone-dry skin and dabbing moisturizer on their lips. After the feverish glow of twilight, and well before the Hollywood moon rose in the sky, a call came into Communications Division from east Hollywood that set a tone for the evening. Despite the immigrant mix in the area that made the school district a Tower of Babel, there were not many African American households within the geographic boundaries of Hollywood Division. The "shots fired" radio call took them to the cottage of a black family who were not African Americans but recent immigrants from the Dominican Republic.

When 6-X-32 pulled up in front of the cottage of the person reporting, Jetsam unlocked the shotgun and took it with him to the door. He was followed by Flotsam, who was driving that evening.

The call had come from a Dominican neighbor of a Salvadoran family from whose house the gunshot had emanated. The person reporting was a Dominican woman who worked as a waitress at a Mexican restaurant on Western Avenue, and she was waiting for them. She was middle-aged and looked to the surfer cops like she ate too many of her restaurant's gorditas. Although she was only five feet tall, she easily outweighed Flotsam, who towered over her.

"I hear somebody fire a gun," she said. "Een there!" And she pointed to the ramshackle residence next door.

By then, 6-X-66 had squealed to a stop, and Hollywood Nate and Snuffy Salcedo jumped out to back up the surfer cops.

Snuffy spoke briefly to the woman in Spanish and was told that she did not know the Salvadoran family, who were recent arrivals to the neighborhood. She thought there was a mother, and a man who might or might not be the father, and at least six children, maybe more. They all lived in the two-bedroom rented bungalow, which was owned by the same slumlord who owned the house of the Dominicans. And then she added that there was also a very old *abuelita* living there.

"A grandma?" Hollywood Nate asked, and Snuffy nodded.

"There's a big houseful of people in that little crib," Snuffy said.

Before the surfer cops got to the front porch of the Salvadorans, a team from Watch 3 arrived to cover the back door. Just then, a detective car pulled up in front, and the night-watch detective, Compassionate Charlie Gilford, got out, wearing a food-stained tan cotton blazer and sucking his teeth, as usual. He was wanting an entry for his log in order to prove that he did leave the station from time to time to assist the bluesuits, and not just to grab a free meal at places where a plate of greasy fare was a full pop to coppers on the beat and half price to anyone else with a badge.

Nate always thought that one of the great mysteries of Hollywood was how the lazy detective—who took the night-watch assignment only to avoid the real work of handling a daytime caseload—could always manage to find a new necktie that was even uglier than the last one he wore. The base color of this one was uncertain because of the swirl and patterns of garish clashing colors snaking over the entire tie, but it was a cinch to hide salsa stains. Nate figured that Charlie showed up only because he had heard the hotshot call, being a few blocks away leeching freebie tostadas by badging the boss at the local taco shop.

When Compassionate Charlie was halfway between the car and the house, he saw that he'd arrived too soon. The uniformed coppers hadn't made entry and secured the situation yet, so he stayed where he was instead of walking into a potentially dangerous incident.

Jetsam angled off at one side of the screen door and tapped on it with the muzzle of the Remington 870 shotgun. Flotsam held his Glock down by his right leg.

"Police!" Jetsam yelled. "Anybody inside, step out now with your hands on your head!"

The inside door opened slowly and seven Salvadoran children, most of them in T-shirts and shorts, emerged onto the porch with their hands on their heads. They ranged in age from about four to thirteen. Three of the youngest were crying and the older ones were plenty scared. The one who looked about thirteen had his hair buzzed down to the scalp and was already wearing wannabe gang rags: a plaid flannel shirt and a baggy pair of denim shorts that extended well below the knees and were hanging halfway off his butt. He was apparently trying to connect as a junior with one of the gangs in the area, possibly the Salvadoran's Mara Salvatrucha, aka MS-13, the largest gang in the world.

"What happened in there?" Flotsam asked him.

"My big brother got shot," said the boy in good English.

"Who shot him?" Jetsam asked, his shotgun held at a ready angle across his chest.

"I don't wanna say," the boy said.

"Where is he?" Flotsam asked.

"He ain't here," the boy said. "He got in his car and went to the hospital."

"Where was he hit?" Flotsam asked, figuring it was probably a gang drive-by.

"Here," the boy said, taking a hand down and touching his left buttock.

"How old is he?" Flotsam asked.

"Eighteen," said the kid. "Can I take my hands off my head now?"

Flotsam nodded and said, "Which hospital did he go to?"

"I dunno," the kid said. "He was really mad and swearing and everything, so he didn't wanna talk to nobody."

"Is your mother home?" Flotsam asked.

"No, she's at work."

"Did one of you shoot him?" Jetsam asked.

"None of us kids," the boy said.

"Then who shot him?" Jetsam asked.

This time the kid burst into tears and shook his head. "I can't tell you," he said, looking toward the bungalow.

"Is the shooter in the house?" Flotsam asked, elevating the muzzle of his pistol, ready for anything.

"Uh-huh," the kid said, and now he really started bawling.

Hollywood Nate and Snuffy Salcedo, along with a second team from Watch 3, deployed near the front porch with their pistols drawn. Flotsam said to them, "The shooter's inside."

Then Flotsam and Jetsam quickly gestured for all of the kids to move from the porch and onto the tiny patch of grass that passed for a lawn. Flotsam nodded to his partner, who nodded back, and Jetsam entered the bungalow quickly with the stock of the shotgun tucked against his hip, followed by Flotsam.

Jetsam yelled, "Police officers! Step out of the bedroom with your hands on your head!"

No answer, but they could hear the television going.

Flotsam crouched, his pistol extended in both hands and moved out of the kill zone. He said, "Now, goddamnit! Come out now!"

Still no answer.

Jetsam advanced in a semicrouch. The gloom of twilight made it hard to see clearly into the darkened bedroom where the television was playing, but they could hear Spanish-speaking voices delivering their melodramatic lines with lots of intensity and plenty of volume. But that was all they heard.

"Come out!" Flotsam ordered again.

Jetsam, his back to the wall and still inching forward, craned his neck, and peering around the doorjamb, he found the shooter.

She was sitting where she always sat, on a lumpy Barcalounger with her legs up, intently watching an old TV that sat on top of a chest of drawers. The antenna wire ran from the TV set to the window, where presumably it led to a roof antenna.

A rusty old .32 caliber revolver was lying on a table beside her, next to a telephone.

121

Jetsam said, "Bro, get in here and check this out!"

Then he entered the tiny room, moving quickly to the table, and picked up the revolver, with Flotsam right behind him.

She hardly looked at them but seemed to concentrate harder on the program, where a shirtless man on a tropical beach at night was kissing a voluptuous woman who sighed and said, *"¡Carlos, Carlos, mi amor!"* He answered with, *"¡Isabel, mi vida!"*

"Dude," Flotsam said. "She's like, a hundred years old."

As it turned out, he wasn't far off. At first glance, she seemed mummified. The ancient Salvadoran woman was the color of mocha coffee with curdled cream. Her hair, what there was of it, was a patch of colorless frizz. Her milky eyes were sunken deep within their sockets, and her eyelids looked like crumpled tissue paper. Her crusty lips hung open, baring blackened gums and a few amber teeth. She wore a faded cotton dress large enough for two of her, and fuzzy Donald Duck bedroom slippers. Her bare arms and legs were brittle sticks, and her crinkling flesh was parchment-dry and looked too delicate to withstand the slightest human touch.

Jetsam said, "Bro, what we got here is the über oldster of Hollywood."

"¿Inglés?" Flotsam said to her. *"¿Habla Inglés?"*

The old woman glanced at him with her milky eyes and shook her head and went back to watching television.

"Get Snuffy in here," Jetsam yelled to the cops now milling around on the front porch.

After a moment Snuffy Salcedo entered the bedroom, looked at the woman, and said to the surfer cops, "Are you kidding me?"

Then he squatted beside the Barcalounger and talked to her. She answered softly in a surprisingly strong voice but never took her eyes off the television program while Snuffy delivered a series of questions.

After she gave a few short answers to him, Snuffy said to Flotsam and Jetsam and Hollywood Nate, "Her name's Irma Beltrán. She's the great-grandmother of the kids, and she thinks she's either ninety-eight or ninety-nine years old, she can't remember which. But she's having a big party here on her hundredth birthday and there's gonna be *pupusas* and *curtido* and *tres leches* birthday cake. And we're all invited."

Flotsam and Jetsam looked at each other, and Jetsam said to Snuffy, "Ask her who shot the kid."

"I already did."

"Don't keep us in suspense, dude," Flotsam said.

"She shot him," Snuffy said.

"Maybe she's covering for somebody," Jetsam said hopefully. "Maybe for the kids' father?"

"She's very definite," Snuffy said. "She shot him."

"Ask her if it was an accident," Flotsam said. "I'll bet it was an accident."

Snuffy spoke to her again and listened to her answer and said, "Nope. She said she shot him on purpose." Then, enjoying the surfer cops' discomfort, Snuffy said, "Want me to read her the Miranda rights? A felony bust will look good on your recap."

Ignoring the wisecrack, Jetsam said, "Ask her why she shot him."

"I already did," said Snuffy. "She shot him because he wouldn't stop talking on the phone when she's trying to watch her favorite *novela*."

After a moment of deliberation, Flotsam said, "So what're we gonna do with her?"

"This is one shooter I ain't handcuffing," Jetsam said. "You touch her and she might crumble into pieces. Maybe into powder. You'll need a dustpan to pick her up. Maybe we better call a supervisor."

"Aw, shit!" Flotsam said. "Ask her if maybe she was just sorta trying to scare him away from her telephone and cranked one off sorta in his general direction, and it sorta accidentally nailed him in the ass."

Snuffy Salcedo spoke to her again and listened to her answer, and then turned to the other cops and said, "She says she always hits what she aims at. And would the big policeman please move away from the television set because she thinks Carlos is very handsome and this is a really good part."

Flotsam stepped aside so Irma Beltrán could see what Carlos was going to do now that he had Isabel lying helpless on the sand in a swoon from his blazing kisses. Isabel's right breast was partially exposed now and that even got Jetsam engrossed in the program.

Then Flotsam said to his partner, "Keep your mind in the game, dude, and pay attention here. We got a Hollywood moon coming up tonight, so maybe she caught an early lunar vibe and this ain't all her fault. Think of a graceful way outta this so we don't gotta move her from that chair."

Hollywood Nate said, "Just book the gun. The kid probably went to the ER at Hollywood Pres. By now he's chill. I bet he'll sign off that the old lady capped him by accident, or maybe you can suggest that he did it himself while practicing his quick draw. And you might remind him to stop using the phone when Granny Oakley's watching her soap operas."

Just then, Compassionate Charlie Gilford sauntered into the crowded little bedroom, and said, "What's taking you guys so long?" When he saw Irma Beltrán, he froze and said, "What the fuck's Norman Bates's momma doing here?"

"She's the shooter," Flotsam said. "It was an accident, though. She thought the gun was the TV remote. It could happen to anyone."

"Put her back in the fruit cellar!" Compassionate Charlie said with a shiver of distaste.

"We think the victim's at Hollywood Pres," Flotsam said to the detective. "He's her great-grandson. Butt shot is all. No biggie."

They were interrupted when a copper from Watch 3 came into

the crowded room and said, "Breaking news. The oldest of the kids just told us his great-grandma's a hundred and three years old."

Hollywood Nate said to the detective, "This might win the Hollywood moon award, Charlie. This has got to be the longevity record for local female shooters. A hundred and three!"

Compassionate Charlie sucked his teeth for a few seconds, then shrugged and said, "So what? Something weirder will happen around here tonight." And then he added the mantra heard so frequently in that geographic police division: "This is fucking Hollywood."

The detective took a notebook from his pocket to find the number for Hollywood Presbyterian Medical Center, but when he walked to the table and reached for the telephone, both Flotsam and Jetsam scared the crap out of him when they yelled in unison, "Don't touch the phone!"

Jonas Claymore wasn't affected by the full moon over Hollywood. He was in bed with a heating pad on his lower back, bitching even when Megan Burke came in with a watson for him that she'd scored along with two OCs in trade for the stolen TV set.

"Is the pain as bad as yesterday?" she asked.

"What the fuck do you think?" Jonas grumbled. "Christ, the heat ain't helping at all. Rub me down again with that hot gel, will ya? Oh, my fucking back. I'd like to go back there and toss that mutt a hamburger loaded with rat poison."

"You should watch TV or something," Megan said, sick of his whining. "If you could just get yourself out of bed, you'd feel better."

"Easy for you to say," Jonas said. "Make me something to eat, will ya?"

"What do you want, Jonas?"

"Oh, maybe prime rib with garlic mashed potatoes. Or a filet mignon with grilled onions. Whadda you mean, for chrissake?"

Megan sighed and said, "I'll see if there's a can of tomato soup left. If there is, do you want crackers with it?"

"Surprise me with your culinary art," Jonas said.

"Maybe it was an omen," Megan said. "Being attacked by an animal on our first crime. Maybe we should stop while we can."

Jonas said, "Didn't you kinda get a rush from snatching that TV from that house? I was hoping that maybe for a little while you could get into grabbing small stuff to trade for ox. I mean, just till we get on our feet. Then I was hoping you might be ready to try going into one of those big houses up in the Hollywood Hills."

"I still think it's scary."

"I told you from the jump, we won't do anything that ain't safe."

She thought about it and said, "Okay, I guess maybe I'm in. Temporarily. Just till we're on our feet."

"I'll be good to go in a couple of days," Jonas said. "Now, how about that food?"

She was gone for fifteen minutes, and when she came back, she had a bowl of tomato soup and a few saltine crackers on a paper plate. Jonas picked up a cracker and it was so soggy it bent in his fingers.

"Is it okay?" Megan asked when he tasted a spoonful.

"Savory," Jonas said. "One of your better dinners, I'd have to say."

★ TWELVE ★

VIV DALEY AND Georgie Adams had been removed from the field after the shooting of Louis Dryden and would not be returned to field duty until a BSS shrink and the chief gave an okay, per LAPD policy. That left only two women working the midwatch on that night of the Hollywood moon. P3 Della Ravelle, a twenty-two-year cop, was the Field Training Officer for P1 Britney Small, who was born a year after her FTO had been appointed to the LAPD. They were working 6-X-46, and Della Ravelle was driving, with young Britney Small doing the report writing.

Britney Small, who was in the last phase of her probation, was one of the most reticent and shy women that Della Ravelle had ever encountered in law enforcement. But her former FTO, a highly disciplined Korean American cop named Rupert Tong, had always given her glowing evaluations, so Della figured the probationer must've been assertive enough when she needed to be. Tong had transferred to a long-awaited detective assignment at Robbery-Homicide Division, and Della Ravelle was taking over Britney Small until the end of her eighteen-month probationary period, two months hence.

Since Britney Small was so near the end of her probation and Della Ravelle was so laid-back, Della insisted that the boot not keep calling her ma'am. Britney had never stopped calling Rupert

Tong sir until their last night together, when the former Navy SEAL said to her, "Be sure and let me know if you need anything or have any questions about something you've learned from me. You've got my cell number."

It was only after Britney had said, "Thank you, sir, and good luck to you," that he'd smiled broadly and given her a farewell hug, saying, "You're a real copper already, Brit. You can call me Rupert anytime."

Britney Small was so willowy that Della Ravelle called her "my bluesuit ballerina." The creamy-faced rookie loved working with this female FTO, telling her on their first night together that it was great to work with someone even older than her mom, for the wisdom it would bring.

"Thanks for that," Della said, thinking what everyone past forty would think at such a moment—Older than her mom? Where did it all go? How the hell did this happen to me?

Della Ravelle was forty-four years old, with smart hazel eyes and a friendly grin for everyone. She had to go to a hairdresser more often than she liked these days in order to keep her hair brown. "I'll dye till I die" was her motto. She was always struggling to lose ten pounds despite frequent workouts in the Hollywood Station weight room, where Hollywood Nate pumped iron almost daily.

She was twice married and twice divorced, with two sons aged nineteen and seventeen, who lived with her in her South Pasadena house. Zach and Jonathan were students, one at Pasadena City College and the other at South Pasadena High School. Della always thought it was nothing more than sheer luck that she had married slightly better the first time, back at a time when she'd wanted children. That marriage was to an IRS auditor who was diligent with his child support payments throughout the years, even though during their marriage he was so nitpicking and clueless that he almost drove her crazy. To him, police work was something that could be analyzed like the tax returns of the deadbeats he delighted in tormenting. He could never understand the emotional hazards of the Job, and the powerful bonds that developed among the blue brethren in Della's strange fraternity of the badge.

The second husband was a worse mistake because he, too, was a cop, an alpha male, LAPD macho copper, mustache and all. They had battled from their honeymoon on, but thankfully the marriage was brief with no children. So now, with the days and nights of hiring babysitters behind her, Della Ravelle hoped to enjoy the six years she planned to remain on the Job before retiring at age fifty to a peaceful future where the size of the moon over Hollywood did not matter a whit.

At 9 P.M. that night, she looked up while driving and said to Britney Small, "Wonder when it's gonna bring its wrath down on us."

"What?" Britney asked.

"The Hollywood moon," Della said. "We're due."

So far, their watch had been routine, but the full-moon motorists were already feeling the effects of it. There had been three traffic collisions on the boulevards, and both Della and Britney had written traffic citations for moving violations. On their third call, they caught a "415 family dispute" on their dashboard computer, indicating the penal code section for disturbance of the peace. Such routine calls often escalated, so on the way to the call, Della said to her probationer, "About these routine four-fifteen family disputes, I want you to always keep in mind that you and me don't go hands-on with people until backup arrives. Don't be shy about using your rover to call for assistance or help if you have to."

"Right," Britney said.

Della said, "A few years ago, two women officers here in Hollywood got into a knockdown street fight with a large, violent guy, and one of the women got badly hurt. A few firefighters on a lunch break were standing there watching the tussle and didn't lift a finger to help the officers. The fire department later sent a battalion chief to all our roll calls to apologize and try to rationalize it, but every copper at Hollywood Station was extremely pissed off. A few of the mouthier ones told the battalion chief that the next time firefighters were being pelted with rocks or shot at by street thugs, we'd sit and watch just like they did. There were very hard feelings for a while. Moral of the story is, you can only depend on your brothers in blue to help in the rough-and-tumble altercations. Your last FTO was a very good copper, but he was a man. Don't ever forget that you're a woman. You're never gonna impress some of the old guys, no matter what you do."

"I've noticed that for sure," Britney said. "The OGs aren't very friendly with female boots."

"I repeat, Britney," Della said. "Don't ever forget out here that you're a woman."

"Roger that," Britney said. "I won't."

Della said, "We can be outstanding police officers but we can't morph into men during the hands-on stuff. And by the way, female scrappy drunks can be worse than men when it comes to down-and-dirty street fights, so be wary in those situations. But we usually have better verbal skills than men, and sometimes we can talk things down just by being reasonable and by being women, where the men can't. Sometimes our gender can de-escalate things. For these last few months of your probation I'm gonna give you a lotta cop-style girl talk that Rupert Tong couldn't give you. You okay with that?"

"Of course, ma'am—I mean Della," Britney said. "I'm really grateful to learn the woman stuff from another woman."

"I'll bet Rupert Tong never talked to you about underwear, did he?" Della said.

"Underwear? Lord, no!" Britney said.

"Well, it's an important thing for women officers to know about. Never rush off to work with your underwear inside out. And don't wear grandma underwear, although at your age I'm sure you never do. This is in case something bad happens. Would you want a bunch of guys in the ER to see you in funny underwear that's inside out?"

"I see your point," Britney said with a giggle.

"And for the same reason, don't go to work without shaving your legs. How'd you like it if a gossipy ER nurse told some of the Watch Five coppers about your stubble? You just know they'd all start calling you 'cactus legs.'"

"No cactus legs," the rookie said. "Got it."

"And don't wear an underwire bra under your vest. I tried to take the vest off Millie Boyle after she got rear-ended in a TC at Hollywood and Vine, right before we put her into the RA. And her goddamn padded underwire bra popped off like it was spring-loaded. One of the midwatch coppers found it on the street and later taped a cell phone photo of the bra to the wall in the roll call room with a note that said, 'Will the person who lost this piece of equipment at the scene of a TC at Hollywood and Vine please claim it with Harry the kit room king.' It was all very embarrassing for Millie."

"No underwire bra. Okay, boss," Britney said cheerfully. "This is real good information to have."

"Poor Millie," Della said. "She married and divorced two lieu-tenants early in her career, so pretty soon every guy she worked with proposed. They'd say stuff like, 'I know you don't like me, but if I marry you I might get promoted to lieutenant, so how about it?'"

It was a two-story house on a residential street several blocks south of Paramount Studios. They heard the yelling from the street when they got out of their black-and-white. Both women grabbed their side-handle batons. The call came from next door, and a young woman in an orange leotard stood on her porch and pointed to the walkway between the houses. There a large-screen plasma TV was shattered to pieces below an open upstairs window. Della nodded to the woman in the leotard, who went back inside and closed the door quickly.

Britney knocked at the door, and after several seconds, one of the potential combatants, a dark-eyed, olive-skinned, beefy woman older than Della, with enough hairspray to be an ozone threat, opened the door. She was dressed in the work uniform she wore at Farmers Market, where she served coffee and pastries at one of the open-air shops. Her husband was her age and even more over-weight, and appropriately enough, he wore a sweat-stained wife-beater. But neither side had yet inflicted any violence. His boozy face was blooming like a rose and he was scowling at his wife.

The cops stepped inside and Britney said, "One of your neighbors called. Is there a problem here?"

The man pointed at the woman and said, "My wife thinks she can cheat on me and I'm supposed to lay down and take it!"

"May we have your names, please?" Della said, trying for some simmer time.

"I'm John Gianopoulos," the man said, "and this backstabbing adultress is my wife, I'm sorry to say."

The woman turned to the older cop for empathy and said, "This fool thinks I'm bonking my hairdresser, Jackie, who happens to be gayer than a bouquet of daisies. In fact, Jackie's shack bitch is a lit-tle guy who's way prettier than me and a hell of a lot younger. And his shack bitch even has tits thanks to hormone therapy. Why would my hairdresser wanna fuck me, for chrissake?"

Britney's look to Della said, Why would *anyone* want to?

In a quiet voice, Della Ravelle said, "Could we all keep it down? You're scaring the neighbors."

"She's killing me," her husband wailed. "Killing me!"

Then both cops took a closer look at him. There were bald patches all over his head. He had only a little patch of eyebrow over his left eye and none over his right eye. Even his arms looked peculiar. The left forearm was thick with black hair but there were large spots of bare skin showing, just as on his head. His right arm had almost no hair left on it. When Della took a closer look, she saw that though he was obviously meant to be a very hairy man, he had no eyelashes at all.

John Gianopoulos was obviously used to having people stare at him. He said to the cops, "She did this to me. I was a healthy man before she tricked me into marriage by saying her uncle would put me in his house-painting business." He pointed to his head and said, "Look at what being with her does to me!"

Britney gaped and said, "Do you have a skin disease? Like mange or something?"

"I have trichotillomania," he said. "Thanks to her evil ways."

His wife shook her head and said, "They call it an impulse-control disorder. He pulls out his hair when he's stressed, which is most of the time. Sometimes he wears a wig, and believe me, it's no improvement."

Della said, "Have you two considered breaking up?"

"I just needed a push," Mrs. Gianopoulos said, "and maybe having you cops coming here is the push I need."

Della said, "It would be a good thing if one of you could leave for a while until the two of you cool down. I think we have a potentially volatile situation here."

"Let him leave," she said. "He can just walk down to the corner saloon and get shit-faced, which is what he usually does anyway."

"And you can leave permanently," he said. "Take everything and go home to your dago mother. Just get out!"

"When I walk outta here," she said to him, "I'll take my clothes and my plasma TV, which I paid for, by the way, and that's all I want from this sick marriage." She looked at the cops and said, "He can keep the pots and pans and the dishes he's never washed and the bills he's never paid."

"Did you just get home from work?" Della asked her.

Mrs. Gianopoulos said, "Ten minutes before you arrived. Why?"

"Did you happen to use the walkway on the west side of the house?" Della asked.

"No," she said. "I parked in the alley and came in the back door. Why?"

"Uh-oh," Britney said.

Della said quickly, "Mr. Gianopoulos, I think it would be wise and better for both of you if you would leave here for a couple of hours. Do it now, please. And we'll have a brief chat with Mrs. Gianopoulos after you're gone."

He took the hint, put on a Members Only jacket that could never close over his huge belly, and walked out the front door, slamming it behind him. After the cops broke the news to Mrs. Gianopoulos about her plasma TV, and after she finished cursing loud enough to scare the goldfish in the living room, Della strongly encouraged her to load her car and head for her mother's house, and no charge for the marriage counseling.

Della concluded with, "We don't want you to kill him in his sleep tonight. You'd be charged with first-degree murder."

"It might be worth it," Mrs. Gianopoulos said with too much sincerity.

"You'll both be way better off if you leave him," Britney Small said. "Mr. Gianopoulos might even start growing eyelashes again."

After 6-X-46 cleared from that call and was heading north on Van Ness Avenue, Della Ravelle said to her probie, "That was a pretty routine family beef, all things considered. But I can think of a dozen ways a he-said-she-said can go sideways. That one went okay because we were calm and we were businesslike and we're women. Even though that dude mighta been crazy enough to toss a two-thousand-dollar TV out an upstairs window, you noticed he was obedient with us. Probably has mommy issues, but whatever, we use our gender to our advantage out here. Right, partner?"

"Roger that, partner," Britney said, and earnestly began logging the call on their daily field activity report.

Della Ravelle watched Britney and smiled and wondered what it would've been like to have a daughter.

Their next stop resulted in a judgment call for young Britney Small. The Hollywood moon was rising higher in the heavens, and they got a call about an illegally parked car blocking the driveway of a residence up near Lake Hollywood. By the time they got there, the car was gone, but since they were there in the Hills, Della took a drive to a lover's lane where the cops used to catch teenagers smoking pot. She figured that nowadays kids would be doing meth or ox if they still parked up there. That part of the Hollywood Hills was full of stunted trees and brush that had to be controlled to prevent wildfires. Deer, coyotes, raccoons, opossums, and skunks lived there, feeding on the leavings of nearby human inhabitants.

Della said, "One time I got a call when a baby deer got hit by a car up here. The fawn was lying on the road, and there was an old motor cop there ahead of me, standing next to his bike and looking at the animal. The motor cop was one of those dinosaurs whose partners probably have to chew his food for him. One of those old saddle-sore vets that everyone calls Boots when they don't know his name. And then another two radio cars rolled up. And when I called in what had happened and asked for animal control to come and deal with it, the RTO conferred with somebody and came back saying there were no animal control people available, and told me we were authorized to shoot the animal."

"Did you?" Britney asked. "Did you shoot the baby deer?"

"I looked at that fawn, at the terror and pain in its eyes and I wanted to put it out of its misery," Della said. "Hollywood Nate was also there, and a unit from Watch Three, and nobody could shoot the fawn, not even the old motor cop, who I figured would just step up and show us what wusses we were. One of the coppers from Watch Three was a real shit magnet who worked gangs in Southeast, down where schoolkids don't have earthquake drills, they have drive-by drills. Anyway, he'd been in three righteous gunfights down there where he killed a couple of guys, but even he couldn't shoot the deer. Fortunately, the poor little thing went into shock and died."

"I kinda like that story, though," Britney said.

"Whadda you like about it?"

"That the LAPD gunfighters couldn't shoot a baby deer. Somehow that makes me sorta proud. Know what I mean?"

Della smiled at her young partner again and said, "Okay, we're coming up on the lover's lane here. It's a piece of land that goes out a ways. The coppers call it Point Peter Puffer."

Then they spotted a car in the darkness and Della switched off her headlights and turned down the radio and let their car drift closer. It was a white Honda Civic, and it was bouncing and rocking like the hydraulic-aided, tricked-out lowriders that parade up and down Ventura Boulevard in the Valley.

Della said, "They're not doing dope at the moment, that's for sure. But maybe they smoked some to prime the pump, and maybe we can find what's left there in Daddy's car. Wanna check them out?"

"Sure," Britney said. "I'm good to go."

Della let the black-and-white roll into the parking area as close as she could without alerting them. She parked and they got out quietly, leaving their car doors open, and approached in the darkness, Della on the driver's side and Britney on the passenger side. They looked over the roof at each other, turned on their streamlights and jerked open the doors.

Britney said, "Get outta the car!" And she shone her light onto the couple in the backseat.

Della saw the situation first and said, "She can't."

The amorous couple was not in Daddy's car. A sweating middle-aged man was on top, his pants pushed down around his ankles. The woman on her back underneath him didn't look as frightened as he did. In fact, Britney later remembered seeing what she thought was sadness in the woman's face. When the man sat straight up, the rookie saw that the woman had no legs, only scarred stumps ending six inches higher than where her knees should have been.

Della looked over the roof of the Honda at her startled partner to see how she was going to handle this one.

Britney decided fast and simply mumbled, "Sorry." And closed the car door, retreating quickly to the black-and-white with Della following.

When they drove away, Britney said, "I don't think I wanna know her story."

Della said, "I'm gonna enjoy being your FTO, kiddo. You've got what they can't teach at the academy—good old common sense."

"There was nothing else to say, was there?" Britney asked.

Della said, "No, but a lotta male coppers woulda tried. The more macho they are, the more they can fuck things up."

At that very moment a pair of seriously macho cops were hoping to assist in an attempt to serve a warrant for murder on a Mexican national from the Arellano-Félix cartel, who was supposedly living in southeast Hollywood on one of the residential streets near Beverly Boulevard. A snitch had supplied information that the fugitive, whose name was Jaime Soto Aguilar, was hiding out with a woman who owned a house in that vicinity, but as to which house, or even which street, the informant could not say. A detective had gone to roll call and requested that all units make a note of the license number and location of any very old cars in restored condition that might be parked in that neighborhood, because Aguilar was a car nut who couldn't resist restoring classic cars. The detective said they'd follow up on any car leads as time permitted. The fugitive's description was given along with information that he had a tattoo of a rattlesnake with dripping fangs coiled around his neck.

Flotsam and Jetsam had listened with interest during roll call, especially about the car, because they had recently noticed a restored Chevrolet Malibu cruising around that area, and a guy who looked Latino was driving it. After noticing the apple-green eye-catcher, they'd discussed how cool it would be to drive a car named after their surfing beach.

When they were not answering calls on that very warm and windless late summer evening, the surfer cops covered every residential street in that vicinity on both sides of Beverly Boulevard. And when the full moon was rising high over Hollywood, they spotted the apple-green Malibu parked on a street that was jammed with other parked cars. Flotsam and Jetsam put their sun-streaked heads together and cooked up a scheme that would require some assistance. Jetsam requested that 6-X-66 meet 6-X-32 in a certain alley off Beverly Boulevard.

When Hollywood Nate and Snuffy Salcedo showed up and the two black-and-whites were parked side by side, Flotsam said, "Post up and keep an eye on that bitchin' Malibu. The owner of that cherry ride's gotta be in a house real close to it. And the owner might just be Aguilar. The license plate don't mean shit. It's registered to some chick named Johnson in Pomona."

"Where're you beach rats going in the meantime?" Nate wanted to know.

Jetsam said, "To collect some noisy junk." Then Flotsam dropped it into gear and off they went.

Snuffy Salcedo said to Hollywood Nate, "This is stupid. If they're so sure the car belongs to Aguilar, why don't they request a stakeout?"

"Because the chances are so remote that it's Aguilar's, nobody would do it," Nate said.

"Then why're we doing it?" Snuffy said. "We were told just to write down license numbers and locations if we saw a restored car."

"Based on my experience, it pays to indulge them," Nate said. "Somehow, Neptune or whoever the surfer god is bestows crazy blessings on those two. Besides, my curiosity is killing me, isn't yours? Noisy junk?"

When the surfer cops returned to the alley in twenty minutes, they had the backseat of their shop, as well as the trunk, loaded with empty cans of all sizes, along with two battered old metal trash cans.

"What the fuck?" Snuffy Salcedo said when he got a look at their cargo.

"We are stupendously grateful for Chinese restaurants," Flotsam said. "You hardly ever find metal trash cans these days."

"And food cans galore," Jetsam said cheerfully.

Flotsam said to Snuffy Salcedo, "Dude, can you drive like Jimmie Johnson?"

Snuffy looked to Nate in utter puzzlement before he turned and said to Flotsam, "What?"

"They work in mysterious ways, partner," Nate explained to Snuffy. "Let's do what they want and see where it goes."

Flotsam said to Snuffy, "Anyways, dude, try to drive like Jimmie Johnson tonight, okay? We want you to go to the top of the street and come screaming down till you're almost opposite that pristine machine, and then lock 'em up. All four wheels. We wanna hear that rubber scream like a whore for a hundred-dollar tip."

"And what will you two be doing in the meantime, pray tell?" Hollywood Nate asked.

Flotsam said, "Me and my pard, we're gonna be dumping the trash cans full of junk onto the street and, like, making more noise than Chinese fucking New Year."

"If the guy that owns that Malibu ain't boning his old lady, he's gonna run to his ride, to see if it's in pieces all over the street," Jetsam explained.

"Even if he is boning his old lady, he's gonna pull right outta her and run to his ride," Flotsam said. "He can find a bitch anywheres, but where's he gonna find a mint Malibu like that one?"

Snuffy looked at Nate again and said, "Know what? On a night this hot, everybody in a no-A/C neighborhood's got their windows open. Maybe it's me being back in Hollywood where anything can happen, but this is so loopy I think it might work."

Ten minutes later, Snuffy Salcedo was parked at the north end of the block, revving the engine of the Crown Vic. When he received a flashlight signal from the other end of the block, he floored it, and the black-and-white roared south until he was twenty yards from where the Malibu was parked and then he stood on the brakes.

The wheels locked up and the car's rear end started sliding until Snuffy got off the brakes and sped past the Malibu and the waiting surfer cops, each of whom was holding overhead a metal trash can full of junk. Snuffy could hear the explosive crash of cans and other metal before he drove into the alley to conceal the radio car.

Flotsam, Jetsam, and Nate hid between houses and behind cars, and within a minute, people were running out of their houses to see which car had been smashed in the collision. Several car owners scurried to see if they still had fenders intact, but only one man, shirtless and barefoot, ran straight to the Malibu.

He was checking the driver's side of the car when he was lit by flashlight beams and a tall blond cop said to him, "Dude, I don't know if you speak English, but if you even fart too loud, I'm gonna blow the eye right outta that rattlesnake."

A shorter blond cop said to him, "No, go ahead and rabbit. I love the smell of gunsmoke in the evening."

Snuffy Salcedo came running back from the alley with tobacco juice dripping down his chin as the fugitive was being handcuffed.

Jetsam said, "Read him his rights in Spanish, bro."

Snuffy Salcedo told Jaime Soto Aguilar in Spanish of his Miranda rights, and when he was finished, the fugitive made one brief comment to Snuffy in Spanish.

"What'd he say?" Flotsam asked.

Snuffy replied, "He said he thinks he's gonna have a heart attack."

"Bitchin'!" Flotsam said. "Tell him we never made a cardiac arrest."

"Do they rehearse this shit?" Snuffy Salcedo asked Hollywood Nate.

"They don't have to," said Nate. "They're in lockstep. I think they were Siamese twins separated at birth and raised apart. Probably by jackals."

During the ride to Hollywood Station with the fugitive handcuffed in the backseat of their shop, Jetsam said to his partner, "Bro, do you think this is, like, unusual enough to qualify for a pizza from Sergeant Murillo? Or does it have to be more like Hollywood weird? Like, more in the freak-show mold?"

While the surfer cops were locking up first prize for the Hollywood moon award, 6-X-46 was down from the Hollywood Hills, and Della Ravelle was still lecturing her probationer in the ways of women in police work.

As she drove east on Santa Monica Boulevard, Della said, "I can talk a lot about common sense, Britney. It's a good copper's most valuable trait. Things're gonna be a whole lot better for you on this Job than they were for women like me back in the day. When I was a boot, the old guys never got tired of playing little tricks on us. Like when I worked Central, I can remember a time when a couple of OGs had me do a pat-down search on a basehead down on skid row who was wearing spandex. After I patted her down and told them she's clean, my P3 said, 'Good job. I'm gonna write a comment card on you.' Then when I wasn't looking one of the other OGs, a former SWAT guy who thought he was Mr. Tactical and smoked cigarettes in his teeth instead of his lips, puts his hideout gun on the ground and says, 'You missed this, rookie. She had it tucked under her crotch.'"

Britney said, "What'd you do then?"

"For a few seconds I almost panicked, but then my common sense kicked in and I said, 'No, sir. She was wearing spandex and there were no bulges on her except the ones nature gave her.' The OGs had a laugh and I was a step closer to acceptance."

"I try to never forget that it's still a man's world out here," Britney said.

"Yes, but it's lots better now," Della said. "I won't even try to tell you about the sexual harassment we used to put up with. And there were always the goddamn tricks. After a woman boot would search under the seats in her shop before she hit the streets, an OG would invariably drop a bag of rocks or some other kind of dope under the backseat and say, 'What the fuck's wrong with you, baby girl? You missed this.' It got so lame after a while that even they got tired of it. But we had to live with it till they did."

"How'd you finally win the OGs over?"

"By trying to be a better cop than they were without them noticing. And by always staying a woman and making them respect that. I've seen women on this Job trying to become one of the boys, but that never works out. And women have to deal with the impostor syndrome. That's where the woman copper starts to fear that the boss is gonna find out how unqualified she truly is. She starts to believe that she's only faking competence, because every second she's being scrutinized, way more than the men are, and it starts working on her self-esteem. It's like the actor's syndrome, but it's all internal bullshit. You *are* competent and you don't have to fear anything except the people out here who can hurt you. And that's a healthy fear to have."

"You were right, Della," Britney Small said. "I never learned this kind of stuff from Rupert Tong."

Della said, "I'm sure you've already learned on your own that when you meet men away from the Job and they find out you're a cop, they all get a doofus grin and say, 'Can you handcuff me?' I hate that shit. I just tell them, 'Get outta my face, asshole.'"

"You're right!" Britney said. "That already happened to me when I went out to a club with a couple of civilian girlfriends. Lame, isn't it?"

"You're way lucky to be here in Hollywood for your probation," Della said. "I remember the first time I found a gun after transferring here. Of course, guns recovered on radio calls don't count, only observation guns. So one night on Hollywood Boulevard when the beat officers and a midwatch unit were jamming some Rolling Sixties gangsters who came up from Watts, I spotted this brother bopping along the Walk of Fame, pretending to be a tourist watching Tickle Me Elmo posing for pictures. But I saw that when he sauntered past one of the Rolling Sixties, he tried to take a little two-inch wheel gun from one of the bangers who hadn't been patted down yet. I drew down on him and yelled for him to freeze and get down on his belly, and when everything settled and they were all proned out, I recovered my first obs gun here in Hollywood Division. And the sergeant we called the Oracle showed me off around the station and told everyone how I'd caught a gangster dumping a strap, and the watch commander wrote me an attagirl, and it was pretty cool. Of course it wasn't a big burner, but size does not matter when it comes to guns."

Britney said, "I've got a couple of classmates who're doing their probation in Central Division. After hearing you describe it, I'm real glad I caught Hollywood, believe me."

Della was silent for a moment, remembering how it had been back then, remembering the smell of skid row, the fluffy acrid miasma. And then she said, "I truly hated being a boot down there.

The smell of shit and piss and rotting flesh and general decay was everywhere in those days. It got into the fabric of our uniforms. People had lots of scabies. You could grab someone and your hands would slip right off their wrists. I got scabies twice from searching skid row hookers. They were like itchy fleabites. They get on your arms, your thighs, and your stomach. Good thing I never got them on my gizmo."

"Gross!" Britney said.

"And the guys enjoyed it when I had to search the obese ones who liked to hide crack under their humungous breasts. Their tits would be sticky. The guys would say, 'Sticky boobs hide crack.' Once I was searching this monstrous woman in a muumuu who was so fat they claimed she'd flipped a bus bench. And I thought I found a stash in the rolls of fat around her middle. But when I dug it out, it turned out to be an Oreo cookie and some Doritos she was keeping there to snack on. The guys really enjoyed watching me running like mad to a faucet to clean up."

"Disgusting!" Britney said.

Still reminiscing, Della said, "That wasn't even the real bad stuff. Once we found a dead baby in a backpack. It had blue eyes."

Della stopped talking then and they rode in silence. Della broke the silence when she said, "So whadda you think we should do about code seven tonight? My dad sent me three hundred bucks for my birthday, so I'll treat. We can do sushi on Melrose or a spicy chicken salad in Thai Town or maybe some rice and lamb in Little Armenia. No noshing on manly burritos and burgers for the girls of Six-X-Forty-six. Sound good, partner?"

"Can we wait awhile?" Britney said. "For some reason, I don't seem to have an appetite right now."

A trap that had been set by the narks two weeks earlier prompted a radio call on that night of the Hollywood moon that made Britney Small the talk of the station for days to come. A tip from a citizen had led narcotics detectives to the backyard of a vacant house that had been in foreclosure for a number of months. A local Realtor happened to be checking out the property one afternoon and he recognized a large number of cannabis plants on one neat little patch of ground in that overgrown backyard. The Realtor phoned the office of the narcotics detectives, who were housed a block from the main police station, and had a chat with a detective there.

The resourceful detectives not only confiscated the marijuana but they left a note pinned to an olive tree in that yard. The note said, "Sorry about your grow. Call if you'd care to negotiate." They left a cell number used for situations like this and were happily surprised when a call came in the very next day. The caller offered $500, no questions asked, for the return of the plants. A female undercover cop met the pot grower by the parking lot of the Hollywood Bowl, and after the grower made his offer in person, he was arrested by other narks watching the action through binoculars.

The marijuana cultivator was a two-striker who wanted to deal and was eager to give up associates and fellow dealers. He offered the narks information about a male nurse of an anesthesiologist in Venice who had a shaky medical license. The nurse resided in an apartment building in the Las Palmas neighborhood, where he provided his client list—consisting of many drag queens and transsexuals—with forged prescriptions supposedly written from a medical office in Culver City.

One of the things that the two-striker had said, resulting in a search warrant, was, "The quack's nurse writes enough scrips in there to smoke out every dragon and trannie in Hollywood." And hoping to curry favor he added, "But he's bipolar and mega-goony most of the time, so watch out. I've been told he might have a gun in there."

Two teams of narks and their D3 had intended to serve the warrant on the night of the full moon. The nurse was supposed to be at home with his lover, a post-op transsexual called Molly Black, who had been Marvin Black in another life and whose last surgery had completed the gender transformation. At the last minute, one of the teams of narks was pulled away for the arrest of another prescription drug dealer whom they'd been trying to get for months. The three remaining detectives needed a backup team, so they put in the call for a patrol unit to meet them on Las Palmas Avenue. The call was given to 6-X-46 of the midwatch.

Britney Small was excited about this one and wondered if the full moon was going to produce something weird enough for them to win the pizza prize. Also, she'd never been on a forced-entry raid of any kind, and she was stoked when the detectives asked her and Della to accompany them to the third-floor apartment. Their D3 decided to watch the outside window in case evidence came flying out. The entry team wanted women officers with them because of the post-op tranny in there. She was now officially a woman and would have to be searched by a woman.

After they were quickly briefed near Las Palmas Avenue under the white glow of the full moon, they were ready. The two narks who were making entry wore LAPD raid jackets, and the younger one carried a metal ram, the first one that Britney had ever seen.

The older nark said, "No more kicking doors for me. I kicked clear through a plywood panel last year and tore my Achilles tendon."

The younger of the narks, who Britney thought was pretty cute, kept smiling at her, and Della whispered, "Watch out for him. He's got a rep. A real vampire, and he likes fresh, young blood."

After they entered the building and ran up the staircase, Britney was pleased to see that she was not as winded as the narks, and certainly not as winded as Della Ravelle, who was toting the shotgun just in case the rumor was true about the nurse being strapped. They hurried along the darkened corridor to the apartment, and the two narks stood in front of the door with the ram at the ready.

Della angled on the left side of the door and Britney on the right. On the preplanned signal, which was a simple nod to Britney, she was to bang on the door with her baton and give the command. She was surprised how hard her heart was pounding.

Della shone her light onto the door so that the younger nark could accurately slam the ram right next to the dead-bolt lock. Della held the shotgun muzzle up, and Britney had her pistol drawn and muzzle down against her right thigh, with her adrenaline peaking.

The older detective on the left of the ram nodded to Britney, who yelled, "Police! Open the door!"

They heard what sounded like a feminine scream from inside and high-pitched voices yelling to each other and footsteps scurrying. The detective didn't hesitate and slammed the ram once against the heavy door, but it didn't budge. And then the moment occurred that made both detectives actually burst out in roars of laughter before the young one rammed the door a second time.

The door crashed open and the nurse and his tranny lover were caught throwing bags of prescription drugs out the window, where the D3 ran around catching them like a Dodgers center fielder. Lots more detective snickering continued all during the arrest, and even Della Ravelle tried in vain to control her own giggles. It had all been triggered by a moment that won for Britney Small a consolation-prize burrito from Sergeant Murillo for an unforgettable moment on the night of the Hollywood moon. All of Hollywood Station talked about it for days.

When Della Ravelle saw that the battering ram hit six inches higher than the dead-bolt lock on the first attempt at forced entry, she had shouted to the detective, "Lower! Lower!"

But it was Britney Small, in a fever of high-pitched excitement, who had instantly obeyed that command from her FTO. She dropped her voice a few octaves, gamely trying for baritone, and repeated, "Police! Open the door!"

★ THIRTEEN ★

THE CALL FROM Nigel Wickland came at 8 A.M. on Monday. Raleigh had just finished cleaning up the dishes after taking a tray of Cream of Wheat and stewed prunes to Marty Brueger. The old coot was watching something on E! that he'd recorded the night before. Raleigh thought how interesting it was that the young bubbleheads and the old bubbleheads enjoyed the same shows. He figured there must be some demographic dynamic at work here that he didn't understand.

The caller ID showed "Wickland Gallery" on the display. He picked up the phone and said, "Yes, Nigel?"

"We should practice not mentioning each other's names when we speak," Nigel said with that superior tone of his.

Raleigh suppressed his annoyance and said, "Okay, double-oh-sixty-nine, what's on your mind this morning?"

A silence while Nigel suppressed his own annoyance. Then he said, "This is it. I'm coming today."

That got Raleigh's attention. He felt a cold rush of fear in his belly, and he said, "What time today?"

"What time do you prepare lunch for..." Nigel paused, trying to keep from mentioning Marty Brueger's name.

"The geezer," Raleigh said. "About twelve thirty. Then it's nap time from about one until three."

"I'll see you at one," Nigel said. "Precisely."

Raleigh scowled at the receiver when he put it back on the cradle. "Precisely." That was so like the boarding school assholes who frequented the London bistro and left him nothing but their pitiful Brit gratuities. They'd tipped on average less than car-wash employees in Los Angeles might tip for food and service. Well, he'd be ready *precisely* at 1 P.M., and then he'd see if that teabag was the mastermind he purported to be. Raleigh tried to concentrate on his daily chores, making sure that he had the household schedule and Leona Brueger's instructions carefully notated.

The swimming pool cleaner came on Tuesday mornings unless Raleigh called to change the time. Ditto for the gardening crew, who came on Thursdays at about noon. Leona Brueger had offered to hire Raleigh a housekeeper for a biweekly visit or give him an extra $1,200 a month and let him hire his own help. He opted for the money, figuring he could find some Mexican housekeeper in the neighborhood who would drop in once a week to dust, vacuum, and clean his bathroom, and do whatever needed doing in Marty Brueger's cottage. That would cost him less than $400 a month and he could pocket the rest. So far, he'd been doing the light housekeeping himself and hadn't needed to hire anybody.

He decided to drive to the supermarket and pick up the week's groceries just to have something to occupy his mind for the next few hours. Marty Brueger would need more of that pricey Irish whiskey he liked, and Raleigh could pick up a bottle of Jack Daniel's for himself. Working in the catering business had taught him that bars on the west side of Los Angeles could get by if the only booze left on earth was Jack Daniel's and just about any premium vodka. But of course the codger in the cottage insisted on whiskey that required an extra stop at a liquor store on Hollywood Boulevard.

Raleigh went to his bedroom for his wallet and car keys and studied himself in the mirror. He imagined what he would look like with a little bit of help, like maybe that chin tuck he'd been thinking about. And a slight eye lift would help, as well as a hair transplant. He knew he'd need serious liposuction to unload the depressing blubber that encased his torso like a truck tire. Well, now he'd be able to afford all of that and more. Lots more. It certainly was not too late to meet an older woman of means, maybe one who lived in the Hollywood Hills, maybe in a house like Casa Brueger.

Raleigh tried to affect a confident self-assured smile at the mirror, but he thought he saw fear in the pale, watery eyes looking back at him.

Jonas Claymore woke up first, as usual. He extended his legs over the side of the bed gingerly but was surprised not to feel the stab of back pain this morning. Then he put his hands on his bony knees, leaned forward, and pushed himself upright. There was a twinge but nothing he couldn't handle.

He gave Megan a smack with his open hand on the bottom of her foot, and she sat up saying, "Huh?"

"I'm feeling okay today," he said. "It's time to go to work."

She began coughing almost at once and was feeling her own burning pain in her shoulder joints and knees. She hoped there were some perks left or even some zannies lying around.

"I'm glad you feel okay," she said. "Because I don't feel okay."

"A chick your age should be able to bounce back," he said. "You oughtta take better care of yourself. Do some workouts once in a while. We gotta get some cash to tide us over. When was the last time you called your mom?"

"Maybe a month," she said.

"Go take a shower," he said. "Clear your head. Think about asking your mom to give us another loan. Tell her you'll pay her back with a high rate of interest."

Megan got painfully out of bed, walked to the little bathroom, and said, "Sure. My mom's gonna believe I'll pay her back. Like she believes in honest lawyers and leprechauns."

"We're gonna cruise today," Jonas said. "Nothing serious yet. Just cruising and casing. We ain't making the same mistakes the Bling Ring made. We'll make sure we know what's what before we ever set foot on anybody's property, unless we spot some easy pickings like we did the last time. Then we go for it."

Megan sat down on the toilet and said, "How easy was it last time, Jonas? You've been flat on your back for days." And she slammed the bathroom door before he could whine about hearing her pee.

At 12:30 P.M., Raleigh Dibble was sitting in the kitchen of the Brueger home, waiting and clock-watching. He'd done every chore he could think of. He tried to consider every way that Nigel Wickland's plan could go wrong, but whenever he did, he thought of what it would be like to stroll into a bank and put half a million into a safe-deposit box and some mad money into his checking account. But why did it have to be only half a million? Nigel had told him that his European auctioneer claimed that a million was the *least* they would get in today's market for the two Impressionist works. Maybe they'd get 1.2 million. Maybe 1.5 million! Or maybe it was crazy to aim for the stars at his age. But since this was all about art, why not dip the brush of imagination into the colors of fantasy and boldly paint a portrait of a future life? Then again, isn't that what people who end up looking at the stars through steel bars and chain-link did? Right before somebody pisses all over their palette?

When the phone gave two brief rings, indicating someone was at the gate, Raleigh jumped from the kitchen chair. He looked at his watch and saw it was 12:50. Not *precisely* 1 P.M., but he was glad Nigel was early. His hands were shaking when he picked up the receiver and said, "Yes?"

"It's me," Nigel said.

Raleigh pressed the key to open the electric gate and went to the door. Nigel pulled into the faux-cobblestone driveway in his Chevrolet cargo van and made the circle, parking by the entrance door. Raleigh stepped out and walked to the driveway as Nigel got out. They were both too nervous to even think about shaking hands. Nigel opened the side door of the cargo van.

Raleigh looked at "Wickland Gallery" on the side of the van and said, "I'm surprised you brought your own wheels, Nigel. A man as careful as you."

"I had no bloody choice," he said. "I told Ruth that our van needs a tune-up and I asked her to bring her brother's truck to work today. She said she would, but then she called in sick. Believe me, I don't want some nosy neighbor asking Leona what the Wickland Gallery was doing at her house while she was gone. But I didn't think your frayed nerves would withstand a postponement, so here we are. Now that I look around more carefully at this place, there's no need to be worrying about nosy neighbors."

Just like him, Raleigh thought. He fucks up and covers by blaming it on my nerves.

Of all the things that Raleigh did have to worry about, he figured the Wickland Gallery van was the least of it. The Bruegers' mini-estate was secluded by many olive, lemon, and orange trees, and especially by the wall of junipers planted both inside and outside the encircling five-foot wall. He doubted if anyone would notice or even see the van when it entered.

"Help me unload the equipment, will you?" Nigel said.

For the next few minutes, they carried into the house a tripod, two floodlights on lightweight stands, and two umbrella reflectors. Nigel carried the Canon 350 digital camera that he believed was simple enough for him to handle.

The moment they were inside, Raleigh began worrying about Marty Brueger. He ran to the French doors and looked out at the cottage to make sure the old man was inside and not strolling in the garden.

Nigel was trying to take careful measurements of both canvases and he said, "For god's sake, Raleigh, can't you relax a bit and help me?"

Suddenly Raleigh's nerves began to crack, and he said, "How much practice did you do, Nigel?"

"I've been practicing nearly every day for two weeks," Nigel said. "My friend at the lab and I both made different mistakes, but eventually we learned from those mistakes. The last few times I photographed a painting of similar size, it turned out perfectly."

"Did you use the same camera?" Raleigh wanted to know.

"Yes, and the same goddamn tripod and the same lights. Now please close the drapes and stop fretting. You're making me nervous."

It was the first time that Raleigh had ever closed the heavy drapes in that part of the house and he was surprised how dark the great room and corridor became. Then he realized that the drapes were lined with blackout material because the Bruegers used to show movies in that room. There was a screen that lowered from the ceiling at the touch of a button.

Nigel pulled two pairs of latex gloves from his pocket and said, "Put these on. I don't want our fingerprints on these pieces."

"Why do we need to worry?" Raleigh asked. "According to you, they're not even going to notice anything for months. And the moving guys will be handling the pictures, won't they? Their prints will be all over them."

"Just do it, Raleigh," Nigel said. "Why do we have to debate everything?"

Raleigh pulled on the latex gloves and said, "I thought there was no risk here."

"All the so-called art lovers in this town hang their pictures too high," Nigel complained as he set up his umbrella lights. "These baroque gilded frames are just what I'd have expected from Sammy Brueger and his ilk."

Raleigh thought the frames looked okay. And who gave a shit

about the frames anyway? He couldn't stop himself from checking his watch obsessively.

It took Nigel Wickland nearly an hour to carefully remove both canvases from their frames and rehang them from little wires that he carefully stapled to the stretcher bars.

Then Nigel said, "Get me something steady to stand on. A small stepladder, perhaps."

Raleigh ran to the laundry room and came back with a six-foot ladder, opened it, and placed it behind Nigel. And trying to be helpful, Raleigh turned on the lights over both paintings.

"No, no!" Nigel said petulantly. "We must have the painting lights off."

After he sulked for a moment, Raleigh said, " I don't know anything about photography. Will these be developed as slides or what?"

"Digital photos, just as I told you before," Nigel said. "The lab will download them onto a computer and blow them up to any size we want. And thanks to my trial-and-error rehearsals during the last two weeks, I know precisely how large I want them."

There he goes again, Raleigh thought. *Precisely.*

Nigel put the ladder where he wanted it and placed the umbrella lights at each side of the largest painting, *The Woman by the Water,* which looked to Raleigh to be almost four feet tall and nearly five feet wide.

Nigel stood on the first step of the ladder and said, "Move that light a bit to the left. They must be level with the painting."

Raleigh did as he was told and Nigel said, "That's too much. Come back half an inch. There. That's good. Now do the same with the other one. I've got to make sure to line it up so that there's no perspective."

"Okay, just get it done!" Raleigh said.

Still looking through the viewfinder, Nigel said, "And I must get the piece as big as I can get it within the frame."

Raleigh was sweating and thinking, It's only the lights that're making me sweat. I'm not really that scared. Then he blurted, "What if Marty Brueger comes here to the main house and starts banging on the door?"

"Bloody hell!" Nigel said. "I'm trying to compose this shot!"

Raleigh's courage was leaking out like the sweat that was running from every pore, and he said, "What if somebody comes by for some other reason and catches us? What would we say?"

Nigel sighed and stepped off the ladder. He took the inhaler from his pocket and had a puff. He waited a moment and said, "Well, then, we would simply tell them that as Mrs. Brueger's art adviser, I decided to photograph the paintings to have the pictures put onto greeting cards as a surprise for my dear client."

"And then what would we do?"

Nigel took a deep breath, blew it out, and said in sheer exasperation, "And then of course we would abandon this little project and I would go back to being a gallery owner on the verge of bankruptcy. And you would continue as a domestic servant who will spend his old age living off welfare and Social Security. Now, will you please act like a man so we can proceed and get this job done?"

Raleigh glared at him for a long moment, feeling the anger swell his throat. This flouncing Nancy boy was telling him to act like a man? But all he said to Nigel was "Okay, let's proceed."

Nigel got back on the ladder and aimed the camera again. Before he shot his first picture he calmed himself by talking, and he said, "I chose these Impressionist pieces precisely because Impressionist art is blurry. It is, after all, the artist's impression, is it not? The Impressionist artist is not interested in photographic clarity. They're perfect for our needs."

Raleigh gave up counting the shots that Nigel took. Finally Nigel said, "Voilà! It's done. Now to *Flowers on the Hillside*."

"Damn!" Raleigh said. "That took too long. The second one

won't take as long, will it? Marty Brueger will be waking up pretty soon."

"Not a problem," Nigel said. "The second one will go fast."

For the very first time, Raleigh took a look at the other painting. It was a blur of colors that suggested a field of flowers on a hillside with something that looked like a windmill in the distance. "This one's worth almost as much, huh?" Raleigh asked. "It's a lot smaller."

"You have no idea," Nigel said, moving the light stands and the tripod. "*Flowers on the Hillside* could possibly fetch even more than *The Woman by the Water*. Now, let's position everything exactly as we did before."

At that moment, Raleigh had a head-slapping thought: What if these paintings did bring in way more than a million as he'd fantasized? What if they brought in 2 million? How would he ever know? What if Nigel told him that the recession is bad in all the cities he'd mentioned? What if he claimed that he could get only $300,000 for both pictures? How would he ever know if Nigel was lying? He quelled his suspicions by reminding himself that this was only the first phase of the scheme.

Raleigh decided that he needed to work out some details with his prissy partner before Nigel came back to do the switch. But how would he do that? He knew nothing about the European auctioneer and what the art could reasonably fetch. Was he completely at the mercy of Nigel's true intentions? The more he came to dislike Nigel Wickland, the more worrisome the scheme became.

Ten minutes later the phone buzzed from the cottage and Raleigh uttered a choked-off cry. Then he said, "It's Marty Brueger!"

Nigel lowered the camera and said, "Go tend to him, then. Christ, he's virtually senile. You can handle it." And he went back to composing his shot.

Raleigh hurried out the side door and ran to the cottage. When he entered, Marty Brueger was in his pajamas, looking as though he'd forgotten why he rang.

"Yes, Mr. Brueger," Raleigh said. "Do you need something?"

"My teeth," Marty Brueger said. "Where's my teeth?"

"Aren't they in the glass where they usually are?"

"Don't you think I looked there?" the old man said.

"We'll find them, Mr. Brueger," Raleigh said. "Why don't you just sit in your chair and relax and watch *The Girls Next Door*? That Hugh Hefner's really a card, isn't he?"

"It's not on now, Raleigh, and I can't find the most recent videotape."

"You don't need videotape anymore, Mr. Brueger," Raleigh said. "All of your favorite shows have been recorded for you, remember?"

"I always forget how to do that TIVO shit," Marty Brueger said.

"I'll go over it again with you," Raleigh said. "Everything's there for you anytime you want to watch. You just go to your stored programs and select whatever you wish."

"Even *Showbiz Tonight*?" Marty Brueger asked.

"Every single episode," Raleigh assured him. "You've got them there waiting for you."

"I still need my teeth," the old man said.

"I'll do a thorough search for them," Raleigh said.

"If you find them, I'd like to go to one of those new trendy places for dinner," Marty Brueger said. "Like Mr. Chow's."

"Mr. Chow's has been around a long time," Raleigh said. "It's not new but it's still very popular with movie people."

"Spago isn't new anymore either, is it?" Marty Brueger asked.

"No, sir," Raleigh said. "I think it's older than Mr. Chow's. And you might see some celebrities there as well."

"It's funny how time plays tricks on your memory," Marty Brueger said. "Do famous people still go to the Polo Lounge for lunch? People in the business who're my age?"

Raleigh thought, There's nobody in the business your age, but he said, "I think so. I'll find out for sure."

"Talking about restaurants has made me hungry," Marty Brueger said. "Maybe I'll stroll up to the house and look for something in the fridge that I can eat without teeth."

"No, no, Mr. Brueger!" Raleigh cried. "Just sit down and relax. I'll fix you something tasty for a snack, but first you need something to chew with, don't you?"

"I'll tell you, Raleigh," Marty Brueger said. "It's a sad time in a man's life when his dick's gone missing and he can't even find his fucking teeth."

While Raleigh Dibble searched for Marty Brueger's teeth, Jonas Claymore and Megan Burke were driving toward Woodrow Wilson Drive, eyeing many potential targets, as well as checking their maps and addresses for any homes belonging to stars or celebutants.

"I think Outpost has some juicy targets," Jonas said to Megan, who had downed two perks and was zoning as he drove. "But I like it way up here, too."

"I think we're going to die like Bonnie and Clyde," Megan said bleakly.

"Who?"

"The old movie? You know, about the bank robbers? A guy and a chick rob banks and it's all a trip until they get shot to pieces. I think that's how we'll end up."

"Who wants to get old?" Jonas said.

"Yeah, but it might be nice to get old enough to walk in a bar and buy a drink without showing a phony ID. Is that asking too much?"

"You got no imagination," Jonas said.

"Yes, I do," she said. "I can imagine us checking out like Bonnie and Clyde now that we've decided to really go bad."

Ignoring her, Jonas said, "I musta seen a hundred houses that look good to me. Like that one there."

He pointed out one of the many Spanish Colonial Revivals, usually done in the mission- or hacienda-style with a red-tile roof and white-plastered walls. This one was large, with a detached guesthouse and a solid barrier of junipers that almost hid the main house from view except from the road above. Jonas pulled to the side and stopped.

"Get out for a minute," he said.

"What for? I'm tired!"

"You're always tired," he said. "Get out."

Megan opened the door, mumbling, got out, and shuffled along behind him. He strolled over to the junipers and pulled two of them apart, peeking in at the property.

"See," he said. "This place has more land than the others. Do you know what land costs up here?"

Megan just shook her head, and Jonas said, "Plenty, that's how much. I bet there's a tennis court down behind there. This is the kinda place we should go for. But not now. Look, there's a van down there by the garage. It says something on the side but it's parked at an angle, so I can't read it. Probably a delivery guy or a plumber or something."

"Can we go home now?" Megan said.

He said, "What we gotta do is come back here sometime when there's no car in the driveway and no gardeners around and ring the bell."

"There's a big gate," Megan said.

"We ring the bell at the gate," Jonas said. "There must be one. And if there's no answer we go over the wall and check it out and see what we can see."

"And what if there's another dog like last time?" Megan said. "Maybe a vicious guard dog?"

That stopped him. His back was still sending him messages

from time to time. He said, "Okay, we'll come by a couple more times on other days before we try out a house like this. Meanwhile, we can go for more conventional places where we can see the yards and figure out if there's a guard dog or not."

"Let's go home and I'll call my mom," Megan said.

"For what?"

"I'll beg her for a loan of two hundred. I'll say that I'm staying with a friend and we're being evicted on Saturday unless we can come up with the money. She always says she'll never give up on me. I'm her firstborn and I don't think she'll let me down. Not that I'm proud of it." She paused and said, "I just need a taste of ox."

Jonas pressed hard on the small of his back, groaned, and said, "I wonder why God is letting me get knocked on my ass so much lately?"

Raleigh Dibble found Marty Brueger's missing dentures in the trash can by the toilet, but how they got there was anybody's guess. He figured it was the result of too much Irish whiskey. If the old man had any cash to speak of, that probably would've ended up shit-canned as well. But only Raleigh had access to the modest checking account at the local bank that Leona Brueger had left for groceries and other items in order to keep the house running smoothly while she was gone. She had opened the account with $4,000 and told him to phone her in Tuscany if any sort of emergency came up requiring more funds.

"Mr. Brueger," Raleigh said, "why don't you sit in your chair and watch *Oprah* or something? I'm going up to the house now to make you a nice snack. How about one of my special omelets?"

Marty Brueger nodded and said, "Got any more whiskey in the butler's pantry up there?"

"No, but I'll run out and get some later," Raleigh said.

"Why don't I go up there with you and look?" Marty Brueger said.

"No, Mr. Brueger!" Raleigh said. "Just rest. There might be another bottle. I'll be right back."

"I'll have all the rest I need pretty soon," the old man muttered.

Raleigh was a wreck by the time he got back to the house. But he was overjoyed to see that the floodlights had been turned off in the great room, and the tripod was lying on the floor. Nigel Wickland had finished.

Raleigh said to him, "Did you get it done the way you wanted?"

"It's a wrap, as they say in Hollywood," Nigel Wickland said with a satisfied grin. "The next trip here will be far briefer. These are all conventional frames, even if the paintings are not of a common size. It'll be easy enough to make the poster board fit nicely. I think Sammy Brueger had them reframed with those ghastly ornate monstrosities in the past dozen years or so."

Raleigh was so relieved, he felt like sitting down. Now he had a headache, and he was a man who seldom got one. "When're you coming back?"

"It depends on how it goes at the lab," Nigel said. "I'll apply as much pressure as I can to my friend and I'll offer him a bonus of several hundred dollars if he can speed up the process. But it can't be done overnight, you know."

"Will you call me as soon as it's done?"

"Of course," Nigel said. "But be careful never to use your name if you ever ring my office again. And don't use my name when I ring you here. We must proceed precisely as planned."

We're going to come to a new understanding before we're through, Raleigh thought. But all he said was, "Yes, precisely."

★ FOURTEEN ★

VIV DALEY AND Georgie Adams were "off the beach" and cleared for street duty while Force Investigation Division worked on building a twelve-inch-high stack of reports that would be presented to a Use-of-Force Board within nine months of the officer-involved shooting of Louis Dryden. Viv was not as jocular as she had been before that night, and nor was Georgie. Neither would ever speak of Cindy Kroll or her murdered baby again, at least not to each other.

They both had been ordered down to Chinatown, where Behavioral Science Services had their offices, and each one spoke with a BSS psychologist about the event in Little Armenia. Georgie had given brief answers to every question that the shrink asked regarding the taking of a human life. He said that he'd killed a few insurgents in Iraq and that this had felt no different to him afterward. He simply shook his head when he was asked if he had gone upstairs and seen the strangled baby. Both officers had the typical cop's distrust of shrinks from having seen and heard all that the profession had done with their "expert" opinions as witnesses for and against the prosecution in criminal cases.

Viv said that as far as she was concerned, they had killed a boogeyman and she felt not a shred of doubt or remorse about his death. She was less forthcoming when asked by her questioner to talk about what she'd seen in Cindy Kroll's apartment. The psychologist was a generation older than Viv and had gentle eyes and a motherly manner. At the very beginning of their session, she had come from behind her desk to sit next to Viv in one of the two client chairs. She asked Viv to call her Jane, but Viv never used the woman's given name at any time during that meeting.

When pressed repeatedly about her feelings concerning that horrific event, Viv reluctantly admitted to the psychologist that she'd grappled with impulses to contact the Department of Children and Family Services about the surviving child of Cindy Kroll. Viv said she'd thought about inquiring into the possibility of fostering the toddler, who she'd learned was named Carly, at least until a responsible relative could be found or until the child could be placed for adoption.

But Viv then added, "Of course, that was a silly thought. It made no sense at all. Here I am, a single woman with a job that requires me to work half the night, and then of course I have to sleep half the morning. Why would they ever give an infant to someone like me to foster?"

"I agree with you that they certainly would not," the psychologist said. "Still, you say you had impulses about being a foster parent, even if it was impossible given your lifestyle. Why was that, do you think?"

"I don't know," Viv said. "Pity, I guess. It was all so...pitiful."

Viv refused to do more than shake her head when asked if she felt any residue of guilt or responsibility for what had happened to Cindy Kroll and her baby that night, and Viv bristled when the psychiatrist pressed her on it.

"Why should I?" she said.

"You shouldn't," the shrink replied. "But sometimes our unconscious mind doesn't understand words like *should* and *shouldn't*."

"Well, I don't," Viv said. "Just because I had a random thought about how that apartment could be attacked doesn't mean I had a premonition or something. I'm not a mentalist, you know."

"No," the psychologist said. "You're not. You were less cynical than the two detectives and your partner."

"What do you mean?" Viv asked suspiciously.

The psychologist said, "Police officers become prematurely cynical from seeing the worst of people and ordinary people at their worst. They don mental and emotional armor in self-defense. They tend to scoff at anything extraordinary. Your suggestion regarding the ladder and the roof was rebuffed as far-fetched, but it wasn't. You were not cynical. You were trying to be a good police officer by imagining a very unlikely scenario that ultimately came true."

Viv didn't say anything and the psychologist said, "Had you ever seen something very horrific before? Something involving helpless children?"

Viv hesitated and then said, "I remember one case when an Eighteenth Streeter who called himself the Tax Collector pistol-whipped a street vendor for not paying protection money. He decided he needed to teach all the vendors a lesson and he shot the man's baby right there in his stroller."

The psychologist shook her head slowly and said, "I can only imagine how you felt when you got there."

Viv said, "And there was the time we got a call that taught me why detectives who work child abuse are the only coppers who're never asked about their work by their civilian friends. The call came right after we cleared from roll call. This tot had been burned real bad in the bathtub and his mother said it was an accident. Except that his flesh was burned off from his elbows, straight down from that demarcation line. That meant that the child had been held by the wrists and put down into the scalding water. It turned out that the mother's boyfriend did it when he got frustrated during a potty training session. When the man was arrested, he said he didn't know the water was that hot. I was told later that they had to put the skin from dead people on the third-degree burns. It happened on the child's second birthday. His name was Stevie."

The psychologist said, "You know that you can come back and see me anytime, Vivien. You don't have to wait until you're ordered to come here."

Viv gave the shrink a lopsided smile and said, "Don't you know that cops consider it wussy to run down here and talk to you people?"

The psychologist smiled and said, "Oh, yes, how well I know. We have a lonely job around here because of the rampant machismo and super-self-reliance of your colleagues in blue. Believe me, I know all about that."

"Well, then, you get it," Viv said and fell silent.

The psychologist was quiet for a moment watching Viv gaze through the window as though she'd like to escape. Then she said, "Had you ever felt a strong impulse to foster a child before the incident in Little Armenia?"

"No, I hadn't," Viv said, and looked at the shrink again with a hint of defiance. And again she said, "Why should I?"

"You shouldn't," the psychiatrist said. "But this case was different, wasn't it? This had to do with Carly's mother and her baby brother, and feelings of great…discomfort that you were experiencing because of what happened to them. Isn't that true?"

"Maybe," Viv conceded. "Are you trying to tell me that you think I do feel somehow responsible?"

"That man Louis Dryden was responsible," the psychologist said. "Cindy Kroll bore some responsibility also. She refused to go to a shelter where she and her children would've been safe until your detectives could have contacted Louis Dryden and warned him to stay away. You are obviously an extremely responsible person, Vivien, but none of this should become your burden. Given all that was known, the actions of you and your colleagues were reasonable and understandable. This event was an anomaly."

"Have we been talking about some sort of…hidden guilt feelings here?" Viv asked. "Is that what we're talking about?"

"If we are, I hope we can dispel it," the shrink said. "The event itself was exceptionally horrific. You saw things that night that nobody should ever see."

"I suppose so," Viv said. Then she said, "That incident in Little Armenia…it would rattle anybody, wouldn't it?"

"It certainly would," the shrink said.

"And on top of that…"

The psychologist was quiet until she finally said, "And on top of that? What, Vivien?"

"Carly was so traumatized and confused that she kept…she kept calling me…Mommy."

Both women were silent and Viv was startled to taste tears in her mouth. And then she broke down and wept in her hands. The psychiatrist moved a box of tissues from her desktop closer to Viv Daley's chair and waited for her tears to stop.

At midwatch roll call that evening the word was passed from cop to cop that one of the Department's highest-ranking brass had been caught on a dark street in south L.A. with a hooker in his car. And she was not some special Beyoncé look-alike but just a grungy old streetwalker who probably had every known STD and some new ones that weren't yet cataloged. When he badged the patrol unit that caught him, he offered the lame excuse that he was "interrogating" the hooker, who quickly got out of his car and continued on her way.

The two cops assured him that this contact would remain confidential, but by the end of watch they had each texted more than a dozen coppers, who each texted a dozen more, in a chain that didn't end until everybody in the LAPD and beyond knew about it. It was a perfect example of how well things remain confidential in police work, and why cops howl in laughter when cop-hating commentators on TV refer to "the blue wall of silence" or "closing ranks" in controversial cases involving allegations of excessive force and other misconduct, usually involving ethnic minorities.

On that subject, Sergeant Murillo said at roll call, "I could offer to buy a brand-new car to any copper around here who could keep something on the down-low for even one day, and I'd never have to worry about ever touching my life savings. Which I think amounts to about four hundred dollars last time I checked."

After they cleared for calls that evening, Flotsam and Jetsam were not on the street five minutes before a late-model Mustang cruising slowly in the curb lane blew a stoplight on east Sunset Boulevard and caused several drivers to jump on their brakes and yell curses.

"You're up," Jetsam said and did a U-ee, pulling behind the Mustang with his lights flashing. He honked the horn to get the driver to notice.

The driver was so busy talking on his cell phone and driving so erratically that they thought he was DUI. When he finally saw them in his rearview mirror, he pulled to the curb. He was fumbling around so much that they thought he might be trying to hide some contraband or even a weapon, so both cops jumped out quickly and ran up to the Mustang, Flotsam on the driver's side with his hand on his Glock.

Jetsam approached on the passenger side, and since it was still light, they could both see well, and what they saw was a white-collar guy with his shirttail hanging out his fly.

Flotsam said, "License and registration, please."

The tall cop looked across the Mustang roof and grimaced at his partner. Since this was sometimes a whore track after dark, it figured that the motorist was looking to pick up a hooker on the way home from work. It was reasonable to assume that maybe he was doing some phone sex at the same time and it all got to be a libido overload.

Flotsam wrote the ticket on the hood of their shop, and Jetsam said, "Bro, whatever you do, don't shake hands with him."

Flotsam got back to the car and handed the man the citation book and his ballpoint pen. While the driver signed the ticket, Flotsam looked at the damp spot on the man's shirt where he'd wiped his fingers, and said, "You can keep the pen, sir. Compliments of the city of Los Angeles."

Hollywood Nate and Snuffy Salcedo got a message on their dashboard computer regarding "a female 5150 at Hollywood and Highland" on the Walk of Fame. Snuffy punched the en route button, and Nate glanced at the message and said, "A female mental case on the Walk of Fame. How remarkable. That description could apply to *anybody* on Hollywood Boulevard, since gender around here is always questionable anyway."

"I wonder which wack job it is," Snuffy said.

"Just pick anyone that's off the hook and making more noise than the others," Nate said.

When they got to the famous intersection and started cruising westbound very slowly, it didn't take long to spot her among the tourist throngs. She was a black woman about forty years of age who weighed upward of two hundred and fifty pounds. Her hair was dyed the color of a traffic cone, and her costume consisted of a man's olive-green battle jacket, World War II vintage, complete with combat ribbons. From her ample waist south, she wore Day-Glo pink tights and cowboy boots. She was banging two trash can lids together like cymbals and chanting gibberish. Of course, tourists and Street Characters scattered when she got near them, but there was one who did not move fast enough.

The cops saw her suddenly bang Wonder Woman on the head with a trash can lid, and that was enough for 6-X-66. She was an apparent danger to herself and others.

Hollywood Nate pulled to the curb and said, "This one will do, but she's probably not the looniest on the boulevard by any means."

"Loony but not lonely," Snuffy said. "There's always someone inside their heads to talk to."

The woman was cheerful and smiling when both cops approached her on foot, and Nate said, "Could I please see your cymbals?"

She proudly handed him the trash can lids, saying, "Okey-dokey."

"I'll bet you have lots of cymbals," Nate said. "How would you like to come with us and play for some nice folks?"

"Okey-dokey," she said.

"What's your name?" Snuffy asked.

She pondered until some cognition kicked in, and she said, "Pearl."

"I'm Snuffy and he's Nate."

"Whoopdedoo!" Pearl said, happy to meet new friends.

Pearl was so affable and even cute that Nate said, "I don't have the heart to hook her up, partner. Let's try her out in the backseat without the cuffs. If she kills you with a hidden hat pin, it's all my fault."

Nate opened the rear door and Pearl got in, fastening her seat belt without being told to do it.

"She's done this before," Nate said.

Snuffy looked at her through the cage and said, "You really shouldn't whack people on the bean, Pearl. It's very naughty."

"Very naughty, very naughty!" Pearl agreed.

Snuffy said quietly to Nate. "A good sign. Utter remorse."

As they drove east on Sunset Boulevard at twilight, they began to realize that Pearl had a peculiar tic where she not only repeated fragments of what she'd just heard but seemed to take particular delight in it if she was told to stop.

At one point Snuffy looked at a silver Porsche cruising past and said to Nate, "Don't you love that too-cool nine-eleven?"

Pearl said, "Too-cool!"

Nate turned to look at the Porsche and said, "Yeah, it's sweet."

"It's sweet!" Pearl said.

Testing her, Snuffy said, "Don't say it's sweet, Pearl."

"It's sweet, it's sweet!" Pearl said with more enthusiasm.

They rode in silence for a while, heading for Parker Center, to the Mental Evaluation Unit for a commitment approval. After that, they would transport her the few miles to the USC Medical Center on the grounds of the old county hospital. These were the last weeks for the venerable LAPD main headquarters building before it would be abandoned and torn down to the ground. Everything was in the process of being moved to the new Police Administration Building, literally in the shadow of City Hall.

The new PAB was across the street from the Department of Water & Power, whose building the cops said looked like the Death Star in the *Star Wars* movies. There was extremely inadequate parking in the immediate area of the new PAB, and the Department of Transportation was only too eager to write tickets to any radio cars that they found temporarily parked in white and yellow zones. Of course, that produced noisy internecine bitterness.

Outside the new building were large, expensive, and controversial metal sculptures that were meant to give the impression of six bears and two monkeys. The cops figured that soon enough they'd be arresting sex offenders for humping them. The building was designed in such a way that the glass windows facing north caught the reflection of City Hall, which was directly across First Street. The coppers said that the dominant City Hall reflection seen from the new building was a chillingly sinister omen of what the future had in store for them.

As they were nearing their destination, Nate said to Snuffy, "Do you get all nostalgic going back to Parker Center, where you spent all those years driving for those sixth-floor power freaks?"

"Power freaks!" Pearl said.

Snuffy said sotto to Nate in order to keep Pearl quiet, "Mister is the one I'll always remember. One of his favorite movies is *North by Northwest*. You know, the Hitchcock movie where Cary Grant and his chick get chased over the presidents' faces on Mount Rushmore?"

Ever the movies buff, Nate whispered back at him, "Of course. That chick was Eva Marie Saint."

Snuffy forgot to whisper and said, "Yeah, well, I think the reason Mister loves that movie is because he always saw *his* face up there. He imagined they were running across *his* eyebrows and jumping on *his* upper lip."

"His upper lip!" Pearl said.

"I wish she'd stop that," Nate said. "It's getting on my nerves."

Snuffy said to Nate, "Lower her window halfway. I wanna try something."

When the window beside Pearl came partly down, they were stopped at an intersection on east Sunset Boulevard in the Silverlake district, where there was urban renewal going on, with younger people moving into apartments and lofts. Waiting to cross the street was an attractive woman talking to a guy in a Joseph Abboud suit who had that self-important, young professional look, water bottle and all.

Snuffy said, "Pearl, do *not* call that man a yuppie dipshit."

Pearl looked at the man, and when the light turned green and they were moving, she startled the couple by yelling, "Yuppie dipshit!"

Snuffy whispered, "She'll say exactly what we tell her not to say. There's gotta be something we can do with this."

As it turned out, there was. When they got to Parker Center and parked underneath, Snuffy felt a chill of remembrance. Here he was, back in the place where he'd worked for so many years. The criminal element referred to it as the Glass House because of the walls of windows on the north and south exposures. The faces of the various chiefs he had driven for and protected swam before his eyes. For a moment he struggled to remember something good about those recent years. His reverie was shattered and he could hardly believe it when the door leading from the building to the parking lot opened. Snuffy saw one of his old friends and fellow security aides. And who emerged behind the aide but the Man himself!

As Nate pulled into a parking space, Snuffy said quietly, "It's Mister! Jesus, Mary, and Joseph, it's Mister!"

The chief and his aide were both wearing uniforms on this day, and the security aide paused when the chief said something and looked at his watch.

Snuffy whispered to Nate, "He's probably trying to remember how many stoplights there are between here and where they're going, and he's gonna decide exactly how long it should take them to get there."

The chief and his aide had to pass right by the space where Nate had parked their shop, and Snuffy scooted down in his seat, concealing his face with his hand, pretending to write in his log.

He whispered to Nate, "Partner, this is destiny." Then he turned toward the cage and said, "Pearl, pay attention to this. Do *not* call that man an egomaniac."

When Mister and his aide were passing the car, Pearl stuck her face out and yelled, "Igloo maniac! Igloo maniac!"

The chief of police flinched and glanced sharply to his right. He saw Pearl smiling beatifically through the open car window. He ignored her and kept on walking toward the SUV with the ominous tinted windows. His security aide opened the door for the chief and he got in.

Hollywood Nate said sotto, "So that's your idea of get-back? Snuffy's revenge has come down to calling the chief of police a crazy Eskimo?"

Snuffy Salcedo whispered back, "When you get right down to

it, she mighta got it right. He's been giving the L.A. media and City Hall a major snow job for the past seven and a half years."

When they got out of the car and entered the building, Snuffy said, "Anyways, Pearl did her best. On our way to the funny place, let's stop and buy her some ice cream."

"Ice cream! Whoopdedoo!" Pearl cried, and yodeled merrily as she frolicked along the corridor and into the depressing basement office of the Mental Evaluation Unit, inside the doomed old building that for more than half a century lawbreakers had called the Glass House.

FIFTEEN

MARTY BRUEGER SAID to Raleigh Dibble, "It's Thursday and I'm sick of sitting around here. If I'm gonna stroke out and die, I want it to be in Chasen's eating a big bowl of chili."

Raleigh said, "Mr. Brueger, Chasen's has been closed for a very long time, don't you remember?"

"Oh, shit, that's right," Marty Brueger said. "Oh, my mind."

Raleigh was removing the breakfast tray from the table in the cottage and trying to keep his game face on, even though the old coot was starting to smell ripe. It took an effort for Raleigh not to turn away when he needed to take a breath. He also wanted to trim the tufts of hair sprouting from the geezer's ears.

"Elizabeth Taylor loved Chasen's chili. I saw her there many times," Marty Brueger said.

"Yes, I know," Raleigh said.

"She was usually with her husband, Rex Harrison."

"Richard Burton," Raleigh said.

"What's he got to do with it?" Marty Brueger said.

"She was married to him. Not to Rex Harrison."

"Oh, shit!" Marty Brueger said. "Don't ever get as old as me, Raleigh. Take the gas pipe before you do. An old man's life is for shit!"

"There, there, Mr. Brueger," Raleigh said. "Why don't you take a nice bath? It'll make you feel better."

"All right. Then I wanna talk about going someplace. I'm sick of this fucking place."

"Do you need help getting into the bath?" Raleigh asked.

"Raleigh, the day I can't go into a walk-in shower and sit on a bench and turn on the water, that's the day I'll ask you to go out and buy me a gun."

"Okay, Mr. Brueger," Raleigh said. "I'll give you an hour and then I'll come back and we'll talk about an outing. Maybe we could drive to the beach and look at the pretty girls. You said you used to like to do that. Or maybe we could go to the movies in Westwood. Or maybe—"

Marty Brueger interrupted Raleigh with plaintive eyes that looked somehow touching through those Coke-bottle glasses. He said, "I can't even remember the last time I was able to get an erection. I should have had it carbon-dated."

This time it was Megan Burke dragging Jonas Claymore out of bed. Jonas had done way too much Vicodin before going to sleep and he'd washed it all down with screw-top wine. He opened his eyes in utter disorientation when she shook him and said, "Jonas, wake up! You gotta get up right away."

"What?" he said. "What?"

She said, "Mr. Casper's on his way."

Jonas raised himself on his elbows and said, "Who?"

"Your landlord, that's who," Megan said. "He just phoned your cell and he wants his rent money. Twelve hundred dollars."

Jonas yawned, sat up, and said, "It ain't no thing. Give it to him. You got it from your old lady, didn't you?"

"Jonas, focus! I got two hundred from my mom, remember? And we spent half of it last night. Do you remember saying you wanted vike and vino?"

"Oh, Christ," he said, vaguely remembering. "Is that all this fucking world's about? Greedy rich people keeping people like us as serfs and slaves?"

"You have to talk to him," she said. "He says he'll shut off your water and have you evicted."

"Like hell he will," Jonas said. "That little slumlord kike can't push us around."

"Get dressed," Megan said, "and think of something."

"Okay, that does it," Jonas said. "We're going up to the Hollywood Hills in earnest today. No more casing. This is the real thing. Where does Paris Hilton live these days? Anybody can walk into *her* crib and she won't even know it."

While Jonas was trying to swallow a bite of scrambled egg with stale toast, Megan tried to tidy up the little apartment. She stacked the pizza boxes and paper plates on top of the fridge and piled the other debris in the kitchen sink, since the trash can was full of soft-drink cans and candy wrappers.

Then she hurried into their tiny bedroom, and Jonas said to her, "Where you going?"

"To make the bed. In case he goes in there to check things out."

"Get the fuck back here," Jonas said. "You think I'm gonna let that little hebe cocksucker walk into our bedroom? He's gonna talk to us from outside the door."

"No, Jonas!" Megan said. "We have to invite him in. You need another rent extension, so you have to be nice to the man. You get more flies with honey, right?"

"We got more than enough flies in this fucking place," Jonas said. "We don't need no more."

He was making a halfhearted attempt at brushing his teeth in the bathroom when the knock came at the door. He heard Megan say, "Good morning, sir. Come in, please. I'm a friend of Jonas and I'm visiting for a couple of days."

Jonas was shirtless and shoeless when he entered the living room in his last pair of jeans that still had the knees intact. He gave the landlord a sulky nod and said, "Good morning."

Contrary to Jonas Claymore's description, Mickey Casper was not little. He was several inches shorter than his lanky young tenant, but he had impressive arms, a chest that stretched his cotton shirt, and veined hands that belonged on a larger man.

He spoke with a very slight Israeli accent and said, "Jonas, I told you last time that I don't need this aggravation month after month. I'm going to have to ask you to leave."

Jonas said, "I got laid off from my job, Mr. Casper. Times are tough right now. We need you to be patient till I get another job."

"This has been going on too long," the landlord said. "I'm giving you notice."

"Now, wait a minute," Jonas said. "I got an interview today with the manager of a Starbucks. I'll be going to work on Monday if he likes me. And I know he'll like me. He said I'm just what he's looking for."

"Which Starbucks?" the landlord asked.

"The one at Sunset and Cahuenga," Jonas said.

"There is no Starbucks at Sunset and Cahuenga. I know that area very well," the landlord said.

Jonas stared at the man, trying to think of what to say, but the fucking headache was killing him. He couldn't think.

Megan said, "Could you please just give him a couple of weeks, Mr. Casper?"

"I'm sorry," the landlord said. "This has been going on too long. I've giving you notice, Jonas."

At that moment Jonas's headache peaked and he exploded with, "Okay, you little kike bastard, but for now this is my residence. Get out."

The landlord went pale around the mouth and started to speak but then changed his mind. He walked toward the door, but it wasn't fast enough for Jonas Claymore. As the landlord stopped and was about to say something, Jonas gave him a little shove and said, "Get the fuck out now!"

The landlord reacted with a blow to Jonas's solar plexus. It was a punch that only moved eight or ten inches but it was delivered with power and in exactly the spot where he was taught to hit when he'd done some boxing as a young man. Jonas sucked in a breath, started coughing, and went down on one knee and then flopped onto his back.

The landlord directed his fervent apology to Megan, saying, "I'm sorry, miss. I didn't mean to respond like that, but you saw that he pushed me. It was instinct on my part. I'm sorry."

"I didn't see him touch you at all, Mr. Casper," Megan said. "I hope you didn't crack his ribs or something."

Then she knelt beside Jonas, who was mooing like a cow, and said, "Jonas, are you okay? Can you talk?"

Jonas just shook his head slowly and Megan said to the landlord, "I think you'd better leave, Mr. Casper. I'll have to take him to Cedars ER. It could be very serious."

"He shoved me! You must have seen it," the landlord said. Then he added, "Look, Jonas, I'll...I'll give you another two weeks, okay? If you come up with the money then, we can see what's what."

"All right, Mr. Casper," Megan said. "And now, if you'll please go, I'll get him to the ER to see if there's been any damage done."

After the landlord was gone, Jonas rolled over and said, "Fuck! I don't know which hurts more now, my back or my gut."

"That was impressive, Jonas," Megan said.

"What impressive? What the fuck you talking about?"

"The way you goaded him," she said. "The way you made him hit you."

"Are you just stupid or what?" Jonas said, struggling to stand. "He sucker-punched me. That was no act. We're gonna sue that fucking Jew and take everything he's got. My guts're destroyed. Help me up."

"It'll take a long time to sue him," Mcgan said, "since you don't even know a lawyer. And I don't think this is the kind of case that lawyers are going to rush to handle. But meanwhile it bought us some time. If we're ever to do what you've said we have to do, it's now or never. We've got no ox, no perks, and no norcos. We're screwed, Jonas. Life is just one long screwing for losers like us."

His headache was thumping now. His brain felt swollen. He went into the bathroom and splashed cold water on his face and looked in the mirror. It took him a moment to count how many times he had been knocked on his ass in this terrible month. Then it hit him: That stupid bitch just said we're losers!

Marty Brueger had opted for a nostalgic visit to the Griffith Park Observatory that day, but when they got there, he didn't care to go inside. He wanted to sit in the car and gaze at the building, with Raleigh wondering what was going on in the old coot's head. Was he remembering some girl he took there ages ago? Was he thinking about those long-dead actors James Dean and Natalie Wood and Sal Mineo in *Rebel Without a Cause,* where this building was featured? Raleigh Dibble didn't have the interest or energy to inquire. He kept thinking of what he could do with half a million dollars to change his situation in this world.

Then, just as impulsively as he had asked to be driven there, Marty Brueger said, "Okay, Raleigh, let's go home. I need a nap."

"Would you like to have lunch somewhere?" Raleigh asked.

"No, just stop at the liquor store and get me some more of that special Irish whiskey. Three bottles this time."

After they had bought the whiskey and got back to the house, Raleigh made sure that the old man was tucked in with a tumbler of whiskey next to his dentures, and he said, "Have a nice sleep, Mr. Brueger. What would you like for supper?"

"Cyanide," Marty Brueger said before closing his eyes. "Just pour it in the whiskey and don't bother me till it's over."

That was the first time that Raleigh Dibble felt truly sorry for the old geezer. When he got back into the main house, his cell rang, and he looked at the number of the Wickland Gallery.

He felt a tightness in his throat when he said to Nigel Wickland, "Okay, what's going on?"

"Progress has been fantastic," Nigel said. "We're going to do it tomorrow."

Raleigh's bowels began to rumble. Tomorrow! They were really going to do it. He'd been longing for this call, but now it terrified him. "What time?"

"When the old man's napping. How about one o'clock?"

"Well . . . okay."

"Why do you hesitate?"

Raleigh knew it was just nerves on his part, and he said, "No, it's fine. But stay on your cell in case there's a change for any reason."

"Why would there be a change?"

"How the hell would I know?" Raleigh said. "Shit happens, Nigel. Just keep your cell handy, okay?"

"I told you *not* to use names, damn it," Nigel Wickland said.

When Raleigh closed his cell, he muttered, "Arrogant fucking fairy."

Then his bowels rumbled again and he ran to the bathroom.

Megan was even more exhausted and pain-racked than Jonas by the time they finished their work. It had been a day of endless cruising past celebrities' addresses that they found online by using the rented computer at the cybercafé, a commercial enterprise where a hundred computers were operating 24/7. The cybercafé was a favorite haunt of identity thieves, hookers, drug dealers, and scam artists of all kinds. Jonas had insisted on spending a lot of time there these days, seeking out the addresses that he was convinced would bring them the fortune that the Bling Ring had had in their grasp but lost because of careless planning.

When they finally got back to their apartment, Megan said, "Jonas, I'm hurting bad. My elbows, my knees, everywhere." And then she started that incessant coughing that was getting on his nerves.

"I'm the one that got suckered by that kike asshole," Jonas retorted. "What're you complaining about for chrissake?"

"I'm telling you, I'm in pain. I think I've got arthritis," she said.

"Yeah, arthritis at twenty," he said. "Sure."

"I need something for the pain!"

"You're jonesing," he said. "I told you it'll go away as soon as we can make some money to buy enough ox. As soon as we get it together, I'm sending you for a quick trip to rehab for a spin-dry."

"Sending me to rehab?" she said. "We can't afford rehab. Anyway, I never smoke as much as you do. Why don't you go to rehab?"

"I don't wanna talk about this every time you get sick," Jonas said. "Just go fix supper, will ya? I gotta look at our star maps. I think tomorrow we're gonna shoot for our first real target. We're gonna get serious at last. I got four celebrity cribs picked out and we're gonna get inside one of them. We need sleep so we can keep our heads clear."

Speaking of his head made him realize that his headache was almost gone, so he thought he could maybe use a sleep inducer.

"We got any wine and watsons left?" he asked. "That should fix me up till tomorrow. Like my mom used to say, I'll be right as rain then."

"We had real rain in Oregon," Meg said despondently. "This goddamn place is just a glitzy desert."

SIXTEEN

SERGEANT MURILLO LIKED to send the troops out on the streets in good spirits, so he invited humorous comments as soon as he finished reading the crimes and other roll call material. He said, "Has anything noteworthy happened lately that you would like to share?"

Flotsam said, "Yeah, Sarge, the other night we got a call from a drunk hooker on the Sunset track who made an ADW report against some dude that kicked her in the giz when she refused to boink him for twenty bucks. When we got her to the ER, the doctor examined her and said there was something weird about her labia. She thought he said Libya, and she goes, 'I ain't no terrorist. I'm an American.'"

That one got a few hoots and some thumbs-down from skeptics who didn't believe it happened. And then Snuffy Salcedo said, "We pulled over a guy on Cahuenga last night for busting a light, and when I said he had a mutilated driver's license, he said, 'My license don't mutilate for another year.'"

That one got more hoots and a few thumbs-up.

Before he dismissed them, Sergeant Murillo made an announcement that concerned Britney Small and Della Ravelle.

"Six-X-Forty-six," he said, "I'd like you to stop by the library on Ivar and talk to the librarian about the Wedgie Bandit. He's at it again."

The veteran midwatch cops groaned at the news, and Sergeant

Murillo said, "For you new people, the Wedgie Bandit is a white male, about thirty years old, five ten, one forty, brown and blue. He usually wears long-sleeved jerseys or sweatshirts, jeans, and tennis shoes. And he is an unparalleled menace to the safety and security of Hollywood's citizens. It's imperative that we get this villain off the street."

Snuffy Salcedo said, "Wedgie Bandit? Why do they call him that?"

Sergeant Murillo said, deadpan, "He assaults any unsuspecting person he encounters with very forceful wedgies."

"With wedgies?" Snuffy said.

"Do you know what a wedgie is, Officer Salcedo?" Sergeant Murillo asked. "It's very unpleasant. How would you like someone to give you one?"

"I know they're unpleasant, boss," Snuffy said, "but why does he do it to strangers?"

Sergeant Murillo said, "That is the question that the watch commander wants answered, and the station captain, and the division captain, and the bureau commander. I wouldn't be surprised if the chief of police wants to know his motive. When he's caught, we'll find out why he does it, but we can't catch him. Six X-Thirty-two almost caught him one time, I believe. I'm not sure what happened."

Flotsam said, "Yeah, my little pard here chased him through Griffith Park, but the Wedgie Bandit left him panting on the grass with his tongue hanging out like one of them Frisbee-chasing border collies that scoot around there all day."

"He runs like a cheetah," Jetsam said defensively.

Sergeant Murillo said, "You all should be aware of how serial wedgies are committed. This fiend just walks up behind victims of either gender, even senior citizens, and grabs a handful of underwear from the back and pulls up as hard as he can. Then he beats feet and vanishes."

Jetsam said, "I almost had that little booger eater till he ran right through a bunch of bird-watchers that're always out there looking for the Painted Redstart, whatever the hell that is. One of the old babes was, like, taking a bunch of pictures with a telephoto lens and another one was chirping with a birdcall. And pretty soon both were sitting on the grass after he bowled them over. I'm only surprised he didn't stop long enough to give one of them a wedgie."

Flotsam said, "Sarge, remember the time the vice unit helped us out and put an undercover guy out there, and the bandit snuck up behind him and gave the UC cop a wedgie? And got away again!"

"Yes, he's been imaginative and resourceful," Sergeant Murillo said, still deadpan. "If a unit from Watch Five can jam him tonight, I will buy *two* large pizzas with the works for that team. Of course, with the price of two pizzas, I hope you'll wait until about, oh, two thirty for me to buy them, when they're older and cheaper, at an hour when only coppers will eat them."

Hollywood Nate said to Britney Small of 6-X-46, "Be super-careful at the library, Britney. Make sure Della's got your back at all times. It'd be a real feather in his cap to give a uniformed female copper a wedgie."

Britney blushed and the troops hooted and whistled and were all ready to go out and do police work.

When Watch 5 cleared and was on the streets, there was a cyclist causing a disturbance on Santa Monica Boulevard. But this wasn't any ordinary cyclist. He was unique even for this attention-getters Mecca. This cyclist kept cruising on the sidewalk past a beauty shop, honking a horn attached to his handlebars. He wasn't satisfied until he got several women to go to the windows with their hair rolled in goop and tinfoil, with strands protruding in all directions. Then he'd ride no hands and wave at them.

The cyclist was reptile-thin, of indeterminate age, with his hair done in purple spikes, and as far as face metal went, there was nothing left to pierce. He had rings or studs through his nose, ears, eyebrows, lips, and tongue. He was inked on most of his upper body and had only a bit of bare flesh untatted from his knees down.

He wore flip-flops and violet short shorts decorated with sparkles. The proprietor of the beauty shop, a no-nonsense Cambodian woman, went outside several times and yelled, "You stop this! You go way! I call police!"

But that only made him emit a lunatic laugh and honk his horn and make another pass in front of the beauty shop window.

Finally one of the customers said, "I'm sick of this shit!"

She went outside, still wearing her black wraparound smock, and when the cyclist cruised by again, she shouted, "Hey, freako! Get outta here!"

All she got was the cry of a loon, and he sped right past her no hands as she yelled, " You asshole!"

Which turned out to be the apt epithet. She got a good look at him from the back, and when she ran inside to call the police, she said to the other women, "There's no seat on the bike!"

Six-X-Seventy-six got the call about a "415 cyclist" at the beauty shop, and Viv Daley said to Georgie Adams, "The message doesn't say how he's disturbing the peace."

"In Hollywood it could mean anything," Georgie said. "Probably DUI and doing wheelies to impress the ladies while they're getting their hair bleached. I'm glad you don't go in for that highlights stuff, sis. It's so lame and boring. I think half the people in Hollywood do it these days, even Flotsam and Jetsam."

"Those surfer boys swear their golden streaks are from the sun and surf," Viv said as she turned eastbound through the Sunset Boulevard early evening traffic.

"Yeah, right," Georgie said.

"Where the hell does all this traffic come from?" Viv said.

"It can't be explained," Georgie said. "I think it's immaculate congestion."

JOSEPH WAMBAUGH

When they arrived at the beauty shop, the outraged proprietress met them at the curb and pointed to the cyclist, who pedaled off in the opposite direction very fast upon seeing the black-and-white.

The Cambodian beautician tried to explain to them in broken English about the cyclist causing a disturbance, but "Look at ass!" was the best they could get from her.

Not knowing what that meant, 6-X-76 made a dodgy U-turn through the traffic and caught up with the cyclist. Viv beeped her horn and gestured for him to stop, and when he did, she pulled the Crown Vic to the curb beside him.

"What the hell was that woman trying to tell us?" Georgie said. "I don't get it."

They got out and approached the cyclist, who was still astride his bike with one foot on the sidewalk. Since he was wearing only the sparkled short shorts, there was no need for a pat down.

Georgie said to Viv, "The dude's got enough face metal to trade at a junkyard for a 'sixty-eight Torino."

"First of all," Viv said to the cyclist, "you're riding a bike on the sidewalk. Secondly, you were beeping your horn and causing an unnecessary disturbance." Then she took a closer look at him and said, "Get off the bike, sir."

Obediently he swung his leg over the saddle, except there was no saddle. Georgie looked at the steel seat post and said, "What the hell?"

Viv said to the cyclist, "Turn around sir and face away from me."

He smiled amiably and complied, and she got a rear view of him and said, "Don't look, Gypsy. You're too squeamish for this."

But Georgie looked anyway and saw the opening in the shorts. After that he refused to look at either the man's shorts or the metal seat post.

"You talk to him," he said to Viv Daley. "I'm getting nauseous."

"Sir," Viv said to the cyclist, "where's the seat that goes on this bike?"

"Wore it out," he said.

"Why don't you buy another one?"

"I got used to this," he said. "It's more comfortable. And I think it gives me greater control of the bike. Why? Is there any law against it?"

"You're exposing yourself indecently," she said.

"No, Officer," he said. "I'm all covered, if you'll notice. The hole in my shorts is only an inch and one eighth in diameter to fit snugly over the metal post. So you see, I'm not indecent at all."

Viv said patiently, "If I don't write you a ticket for riding on the sidewalk, will you promise me to go home and get yourself a bike seat and never ride like this again, even if it gives you greater control of your bike?"

His mouth turned down at the corners. No mean feat with all the lip rings and studs, and he sighed and said, "If you say so, Officer. I want to always obey the law."

"Okay," Viv said. "Walk your bike home, sew up your shorts, and buy a bike seat ASAP."

When they got back in the car, Georgie Adams said, "We should get a pay bump for dealing with Hollywood weirdness."

Viv said, "The next time you go for a bike ride…"

"Please don't clown me, sis," Georgie said. "I'm feeling queasy. There's stuff out here that you people with X chromosomes can handle but us Ys can't. This is definitely one of them."

That evening started out on an annoying note. There was a disturbance at a house just off Franklin near Bronson Avenue where there had been any number of disturbances in recent years. A Goth family who played their role to the hilt occupied an old two-story house. Every family member, including children under the age of ten, was always clothed in black. And their parents, a pair of scarecrows in their late forties, usually wore theatrical makeup with their hair dyed black, parted in the middle, and combed down to their shoulders. It was said that the wife had a trust account that provided the money for the spooky games they played, as well as for their toys and exhibits. The cops referred to them as Mr. Goth and Mrs. Goth.

In their large living room were three coffins and an antique embalming table. In two of the coffins there were mannequins that popped up and scared the hell out of anyone who had never been to the house before. The Goths had drug parties in that living room, which detectives had tried unsuccessfully to infiltrate. The couple would probably be chosen as the area's most despised householders by the cops at Hollywood Station because they were Addams Family wannabes. And in their efforts to be "authentic Goths," they sometimes invited what they considered to be interesting party guests to their home, who often ended up being more than troublesome to their hosts.

Six-X-Sixty-six was called to the Goth residence just after midnight, and Mrs. Goth was waiting on the sidewalk in front. She was in her Morticia costume: a straight, black, floor-length, form-fitting gown with a neckline plunging almost to her naval. Her lashes were an inch long and her eye shadow was so black and heavy, it looked like patches of corduroy.

Hollywood Nate and Snuffy Salcedo followed her into the residence, and Snuffy paused to gape at the coffins with mannequins lying in repose. The candelabras, which contained not wax candles but electric fixtures, were lit, and baskets of plastic flowers surrounded the coffins. The antique embalming table was in a spotlight and made to look like a medical surgery in Victorian times, and the sound of an organ playing a funereal dirge was coming from stereo speakers in the walls.

Mrs. Goth said to them, "One of our guests won't leave and go home. We don't really know him very well. He's a friend of a friend, and, well, he's a bit frightening."

Hollywood Nate, who had twice been called to the Goth house

for similar disturbances and thought they were about the lamest of Hollywood's present crop of attention getters, said, "Upstaging you, is he? When you're supposed to be the weird and scary ones."

Mrs. Goth was trying to decide how to respond to that impertinence when Snuffy Salcedo said, "Did you tell him to go home?"

"A dozen times," she said. "He's a very difficult and very strange man."

They could hear a television going, and Snuffy said, "What's he doing in there?"

"Watching porn," she said.

Hollywood Nate asked, "Where'd he get it?"

"My husband gave it to him," she said. "A mistake. My husband sometimes gets enthusiastic when he's with barbarians, and he tends to indulge them."

"Where's your husband?" Snuffy asked.

"With our children."

"In the house?"

"No, he took them for a hamburger until it's over. He always leaves me to deal with the party detritus."

"Until what's over?" Snuffy Salcedo asked.

"Whatever happens between you and him," she said. "He claims his name is Rolf Thunder. That's all I know."

"Let's have a look at your barbarian," Snuffy said.

Mrs. Goth just gestured down a darkened hallway.

Snuffy Salcedo led the way to a lighted sitting room and quietly pushed the door open a few inches to take a peek inside. Rolf Thunder sat in a La-Z-Boy recliner in the lamp-lit room eating potato chips and watching porn. They could hear the heavy breathing and orgasmic moans coming from the video. One hand was holding an object on his lap.

Snuffy Salcedo came back into the corridor and said to Mrs. Goth, "What's that on his lap?"

"A penis pump," she said.

"Where did he get it?" Nate asked.

"My husband lent it to him," she said. "We didn't know he'd fall in love with it and decide to spend the night playing with it."

Snuffy Salcedo turned to Nate, who had not yet had a look at Rolf Thunder, and said, "Let's get some backup here."

"Any particular reason I should know about?" Nate said.

"About two hundred eighty of them," Snuffy said. "That's about how many pounds he weighs. And I'd guess it's spread over about six and a half feet of very large and heavy bones. And on his shoulder he's got some White Power jailhouse tatts, so I'm pretty sure he doesn't like Mexicans. And he won't like Jews either, so hide your nameplate."

Nate said, "Are you sure we'll need backup? He's only one guy."

Snuffy said, "Partner, I got a real bad feeling about this one. He's only slightly smaller than a bulldozer and he's ready to tear things down. Take my word for it. I'm older and wiser than you."

Hollywood Nate walked back to the living room with Snuffy to make the backup request on his rover. Like all male cops with sufficient machismo, Hollywood Nate was reluctant to request code 2 assistance, and only once or twice in his entire career had he resorted to a code 3 "officers need help" request. He just spoke into the rover and subtly requested "a unit to assist" at the Goth family address.

He got two units: 6-X-46, with Della Ravelle and Britney Small, and 6-X-32, with Flotsam and Jetsam. Mrs. Goth walked to the street to meet the arriving radio cars, and she looked decidedly uncomfortable to see Flotsam and Jetsam get out of their black-and-white. They had been called to the Goth house on other occasions.

"Dude, I truly hate these Goth show-offs," Flotsam said to Jetsam. "They are mega-phony."

When the surfer cops entered the living room of the house, Snuffy said to them, "I got a bad vibe going here. An acquaintance of this lady and her husband does not want to leave their premises and I think he ain't gonna listen to reason."

"Have you talked to him yet?" Flotsam asked.

"Not yet," Snuffy Salcedo said.

"Why not?" Jetsam asked.

"He's busy pumping his penis," Snuffy Salcedo said. "I figured it's best to wait till he's finished."

"What?" said Flotsam.

Just then Della Ravelle and Britney Small entered the house to join the other cops, and Snuffy said to them, "I'm glad to see you have your regular batons with you and not those cheesey expandable ones. I would prefer we had Louisville sluggers for this gig. I suggest you be ready with Tasers and pepper spray. And an M-sixteen if you got one."

"Who're we evicting this time?" Della asked. "King Kong?"

"Pretty close," Snuffy Salcedo said. "If King Kong was a skinhead with jailhouse swastikas on his twenty-two-inch neck and a pentagram inked on the side of his shaved melon. And if King Kong liked penis pumps."

"What?" Britney Small said.

"Do you want us to try talking to him first?" Della asked. "The woman's touch?"

"It's our call to handle," Hollywood Nate said. "We wanted backup just in case."

Snuffy Salcedo led the way to the sitting room, followed by Hollywood Nate, with the other four midwatch cops standing outside in the corridor near the living room.

Snuffy pushed open the door and saw that nothing had changed. Rolf Thunder was still watching porn and still wearing the penis pump. He looked to be in his late forties, about the same age as Snuffy Salcedo.

He didn't look up until Snuffy said, "Mr. Thunder, we need to talk."

Only then did the man glance at Snuffy with unfocused brown eyes, and Snuffy could plainly see that the guy was fried, probably on crystal or some other lowlife drug. Rolf Thunder didn't say anything to Snuffy but just went back to watching the porn video.

Hollywood Nate stepped in behind Snuffy and said, "Dude, you're gonna have to get up and leave here, so you might as well understand that. You got any ID?"

Finally, Rolf Thunder spoke without looking at Nate, saying, "Yeah, do you?"

"I'm wearing mine," Nate said.

Rolf Thunder then looked at both cops and smirked. "Are you bad cop?" he said to Nate. "And what's little homeboy, good cop? Do you two make tamales after work and sleep together or what?"

When he grinned, they saw at least three teeth missing from his upper grille. The man had a simian brow and flaring nostrils exposing what looked like a nose full of steel wool. His jaw was massive and square with a bulldog underbite, and he looked like he could chew through handcuff links. Flotsam and Jetsam stood in the doorway so the giant could clearly see how badly he was outnumbered.

Rolf Thunder looked at the surfer cops and said, "Oh, so you brought a couple of the other girls along. I like blond candy. We woulda had fun with them up at Corcoran."

"Yeah, we get it that you're a badass ex-con," Snuffy said, "so don't even go there."

"Our posse's got lots of pain tools and we jump ugly," Nate said. "So chill and think it over."

Rolf Thunder's massive jaw muscles flexed and he looked at Hollywood Nate and said, "Up at Corcoran the screws called me 'Bio-hazard' because everyone I choked out shit his pants."

Jetsam said sotto to Flotsam, "Bro, there's some very bad juju here."

Flotsam said sotto, "This dude's more dangerous than a Toyota floor mat."

"Get your savage on, bro," Jetsam said.

Della Ravelle whispered to Britney Small, "If this turns into a melee, don't try to be a man. Stand back with your Taser and your baton and pick your shots. And don't be shy about calling for help if we need it."

Britney's blue eyes were wide when she nodded at her partner and waited, pepper spray in one hand, baton in the other.

Back in the sitting room, Snuffy Salcedo said, "How about you just get outta that chair now."

"Sure, homie," Rolf Thunder said, standing up so fast that both cops took a step backward. He was still wearing the penis pump on his drooping member.

And he was even bigger than Snuffy Salcedo had thought. He was tall enough to look down at Flotsam, and Snuffy's estimate of 280 pounds was way off. They all figured he weighed three bills if he weighed an ounce.

"Take that thing off," Snuffy Salcedo said, pointing to the penis pump.

"You take it off, sweetie," he said to Snuffy with a wolfish grin. "But then you'll have to marry me."

Hollywood Nate said, "Turn around and put your hands behind your back."

The behemoth drilled Nate with death-ray eyes and said, "Why don't I put them behind *your* back, cupcake?" Without another word he lunged forward, roaring, and grabbed Hollywood Nate in a bear hug and began crushing him.

Flotsam, Jetsam, and Snuffy Salcedo swarmed Rolf Thunder. Jetsam tried pepper spray and got the side of Rolf Thunder's face as well as his partner's. Flotsam bellowed from the burn but the giant didn't flinch, and he released Hollywood Nate, only to start throwing wild punches that mostly missed their target. But even blows that hit them on the chest or back were stunningly painful and knocked the wind out of them. He managed to break free and run into the hallway, crashing into Britney Small and sending her sprawling. When he reached the living room, he made his stand.

Mrs. Goth let out the most chilling scream that had ever emanated from a house that featured recorded screams and other spooky special effects. She ran outside, where neighbors had begun to gather. And all the time the recorded organ played a funeral dirge.

Britney Small leaped to her feet and ran into the living room after Rolf Thunder, but Della Ravelle grabbed her by the back of her Sam Browne belt and said, "Don't jump into that. Stand back and pick your shots!"

And since female officers did not have to struggle with machismo, Della felt no compunction about putting out a code 3 call on her rover, which she knew would bring units from everywhere, and fast.

The four male cops charged into the great room in a bunch and hit Rolf Thunder high and low. Flotsam received a punch on the side of the head and it knocked him off his feet and set his ears to ringing. Jetsam dug two baton thrusts into the big man's belly, but it didn't faze him. Hollywood Nate smacked him on the elbow with his baton, but the giant only backed up a couple of steps and waited, hands hanging low at his sides and grinning.

Snuffy Salcedo drew his Taser and said, "Back away from him!"

When the other cops backed off, Snuffy Salcedo fired the Taser into the big man's chest from five feet away. The blue thread of light snapped and Rolf Thunder stood straight up and grimaced from the 50,000 volts.

But then to the horror of all present, he pulled the dart out and said, "You jist opened yourself a can of whup-ass, homie."

He charged Snuffy Salcedo and Hollywood Nate both, taking one of them in each arm and driving them into the wall, and that stopped the organ music. Flotsam jumped onto the back of the giant and tried to get a choke hold, which vocal police critics considered to be de facto excessive force in almost all cases. But Rolf Thunder was stronger than Flotsam and pried his grip loose and swung a roundhouse that caught Snuffy Salcedo between the eyes, shattering the bridge of his nose.

Rolf Thunder scrambled to keep his feet before he was driven into the nearest coffin by Jetsam, who hit him low with his shoulder. When the giant went down, Della Ravelle whacked him across the knees with her baton and Britney Small shot him with another Taser dart but with the same effect. He stiffened, grimaced, and pulled out the dart.

When Snuffy Salcedo stood up with blood pouring into his mouth, he hit the giant across the forehead with his baton, knocking him backward against the second coffin, which dumped the mannequin onto the floor, where its mechanism was triggered. It kept popping up in a sitting position over and over like a lunatic cheerleader enjoying the macabre violence.

Rolf Thunder got up and ran at Flotsam, and the two tall men crashed into the antique embalming table, spilling all of the paraphernalia onto the floor. Then Jetsam was on Rolf Thunder's back, trying for another choke hold, but he was spun around and hurled into another coffin, where a second mannequin was ejected. It fell across Flotsam and they lay together like lovers for an instant until the surfer cop pushed it off and scrambled to his feet.

At that point, Hollywood Nate kicked Rolf Thunder in the groin, and that doubled him over for a moment, giving Jetsam and Snuffy Salcedo time to begin whacking him anywhere and everywhere with their batons, including a few head strikes that sounded like rifle shots. Britney Small stepped in close and gave him a good dose of pepper spray, which missed the other cops this time and entered the mouth of the giant.

The pepper spray got him coughing but he still got to his feet somehow. That gave Jetsam the chance to drive the end of his baton into the big man's groin, the only place where he seemed vulnerable, and Rolf Thunder dropped to his knees, clutching at his throat and at his groin. And when he was in that position, Snuffy Salcedo, his face a blood mask, played catch-up and smashed Rolf Thunder across the face with his aluminum baton, doing more damage to the giant's nose than his own had suffered.

At last, Rolf Thunder tumbled to the floor on his back, concussed but still not completely unconscious. He writhed and struggled to breathe and pulled his legs up to protect his groin. Both surfer cops jumped on him and with the help of Snuffy Salcedo got his hands twisted behind him. They feared for a moment that the handcuffs would not fit around those enormous wrists, but after a struggle they managed to get the first few ratchets to grip and hold.

Breathing hard, Flotsam said to him, "They'll stretch with wear, dude."

Della Ravelle made another call on her rover to request two rescue ambulances, one for their prisoner and one for Snuffy Salcedo, who was sitting on an overturned coffin, trying to stanch the blood from his nose. The creepy mannequin kept popping up and looking at Snuffy until he hauled off and smacked it with his baton, knocking its head clear off.

Everyone else was sitting or standing, wheezing and chuffing and panting, and Rolf Thunder lay still for a moment and then croaked out some words. He said, "Wasn't that fun?"

Snuffy wiped his bloody face on his uniform sleeve and said breathlessly, "Yeah, you masochist freak, that was tons of fun. I only wish I could put a few forty-caliber rounds in your belly to show you a real good time."

"Yo, homie," Rolf Thunder said, his own face a mask of blood from shattered bone and dislodged teeth, "can't you handle a little sound and fury?"

"Go outside and wait for the RA, Snuffy," Hollywood Nate

said. "We'll deal with Sasquatch. When he gets to County USC, he's gonna need a needle and lotsa thread."

His partner nodded, got up painfully, and shuffled to the open door, where he could hear the sirens on their way. Black-and-whites responding to Della's help call were screeching to a stop on the street in front, and a wall of bluesuits came running toward Goth House.

Inside the living room, Hollywood Nate pointed to the penis pump, held in place by a constriction band, and said, "We should get that thing off him."

"Not me, dude," Flotsam said. "That's way beyond my pay grade."

"Ditto," said Jetsam.

Flotsam said to Della Ravelle, "Would you mind taking that thing off him, Della?"

"Do it yourself," she said.

"I never touched another guy's junk before," Flotsam said.

"You've touched your own often enough," she said.

"That's different," Flotsam said. "Mine belongs to me. I even got a pet name for it."

"Don't look at me," Jetsam said. "I ain't touching it. Come on, Della, you probably touched lots of them in your time."

"Go screw yourself, surf rat!" Della said.

"No, wait," Jetsam said. "I'm just saying, like, a woman of your . . . maturity, like, probably in her lifetime . . ."

"Aw, shit," Della said, and went over to Rolf Thunder, who was lying handcuffed in a fetal pose and going in and out of consciousness now. She knelt and loosened the constricting band and removed the penis pump and tossed it at Jetsam, saying, "Here, would you like to book this as evidence?"

The surfer cop leaped aside like the thing was radioactive as the penis pump flew past him.

Snuffy Salcedo was taken by ambulance to Cedars-Sinai

Medical Center, where an ER doctor said that his nose would probably be "almost like new after surgery." He was told he'd be kept
overnight for observation and surgery in the morning.

When 6-X-46 was alone in the women's locker room at Hollywood Station, Della Ravelle helped Britney Small apply an ice pack
to her right eye where she'd been slammed by Rolf Thunder's elbow
as he'd bolted into the coffin room to make his stand.

"Keep the ice on it till the second-guessers get here," Della said.
"You've got a mouse growing already and it's turning purple."

"I'm in better shape than any of the guys," Britney said, touching the swelling gingerly.

"This has been a learning experience for you, girlfriend," Della
said. "You see how male coppers are? They pride themselves on
never putting out an officers-need-help call. Their machismo pre-
vents even an assistance call. There's just a whole lot of cowboy in
them. If I'd been running that show, I would've backed off in the
beginning and at least put out the code-two call the second Mr.
Frankenstein made it clear he was gonna go the hard way. But with
six of us there, no guy gunslinger would ever humble himself to do
that. Well, girl, now you've seen some real whup-ass. And now you
see that all the grappling holds and everything else you learned at
the academy are worth shit out here in the real world when you
come up against a walking reign of terror. I know you're brave, but
what good would bantamweight Britney Small have done in the
midst of half a ton of raging beef crashing around that room? If
you ever face something like that by yourself, just remember that
you carry a forty-caliber Glock, and if your back's to the wall, do
not hesitate to pull and kill the bastard before he kills you. Don't
think about whether you're justified by policy or by law. Remember the old copper saying: It's a whole lot better to be judged by
twelve than carried by six."

Because of the kind of violence inflicted, which could have
included choke holds, baton strikes, and kicks, Force Investigation

Division had been immediately called out to determine if all action was in policy. The five ambulatory cops spent the rest of the night being interviewed at Hollywood Station, where they tediously had to deconstruct the battle and justify each move they made.

What they all *wanted* to say to FID was "When it comes to subduing a monster with no pain receptors, the Marquis of Queensberry's just some tranny on Santa Monica Boulevard. So stop fucking with me!"

Rolf Thunder, whose true name was Filmore McClain, was transported to the jail ward on the thirteenth floor at USCMC, the old county hospital, and later told investigators that it had all been worth it and he had no complaints. The institutionalized man said that he'd enjoyed his vacation in the free world for a while but that it had gotten too stressful. He said he had been trying to find a fun way to violate his parole and go back to prison, which was the only place he'd ever been really happy. It was where he could be taken care of and kick back and never have to make decisions and experience life the way he'd always known it since he was fifteen years old. Prison was security. Prison was home.

The only positive note that the male cops took from the event at Goth House was that after the battle they all got a good look at the penis of the giant when he was strapped onto the gurney by paramedics.

Della Ravelle noticed their satisfaction and later said to Britney Small, "Did you see the smug little smiles on the surfer cops and Hollywood Nate when Jumbo was on the gurney? What they'll remember most about the war at Goth House is that their little willies are just as big as Goliath's. They might even stop using male-enhancement products."

★ SEVENTEEN ★

RALEIGH'S SLEEP WAS fitful and fraught with strange dreams that he could not interpret. He awakened every hour or so until he gave up and rose at 5:30 A.M. He watched TV with his breakfast but couldn't eat much. Then he took Marty Brueger's breakfast on a tray to the cottage, but he found the old man still sleeping. He left the tray and walked back to the main house and tried to read the *L.A. Times,* but he could not concentrate.

His thoughts kept returning to the months he'd spent in federal prison, where he'd met several inmates who had served very hard time in state penitentiaries. One of them told Raleigh that comparing Club Fed to state prison was like comparing hemorrhoids to colon cancer, and the inmate was a man who had suffered both.

There was still time, Raleigh thought. He could pick up the phone and call Nigel Wickland, using both his given name and surname just to piss him off, and cancel the whole thing. After all, his life in the Brueger house was pretty good, and he'd never been a greedy man. Why should he risk arrest and trial and a sentence at one of the nightmare factories run by the state of California, where each hour of each terrible day his life would be put at risk? This was madness, this fantasy that had been sold to him by one of those "toffee-nosed poofs," as his fellow workers in the London bistro used to call the upper-crust homos.

He went to the butler's pantry and got a notepad and pen and began making a list of all the ways in which this thing could go sideways. When he got to number six, he tore it to bits and then set fire to the paper scraps in the sink. He sat down again. Then the phone buzzed, and he picked it up, knowing it was the cottage line.

"Yes, Mr. Brueger?" he said.

Marty Brueger's morning voice said, "I'm sick of this fucking place, Raleigh. With Lorena away, I feel like a prisoner in solitary confinement."

"I'm sorry, Mr. Brueger," Raleigh said. "Maybe we can take a drive later this morning? Is there somewhere you'd like to go? We can take any one of Mrs. Brueger's cars. How about the big Mercedes? You could sit in back with a flask of whiskey and take in the sights and I'll be your chauffeur."

"I was thinking about a longer drive," Marty Brueger said. "I was thinking maybe you could take me to Palm Springs and I could look at all the old places I used to know when Sammy and me were young bucks."

And there it was! One of the ways things could go sideways, and it wasn't even on his list. Palm Springs was three hours away. He couldn't take the geezer to Palm Springs and be back by 1 P.M.

"Mr. Brueger," he said. "It's still too hot in Palm Springs. In a couple of months it'll be nice there and we can go and get a hotel for an overnighter. You could gamble in the Indian casinos. Maybe catch a show. But you don't want to go to Palm Springs now."

"I'm lonesome," Marty Brueger said. "Come on over and let's talk about it. Or I can come up to the house."

"I'll come to you, Mr. Brueger," Raleigh said.

He hung up and thought about this. Was it fate, destiny, or divine providence? Today of all days, something had made that old man decide he wanted to go to Palm Springs. Something or somebody was trying to help Raleigh out of the incredible scheme concocted by Nigel Wickland. All he had to do was call the man and tell him that Marty Brueger wanted to go to Palm Springs today, which was the truth. After that, he could tell an untruth and say that Marty Brueger had decided to move into the main house because he was lonely. And with Marty Brueger in the main house, it would effectively end Nigel Wickland's plot to make a million dollars. Raleigh could save face with that pompous limey, as if he needed to, and the bad dreams would be over.

Suddenly he felt like a free man. He felt wonderful. He sauntered down the walk to Marty's cottage and literally stopped to smell the roses. He knocked twice, as he always did. He entered and found Marty Brueger on the floor in the bathroom, wearing only urine-soaked underpants.

"Mr. Brueger!" Raleigh ran to the old man, stripped off his underwear and carried him to his bed.

Marty Brueger looked at him and said, "Wa-wa-wa..."

"Are you trying to say my name, Mr. Brueger?" Raleigh said in panic. Then he muttered, "My god, it's a stroke!"

Raleigh Dibble picked up the phone and dialed 9-1-1.

Megan Burke was shocked to be awakened by the smell of actual food. She opened her eyes and found Jonas sitting on the bed, fully dressed, with a glass of orange juice in a Styrofoam cup and an Egg McMuffin on a plate.

He said, "I got up early. This is the first day of our new life as successful people. I went out and had breakfast and brought yours home. We gotta be healthy and strong today. Eat, baby, eat."

Megan rolled out of bed with her feet on the floor, stood up painfully, and lurched into the bathroom. Jonas went to the kitchen, and she could hear water running. When she finished in the bathroom, she saw the plate of Egg McMuffin on the kitchen table with the orange juice. And he was actually making the coffee, another first.

"We ain't doing drugs today, Megan," he said. "We're working and we ain't coming home till we hit a target. We're aiming for nothing but bull's-eyes today. We're finding a likely crib and we're going in. Nothing can stop us."

Megan sat and sipped some orange juice and nibbled at the Egg McMuffin without interest. She thought, Right, I don't get to do any drugs today, but look at him! She figured he'd had a taste of something, the way he was amped. It made her surly and resentful. She always got the short end because he was the man, or so he thought.

"Come on, sweetie, take bigger bites," he said. "And chew, chew, chew."

She had a momentary fantasy of picking up a kitchen knife and cutting his throat.

Raleigh's panic had subsided before the ambulance arrived, and after they'd loaded Marty Brueger in and taken him to Cedars-Sinai, he went into the main house and took a shower. He had the old man's piss on his clothes and he wanted to stand under hot water for a long time. The paramedics had verified that it looked like a stroke, and they had wasted no time in getting their patient out of there, so now Raleigh was alone for the first time in Casa Brueger. He needed to think, but first he needed the shower.

When he finally was out and had toweled off, Raleigh stood before the mirror and thought about all the things he had planned to do with his fifty thousand tax-free dollars. He was going to be physically transformed, easily losing ten years from his appearance, thanks to the cosmetic magicians on the west side of Los Angeles. He had also planned to purchase a modest condo, his own home at long last. And there was the dream of hooking up with an older wealthy woman, like the kind he'd met through his catering business. And why not? He could cook and he knew food and wine. He could manage a house and he could drive. And he was, if he did say so himself, a presentable companion who could converse with any-one. But what was going to happen now that Marty Brueger had suffered a stroke? Was this yet another act of providence, or fate, or destiny? If so, what did it mean?

Then again, if he did go forward with Nigel Wickland, it would make it all far easier and less stressful with Marty Brueger off the property and in the hospital, wouldn't it? Things would be simpler and safer in many ways. But he didn't dare keep the fact of Marty Brueger's hospitalization from Marty's sister-in-law, Leona Brueger. He had to phone Tuscany. That much was certain. But what would she say and do?

Ten minutes later Raleigh made a call, but he did not phone Leona Brueger in Tuscany. He phoned Nigel Wickland's cell phone.

When Nigel answered, Raleigh said, "The old guy's had a stroke. He's at Cedars."

Nigel Wickland did not speak for several seconds and then said, "All right, that doesn't change anything."

Raleigh said, "Doesn't change anything? What if she decides to come home? He's an old man in poor health. He might die at any time."

"She doesn't care about him any more than she cared about his brother," Nigel said. "Tell her it's a stroke but downplay it. Let her know that you think he'll be fine and that they should continue with their long holiday and you'll let them know if something untoward happens."

Untoward, Raleigh thought. The supercilious asshole always had to use his boarding school vocabulary. "What if they still decide to come home right away?"

"They won't, I promise you," Nigel said. "She'll be happy if the old bastard dies. So calm yourself."

"I'll talk to you later," Raleigh said.

"You'll see me later," Nigel said. "Nothing has changed."

When Raleigh finished the call, his bowels began rumbling again and he ran to the bathroom.

An hour later, after more dithering, Raleigh called Tuscany and got Leona's voice mail. He said, "Mrs. Brueger, it's Raleigh Dibble. Please call me as soon as you get this message."

At 12:30 P.M., thirty minutes before Nigel Wickland was due to arrive at the Brueger house, Raleigh was stunned to hear a vehicle in the driveway. He ran to the main door, opened it, and saw the gardener's truck parked on the faux-cobblestone driveway. The electric gate was wide open as was always the case when the crew was there tending to all greenery on the outside as well as the inside of the garden walls.

Raleigh ran out and said to the first worker he saw, "What're you doing here today?"

The Mexican shrugged and said, "No Eeng-lish."

In utter frustration, Raleigh dashed around the property, looking for the boss, a burro of a man named Angel.

When he found him he said, "Angel, what're you doing here today?"

"Mee-sus say to come today to reseed all the grass," the gardener said. He took a pocket calendar from his back pocket and showed Raleigh that the date had been circled.

"Oh, shit!" Raleigh said. "Can't you do it some other day?"

The gardener looked at his crew of five men, who were already pruning and trimming as well as scalping the lawn, and he said, "No, sir. Sorry. Thees ees the day I can be here."

Raleigh said, "Okay, please try to hurry."

He went out to the street, looking at his watch. He didn't see the van from Wickland Gallery yet, so he hurried back to the house, picked up his cell phone, and dialed Nigel's cell number.

He got voice mail and felt like throwing the goddamn phone through the window. He ran back out to the street and trotted fifty yards down the winding road until he had to stop to catch his breath. He was standing there panting when he saw the cargo van make the turn in the road and climb the street toward him.

Raleigh stepped into the middle of the road and waved his arms. The van came to a sudden stop and Nigel Wickland said, "What the hell are you doing?"

"The gardeners are here!" Raleigh said. "There're Mexicans all over the place. I couldn't stop them."

"You said the gardeners came on another day. Not today," Nigel said.

"I know, but this is something special that Mrs. Brueger set up. She didn't tell me about it. It's not my fault."

"Not his fault," Nigel said, looking away.

Raleigh said, "First Mr. Brueger has a stroke, and now this. Maybe fate's trying to tell us something."

"Don't you lose your nerve!" Nigel said. "I've planned this and spent a lot of money, and worked on this without proper sleep or rest. I've got two perfect pictures in this van that are identical to the originals. And we're going through with it, Raleigh."

"With the gardeners here?"

"How long will they be here?"

"I don't know. Usually only a few hours, but this is a special job."

"Shit!" Nigel said. "Did you phone Leona about her brother-in-law's stroke?"

"Yes, but I only got her voice mail. I left a message for her to call me."

"Christ!" Nigel said. "Call me the minute you find out when the gardeners are leaving."

"I will," Raleigh said. "If you'll turn on your cell phone."

Nigel reached into his pocket and took out his cell phone, looked at it, and said, "Right."

Then he pulled into a neighbor's driveway, turned around, and drove back down toward the flatland.

Raleigh was surprised at how much satisfaction he'd gotten in demonstrating to Nigel Wickland that his cell had been turned off and he wasn't so fucking perfect. He hurried back to the house, but the way the lawns were being scalped, it didn't look like this would be a quick job. When he got inside the house, he checked the answering machine. He distinctly remembered giving Leona Brueger his cell number as well. He wondered if she'd lost it. He turned on the TV just for the noise it made.

That lovely day in early autumn was the longest day in the life of Raleigh Dibble. Leona Brueger never called. At 4:50 P.M., the gardeners finished their work and Raleigh notified Nigel Wickland that they were gone. Then he went into the bathroom and threw up.

Nigel Wickland rang the gate bell at 5:30 P.M., and Raleigh buzzed him into the Brueger compound. Raleigh walked outside and watched Nigel turn his cargo van all the way around and park it facing the gate.

When Nigel got out of the van, Raleigh said to him, "What's the three-sixty for? A quick getaway?"

Nigel ignored that and said, "Help me with the material."

He was wearing white coveralls with "Wickland Gallery" embroidered over a breast pocket. He opened the side door and put his ring of keys on the van roof temporarily, in order to free up both hands. He picked up his toolbox and handed it to Raleigh. Then he removed the two photographs on poster board, each individually wrapped in a furniture mover's blanket. He leaned them carefully against the garage door and went back to the van for a floodlight and a light stand.

"What's that for?" Raleigh asked.

"I want good lighting in that dark corridor when I do the switch," Niegel said. Then he handed the floodlight and light stand to Raleigh and said, "Take all of this inside. I'll carry the pictures."

While Raleigh was walking into the house, Nigel closed the door of the van and picked up the photo reproductions.

After they carried everything across the Mexican-tile floor in the foyer, Nigel rested the blanket-covered pictures against a wall and said, "I could use a cold drink. Get me a Perrier, will you?"

With an edge to his voice, Raleigh said, "You'll settle for another brand if I can't find Perrier, won't you?"

"Yes, yes," Nigel said with a dismissive toss of his head. "Any mineral water will do."

"Does it have to be carbonated?"

"For heaven's sake, Raleigh, no! It need not be carbonated."

Raleigh left Nigel to his work and walked into the butler's pantry, muttering. He scooped a few little cubes from the ice maker into a tumbler and filled it with water from the faucet.

When he came back, Nigel was adjusting the floodlight, and he took the glass, drank half of it, and said, "Thanks. I was thirsty."

Raleigh said, "That's Vichy Catalan mineral water. I hope it's okay."

"Yes, perfect," Nigel said. "Put these on." He removed a pair of latex gloves from the back pocket of his coveralls and gave them to Raleigh. Pulling a second pair onto his own graceful hands, he said, "Now, carefully remove a blanket from one of my pictures and spread the blanket on the tile floor. Be very careful in handling them."

Raleigh obeyed while Nigel got the floodlight shining down onto the mover's blanket that Raleigh had spread. Then Nigel carefully removed *The Woman by the Water* from its place on the wall and, carrying the painting to the blanket, placed it facedown.

"Bring me my toolbox," he said to Raleigh.

Raleigh did as he was told and was putting the toolbox on the floor next to Nigel just as the house phone rang.

"Is that the gate?" Nigel asked.

"No, the gate has a special ring," Raleigh said, and he ran to the kitchen to answer it.

When he picked it up, he heard the grating voice of Rudy Ressler, who said, "Raleigh? This is Mr. Ressler. We got back last night from a couple of days in Rome and were so tired we crashed. I just got up to go to the bathroom and noticed your voice mail. What's up?"

Raleigh said, "Mr. Ressler, I'm sorry to say that Mr. Brueger has had a minor stroke. At least I think it's minor. He's in Cedars-Sinai. I wanted Mrs. Brueger to know right away."

The line was quiet for a moment and then the director said, "Leona's dead to the world. It's three o'clock in the morning here. I'll tell her when we get up. I gotta go back to bed now. This whole scene over here is supposed to be restful, but don't believe it. Every fucking thing that could go wrong with this villa has gone wrong. I'll call you when we get outta bed."

"Okay, Mr. Ressler," Raleigh said. "When you tell Mrs. Brueger about it, please say that there's no cause for alarm. I'm sure he'll be fine. He's a tough old man."

"Yeah, okay, Raleigh," the director said. "I'll call you in a few hours."

Raleigh hung up and returned to the foyer, where Nigel Wickland had *The Woman by the Water* removed from the frame and leaning against the wall under the light stand.

"That was Rudy Ressler," Raleigh said. "They've been away from the villa for a couple of days. I told him about Mr. Brueger."

Nigel stopped working. "And?"

"He said he'd talk to Mrs. Brueger when they get up in the morning and then get back to me."

"Did you tell him it wasn't serious?" Nigel asked petulantly.

"Yes, I told him," Raleigh said, thinking he'd give a sizable piece of his share of the money just to never see this bastard again or hear his flutey voice.

Next, Nigel took down *Flowers on the Hillside* and carefully placed the framed painting on the mover's blanket. He began painstakingly removing the fasteners from the stretcher bars while Raleigh looked at his watch. That exercise took nearly fifteen minutes. This wasn't supposed to be such a lengthy ordeal.

When Nigel was finished, he gingerly lifted the smaller painting from the frame, brushed some dust and wood residue from the edges of the canvas, and leaned it against the wall by the larger painting.

"That's a million dollars resting against the wall, Raleigh," Nigel said.

Raleigh looked at him, at his narrow patrician nose looking as though it wanted to sniff the paintings like a dog. The man was actually leering. His greed had completely overcome any normal fear factor. And that made Raleigh Dibble even more frightened of this entire goddamn scheme.

Megan Burke was feeling better now that the watsons had kicked in. At least the pain in her knees and other joints had diminished. They had almost attempted entry at five separate houses, but each time something had happened. At one of them, the Hispanic housekeeper answered the door after they were positive that nobody was at home, just as Jonas was ready to attempt entry through a window. At another one, a newspaper in the driveway convinced Jonas that the residents were at work, but then a yappy dog ran out, and Jonas dashed back to their car and said, "Fucking dogs! I wish all the goddamn bucket heads in this town would eat them like they do in their fucked-up countries. You don't see dogs running all over the yards in China, I bet."

Something happened to frustrate Jonas at every residence that looked likely. Megan was afraid the pain would return and she was thirsty and tired. She'd always liked the sky over Hollywood at twilight, and there was a beautiful sky up there now, with red and gold and violet splashing across the heavens as the sun was sinking into the Pacific Ocean. Back when she felt healthy and hopeful, she'd had a fantasy of trying to paint the twilight sky over Hollywood. That seemed like a lifetime ago, back when she felt healthy and hopeful.

Jonas parked for a moment off Woodrow Wilson Drive near Mulholland and said, "Let's cruise a little ways down and have a look at that big place again."

"What big place?" Megan asked.

"The Spanish-style place with the wall around it and the big house with a guesthouse? That one. Remember we peeked through the trees at it?"

"We've looked at so many, I don't remember," Megan said.

"All you gotta do is trust me," Jonas said. "I got a memory like a rhinoceros."

"A rhinoceros," she muttered. "Oh, god!"

★ ★ EIGHTEEN ★

THE MIDWATCH ROLL call was a bit subdued at first. It was always that way after an officer had been hurt. Although Snuffy Salcedo had not been seriously injured, he had gone through surgery that morning at the hands of a plastic surgeon who came recommended by the specialists at Cedars-Sinai Medical Center. Hollywood Nate Weiss, who had not gotten much sleep after the incident at Goth House and the interrogation by Force Investigation Division, talked to Snuffy on the phone before coming to work. Snuffy had taken full responsibility for the "unintentional" baton blow to the face of the colossus as well as all other "unintentional" head strikes. And because baton head strikes generated nearly as much paperwork as officer-involved shootings in the closely monitored LAPD, he was officially removed from the field until FID was satisfied and a shrink from BSS as well as the bureau chief gave the okay for his return. And that was just fine with Snuffy, who needed time off to recuperate. He told Nate that his injuries made him look like a raccoon that got mauled by a grizzly.

It had always been a matter of pride in a warrior culture to quickly return to duty after a battle, but Jetsam had to take a few sick days. He had been stricken with a muscle spasm in his neck that began when he was being questioned by FID and got worse after he went home to his apartment and tumbled into bed. When he woke up at 2 P.M. the next afternoon, he could not turn his head without great pain and had to see a doctor.

The remaining combatants sitting at roll call, Hollywood Nate and Flotsam, had suffered hematomas, contusions, abrasions, with even a couple of lacerations—the whole ball of bash—and their movements were slow and painful, but each cop was serviceable. Oddly enough, the only one with a genuine black eye was Britney Small, who sat next to Della Ravelle at roll call wearing a black eye patch for laughs, but she took it off when all the cops begged to see her shiner and wanted cell phone photos.

Sergeant Murillo had to change the lineup and team Hollywood Nate with Flotsam in 6-X-32, since they were both missing a partner, and before dismissing roll call, he said to them, "If any citizens ask why you both have bumps and bruises, explain that they came from fighting a bad guy. We have enough of a PR problem around here without people thinking we're lumping up each other nowadays."

As all the troops touched the photo of the Oracle before leaving the roll call room, Hollywood Nate Weiss wondered if maybe Snuffy Salcedo had failed to touch the picture yesterday. He couldn't remember seeing him do it.

Twenty-five minutes after roll call ended and the midwatch was on the streets, Jonas Claymore, accompanied by Megan Burke, made a rolling stop on his way to a last pass up into the Hollywood Hills before darkness. So far, it had been another fruitless search for a residence to burgle. Jonas heard the toot of a horn behind him and looked in the mirror to see a black-and-white with lights oscillating.

Georgie Adams was driving, with Viv Daley riding shotgun in 6-X-76, and they had just responded to a call far from their beat. They were up north in 6-A-15's area and complaining about it when they spotted the VW bug roll through the stop sign. They pulled over the old Volkswagen on Mulholland Drive.

"You're up," Georgie said, and Viv grabbed her citation book.

Jonas said to Megan, "Can anything more happen to me this fucking month?"

Megan was trying to massage her knees and said, "Jonas, I'm in pain. We've got to at least get some norcos or perks."

Viv approached on the driver's side and said, "Your license and registration, sir."

Jonas took the registration from the glove box and handed it to Viv along with his driver's license, saying, "Look, Officer, I'm outta work and we're hurrying to a job opportunity in the Hills. Some rich people need a handyman around the house. See, we got a sick five-month-old baby at home and this job is important. Can't you give us a break?"

"Is this lady your wife?" Viv asked.

"Yeah, my wife," Jonas said, but amended it. "Well, we're not officially married, but now that our baby's here, we're gonna take care of that."

Jonas Claymore could not have known that he had exactly the right officer from Hollywood Station at this time to be telling about an infant in need, and Viv Daley said to Megan, "Who's taking care of your sick baby?"

Megan Burke's pain threshold had been reached, and she turned her welling eyes to the cop and said, "My...my mom!" And the tears spilled down her face.

"Okay," Viv said, handing Jonas Claymore's license and registration back to him. "Make complete stops. You don't want your baby growing up an orphan."

"God bless you, Officer," Jonas said.

When Viv and Georgie got back in the car, he said, "They looked like tweakers."

"Gypsy, you're a cynic," Viv said.

"Didn't they look like dopers to you?"

"They certainly did," she said.

"So why'd you kick them?"

"I thought maybe they were telling the truth about a sick baby at home."

Georgie Adams didn't say any more about it. They didn't talk about infants in need.

After Jonas started driving again, he said, "That was fucking fantastic the way you turned on the water! You even had me believing it."

"I wasn't acting, Jonas," Megan said. "I'm hurting."

"You gotta man-up," Jonas said. "We got work to do."

"I can't," Megan said. "I feel like I'm dying."

He looked at her closely then and pulled to the side of the road. He said, "As soon as we get a stake, you're going to rehab. Here, get your watsons on." And he reached in the pocket of his jeans and took out two Vicodins that he'd been keeping for an emergency. She snatched them from his hand, popped them in her mouth, and chewed them up.

Nigel had the poster-board photograph of *The Woman by the Water* nailed snugly in place, and it fit even more perfectly than he had hoped. He lifted the baroque frame under the floodlight and said, "I am a genius!"

"I'll try to always remember that," Raleigh said.

Nigel carefully hung the frame with the poster-board impostor in it, stood back, adjusted it on its hanger, stood back again, and said, "Could you tell the difference between this and the original under normal lighting? That is, if you were someone who seldom studied this piece or any of the other art that you own? Simply put, if you were silly Leona Brueger or her idiot boyfriend?"

"I have to say, you did a great job," Raleigh said grudgingly.

"Okay, now we do the second one and we're finished," Nigel said. "Could you get me another glass of that refreshing Vichy water?"

Nigel carefully covered *The Woman by the Water* canvas with the mover's blanket and tore off strips of masking tape to secure the corners of the folds while Raleigh refilled Nigel's glass with tap water and a few ice cubes.

When Raleigh brought the water back, he didn't see that Nigel had moved one of the paintings. *Flowers on the Hillside* was leaning against the opposite wall, and when Raleigh stepped around the light stand, he accidentally kicked it and it fell over.

"Goddamnit!" Nigel screamed. "You clumsy fool!"

"I'm sorry," Raleigh said. "I didn't see it. You moved it."

"Bugger all!" Nigel said, as he ran to the painting and picked it up, examining it under the floodlight.

"It fell on the back of the canvas," Raleigh said. "I didn't hurt it."

Nigel took deep breaths to calm himself and said, "All right." Then he took the water tumbler from Raleigh and drank.

When he put the tumbler down, he said, "We're bundling this piece now before you destroy it. Help me."

Raleigh spread the mover's blankets on the tile floor, and each painting was wrapped separately in a blanket and secured with duct tape.

When they were finished, Raleigh said, "I'm getting these paintings into your van before something else happens to make you have a fucking stroke like Marty Brueger."

Nigel saw that Raleigh's waning diffidence had morphed into mounting anger, and he was about to say, "No, I'll do it," but instead he said, "Okay, I'm sorry I blew up. Yes, take them to my van, but be as careful as you have ever been in your life. Lay them down on the floor of the van, near the rear door. I'll secure them in place when we finish here."

Raleigh picked up the blanketed bundles and started for the door, when Nigel said, "Wait a minute. You'll need the keys." He felt his pocket and said, "I must've left them in the van." Then he began to fit the poster-board photograph of *Flowers on the Hill-side* into the smaller gilded frame, having to make more adjustments before getting it shimmed snugly into place.

When Raleigh got outside, carrying a bundle under each arm, there was not much left of twilight. Darkness was falling fast on the Hollywood Hills. He had to lean both bundles against the front fender of the van in order to open the door. After he got it open, he picked up each bundle separately and crawled into the van twice, placing each painting on the floor, neither bundle touching the other.

When he was finished, he closed the van door and heard the phone ring. He thought, Mrs. Brueger!

Raleigh ran into the house, raced across the foyer to the wall phone, picked it up, and said "Hello?"

A voice said, "Hi. My name is Amber. May I please speak to the lady of the house?"

Raleigh said, "She's on the floor right now," and hung up. He looked at his watch and saw that it would be almost dawn in Tuscany. His nerves. His goddamn nerves were shredded.

There wasn't enough daylight left for Jonas Claymore to see clearly from his vantage point, peeking over the wall between two junipers. Jonas whispered to Megan, "What's up with that? Did you check out how careful he put that stuff in the van?"

Megan could make out the lettering on the side of the van and whispered, "Wickland Gallery. It's gotta be art or something."

Jonas said, "Whatever it is, it's gonna belong to us in about two minutes."

"You're going down there?" she said.

"Yeah, go start the engine. When I come over the wall be ready to move."

"They looked like pretty big things he was carrying," she said. "Whatever it was might not fit in the VW."

"We'll make it fit," he said, and in a few seconds he had squeezed between the junipers and pulled himself up and over the wall.

Jonas scrambled down the little hill that was planted with ivy to hold the soil. In a moment he was creeping along the cobbled driveway. When he got to the side of the cargo van, he grabbed the handle, opening the door as quietly as he could. He peered inside, and even in the darkening shadows he could see that Megan was right. The two bundles were too large to fit in the VW. He crawled inside and lifted one and saw that it was not heavy. He guessed that they were paintings. He thought that in a house like this they must be valuable. Maybe worth five grand, maybe even more. But they were too big to transport in the VW bug.

He was feeling frustration overload and crawled out of the van quietly, ready to scurry back to safety. But while standing outside the van, the tall young man saw that just above eye level on the roof of the van was a ring of keys, where Nigel had put them. He closed the van door quietly and grabbed them, easily locating the ignition key.

Inside the Brueger house Nigel Wickland was so overjoyed, he was actually whistling softly, and he just about had the smaller Impressionist painting shimmed into place inside the gilded frame.

Nigel said, "Raleigh, hand me that small screwdriver from my toolbox. The one under the—"

"Shut up!" Raleigh said. "What's that?"

"What's what?" Nigel asked.

"It's a car engine," Raleigh said. "It's your van!"

Raleigh bolted for the front door and switched on the driveway lights in time to see the cargo van stopped momentarily at the security gate until the electronic beam caused the gate to swing open wide.

"Hey!" Raleigh screamed. "Hey!" And he began running after the van, which sped through the gate and headed down the hill, followed by an old Volkswagen bug.

"Hey," Raleigh said weakly as the gate closed with him inside.

Raleigh stood there staring at the left taillight of the VW bug, the right one having burned out. The little car chugged down toward the flatland, growing smaller, its one eye winking at Raleigh Dibble as it descended in the darkness.

Megan Burke had an epiphany as she followed her partner down from the Hollywood Hills after his shocking theft of the van. She thought of how she had told Jonas, "There are some things I won't do." But she was doing them. First the old woman's TV and now this van. And she thought, I am a thief. I have become a common thief. My life is in ruins. Hollywood is killing me.

Nigel Wickland was standing in the foyer, looking forlorn and helpless, when Raleigh jogged back into the house.

Raleigh said to him, "Why did you leave the fucking keys in the van? Goddamn you, why didn't you put them in your pocket?"

Nigel's voice was a rasp when he said, "I told you I had left them in the van, you blockhead. Why didn't you bring them in?"

"The keys were your responsibility, not mine, you fop," Raleigh said. "Now what do we do? Now what?"

Nigel turned his back on Raleigh and walked back to the unfinished job. He stood under the floodlight, tall and gaunt, his white hair sparkling beneath the glow. Nigel Wickland had a dizzying moment when he felt like a doomed protagonist in a Shakespearean tragedy. And like Lear he screamed.

Raleigh's shock and terror were pushing him into a kind of somnambulate state, but Nigel Wickland's primal scream jolted him out of it. Raleigh froze in place, standing in the foyer watching Nigel Wickland collapse into himself and drop onto the floor on his knees. Then the gallery owner started to weep, and he reached for his inhaler and took two puffs, inhaling deeply and holding his breath until he had to exhale and weep some more.

Raleigh tiptoed past him to the butler's pantry for a fresh

tumbler. He threw in some ice cubes and filled it under the tap. When he returned to the foyer, he put it down beside his crime partner and said, "More Vichy water?"

Nigel wiped his eyes on the sleeve of his coveralls and said, "We're finished, Raleigh. I think I shall shoot myself before going to the penitentiary. I'm too old for prison."

For the first time the roles were reversed and Raleigh Dibble felt that it was up to him to salvage something from this catastrophe. But what?

He said, "Shouldn't we call the police? The cops may get lucky and catch them before they get too far away."

Nigel stopped weeping entirely and let out a scary laugh, shook his head, and said, "You are really the most benighted human being I have ever met."

"It's not too late," Raleigh said. "The cops might get them."

"It's too late," Nigel croaked. "Too fucking late."

"Nigel!" Raleigh said desperately. "Even if they get the paintings they'll probably just dump the van down on one of the boulevards and the police might get fingerprints or DNA or something, and locate them. And they might get the paintings back. I'm calling the police."

Nigel got to his feet then and said, "If you touch that phone, I swear I will kill you."

"But why not call them, goddamnit?"

"Because, you fucking fool," Nigel said, "the *last* thing we want is for the police to arrest the miserable scum who stole my van!"

Raleigh's mind was racing now as his panic grew. "But they might catch them before they dispose of the pictures and we could get them back and everything could be okay before Mrs. Brueger gets back from Tuscany and—"

Nigel interrupted, saying, "What do you suppose the police would do if they arrested the thieves and recovered the paintings?"

"They'd find out from the crooks where they stole them, and they'd come here and give them back."

"Think," Nigel said, "if that's possible. They would *not* bring them here. They would impound the paintings as evidence. They would need the owner of the paintings to testify in court that they were taken from her home. And the owner of the stolen van, who happens to be your partner, would also have to testify how and where the vehicle was stolen." His voice rose when he said, "So you see, Raleigh, it would all unravel like a filthy fucking ball of yarn that a terrier has dragged through a kennel full of dog shit!"

"You can still report the van as stolen," Raleigh said, his mouth dusty dry, "if you say it was stolen from your gallery or someplace other than here."

Nigel looked toward the garish floodlight, then at the poster-board counterfeit hanging on the wall, and then closed his eyes and said, "I've partnered with a madman. He is insane." Nigel opened his eyes and said, "For the reason just explained in the Queen's English, I cannot risk that the police might get lucky and arrest somebody. Because as soon as they make the vile cretin confess, it would all come right here to this house, where Leona Brueger would ask the police how it was that my van was stolen from her driveway on this lovely night. And then the cock-up would be plain even to the stupidest policeman. Even to Leona herself."

"What will you say if the van turns up somewhere? Maybe it'll be parked in a red zone and get impounded."

"Then I shall be notified and will pay the impound fee and pick it up, saying that I lent it to my wayward nephew and look what he did with it. The best thing that could happen now is if the thieves get in a fiery crash and kill themselves and burn the goddamn paintings to ashes." That made Nigel's eyes well, and Raleigh thought he might start bawling again.

"And what's going to happen to us if the thieves take the

paintings to an art dealer here in town? Maybe to an auction house and try to sell them?"

"I believe that their provenance would be discovered soon enough," Nigel said, looking like a man on a gallows. "And the police would be called in without hesitation, and whether or not they caught the thieves, they would end up here at this house, and through Leona Brueger the police would quickly discover the switch. In which case I might decide to test the aging ammunition in my pistol. I'm too old for prison."

Raleigh sat trancelike while Nigel completed mounting the poster board into the frame belonging to *Flowers on the Hillside*. After that, he placed the framed poster board on the original hanger and said, "The work is finished and perhaps so are we."

"I'm getting sick," Raleigh said, and ran to the powder room off the foyer. When he returned, he was pale and beads of sweat had popped out on his upper lip and forehead. He wiped his mouth with a hand towel bearing the Brueger monogram.

He said, "Nigel, I'm desperate. I have one last idea. Please hear me out."

Nigel was putting his tools away and folding the light stand and didn't stop working when he said, "Go ahead. Impress me with your acuity."

Raleigh said, "What if we take the framed poster-board pictures and get rid of them? Burn them up somewhere or break them into pieces and drop them in a Dumpster. And I drive you home and come back here and call the police and say that home-invading robbers got in through an unlocked side door and put a gun on me and stole the pictures."

"Oh, that is brilliant!" Nigel said. "I'm sure they would believe a fucking domestic servant who has only been employed here for a matter of weeks. And who happens to have a prison record. Oh, yes, and I wonder what you would say when they asked you to submit to a lie detector? And in the hopefully unlikely event that they catch the thieves, it would make it ever so much easier to figure out what was going on here, especially after they were able to place my van at the crime scene. Oh, there would be such a jolly time at the station house when they brought you in handcuffed. Do you know what the joke would be for weeks to come?"

Raleigh sat down on a carved antique chair with a needlepoint cushion, his chin hanging almost to his chest, and said, "Tell me the joke. I'm dying to laugh."

Nigel said, "The joke would be, the butler really did it."

Raleigh's head was still spinning when he drove Nigel in the Brueger Mercedes to his Beverly Hills gallery, where his car was parked. Neither spoke for the first twenty minutes. Then Raleigh said, "If the paintings never surface, things can proceed as originally planned, right? You'll help Mrs. Brueger pack and ship all the art to her storage facility just as you said?"

After a moment Nigel said, "Yes. Just as I planned. Except that I've spent a few thousand at the photo lab and I've lost a van, at least for now. And I believe that I've lost several years from my life as a result of this disaster. But if that should happen, I would be so happy that I'd throw a party and invite everyone I know. Except you."

Raleigh continued his train of thought and said, "So a long time from now, if the switch is discovered when the art is taken from the storage facility, it'll be blamed on one of the transporters or a storage yard employee, right?"

Nigel sighed and said, "From your lips to God's ear."

"A part of me would feel okay if that happened," Raleigh admitted. "Maybe we dodged a bullet. I could just go back to being what I am and you can go back to being—"

"Bankrupt," Nigel said.

"Whatever," Raleigh said. "At least we won't be in prison if those crooks never get caught."

"Raleigh," Nigel said suddenly, and this time his tone had

softened. He sounded almost conciliatory. "If anything untoward should happen..."

There it was again, Raleigh thought. *Untoward.*

"Yes?"

If something did go wrong sometime down the road...that is, if something came back on you, would you really bring me into it? I mean, haven't I suffered enough?"

Raleigh turned to gape at Nigel and almost rear-ended the car in front of him at the stoplight. He said, "Haven't *you* suffered enough?"

"Raleigh, there'd be nothing to gain by informing on me," Nigel said. "What could you really profit from saying that you had a crime partner? I could take a second mortgage on my condominium and sell my business if I had to do it. I could put half of everything I realize from the sale into a trust account for you. I'd do it, gladly."

"You really are a piece of work, Nigel," Raleigh said. "Please forgive my clichés, but you are a piece of fucking work."

"So you'd bargain with my freedom just to curry favor with a prosecutor and have maybe a year or two lopped from your sentence, is that it?"

Raleigh said, "I'd trade your ass to have two months cut from my sentence. Or two weeks. I'd do it for no sentence reduction at all, just to see how you handle your inferiors in the prison yard, you pompous flouncing popinjay!"

There was no more said until Raleigh parked behind Nigel's gallery, where they unloaded the light stand, floodlight, and toolbox.

Nigel Wickland said, "I don't suppose we shall need to see each other after tonight."

"Not in this life," Raleigh Dibble replied, and headed for the Hollywood Hills.

* * *

There was just enough room to park the Volkswagen on Jonas and Megan's street, so Jonas had to double-park the van beside the car of a tenant who seldom went anywhere at night. They were excited when they got the bundles inside and removed the tape and the mover's blankets.

Jonas picked up the largest canvas and placed it on the back of the sofa, leaning it against the wall, and then he stepped back to appraise it.

"It's what you call an Expressionist picture," he finally said to Megan.

"Oh, really?"

"Yeah, it's a picture where the expression on the person's face tells you what the artist had in mind."

Megan said, "You can hardly see the woman's expression if that's what you're looking for."

"That's the way Expressionists paint," Jonas said. "You have to look through the fuzzy brushwork and guess what she's thinking."

"Do you think it's really worth five thousand?" she asked doubtfully.

"Just look where it came from. The crib up there in the Holly-wood Hills is worth gazillions."

"Where will we sell it?"

"I don't know. Not at a swap meet, that's for sure. We gotta do some research."

"How about the other one?"

"Not as much," Jonas said. "It's smaller, and flowers are over-done these days. All the swap meets have lotsa framed pictures of flowers. But we might get a few Franklins for it."

"Do you think you'd better get rid of the van? The cops proba-bly have a report on it by now."

"Yeah," Jonas said. "I'm gonna dump it over on Normandie after I wipe off all my fingerprints. Gimme a dish towel, will ya?"

When they got out to the street, Jonas was barely seated in the van when 6-X-32 pulled up behind him with red and blue lights on and gave a short toot on the horn. Megan, who was about to get into the VW bug, saw them and headed back to the apartment, having to force herself to walk slowly.

Hollywood Nate approached on the driver's side of the van and Flotsam on the passenger side, shining his streamlight in on Jonas's hands. Nate said, "License and registration, please."

"Sure, Officer," Jonas said, his chin quivering. "What did I do wrong?"

"Do I have to tell you it's illegal to double-park like this?" Nate said.

Jonas was so relieved, he felt like crying, and said, "I'm sorry, Officer. I had to make a delivery for my boss. I been working all day and this is the last stop. I'm sorry. Please don't write me a ticket."

Jonas tried hard to keep his hand from trembling when he offered the driver's license to Hollywood Nate, hoping that the registration was in the glove box. Nate didn't even bother to take the license from him. He looked at the side of the van and said, "Wickland Gallery. This doesn't look like a gallery neighborhood."

"We sell good art and crappy art, Officer," Jonas said. "Real affordable stuff. You and the missus should stop by sometime if you're thinking about—"

"Crappy art," Nate said. "I'll keep that in mind if I ever have another missus and need anything crappier than I've got now."

With that, Nate turned and walked back to the radio car. When they were cruising again, Flotsam said, "Why didn't you write that one? Double-parker, dude. One for the recap."

Nate said, "This recession's been tough on working stiffs like that kid. Besides, all my bones hurt. I just wanna sit in our shop tonight and think of ways I can burn the fucking Goth House to the ground."

"That reminds me," Flotsam said, taking out his cell phone to check on Jetsam for the second time.

When the black-and-white pulled away, Megan ran to the Volkswagen and headed toward Normandie Avenue. She drove south for a few blocks until she saw the Wickland Gallery van just past Melrose in front of a liquor store. Jonas was already out and walking northbound when she picked him up.

"I was so scared, Jonas!" she said. "I thought they had a report on the van and you were busted."

"I'm starting to think I can talk my way outta anything," he said. "He didn't even look at my license, so I can't be connected to the van even if they pick it up. Two cops in one day have tried to hack me and I'm still here. This might be, like, kiss-met."

"What?"

"It means that destiny is calling. Something big is in my future. You're lucky you hooked your wagon to a star!"

"I only hope I didn't hook my wagon to a wagon," Megan said. "A beat-up old Volkswagen that might end up driving us both straight to jail."

NINETEEN

RALEIGH MANAGED TO get to sleep as the rising sun was providing the citizens of Hollywood, California, with new hope on the cusp of autumn. Just as he was beginning to dream, the phone rang. He sat up when he heard Rudy Ressler say, "Raleigh, it's Mr. Ressler. How's Marty?"

During all the turmoil at the Brueger estate, Raleigh had hardly thought about the old man, and hadn't even phoned Cedars-Sinai since Marty Brueger was admitted.

"He's fine, Mr. Ressler," Raleigh said. "You and Mrs. Brueger have nothing to worry about. I'll let you know if there's any bad news at all."

"You won't have to," Ressler said. "I've booked a flight. We're coming home."

This time the blast of fear sent blood surging through Raleigh's skull. He jumped out of bed and stood naked and tense. "But Mr. Ressler," he said. "You have several weeks left on your vacation rental. Mr. Brueger is fine. Stay and enjoy yourself."

"To tell you the truth, it's not all that enjoyable," Ressler said. "The villa isn't what it was cracked up to be. The toilets work half the time and the water's never hot enough. This guy Silva who's supposed to be our translator is a greedy little wop who's always in our pockets for something or other. I'm not enjoying it at all and neither is Mrs. Brueger. We're leaving here."

Raleigh caught his breath, swallowed hard, and said, "I see. Do you know when you'll be arriving at LAX?"

"Not yet," the director said. "I'll let you know. We'll expect you to pick us up."

"Of course," Raleigh said. "I'll be in the big Mercedes."

After he hung up, Raleigh Dibble experienced the terror of being utterly out of control. The boiling heat in his head topped a roiling stomach that sent him to the bathroom again.

He phoned Nigel Wickland's cell phone ten minutes later and was not surprised to find his partner awake.

"It's me," Raleigh said.

Nigel said. "Please don't tell me there's something wrong with the replicas."

"No," Raleigh said. "The Bruegers are leaving Italy and coming home."

Silence on the line and then, "My work will be tested a lot sooner than we thought. All right, what of it? Just don't lose your head. The replicas look perfect. Just behave as you always do and it will be fine."

"You haven't heard anything about your van yet, have you?"

"Of course not."

"If you do hear anything . . . let me know ASAP."

"Why?" Nigel said. "Are you going to reimburse me if the thieves strip it?"

"I'll feel a lot better when you get the van back, that's all," Raleigh said. "So just let me know if it gets impounded for any reason."

Nigel clicked off without responding.

Raleigh wondered if Nigel Wickland was serious when he talked about shooting himself if the thieves got caught. If that happened, suicide didn't seem to Raleigh like such a bad idea.

*   *   *

Jonas Claymore and Megan Burke had decided to spend every last dollar she'd wheedled from her mother and buy enough ox to chase the dragon all weekend. This because they would have a windfall as soon as they figured out the best way to approach art dealers with the paintings. It was when he felt euphoric that Jonas got his latest idea.

He tried to roust Megan out of her stupor and was only half successful. He said, "Baby, I got it."

"Got what?" she mumbled.

"It's too fucking risky to be messing with art dealers or auction houses. What I think we should do is make them pay us ransom!"

"Ransom?" she said drowsily.

"Yeah," he said. "We call the Wickland Gallery on Monday morning and we talk to the boss there and we say we know how they fucked up the other night and got their paintings swiped, but we'd like to help get them back. Shit, I could even tell him where to pick up his van as an act of good faith. You on this?"

"Uh-huh," she muttered.

"Then get your head in it. All we gotta do is negotiate the price and tell them if they go to the police, we slash the paintings to pieces. Then we set up a money drop. I seen this done a million times in the movies, so I know all the tricks."

"Tricks?" she said.

"What's the use?" he said. "You're all spun out. I could get more companionship from a hamster."

Jetsam's neck spasm was not responding to muscle-relaxing drugs and he was advised by his doctor to take a few days off and rest at home. When he phoned Flotsam and told him about it, his partner said, "Do what the croakers tell you, dude. There's some good surfing coming down and you don't wanna miss it. So take it easy and rest up."

When Jetsam found out that Flotsam was partnered with Nate, he said, "Bro, I'm glad you got teamed with Hollywood Nate. He is like, so hormonally ingenious and cinematically dialed-in, he might put you onto some scintillating starlets from his movie ventures."

"He ain't done it yet, dude," Flotsam said. "But if he does, I'll save them for when my li'l pard comes back. I won't use them all up without you."

Hollywood Nate was glad that Snufffy Salcedo was still recuperating, because roll call that night would have driven him mad. The watch commander was conducting it instead of Sergeant Murillo, and he was droning on about the chief's pet program, the thing he brought with him to the LAPD from the East Coast.

The lieutenant said, "You should pay particular attention to reporting districts six-forty-three and six-forty-four. CompStat indicates unusual four-five-nine activity there. I'd like some explanations as to why these crimes are happening."

Everyone glanced at one another and eyes rolled, and Sergeant Murillo arrived in the nick of time, entering the room and saying, "Lieutenant O'Reilly, call for you from the captain. About the inspection next week."

"Oh, yes," the watch commander said, and went downstairs to take the call.

Sergeant Murillo sat and said, "Let's see, what were we talking about?"

The whole attitude of the troops changed with Sergeant Murillo in charge, and Flotsam said with a smirk, "The super chief's baby, of course. CompStat. You know, like, let's explain why this crime happened, where it happened, how it happened, et cetera. What I'd like to say is, it happened because some dude's been shooting up too much dope and needs money and he kicked down a door to find some. Period. End of story."

"We can't say things like that," Georgie Adams griped. "With

CompStat, nothing is allowed to be random crime. *Random* is not in the CompStat lexicon. Yet, these're just jump-on crimes, Sarge. They happen."

"But we gotta come up with some goofy answer," Hollywood Nate said, echoing what he'd heard so many times from Snuffy Salcedo. "Because Mister brought it from back East, and the mayor thinks it's some kind of special juju, and the media has bought into it, and it's bullshit."

"It's all about putting the cops on the dots," Viv Daley said. "You put a pin map on a PowerPoint and it's supposed to do some kind of magic numbers-crunching."

Della Ravelle said, "It's nothing but pin maps that've been around a hundred years but without the computers back then. CompStat is supposed to figure out trends, but what if, like Georgie says, most of street crime is random? We're expected to invent trends to justify a theory. Mister is a master at stroking City Hall and conning the media."

Viv Daley said, "Back East where Mister comes from, not everybody has a car, so crimes can come in clusters in a small area, and cops can maybe look for trends there. But L.A. is a city on wheels. Everybody has at least one car. Everybody's in motion. One bad guy can scatter his offenses like cold germs all over the map. Where's the trend?"

Hollywood Nate said, "I'm gonna create a two-sentence book called *CompStat for Dummies*. The book will say, 'It's a computerized pin map, stupid. Now just go in there and do your Kabuki dance for the chief.' Think it'll sell down at PAB?"

It all stopped when Lieutenant O'Reilly came back into the roll call room and said to Sergeant Murillo, "Did you discuss CompStat and its importance?"

"Absolutely," Sergeant Murillo said. "And everybody here is onboard a hundred percent. It's the best thing that's happened to the LAPD since Kevlar vests and semiautomatics."

Lieutenant O'Reilly looked for irony in his sergeant's expression but nodded and said, "Fine. Let's go to work."

The moment 6-X-32 drove out of the parking lot and cleared, Hollywood Nate got a cell call. He didn't recognize the number but answered, and Leona Brueger said, "Hi, gorgeous."

"Mrs. Brueger!" Nate said. "Are you home?"

"Leona, remember?" she said. "And no, I'm not. It's the middle of the night here and I couldn't sleep and started thinking of you."

"That's . . . that's flattering," Nate said.

"I had too much champagne at dinner," Leona Brueger said. "It always wrecks my sleep. How about talking sexy to me until I get drowsy?"

Nate said, "I'm, uh, just leaving Hollywood Station with my partner beside me, preparing to crush crime and terrify lawbreakers. I don't see how I can do that."

"Bad timing," she said. "The story of my life."

"Maybe you'll invite me to a dinner party when you get back," Nate said. "With some of the industry people?"

"You actors," she said. "One-track minds. Okay, I'll let you guardians of law and order do your thing, but how about checking on my house? Rudy told me that our butler sounded a bit stressed the last time he called. Just make sure everything's okay."

"Absolutely," Nate said. "I'll stop by this evening. See you when you get back."

"You'll be seeing me sooner than you think," she said. "Bye-bye, gorgeous."

Nate closed his cell and said to Flotsam, "I need to make a quick stop up in the Hills."

That piqued Flotsam's interest. "Yeah?" he said with a leer. "You got some smokin' hot Hills honey up there? Maybe a stupendous starlet from one of your SAG jobs? How about an introduction? My li'l pard and me, we'll take your leftovers."

"Not exactly that," Nate said. "I met a director who's asked me to check on the house of his girlfriend. They're off in Italy for a couple of months. I've been meaning to stop but I haven't had time."

"What's the girlfriend look like?"

"Old enough to be your mother and mine," Nate said. "But she's still pretty hot."

"The miracles of modern medicine," Flotsam said. "My partner met a chick a year or so ago that was rebuilt from spare parts. T and A, all of it. She looked great, but he said he was scared to touch her for fear something would fall off."

"We'll just take a minute to ring the bell and ask the butler if everything's okay," Nate said. "And I'll leave my card to prove I've been there."

"Is he, like, gonna put you in a movie?"

"That's the idea," Nate said. "I'm thirty-eight years old. My time's running out."

"I'm thirty-five, dude," Flotsam said. "That's the good thing about the surfing life. You can do it till your libido expires and way beyond. There's no sell-by date as long as your knees keep working."

As Nate drove up toward Woodrow Wilson Drive, he said, "Magic hour. This is the best time to shoot movies. The light . . . it's magic up here."

"Dude, when you get to be a star and buy a crib up in the Hills, I'd like to be your part-time houseboy. I know you're gonna have them starstruck Susies all over you, and my partner and me, we could take turns working for table scraps and whatever Bettys you leave still breathing when you're done with your monkey sex."

"I'll try to leave them breathing," Nate said.

"I hear that the homicide teams ain't too fond of the people that live up in the Hills," Flotsam said. "They're, like, way too busy arranging their toothbrushes according to feng shui to talk to coppers. The detectives are, like, 'Well, please give us a call after the kid's yoga, soccer, and lacrosse. It's only serial murder we're look-ing into.' Me, I prefer the people in east Hollywood, who have their kids the old-fashioned way. The brats up here go around saying, 'We're in vitro twins,' or, 'I'm a reversal,' referring to daddy's vasec-tomy turnaround. It's all too weirded for me. But I wouldn't mind one of them trophy bride Hills-honeys who like to get their reli-gion on."

"What's that supposed to mean?"

Flotsam said, "You know, they go, 'Oh my god, oh my god!' when they finally get nailed by someone from their own generation after sleeping so long with semi-erect sugar daddies."

"I'll try to remember all that," Nate said. "When I get to be a star."

Hollywood Nate found the address written on Rudy Ressler's card, stopped at the drive-in gate, and pushed the call button.

Raleigh Dibble's voice said, "Yes? Who is it?"

"Police officers," Hollywood Nate said. "Could you let us in, please?"

Raleigh stood petrified in the billiards room, where he'd been shooting pool to kill time as the hands of the clock on the wall seemed locked in place. And now he was paralyzed by the tele-phone voice. The voice said again, "Hello? Police officers. We need to come in, please."

Raleigh pushed the appropriate phone key, put down the pool cue, and walked into the foyer. He vaguely thought about getting something warm to wear because he knew from experience that a jail cell was a chilling experience, even during an arid day like this, when the Santa Anas were baking the Hollywood Hills.

The black-and-white had already parked in front of the entry arch, and the uniformed officers were getting out by the time Raleigh opened the door, hoping that the handcuffs would not be cinched so tightly this time. He remembered how they'd bruised his wrists when he'd been transported from courtroom to jail.

He thought that it would be detectives who brought him in this time, but then he remembered that detectives might not be working on the weekend, and he would no doubt see them on Monday morning. He decided to tell these uniformed cops that he had no wish to speak to them without a lawyer present, but on Monday he would make a deal with the detectives and spill his guts. The first thing he'd talk about would be the mastermind, Nigel Wickland.

The tall, suntanned cop was looking around at the grounds as though he were a potential buyer. The good-looking one was smiling, and he presented a business card to Raleigh, saying, "I'm Officer Nate Weiss from Hollywood Division. Mr. Ressler asked me to stop by and check on the property. And you are?"

He needed to swallow twice before saying, "Raleigh Dibble. I'm the butler and caretaker here. Mrs. Brueger is away."

"Yes, that's what I was told by Mr. Ressler," Nate said. "I just wanted to introduce myself and tell you that we're keeping an eye on things, and if you need anything from us, call me personally. My cell number is on the back."

Raleigh said with much emotion, "Thank you! Thank you, Officer!"

"Do you know what date they'll be returning?" Nate asked.

"Tomorrow," Raleigh said. "They're coming back tomorrow, I think."

"Really?" Nate said, wondering why Leona Brueger had not mentioned that. The woman was full of secrets and surprises.

Raleigh displayed a lopsided toothy smile that seemed inappropriate to Nate, especially when the butler said, "Mrs. Brueger's brother-in-law had a stroke and they're coming home to take care of him."

"I'm sorry to hear that," Nate said. "Please tell Mrs. Brueger and Mr. Ressler that I stopped by and that we've been keeping an eye on the place since they've been gone. Will you be sure to tell them that?"

"I'll be glad to, Officer," Raleigh said.

When the cops were driving out the gate, Flotsam said, "I was hoping he'd invite us inside. I wanted to take a tour of that crib to see what it's gonna be like when I'm your houseboy."

"He's a peculiar guy," Nate said. "He looked like he just got bad news from an oncologist when we arrived, but at odd moments his smile got beamier than Oprah's ass."

"Who cares? I'll bet the swimming pool's big enough to surf on," Flotsam mused.

"Something's not normal with that guy," Nate went on.

"Dude, you were expecting normal?" Flotsam said. "This is fucking Hollywood."

A short time later they spotted a young man running south on Orange Drive from Hollywood Boulevard, dodging pedestrians, holding something under his shirt. They felt sure he'd snatched a purse from one of the tourists on the Walk of Fame and they closed in on him and caught him two blocks south. They ordered him to put his hands on his head.

He did, and the hidden object fell to the pavement. It was a box containing a pepperoni pizza that he was trying to keep warm until he got back home with his girlfriend to watch *American Idol*.

"See what I mean, dude?" Flotsam said to Hollywood Nate. "It's this geography."

★ TWENTY ★

ON MONDAY MORNING, Jonas was awake early, feeling electric at the prospect of making real money for the first time ever. He felt the old vibration mode as though he'd been doing crystal meth again, which he had not. He believed that his tweaking days were over now that he'd learned the joys of ox. Jonas's hands were shaking noticeably while he was trying to get some orange juice into himself to wash down one of the peanut butter sandwiches that Megan had made for their breakfast.

She swept the little kitchen and made a halfhearted attempt to wipe down the stovetop. But when she opened the refrigerator to give it a wipe, she gave up. There was so much spilled juice and milk and jelly and ice cream on the shelves that she'd have needed a garden hose to clean it.

Megan had even washed a load in the coin-operated washer in the community laundry room that they shared with five other apartments, and she had the clothes in the dryer by the time Jonas finished his sandwich. She was hoping for a word of appreciation.

"Try to dress a little nice for once" was all he said, sneering at her cutoffs and coffee-stained T-shirt.

Even when she was feeling halfway decent he managed to ruin it for her, so she said, "Why? Are we doing lunch at the Bel Air Hotel?"

"Meg," he said, as soberly as possible. "This is gonna be the biggest day of your life. This is way big. You and me gotta look and act . . . professional. In case."

She leaned against the drainboard, one hand on her hip, and said, "In case of what, Jonas?"

"That's the thing!" he said. "I don't know. I'd like to call that house up there if I had the number, but I don't. So we're gonna call the Wickland Gallery and jist—"

"Wing it."

"Right."

Megan said, "Don't think for one minute that I'm going to talk for you on this one. Like when you had me talk to the maid after you got the phone number of that no-name actress whose house we were supposed to burgle. She told me to go fuck myself in Spanish and English both."

Jonas said, "Don't start bitching at me, Megan. Put on something clean and we'll go to the public phones at the cybercafé and make the call. I gotta think of the best way to show the owner that we're serious people he can deal with."

Ruth had opened the Wickland Gallery that morning, which was a bit unusual. Normally, by the time she arrived Nigel Wickland would already have coffee brewing and croissants set out. She was as meticulously groomed as ever and had removed her teal jacket, hanging it in the little closet in Nigel's office.

When he did arrive at 10 A.M., he looked terrible. His eye pouches sagged and his orbs were red-rimmed and watery. His beautiful mane of white hair had been hastily combed, and he was wearing exactly the same shirt, jacket, necktie, and trousers that he'd worn on Friday. That had never happened before in the years she'd worked at Wickland Gallery.

She said, "Good morning, Nigel. Is everything all right? You look a bit . . . tired."

He had a distant look on his face when he said, "I'm knackered, Ruth. I may have to lie down in my office for a bit. I couldn't sleep last night."

"Is anything wrong? Are you sick?"

"Not now, I'm not," he said. "I think the sea bass I ate for dinner had turned. It smelled fishy, and as they say, if it smells like fish don't eat it."

"Where's the van? It's not in the carport."

"Oh, I...I lent it to my nephew, Reginald. Have I ever told you about him?"

"Not that I recall."

"He's a bit one-off, that lad. My sister's boy. Said he needed to move some things from his girlfriend's house, and he promised he'd bring it back by tomorrow."

"I hope we don't need it today," she said.

"The way business has been, that's unlikely," said Nigel Wickland. "Very unlikely."

"I'll bring you some coffee," she said.

Ruth had the coffee poured and had spooned in his sugar and cream when the phone rang. She went to her desk and picked it up.

Jonas had actually come close to paying Megan a compliment when he said, "I ain't seen you in a dress since I met you, Meg. You don't look so bad."

She was wearing a candy-striped baby-doll shirtdress that she'd worn to a dance in high school. Now high school seemed to Megan like half a lifetime ago. Sometimes she felt like checking her driver's license to be sure that she was only twenty years old. The dress came to midthigh and she thought it would look better if she wore heels, but her ankles and knees were hurting too much, so she wore her only pair of flats, on which the soles were worn through. The lip gloss and eyeliner made her feel feminine for a change, and that gave her a bit of a lift.

Jonas was wearing the only sport coat he owned, a green-checked cotton blend. He wore it over a clean black T-shirt with faded jeans and tennis shoes. He seldom shaved his wispy facial hair, hoping in vain to grow it into a real five-day stubble like all the rich young dickheads whose cars he parked, but so far he couldn't produce a manly growth.

When Jonas and Megan arrived at the shopping mall that housed the cybercafé, Jonas said to Megan, "Don't interrupt me when I'm talking to the guy. Just stand there and listen. Remember, this is my game plan and I'm the quarterback."

They chose the public phone that was farthest from the cubicles full of people who rented the computers at all hours seven days a week. Business was brisk on a Monday morning, and the downstairs customer closest to Megan and Jonas was a black man in a tracksuit and very pricey tennis shoes. He was sitting beside a curvaceous blonde with sultry eye shadow, wearing shorts, ankle strap platforms, and an apricot top that came down far enough to just cover her silicone rack but was high enough to display her gleaming navel ring.

Jonas mouthed the words "pimp and whore" to Megan, as if she didn't know. He was so nervous, he dropped one of his quarters and she had to pick it up for him.

When Ruth answered and Jonas asked to speak to the gallery owner, she said, "May I ask the reason for your call? I might be able to help you."

"I gotta speak to the owner of the Wickland Gallery," Jonas said. "It's important."

"I'm sure I can assist you," Ruth said, "if you'll just tell me what it's about."

Jonas said, "My aunt died and I'm inheriting some very valuable paintings. I wanna sell them through your gallery. But I gotta speak to the owner or I won't do business with you."

"Just a moment, please," Ruth said.

Jonas winked at Megan, put his hand over the phone, and said, "Official bitch."

"Officious," she said.

"What?"

"Officious," Megan said.

"What?"

"Never mind."

A mellifluous but weary voice came on the line and said, "This is Nigel Wickland. How may I serve you?"

Jonas said, "I was thinking about how I can serve *you*. I think I may have some property that belongs to you."

The line was quiet and then Jonas heard the sound of a door closing. The gallery owner got back on the line and said urgently, "Who are you?"

Jonas said, "I'm the guy that wants to help you out. Are you missing a van?"

Nigel's heart raced and he said, "Yes, how did you know?"

"Was it stolen?"

"I haven't reported it stolen," Nigel said.

"Bullshit. Don't talk to me like I'm an idiot."

"Yes, it was stolen," Nigel said, changing tack quickly. "And yes, I reported it. Where is it?"

"First we gotta negotiate," Jonas said. "See, I saw the van parked on the street early this morning with some black teenagers inside. I figured they stole it for joyriding. I watched them open the door and start to take out a big wrapped object. I yelled, 'Hey, get outta that truck.' And they ran away. So I looked inside and saw two wrapped objects. And I took them out and I got them at home. I saw the name on the van and called information and here we are."

Nigel massaged his left temple and said, "I see. You're a Samaritan."

"A what?"

"Never mind. I would like to know the location of the van and I would like to get my property back."

"Is there a reward?"

"Yes, I think we can arrange for a reward."

"There's a problem here," Jonas said.

"Yes, I thought there might be," Nigel said, his stomach aflame.

"Who do the items in the van belong to?" Jonas asked.

"Why do you ask?"

"I'm trying to help you, dude," Jonas said. "I'll ask the questions."

"They belong to me," Nigel said.

"Are you sure?" Jonas said. "Because if they belong to somebody else, like one of your customers, then I gotta negotiate a reward with them and not with you, right?"

"Did you unwrap the . . . objects?"

"Yeah, and they look like very expensive art."

"Are they damaged in any way?"

"No. I rescued them from the little niggers jist in time."

Nigel said, "They do not belong to my client. They belong to me personally. I was at a client's home trying to persuade the client to buy the paintings when the van got stolen." Then he added, "No doubt by the black youths that you chased away. So there's no reason for you to deal with anyone but me."

"What did your client say when your van got snatched?" Jonas asked.

"He was as shocked as I was."

"Did you call the cops from your customer's house?"

Nigel paused again and said, "Yes, from there."

"How much were you trying to sell the paintings for?"

Another long hesitation, and Nigel said, "Look, sir, business is rotten during this recession. People do not go out and buy art when they have to tighten their belts. I'm looking at bankruptcy, but if you'll be reasonable, I could offer you a handsome reward for saving my property from the thieves and returning them to me."

Jonas liked being called "sir" but he said, "I'm getting impatient. How much were you trying to sell them for?"

"Eight thousand dollars," Nigel said.

Jonas gave Megan a thumbs-up and said, "And the van must be worth fifteen grand, even though it ain't new. I saved you twenty-four grand."

Nigel was overjoyed now but knew he had to negotiate to keep from arousing the scum's suspicion, so he said, "The eight thousand included my profit. The two paintings are only worth four thousand total."

"You make a hundred percent on your goods?"

"Yes."

"Damn," Jonas said. "I'm in the wrong business. So how about the van?"

"I have it insured, of course. But I should think I couldn't sell it on today's terrible market for more than ten thousand."

"Four thousand and ten thousand," Jonas said. "So a decent reward would be fourteen thousand bucks, right?"

Nigel thought he must not accept quickly, so he said, "Sir, I have a wife and four children. My business is in ruins. And it's your duty as an honest man to return goods that you know are stolen, but I agree that you deserve a reward. For the van and the pictures I would like to offer you a reward of eight thousand dollars."

Jonas said, "Well, I think I should get a reward of twelve thousand."

"Done," Nigel said.

"Done?"

"Yes, I accept," Nigel said. "Now, please, where is my property and where is my van? I'll need the van in order to transport the paintings."

"Is the big one worth more than the smaller one?" Jonas wanted to know.

"A little more."

"I thought so," Jonas said. "It's got better brushwork and the Expressionist artist had a better sense of color and light. So he got her expression jist right."

"You are a connoisseur, sir," Nigel said. "I'm so glad to be dealing with a man of taste and decency."

"One more thing," Jonas said. "I don't want the police to know anything about me and my reward. They might think I was in on this theft."

"I understand."

"Even if they don't think that, they'll say it's my duty as a citizen to return your property and tell you where to find your van. And they might try to screw me outta my reward."

"I wouldn't let that happen," Nigel said. "I'm so very grateful to you."

"Yeah, but the cops might not be," Jonas said. "So I wanna give you your paintings and get my reward in a really private and confidential way."

"I understand."

"That means I'll call you later about where and when we meet. I'll take the money then and tell you where your paintings are."

"I'll have to trust you, is that it?"

"Yeah," Jonas said, "but to show my good faith, I'm gonna tell you where your van is so you'll have a way to transport your art."

"Thank you."

"You got an extra key for it?"

"Yes."

"It's right in front of the Lucky Star liquor store on Normandie, south of Melrose. I'd suggest you pick it up quick because the store owner might call and get it impounded if it sits too long. In fact, there's a parking meter, so you'll probably have a ticket on it."

Nigel gripped the receiver so tightly, his knuckles went white, and he was close to weeping when he said, "I'll go and collect it now, sir. Thank you very much."

"What's your name?" Jonas asked, feeling bold, feeling in control, feeling wonderful!

"Nigel Wickland."

"One thing more, Nigel—" Jonas said.

The call was interrupted by an automated voice, and Jonas had to drop more coins into the coin slot. Then he said, "One more thing. Why did you first try to tell me that you didn't report the stolen van to the cops?"

"Sir," Nigel said. "At first I thought that I was getting a ... ransom call from the person who took my van. It was cynical of me and I'm sorry. I'm only too happy to be dealing with someone like yourself."

"Okay, go get your van. You'll hear from me."

"I shall go now," Nigel said.

"My head's spinning," Jonas said to Megan after he had hung up. "Let's go home and figure things out. Any ox left?"

"A quarter," she said. "Why didn't you ask him for his cell or home number?" Megan said. "Then you wouldn't have to go through a store employee."

Jonas hesitated and then said, "Because my fucking head ain't clear. Let's go smoke that quarter so I can think better."

Nigel opened his office door and said, "Ruth, I need you to give me a ride to east Hollywood. My stupid nephew left my van there all night and I have to pick it up."

Ruth looked up from the inventory list she was checking at her desk and said, "Why in the world would he leave it there?"

"He's a fool," Nigel said. "Thirty-five years old going on fifteen. He's off to Las Vegas with some friends and said he didn't have time to bring it back to me."

Ruth got into her jacket, grabbed her purse, and said, "I hope that's the last time he ever drives it."

"You can depend on that," Nigel said.

Ruth went to fetch her car, and Nigel got the extra van key from his desk. On the drive, he hardly heard Ruth nattering on about the irresponsibility of relatives. When they got to Normandie and Melrose, he thought that the miserable thief had duped him. But then he saw the van half a block south parked in front of a liquor store.

Ruth dropped him off at the van, and Nigel got in and started the engine. He rolled down the window and waved to Ruth. Everything was just as the thief had said it would be. And even though the van was parked in a metered zone, he didn't even have a ticket on it.

Nigel looked at his watch and realized that Leona Brueger probably had not arrived back in L.A. yet, so he drove straight to the Hollywood Hills. He had a few random thoughts about the possibility of pulling this off by himself, but he realized it would be impossible. There were two thieves at least, the one who drove the van and the one who drove the Volkswagen. Nigel needed his moronic crime partner, Raleigh Dibble, and he wanted a conversation face-to-face.

It was astounding to hear Nigel Wickland on the gate phone. Raleigh, still in his pajamas, bathrobe, and slippers, truly thought that he'd seen the last of Nigel. It was infinitely more astounding to look out and see Nigel parking the Wickland Gallery van on the faux-cobblestone driveway.

Raleigh jerked open the door and said, "They caught them?"

Nigel walked right past him into the house and said, "No, they didn't catch them."

"Then how ... what ...?"

"I'm afraid it's come down to a life-or-death situation, Raleigh. It's us or them."

Raleigh and Nigel sat at the kitchen table, and Raleigh listened slack-jawed to the incredible turn of events that resulted in Nigel recovering his cargo van. And when Nigel was finished, he said,

"They've got our paintings. They're blackmailers as well as thieves. Of course, they could testify that I was here in the van, and that you and I had stolen the Brueger paintings before they stole the van. They could put you and me in prison if they wish to. Or I can pay them twelve thousand dollars and hope that the blackmail does not continue for the rest of my days."

Raleigh said, "The important thing is to keep them from being arrested, is that it?"

"Precisely," Nigel said.

"Stop saying that," Raleigh said.

"What?"

"Never mind. Do you have twelve thousand dollars?"

"Just," Nigel said. "As soon as I leave you, I'm going to the bank. It will clean out my reserve account and I'll have trouble explaining it to Ruth, especially since I'm about to lay her off." He paused then, shook his head wearily, and said, "It's the hardworking people like me who are hurt the most by this fucking recession."

"Nigel," Raleigh said after some thought, "if this isn't some kind of police setup and you're able to buy the paintings back, we could still come out of this thing."

"I'm positive it's not a police setup," Nigel said. "With all the things he said to me, it would be considered entrapment. I've watched enough television to know that much. No, he's our louche little thief and he's not in police custody."

"Well, then, if we wait and we do the deal, we're not much worse off, other than you losing twelve grand. Which you can take out of my half million."

"Oh, that is magnanimous of you, Raleigh," Nigel said. "Magnanimous and fucking obtuse."

"One of these days you're going to call me one name too many," Raleigh said, "you arrogant pansy."

Ignoring that, Nigel said, "There is one thing of great concern here. The thieves will spend their twelve thousand on women or drugs or whatever they fancy, and then they might have a bit of a think. They might try to find out about the provenance of the paintings. It's not hard to do since you may have noticed that Sammy Brueger's name, address, and phone number were on a card stapled to the stretcher bar on both pieces. Every art dealer and auction house on the west side of Los Angeles knew about Sammy Brueger and his collection. The thieves could learn the approximate value of the pieces and feel they'd been cheated. Yes, the fucking thieves would then feel that *we* stole from *them*. That would let the cat out and they'd know something is amiss and come after me for everything I've got."

"What could they do? Go to the police and say they stole the van?"

"No, but the worm I was talking to might have a smarter crime partner who could contact Leona Brueger either by letter or phone and ask some pertinent questions about *The Woman by the Water* and *Flowers on the Hillside.* And perhaps offer Leona some information for a price, information that concerns Nigel Wickland and his van. Leona is a fool in many ways, but she can be shrewd and ruthless when she wants to be. She'd put her finger on it. And she'd call the police, and our whole scheme would unravel."

With that, Nigel walked to the larger replica on poster board and said, "Come here, Raleigh. Touch this."

Raleigh complied, and then Nigel said, "Walk down the corridor and touch a few of the legitimate pieces."

"Yes," Raleigh said. "If she literally puts her finger on it, she'll know. They feel completely different from the real paintings."

"Precisely," Nigel said.

"Well, what're you suggesting here, Nigel?"

"I think you know," Nigel said. "Were you able to see anything other than silhouettes when they drove out of here?"

"No, I saw one person in the van and one person in the VW bug."

"Both were men, I presume?"

"I don't know. I suppose so."

"They're thieves," Nigel said. "And blackmailers. They're scum who don't deserve to live."

Raleigh Dibble said, "I'm not killing anyone, Nigel. Not for a million and not for ten million."

"Not even to keep from going to state prison?"

"You'd bring me into it, wouldn't you? You'd tell them everything."

"Turnabout is fair play," Nigel reminded him. "I'd make the best deal I could with the prosecutors. I learned that from you."

"You're a miserable shit," Raleigh said.

Nigel said, "Can you make me a goddamn vodka martini, please? It might make it easier if I should decide to go home and shoot myself."

Raleigh felt like weeping the entire time he was making martinis for both of them. When he was finished, he said, "I gave you a twist instead of an olive. You don't look like an olive person."

"Thank you," Nigel said quietly. "I take that as a compliment."

"Okay, we won't be safe until we get the paintings back," Raleigh said. "That much I can see. So what if we get them and put them back in the frames where they belong?"

"And forget the million dollars?"

"Yes, and just be grateful not to be going to prison."

Nigel thought for a moment and said, "And if the thieves demand more extortion money not to tell Leona Brueger how her paintings got to be temporarily stolen, then what?"

"You just deny everything. You were never here, which I would verify. The person who contacted her with the ridiculous story about her paintings being stolen is just some Hollywood madman. The town is full of lunatics."

"When're they arriving?" Nigel asked.

"I still don't know. I've been expecting a call all morning."

"All right," Nigel said. "Then it depends on when the thieves call me and when we can deliver the money and get the paintings. We would have to get the paintings back here and into the frames before Leona Brueger enters this house again. But we still would not be safe from future danger. Is this what you really want?"

"Stay in close touch with me today, Nigel," Raleigh said.

"Don't worry, I shall."

Raleigh said, "When you threatened to shoot yourself, I was wondering, do you really have a gun?"

"Yes, at the gallery for protection. Why? Could it be that you are possibly coming around to the conclusion that if we are ultimately faced with losing the million dollars *and* going to prison, then we would have no option but to try our very best to remove the thieves from our lives?"

Raleigh drained his martini, shaking his head slowly back and forth. But as he thought about it longer, he nodded slowly and said, "Precisely."

TWENTY-ONE

FOR THE VERY first time since they began smoking OxyContin together, Megan Burke did not join Jonas Claymore in the chasing of the dragon. She swallowed a perk instead, and although it helped ease her nausea and joint pain, she still longed for the euphoria that she got from the ox. Before he zoned, she tried to talk to Jonas about what they were doing.

She squeezed his cheek between her finger and thumb and said, "Jonas, don't get all smoked out on me. We've got to talk."

His voice was thick when he said, "I know. That's why I needed the ox. So I could work on my plan and we could talk."

"I've been thinking," she said. "That guy was very quick to cut a deal with you. Even though he might not believe a thing you said, because to tell the truth, it wasn't too convincing. He might be talking to cops right now, getting ready to set a trap for when he hands over the money. Maybe we should try to find out something about these paintings and simply sell them. Maybe we should stay away from the guy we stole them from."

"Okay," Jonas said. "Later. Man, that was good smoke. I'm toasted."

He was zoning hard and Megan Burke longed to join him, but she summoned all the self-control she had left in her increasingly frail body and mind. She took both paintings from behind the sofa

252

and looked at them closely. She went to the bedroom and got her cell phone and photographed both paintings in case she decided to make inquiries about them. Then she turned them over and saw the framer's cards stapled to the stretcher bars.

She read the name of the customer, Sammy Brueger, along with an address and phone number. It took her a minute to realize that the address was the house where they had stolen the van!

"Snap out of it, Jonas!" she said, slapping his face lightly.

"What?" he said. "What the fuck's wrong with you?"

"The pictures," she said. "They don't belong to the gallery guy! They belong to the guy who lives at the big house. His name's Sammy Brueger. So the gallery guy doesn't really care about making a deal with you for the pictures. He just wanted to get his van back, and now he's gonna work with the cops and maybe set a trap for us when we go meet him for the money!"

"Later," Jonas mumbled, not understanding a single word she said. "I gotta push the off button for a while."

"Fuck you!" Megan said.

She went to the bathroom and touched up her makeup, shocked to see how pale she looked. A touch of blush on her cheeks brought a bit of life to her face, and she tried to separate her eyelashes with a safety pin, but her hands were so shaky she feared she'd poke her eyeball. When she figured she looked as good as she could, she grabbed her purse and Jonas's car keys and left.

This was by far the most dangerous idea she'd ever had, but she was going to act on it. If it worked and if real money somehow came from the paintings, she was going to get away from Jonas Claymore for good. For her freedom, for her sanity, for her life.

When she'd phoned home for that last $200 loan, her mother had said to her, "Megan, your life has gone from bad to worse since you went to Hollywood. You've got no chance until you leave that terrible place and come home to people who love you."

Megan had never told her mother about moving into the

apartment of Jonas Claymore, and she certainly had never told her mother that they were both straight-up drug addicts by now. She hated thinking about all the money she'd begged and borrowed from her mother, who still had Terry, Megan's sixteen-year-old brother, to support. And it hadn't been easy for her mother, with what she made doing a man's work in the department store warehouse. Bitter experience had taught Megan that the more she thought about her mother, and the more guilt that brought on, the more she'd long for the honeycombed tranquillity of an OC high. She was desperate for money now, more desperate than she'd ever been. And it was that desperation that overcame her fear and propelled her back up into the Hollywood Hills in the little VW bug.

During the drive, Megan ran through in her mind several approaches to get access to that house. She wasn't sure what she'd find there, but she wanted to see the man, Sammy Brueger, to get a sense of whether they could work with him now that she knew for certain that Nigel Wickland had lied about being the owner of the paintings. In order to bolster her courage, she kept telling herself that this was just an exploratory visit to test the real ransom target, Sammy Brueger.

She parked the VW bug fifty yards south of the Brueger estate, facing the flatland in case she needed a fast getaway. Then she walked to the gate phone and pressed the button.

"Yes?" Raleigh Dibble said. "Who is it?"

"My name's Valerie Turner," Megan said. "I'm your neighbor from down the road."

"What is it?" Raleigh asked.

"It's my dog, Cuddles," she said. "He's on your property."

"There's no dog here," Raleigh said. "This place is completely fenced."

"He's a Chihuahua," Megan said. "He slipped through the gaps in your metal entry gate. I saw him and I have to get him or I'll get in big trouble with my mom."

Raleigh said nothing, but he pushed the phone key, and the electric gate swung open slowly and Megan walked in. The mini-estate looked bigger from the inside. She was glad she wasn't wearing heels when she walked over the uneven driveway, and she could feel the rough stones through the holes in her shoes.

A pie-faced, chubby, balding man who looked pretty old to Megan opened the door and said, "Have you tried calling him?"

"For the last half hour," Megan said. "I'm glad to meet you, Mr. Brueger."

"I'm Mr. Dibble," Raleigh said. "I look after things here. Mr. Brueger is in Cedars-Sinai. He had a stroke."

"Oh, that's too bad!" Megan said. "I'll tell my mom. I think she knows him."

"You can walk the property and call your dog," Raleigh said. "Let me know when you want to leave and I'll open the gate for you."

"Thank you, sir," Megan said.

She walked around the garage toward the pool that was designed like a lazy lagoon with a six-foot waterfall. "Cuddles!" she called. "Here, Cuddles!"

She thought five minutes was enough. She rang the bell and Raleigh came to the door again.

"Did you find your dog? he asked.

"No, the brat," she said. "I know he's hiding here. He does this when he doesn't want to be found."

"If you'll leave your phone number, I'll call you if I find him," Raleigh said.

"Do you have something I can write on?"

"Come in," Raleigh said, and she entered the foyer while he went to fetch a notepad and pen.

Megan walked into the great room and marveled. She'd never been in a house like this, and the thing that impressed her most was the art. There were paintings everywhere. The corridor along the foyer was lined with paintings, all of them with lights attached to the top of the frames.

And then she saw *The Woman by the Water* and drew in her breath. And next to it was *Flowers on the Hillside*. They were identical to the paintings that she and Jonas had in their apartment! What did it mean?

Raleigh returned with a notepad, and she scribbled a fictitious number.

"I majored in art in community college," she said. "And I'm very interested in art. Do you know a lot about the paintings here?"

Raleigh thought she was a very pretty girl in a waiflike way. She looked so touchingly anemic and vulnerable, and she didn't do that Valspeak where they made every damn sentence sound like a question. He said, "I know a bit."

She strolled along the wall of paintings and said, "This one?" pointing at a small British watercolor that Raleigh knew nothing about, and he said, "I think that's by a German Impressionist. Can't recall his name. An interesting piece."

"Wow!" Megan said, and pointed at an oil painting of red-coated hunters riding to hounds. "This must be British, right? It looks like the scenes you see on public television."

"Yes, I believe it is British," Raleigh said, feeling a sensation in his loins that he had not felt for ages. He couldn't think of the last time he'd slept with a woman. And this tulip of a girl with alabaster skin was flirting with him. He was almost sure of it.

"This is interesting," Megan said, pointing to the replica of *The Woman by the Water*. It had looked identical to the one in their apartment until she got very close. Then it was somehow different, but she couldn't say exactly how. She wondered if this was the original and hers was a copy. Or was it the other way around? And why would Sammy Brueger want a copy anyway?

Megan was thoroughly confused when she said, "My mom has

always said that Mr. Sammy Brueger is a big art collector, but I had no idea."

Raleigh said, "Sammy Brueger is dead. His brother, Marty, lives here. He's the one who had a stroke."

"Oh," Megan said. "I've always heard her mention the name Sammy Brueger. I never met any of the family. How many Bruegers are there?"

"Mr. Sammy's widow, Leona, lives here. Your mother's probably met her."

"I guess," Megan said. Then, "Would you mind if I had a glass of water? I'm pretty hot from roaming around the property looking for Cuddles."

"Sure," Raleigh said. "Come into the kitchen with me. It's a gourmet setup. You might be interested."

Megan followed Raleigh, who took more than one glance at Megan's calves and thought, The girl has natural curves, but she's so thin. She looks so childlike in that candy-striped dress. And then the peril he was facing with Nigel Wickland entered his mind and he lost some of the nostalgic itch in his loins. He hadn't realized how lonely he'd become.

"Would you like a soft drink?" he asked. "Or maybe you're old enough for a cocktail?"

"I'll have a white wine if you'll join me," Megan said.

He saw that look in her violet eyes again. Her smile was playful and provocative, and now he was sure of it. She was flirting with him! "I'd be pleased to join you," he said. "I have a lovely Chardonnay in the wine cellar that I've been saving. Why don't you have a seat in the great room?"

Raleigh went to the wine cellar, which wasn't a cellar but a very large closet lined in redwood and located just off the butler's pantry. He found a good California Chardonnay that still had the sticker label of $180. He put it in a silver bucket, surrounded it with tiny cubes from the ice maker, folded a white linen napkin over the bucket, and brought it along with two crystal wineglasses to the great room.

He placed the bucket on the table between two side-by-side overstuffed chairs, poured the wine into the glasses, and, handing one to her, said, "Mademoiselle."

"Merci," she said, and there it was again. That look.

Raleigh raised his glass and said, "Here's to Cuddles for bringing a new friend to this lonely house."

Megan giggled and said, "To Cuddles."

"I hope it's not too tannic," Raleigh said. "It didn't get a chance to breathe."

"It's great, Mr. Dibble," Megan said, smiling at him over the rim of her glass.

"Raleigh. Call me Raleigh," he said.

"Okay, Raleigh," she said, taking another sip and licking her lower lip.

She was so young! He felt a shiver in his stomach that went clear to his toes. "I'm an excellent chef," he said. "You should let me prepare a meal for you sometime. And your parents, of course."

"That would be nice," she said. Then Megan added, "You said it's a lonely house. Who lives here with you besides Mrs. Brueger and Mr. Marty?"

"That's all. But Mrs. Brueger's getting married soon, and the house will be put up for sale. I'll miss it."

"That's too bad," Megan said. "What will happen to all the beautiful art?"

"It'll go into storage," Raleigh said. "And eventually it'll be moved to their vineyard in Napa. She thinks she wants to live there and make fine wine. That was a common fantasy in pre-recession days. She may change her mind. I can tell you, it's not easy to produce a fine wine."

"This one's sure good," Megan said.

"It's amusing," Raleigh said.

"Oh, that reminds me," Megan said. "A few nights ago...I don't remember when it was...my mom was out walking with Cuddles just after dark, and she said an art truck sped out of your driveway like mad and flew down the hill."

"An...art truck?" Raleigh said.

"She said it had an art gallery name on it or something like that. I didn't get the whole story."

"Nope," Raleigh said, taking more than a sip this time to quell the starburst of fear. "Not here. She's mistaken."

"That's funny," Megan said. "She said the truck came from the Brueger driveway. It scared her because it almost ran over Cuddles."

"No, I've been here every night since Mr. Brueger has been in the hospital. There was no one here in a truck or a car."

"She must've been wrong," Megan said. "She gets a little rattle-brained these days. But speaking of art, what would some of these paintings be worth?"

She looked so innocent, so like the child she really was, that Raleigh longed to impress her. He said, "Valerie, you might not believe it, but there are paintings in this house that're worth half a million dollars."

"Really?" she said. "For one painting?"

"For one painting," he said.

"Wow!" she said, and it made him chuckle with pleasure. Her eyes popped wide like the little purple umbrellas he used to put in mai tais when he was catering parties. Then she said, "I like so many of them. I'd love to have an inexpensive copy of a few of them. I forget what you call copies of paintings."

"Lithographs?"

"Yes, lithographs. Are there any places where I can buy a lithograph of some of these?"

"No, I've been told that each painting you see is an original and there's not another like it on the planet."

"Wow!" she said again.

He loved hearing her say that. "If there was an inexpensive lithograph available for some of these pieces, I'd buy them myself," Raleigh said. Then he looked over the edge of his glass at those violet eyes and said, "I'd present one to you as a gift if I could."

"You're very sweet, Raleigh," Megan said, finishing the wine.

"More, Valerie?" he asked quickly.

"I think I'd better take another look around for Cuddles and then walk home," she said.

Raleigh was about to offer her a few calendar dates to choose from for the home-cooked dinner, when the house phone rang. He hurried to the kitchen phone for privacy, and when he picked up, he heard the now-familiar voice of Rudy Ressler.

"Raleigh," the voice said. "It's Rudy Ressler."

"Yes, Mr. Ressler," Raleigh said. "I've been waiting for your call."

"We're in New York," he said. "It's been hell getting flights on short notice. Unless plans change, we'll be arriving at LAX late tonight, and we are totally drained. You can pick us up and drop me at my house. Then be prepared to do a light supper for Mrs. Brueger before she hits the hay. She'll sleep for twelve hours, at least."

Raleigh felt cold again and his limbs went weak. He had to ask Rudy Ressler to repeat the airline and the flight number. Meanwhile, Megan Burke was standing in the corridor, running her fingers over the poster-board replica of *The Woman by the Water*.

Raleigh hung up the kitchen phone and returned to Megan, now in the foyer by the door. She smiled and said, "Thanks for a wonderful time, Raleigh."

"Yes, it was lovely, Valerie," he said, looking agitated now. "I hope you find your little dog."

"I will," she said. "I'm just going to call him a few more times. He'll come home when he's tired. He always does. Will you open the gate for me?"

"Certainly," Raleigh said.

"One thing, Raleigh," she said. "Could I maybe call you some-time? I really enjoyed talking to you. Maybe we could go some-where and have another glass of wine. I know a good little bistro."

Stunned, he said, "Yes, of course. Call my cell." And he ran to get the notepad and wrote down his number for her.

She kissed him on the cheek and said, "You're a doll."

That kiss from this delightful young woman would have made him happier than he'd been in months, except for the dread he felt over Leona Brueger's homecoming.

He opened the door and watched her striding up the driveway, calling, "Cuddles! Here, Cuddles!"

Raleigh pressed the button on the wall panel inside the door, and the gate swung open. When she was out, he dialed Nigel Wick-land. After the third ring came the voice that he had come to hate.

"Yes?" Nigel said.

"They'll probably be home tonight."

"Tonight?"

"Yes, tonight," Raleigh said. "Has that goddamn thief called you yet?"

"Not a word since the first time," Nigel said. "This is somewhat worrisome."

"This is disastrous," Raleigh said.

"Don't lose your head."

"Stop saying shit like that!" Raleigh said. "I have a right to lose my head. For listening to you and your crazy scheme in the first place."

"If you hadn't left the keys in the van..."

"Okay, let's not go over all that again. Now what?"

"Now we sweat it out, Raleigh. The ball is in the court of my mentally challenged tormentor. Now, either we stay out of prison and make a million dollars or—"

"Don't tell me about the *or* again."

"All right, dear boy," Nigel said. "As long as you are clear that despite your obvious aversion to gays, we two are in bed together for the foreseeable future."

Megan was so excited and her mind was working so furiously, she feared she'd have an accident on the dangerous winding road as the VW descended from the Hollywood Hills toward the roaring traffic below. She only hoped that Jonas had recovered enough to understand the significance of her amazing discovery. Their scheme had changed completely. Before she arrived in east Hollywood, she had decided on a whole new game plan, and Jonas Claymore was no longer the quarterback.

He was standing in the shower when she got to the apartment. She dropped her purse on the kitchen table and entered the bathroom, but Jonas didn't even see her. He was still coming down from the euphoria and never saw her hand reach inside the shower curtain and turn off the hot water. A blast of cold water made him squeal.

"What the fuck you doing?" he said, shutting off the water.

"Here, dry off," she said, handing him a towel that was reasonably clean.

"Where you been?"

"Out," she said.

"Yeah, I figgered that. But where?"

"I was trying to score some ox at Pablo's, but there was nobody there that I knew or even recognized."

"What were you gonna use for money?"

"I was going to try to talk somebody out of a quarter."

"Goddamnit, girl," Jonas said. "How many times I gotta tell you that nobody in Hollywood sells ox on the fucking installment plan. This ain't Bend fucking Oregon. Christ, Megan, is your brain totally wacked, or what?"

"I'm just not as smart as you," Megan said, going to the kitchen for some milk and cereal. Anything to settle her stomach.

When he was dressed in the same jacket, shirt, and pants he'd worn to the cybercafé, he joined her in the kitchen, running a comb through his hair. It looked to Megan like a sopping mound of straw. Like they'd mucked out of the stable back in Bend, where she'd taken riding lessons that her mother couldn't really afford, a lifetime ago.

It was growing harder for Megan to believe that she'd ever been attracted to Jonas. But at times like this, when some inner defense mechanism allowed her to think and remember her past life, she could realize and admit that it had never been Jonas, it had been the ox. They had both mounted the ox and had ridden it into the arena that was Hollywood, and after that wild ride, her world had changed.

She said to him, "I know you're running the game, but I think we should go right to that man Nigel Wickland and collect our money and make arrangements for him to pick up the paintings."

He stared at her and said, "You do?"

"Yes."

"And if he's told the cops about us and they're all staked out there, or maybe have the place wired, then we're busted, right?"

"I don't think we have to worry about that," she said.

"Oh, you don't?"

"No, in fact, I'll do it."

That made Jonas push the calico cat off the kitchen chair and sit. He couldn't believe this new boldness he was hearing. He said, "Yeah, you must be smoked out."

"Yes, you always say that," Megan said. "Maybe I am, and of course you aren't, because you can handle it. Well, what do you have to lose? I'll go in and get the money and tell him where to find the paintings."

"And if it's a setup and the cops move in and bust you, what am I supposed to do, fly to Rio? They'll put you in a room and you'll spill your guts and we'll both be sleeping in jail tonight."

"I give you my word that if it's a police setup, I will not involve you. I'll go to jail and say nothing. My mother's address is on my driver's license, not your address. And she doesn't know your last name or anything about where we live. You'll be safe."

"Megan," he said, "what makes you so positive that the guy didn't tell the cops that I phoned him? Jist tell me that."

"I think he doesn't want to lose his paintings. I think they might be worth a few thousand more than he told you. I think he wants them back, no questions asked."

"How much do you think they're really worth?"

"More than he says."

"And you're willing to risk getting arrested by walking in there and collecting our twelve large?"

"Yes."

Megan could almost see his thoughts whirling. She got some cat food from the cupboard and fed Cuddles, then refilled her water dish. She gave the calico cat a bonus saucer of skimmed milk and stroked her until Jonas finished thinking.

Finally Jonas said, "Here's what I'll do. I'll drop you a block from the gallery. Go in there and talk private with him and tell him if he wants his goods, he has to give you half the money right now to show good faith."

"Six thousand?"

"You got it. And tell him the next meeting will be for the balance and we'll have his property with us. Tell him he'll get instructions by phone. Get his cell number. I ain't going through that official . . . officious bitch again."

"You'll be close by?"

"Right. I'll be parked somewhere and watching. And if this is a setup, I'm leaving you there. And I'm trusting that you'll take the heat and you won't rat me out. I'm trusting you, Megan."

"Okay, you can trust me," she said.

"I never been in jail except once for DUI," he said.

"I've never been in jail for anything, but I'll take a chance," she said. "I think I can do this."

"If he don't have the twelve grand after the talk we had today, then there's something wrong, and you better leave and walk west on Wilshire. Keep walking till I pick you up."

"Let's get going before the gallery closes," Megan said. "I'm getting burbly thinking about it."

TWENTY-TWO

RUTH WAS GETTING ready to lock up when Megan walked into the Wickland Gallery.

"We're about to close," Ruth said. "May I help you?"

"Yes," Megan said. "I'd like to see Mr. Wickland."

"I can help you," Ruth said.

"I'd really like to talk to him personally," Megan said. "Please tell him that I've been sent by the gentleman he spoke to on the phone this morning."

Ruth said nothing but turned and walked through a door behind the showroom to the gallery owner's office and said, "Nigel, there's a young woman to see you. She claims she was sent by someone you spoke to this morning."

He started to jump to his feet but caught himself and said, "Send her in, Ruth. And you may go home. I'll lock up."

"Is this something I should know about?" Ruth asked.

"A man has inherited some art that may or may not be valuable," Nigel said. "There are other parties involved in the family's will and they want a secret appraisal. Mum's the word, and all that."

Ruth said, "Oh, one of those hush-hush appraisals. Okay, see you tomorrow."

When Megan entered the office, Nigel didn't get up. He said, "Close the door, please."

Megan sat in a client chair in front of Nigel's desk and he studied her. "You're not what I expected," he said.

He was pretty much what she had expected: a tall, elegant older man with a mane of snowy hair. She thought that his hands, with long, tapered fingers and manicured nails, were the most beautiful hands she had ever seen on a man.

She did her best to project sophistication and confidence, but her legs were trembling. She smoothed her dress down, trying to cover her knees, but the shirtdress was so short it was hopeless. Her lips were parched and felt stuck to her teeth when she said, "I've come for the reward money."

"Where is my property?"

"Did you get your van back?"

"Yes, but where is my property?"

Megan said, "I believe my partner told you to have the reward money today."

"Yes, you'll get it," Nigel said, looking at this . . . this child who was brazenly extorting him in his own office!

"I'll have to have it now, Mr. Wickland," she said. "Those are my instructions."

"Does your partner really think I'm going to hand over twelve thousand dollars and let you walk out of here with it?"

"I think you will, Mr. Wickland," she said. "And I think you'd be better off talking only to me and not to my partner."

Nigel didn't speak for a moment. Then he smiled sardonically and said, "Young woman, you interest me. I cannot imagine what you could be thinking, but I do find you interesting. What are you trying to tell me?"

Megan said, "I'm trying to tell you that I'm willing to deliver your paintings, but it will cost you the twelve thousand that you had better have with you today. As well as a bonus."

"I might have known," Nigel said with a sneer. "I told your partner that this gallery is on the verge of bankruptcy, and that's the truth."

"Yes, I know what you told him," she said. "The recession has been hard on everyone. But I'm still going to require a bonus."

His fury was mounting, and he gripped the edge of his desk so hard, his knuckles went white, alarming Megan Burke. "And how much of a fucking bonus do you require?" he said, feeling a tremor in his voice. He knew then that he was capable of killing both of them, given half a chance. He kept thinking of the 9-millimeter pistol in his middle drawer.

She said, "One hundred thousand dollars."

He didn't know whether he should laugh in her face or play it differently. He sat back and said, "What could you possibly be thinking?"

Megan said, "I'm thinking that one hundred thousand dollars is a small price to pay for staying out of jail and completing the theft of the two paintings you stole from the home of Leona Brueger."

She watched the blood drain from his face. When he went pale he looked older, and his mane of white hair almost seemed to fade to the gray of his flesh. She was aware that her own heart was hammering in her chest. She was suddenly very frightened of this man, and she said, "My partner is watching this gallery right now, and if I don't walk out of here with the money, you'll be in jail before the night's over."

When he could find words he said, "You little bitch. You fucking little bitch. What're you talking about?"

"The Bruegers have paintings that're worth a lot of money," she said quickly, her teeth clicking together. "They have a very valuable collection."

He thought he understood now. She'd seen the identification tickets that the framers had stapled to the stretcher bars. Perhaps she'd taken the paintings or photos of the paintings to someone who knew or thought he knew their provenance.

"Whoever you've consulted has grossly inflated the value of those paintings," he said. "You can try to sell them, but you'll get arrested when the art dealer calls the police."

"We agree with the second part," Megan said. "That's why we're selling them back to you."

"Young woman," he said. "You are being absurd. I truly don't understand what you think you know about these paintings."

Megan took a breath and said, "I think I know about the pictures in Leona Brueger's house that are identical to the paintings that my partner has safely put away." Then she said, "Well, not identical but almost. They don't feel the same when you touch them, but you did a good job of reproducing them, however you did it."

Nigel Wickland felt that he might faint. All he had to do was open the desk drawer and take out the gun. But there was the other thief, the fucking idiot partner.

She was terrified by the look on his face now. Her voice rose when she said, "Believe me, my partner is watching this gallery, and if I don't return safely to his car, you're finished, Mr. Wickland."

He wished he had a glass of water. He loosened his necktie and unbuttoned his collar. He took the inhaler from his pocket and took a puff, holding it in his lungs for a moment, and then said, "Who *are* you?"

"I'm the partner of the man who has your paintings," Megan said. "And you need them. And you need to keep your plans a secret. That's okay with me. I don't need to know anything about your plans. I don't care how much you sell the paintings for. That's your business. I agree that we'd get arrested if we tried to sell them to a gallery owner like you. So the best thing to do is sell them back to you. I'm not being greedy in charging you one hundred thousand."

"You have been in the Brueger house?" He couldn't believe it, but he said it again. "You have actually been inside Leona Brueger's house?"

"Yes," she said. "And her brother-in-law is in the hospital with a stroke. I believe his name is Marty. Would you like me to describe the house and where the fake paintings are hung?"

Nigel said, "And has your partner been in the house, too?"

"No," she said. "And it'd be better not to talk to him about it if he calls you again. Just do all business through me."

"Yes, I see," Nigel said with a hiss. "You are the one with the brains. He is obviously a cretin. Yes, I shall deal with you."

Megan almost jumped up and bolted when he opened his desk drawer. But he removed a fat envelope and tossed it across the desk. "A hundred and twenty hundred-dollar bills," he said. "Just as your half-wit partner demanded." Nigel added, "Before his ambitious little partner devised a way to increase the reward considerably."

Megan picked up the envelope and put it into her purse, saying, "Thank you. Let me have your cell number, please, and wait for a call from me. If you get a call from my partner on your business phone, just disregard whatever he says and wait for a call from me."

"I think I understand," Nigel said. "Would you happen to know a man named Raleigh?"

"Mr. Dibble's very nice," Megan said. "I met him today."

"Yes, I thought as much," Nigel said. "And how may I reach you?"

"You can't. Just wait for my call."

"And your name?"

"Valerie," she said.

"Does your partner know about your meeting with Raleigh?"

"No, I did it on my own," Megan said.

"Well, Valerie," Nigel said. "Since you and I both seem to be partnered with imbeciles, it does appear that you and I should exclude our partners from all future dealings. I take it that you will never see or speak to Raleigh again?"

"Of course not."

"Then if Raleigh thinks that the paintings have been kept by the thieves and lost forever, nobody would ever tell him any different?"

"Not me," she said.

"And not your partner?"

"He's not part of my bonus plan," Megan said. "He'll be very happy to settle for the twelve thousand that you promised him. He believes the paintings belong to you and he knows nothing about the Bruegers."

"And if I am able to get a mortgage on my home and manage to scrape together one hundred thousand dollars, that bit of business will remain between you and me, correct?"

"Correct. So whatever you get when you sell the paintings will not have to be shared with Raleigh," Megan said. "But that's your business."

"It will take a couple of days, I'm sure," Nigel said.

"Okay," Megan said. "I would like the cash in one-hundred-dollar bills, no later than forty-eight hours from now, just before you close for the day."

"I'll know tomorrow if I can do it," Nigel said.

"You'd better do it, sir," Megan said. "I'll call you tomorrow to see about your progress."

"All right. Always use my mobile number," Nigel said. He wrote his number on a notepad, tore off the sheet, and handed it to her.

Megan said, "And remember, someone will deliver me here and wait for me when I come for the money. My companion will be a hired driver, and he will not know anything about our arrangement. But if I don't walk out of here in fifteen minutes, he will make a nine-one-one call and present the arriving police with a letter that I've written. You will be in way more trouble than you are in now if something bad happens to me when I come to this place of business."

Nigel emitted a bark of a laugh for the first time and said, "You are truly a very bright girl, Valerie. Believe me, nothing is going to happen to you."

"I used to be a bright girl," she said. "And I'm trying to be a bright girl again. That's why I'm here."

Nigel took a hard look again at her undernourished body,

nervous hand movements, and agitated watery eyes, and he said, "Drugs?"

She nodded and said, "You're a smart person, too, Mr. Wickland."

"Not half as smart as you, Valerie," Nigel said. "I should hope that I won't see you some time in the future when your drug money runs out. It would be a big mistake on your part to come at me again."

"Believe it or not, Mr. Wickland," she said, "I'll be using a big chunk of the money to get out of this state and go to a rehab and get clean. And learn how to stay clean."

"And the rest of the money?"

"I'm giving it to my mother."

Nigel laughed heartily and said, "Good lord! You're so convincing that I can almost believe that, too, Valerie."

"Good-bye for now, Mr. Wickland," Megan said. She stood and opened the office door, walking briskly to the street door and out onto Wilshire Boulevard.

After Megan left the Wickland Gallery, Nigel dialed the cell phone of Alec Townsend, the manager of his bank, a personal friend who also frequented the gay bars of west Hollywood.

When he reached the bank manager, he said, "Alec, Nigel Wickland here. Listen carefully. I need to loot my savings account and my commercial account. I must have one hundred thousand dollars as soon as possible. I have a chance to purchase a painting of immense value, but it's a bit dodgy because its provenance is unknown to the seller. Someone else will get it if I don't grab it at once. This investment will produce a windfall profit."

He listened to the bank manager's warnings and protests and said, "Alec, I am not being scammed and I am not being extorted. This is a chance of a lifetime. I want the money in hundred-dollar bills by tomorrow."

After a moment of listening, he said in frustration, "I don't care about your currency transaction reports or your goddamn deposit-demand account. It's my money. And I stand to reap a return of one thousand percent in a few months. Can your fucking bank do that for me?"

He listened again and said, "I'm sorry. I didn't mean to get angry. But Alec, it is my money to risk as I see fit. Can you pull strings and have it for me by the day after tomorrow at the latest? In hundred-dollar bills. I'll owe you, my friend. Please help me."

When Megan Burke left the Wickland Gallery with the envelope in her purse, she had to walk two blocks until a very cautious and supremely nervous Jonas Claymore had the courage to pull the VW bug to the curb beside her.

She jumped in and said, "Go, Jonas."

He almost sideswiped a gleaming Rolls-Royce parked on Wilshire Boulevard and she said, "Watch where you're driving."

"Did you get it?"

"Yes, I got it."

"Let's see it."

"When we get home."

"Now, bitch!" he said.

She looked at him but said nothing. Then she turned the rearview mirror and looked at herself.

"What're you doing?"

"I'm trying to see who I am," she said.

"What the fuck you talking about?"

"I should say that I'm trying to see who I've become. Sitting here with a loser like you who can't utter a complete sentence without using words like *bitch*. In fact, someone who can't utter a complete sentence period."

"Me, a loser?" he said. "I jist got you six fucking grand. Me, a loser? Gimme that money!"

"It's in my purse and you'll have it when we get to the apartment," she said firmly. "Now drive me home."

"It ain't your home, it's my home," he reminded her. "And first I'm stopping at Pablo's Taco Shop and you're gonna give me some of that bank and I'm gonna buy some OCs. And then I'm going home and I'm chasing the dragon, and if you don't like it, move the fuck out. But first gimme what you got in your purse."

Jonas was driving as fast as the rush-hour traffic allowed, and he kept glaring at her, but Megan was past anger, past all intense feelings. She had never been so tired in her life. She reached into her purse, withdrew the envelope, opened it, and handed him five hundred-dollar bills.

"Go ahead, stop at Pablo's," she said. "Get yourself busted. Get me arrested, too. That'd be about what I'd expect from you."

"What you can expect from me is a bunch of good ideas, and this is only the start of it. When we get home, the first thing we do is get rid of those paintings."

Megan looked at him and said, "What do you mean, get rid of them?"

"We got paid for our work, so why do we need to take any more chances with them? I'll give them to Wilbur for some ox. He can unload them at a swap meet."

"No!" Megan said. "I gave the man my word."

Jonas looked at her and said, "Your word? What's this, something you picked up in Sunday school? Your word?"

"It's a bargain," Megan said. "We made a bargain with the man and we took his money."

"So now you're running the show, huh? Well, news flash, girlfriend. That ain't gonna fly. I'm the man. I'm the quarterback and I'll call the signals. You reading me?"

She was silent. Then she sighed and said, "Yes, you're easy to read. You're a comic book. You're what I deserve for riding the ox."

Feeling gravely insulted, Jonas said, "When we get back to the apartment, maybe I'll give you what you got coming and let you take your fucking cat and your clothes and get the fuck out."

"And what do I have coming?"

"I'll have to think about that."

"Think hard," she said. "I faced the man and got the money. I deserve a fifty-fifty split."

She heard him cackle like a movie witch, and he said, "I been saying you're all smoked out. Your brain's more shriveled than your puny tits."

"What split do you have in mind, Jonas?" she demanded. "I walked in there and got the money."

"Okay, I'll be big about it," he said. "An eighty-twenty split. The eighty is for the brains."

"I see" was all Megan said.

They spoke no more until they arrived in Hollywood at Pablo's Taco Shop on Santa Monica Boulevard, where he drove into the parking lot at twilight.

"Please take me home, Jonas," Megan begged. "We can't afford to get busted now. There might be some narks watching this place. Everybody knows it's a hangout for dealers. Please take me home first."

He parked at the far end of the little strip mall and said, "I ain't scared of five-oh. I can smooth-talk any of them. Anyways, I ain't got time to drop you. I want those green beans now, and you do, too."

"I'm not smoking ox with you anymore, Jonas," she said. "Or anything else."

"Hah!" he said. "Let's see what you do when that beautiful snowbird starts to cook."

"All right, get me some perks or norcos," she said. "Anything to get me past the joneses. But I'm not smoking ox with you."

"We'll see," he said with a smirk, and left her sitting in the car. He walked ten yards, stopped, and came back. He reached through the open window and took the keys from the ignition, saying with a wicked little grin, "Can't leave you here with my keys *and* my bank. The temptation might be too much for you."

He got out but left his cell phone in the ashtray, where he always kept it while driving.

He was gone only for a moment when she saw the black-and-white wheeling into the parking lot.

Six-X-Seventy-six had just cleared from roll call, and Viv Daley and Georgie Adams thought it was time for a cruise through the strip mall on a routine check for tweakers and other drug users who did business at the taco shop.

Megan Burke grabbed Jonas's cell phone, opened the door of the VW bug, got out, and walked east on Santa Monica Boulevard as fast as she could. When she was a safe distance away, she stopped and watched the parking lot to see what was going to happen.

Jonas Claymore had to use his hand to shield his eyes from the late rays of the sun. The dying fireball was giving Hollywood a last blast of its power before settling into the Pacific. Jonas peered into an old Mazda and found a dude he'd done business with on a few occasions. What was his name? Earl, that was it.

He was a scrawny little rat-faced tweaker with what everyone said looked like terminal acne. His face was a flaming pus ball, and it was sickening to score from him, but he had pharmacy connections and was usually good for norcos and perks and sometimes OCs.

The Mazda's windows were open and Earl was eating one of Pablo's lard-fried tacos filled with what Jonas thought was probably horsemeat.

"Earl, whazzup?" Jonas said.

Earl looked at Jonas, recognized him, and said, "I'm living the dream, dude."

"I need ox," Jonas said. "I'll take four if you got 'em. And I need a few norcos or perks for my bitch. I'll give you two Franklins."

"Bite it," Earl said, ferociously chewing the taco, grease the color of dishwater running down his chin and dripping onto his cutoff sweatshirt.

"Okay, dawg, I ain't got time to fuck around," Jonas said. "I'll give you three Franklins for the four OCs and maybe a dozen norcos or perks."

Earl held up four fingers and took another bite from the taco.

"Aw, fuck it!" Jonas said, tossing four hundred-dollar bills onto the Mazda seat, which Earl snatched up so fast, Jonas hardly saw his little hand move.

"Go get a Coke," Earl said. "I'll see you inside."

Jonas did as he was told, wondering vaguely where Earl's drugs were stashed. They could be concealed inside the car's headliner, or taped under the dash, or hidden under the spare tire, or even up Earl's ass. He hated to think about that, but he was so desperate, he pushed all questions from his mind and ordered a soda at the counter.

He sat at a table near a Mexican family with a bawling baby and waited. Earl entered after a few minutes and went to the counter, where he removed several paper napkins from the dispenser. He wiped his greasy face with the napkins and when he got to his mouth he spit a tied-off condom into the napkins, dropping the crumpled mess onto Jonas's table before exiting.

Jonas stuffed the wad of napkins into his pocket, put the soda cup in the trash container, and sauntered out, trying to walk casually to his car.

Georgie Adams was driving the black-and-white, and he said to Viv, "Hey, sis, isn't that the guy we stopped a few days ago? The one who said he was heading for a job in the Hills with his crying wife?"

Viv Daley looked at him and said, "Yeah, the one with the sick baby."

"Told you they looked like tweakers," Georgie said.

"Let's jam him," Viv said.

Jonas had reached his VW bug and was looking around, wondering where the hell Megan went, when the black-and-white stopped, blocking his exit, and he saw two cops get out. He recognized the tall woman cop as the one he'd talked out of a ticket, and he said to himself, Do not panic. You did it before and you can do it again. But he didn't like the dark, sinister look of the shorter cop with her.

Viv said to Georgie, "There it is. The over-the-shoulder look."

"Hi, Officer!" Jonas said to Viv. "I remember you from the other day."

"And I remember you," Viv said. "How's your sick baby?"

"Getting better every day," Jonas said. "Thanks for asking."

"Where's your wife?" Georgie asked.

"I was just looking for her. She musta went across the street to buy a doughnut. I'll tell her I saw you."

He started to step to his car, but Viv said, "What's that bulge in your pocket?"

"Bulge?" he said. "Nothing."

"It could be a weapon. It could be drugs," Georgie said. "Did you know tweakers hang out here and do deals?"

"No, I didn't know," Jonas said, aware that his jaw was trembling but unable to stop it. Then he said, "Oh. I almost forgot. It's a bunch of napkins in my pocket. I ate a taco in there."

"How much did the taco cost you?" Viv said.

"I didn't pay much attention," Jonas said.

Georgie said to Viv, "This dude's like a dog. Eye contact makes him jumpy."

"Why didn't you throw your napkins in the trash can?" Viv asked.

Jonas said, "I . . . I brought them to wipe off the windshield. I got a big bug splatter on the glass."

"Go ahead," Viv said. "Wipe your windshield."

"Later," Jonas said. "I don't wanna waste your time."

"No problem," Georgie said. "Wipe your windshield. You gotta have good visibility when you drive on these busy Hollywood streets."

"Maybe I'll wipe it later," Jonas said. "It's my windshield, ain't it?"

Georgie looked at Viv and said, "More contempt of cop from the baseball-cap-turned-backward set."

Jonas said, "All I meant is, what's wrong with a couple dead bugs on the glass?"

Georgie said, "Don't make me use my uppercase voice, dude. You're wasting my minutes."

Jonas reached into his pocket and both cops looked like they might shoot him if he moved too fast. In fact, he heard the male cop say, "Take your napkins out real slow. We're the nervous type."

Jonas removed the big wad of greasy paper napkins with the condom in the middle of it and started rubbing the crumpled napkins across his windshield.

"Wouldn't it work better if you unfolded that wad?" Viv said.

Jonas turned to answer her and the greasy condom fell out of the wad of napkins and landed on the hood of the VW bug, then slid down onto the asphalt by the zip-up black boot of Georgie Adams, who said, "Uh-oh. What *are* they serving in their tacos these days?"

Viv said, "Turn around." And when Jonas did, she handcuffed his hands behind his back.

"You searched me without my permission," he said.

"We didn't search you at all," Viv said.

"This ain't fair!" Jonas wailed.

Viv said, "Dude, your GPS is off. A fair is where you eat candy apples and get your pocket picked. This is a different place."

"Can't you just warn me again?" Jonas whined.

"Yeah," Georgie said. "I'm warning you that those OCs will turn your brain to meat loaf. Now shut the fuck up while I read you your rights."

After seeing Jonas Claymore being handcuffed, Megan Burke

entered a 7-Eleven store and bought cat food and vegetable juice in order to break one of the hundred-dollar bills. The Pakistani proprietor asked if she had a smaller denomination and she apologized but said that she did not. Instead of using Jonas's cell to call a taxi, she asked the Pakistani to do it and tipped him $5 for his trouble. It was the first time in months that she'd had enough money to tip anyone and it was a good feeling.

An Eritrean taxi driver drove her to Jonas's apartment in Thai Town and she tipped him another $5, and used the key that Jonas kept hidden behind the exterior wall sconce to open the door. The calico cat ran to her, and Megan put her groceries down and picked her up, hugging the purring feline to her face.

"You're going to Oregon, Cuddles," Megan said. "I think you'll like it there."

Then she called the only dependable drug dealer she knew, even though he often came on to her when Jonas wasn't with her. He was a revolting street creature who always reeked of body odor and onions, but she needed him badly now.

Megan called on Jonas's cell and he answered as always on the second ring. She said, "Wilbur, it's Megan. We need norcos and perks. Twenty of each. As fast as you can get here. We'll pay twenty-five bucks extra for home delivery."

Wilbur said, "No OCs?"

It took all the willpower she had to say, "Not this time."

"What's wrong?" he said. "Ain't Jonas with you no more?"

She said quickly, "Yeah, he's sick in bed."

"Why don't you drive over to my place?" Wilbur said. "Save the twenty-five. I got some beautiful leaf you might like. Makes you feel gooooood."

"I can't leave Jonas," Megan said with a shudder of disgust. "Could you hurry, please?"

When she closed the cell, she vowed that the business would be conducted outside the apartment, no matter how much Wilbur liked privacy. She would not let him slither inside, where he'd discover that Jonas was not at home.

She bent down to pet the cat again and said, "Cuddles, we just have to survive the next two days somehow. And then we're going home at last."

She called the airline that had brought her to Los Angeles from Oregon, and while she was inquiring as to ticket prices, Cuddles leaped onto the kitchen table, putting her face against Megan's and purring in her ear. Megan thought that Cuddles was trying to tell her that she wasn't in this thing all alone.

When 6-X-76 brought Jonas Claymore into the station and was putting him in the holding tank, Hollywood Nate passed them on his way to the report room. He glanced at Jonas through the heavy viewing window of the holding tank and stopped.

"Hey, Gypsy," he said to Georgie Adams, pointing at Jonas, who was sitting on the bench in the little room. "What'd he do?"

"Bunch of pills," Georgie said. "Ox, perks, that kinda shit. Do you know the dude?"

"He was double-parked in a van the other night and I warned him to move on," Nate said.

"Yeah? He seems to get a lotta warnings," Georgie said. "We also gave him one a few days ago."

"Was he driving a cargo van at the time?"

Georgie shook his head and said, "A VW bug."

"He works for an art gallery," Nate said with a grin. "He'll sell you crappy paintings on the cheap."

"Not him," Georgie said. "He's unemployed."

"Bullshit," Hollywood Nate said. "Open the tank for a minute."

Georgie opened the door, and Nate said, "Hey, man, remember me?"

Jonas gave Nate a glum look and said, "No."

"You were double-parked in Thai Town delivering crappy art. Remember?" Nate said.

"You got the wrong guy," Jonas said, alert now and worried.

"Dude," Nate said. "You were driving a fucking van. It had the name of an art gallery on it. Wicker. Something like that."

"Not me, Officer," Jonas said. "I'm outta work. This officer and his partner stopped me last week when I was on my way to a job interview up in the Hollywood Hills." He turned to Georgie Adams and said, "Ain't that right, Officer?"

"Wickland," Nate said. "It was the Wickland Gallery. You were doing a delivery for them."

Jonas managed his most sincere smile and said, "I look like a bunch of people, Officer. This always happens. People confuse me with somebody else. No, it wasn't me. I'm unemployed."

Hollywood Nate looked at Georgie Adams and said, "I even remember his voice. It's him. What the hell's going on here?"

Before Nate and Flotsam went back into the field, Nate decided to call the Wickland Gallery, but he got a recorded message giving the gallery's daytime store hours. Then Nate called the Beverly Hills Police Department and tried to find out if there had been a van reported stolen by the owner of the Wickland Gallery on Wilshire Boulevard. Viv Daley was on the computer, doing what she could without having a license number to work with. All responses were negative.

"Better leave a note for the detectives or call them in the morning," Viv suggested to Hollywood Nate.

"He was double-parked in front of an apartment building," Nate said. "I wish I'd seen which apartment he came out of."

Georgie said, "If that van wasn't hot, then Jonas Claymore does work for the Wickland Gallery and he was doing something extracurricular over there in Thai Town that night. It could mean anything."

Flotsam said to Hollywood Nate, "Dude, maybe he lives there and went home to check his voice mail. Or, like, maybe his girlfriend lives there and he went by for a quickie and he don't want the boss to know about it."

Georgie said, "The art gallery oughtta clear it up for you one way or the other."

"Yeah, it's probably nothing much," Hollywood Nate agreed. "I'll call the gallery tomorrow before I send the detectives on a wild goose chase."

Raleigh Dibble had been trying all evening to reach Nigel Wickland on his cell phone, but all he got was voice mail. He was certain that Nigel was avoiding him. At 7:30 P.M. Raleigh became convinced that fate had provided a gift of unfathomable worth. Rudy Ressler phoned and said that they weren't coming home yet. They'd decided to stay over in New York to visit old friends of Leona's because she was exhausted from the long journey.

"I don't mind telling you I can't wait to get back to L.A.," Ressler said to Raleigh. "This doesn't make me happy. By the way, how's Marty?"

"Serious but not critical," Raleigh said. "He's in and out of consciousness. I call every day." They had bought him time!

"I'll call when we're sure of our flight, but right now it looks like Wednesday," Rudy Ressler said. "I think we'll be at the Waldorf for old times' sake. That's where Leona and Sammy went on their honeymoon."

"Enjoy yourself in New York," Raleigh said. "Why don't you take in a Broadway show? Stay as long as you like. Everything here is out of control."

"'Out of control'?" Rudy Resssler said.

"No, I said *under* control," Raleigh said quickly.

When Raleigh hung up, he tried again to reach Nigel Wickland, who at last answered.

"Where the hell've you been?" Raleigh said.

"I've had a very busy day. What's happened?"

"You tell me. Did they make contact today? What've you heard?"

"Nothing," Nigel said. "There was nothing to report since his first call to me, so I didn't phone you."

"Well, I phoned you. Half a dozen times."

"My mobile went dead. I forgot to charge it. I'm sorry."

"Next time I'm calling your gallery phone whether you like it or not," Raleigh said.

"Don't do that," Nigel said. "Ruth is already getting suspicious."

A pause and then, "Suspicious about what? Is something going on?"

"No, I just meant that she's observing my anxious behavior and asking me if there's anything wrong. She's not used to having people wanting to speak to me personally. She's not stupid, Raleigh."

"Okay, keep your cell phone charged and in your goddamn pocket. I have some good news to report. Mrs. Brueger won't be coming home until the day after tomorrow at the earliest. We have time, Nigel!"

"Time?"

"Time to return the paintings to this house and get ourselves out of this nightmare. And if those thieves ever come at you again with demands, you just lie and deny and nobody can prove anything."

"Yes," Nigel said, "but restoring you to your former blissful existence depends on the thieves phoning me, doesn't it? I have the twelve thousand they want, but I can't do a thing until they make contact, so calm yourself until then."

"Calm myself?" Raleigh said. "I'm having erratic heartbeats.

Any day now I could stroke out and end up in the hospital bed next to Marty Brueger."

"Raleigh," Nigel Wickland said. "If our thieves perform as planned, I'll pay them off and we'll return the paintings to their vulgar frames in the home of your parvenu mistress. But I should've thought it would be better to risk being in a hospital bed next to a Marty Brueger than to spend the rest of your life as a domestic servant, wiping his ass or the ass of someone like him. But I guess you've already made your career choice, haven't you?"

When Raleigh hung up, he thought, What an offensive, elitist, supercilious fucking faggot! He hated Nigel Wickland more than he'd ever hated anyone. His face was aflame and his hands were shaking when he went to the butler's pantry and poured a stiff shot of Jack Daniel's. Then he felt his pulse again. It was beating more erratically than ever.

He went into the great room and sat, trying to get some comfort from the wealth surrounding him. Something was nagging and it didn't come to him until after he'd finished the Jack. Then he realized, the thief surely should have called Nigel today but Nigel didn't seem at all upset about it. What had Nigel said about his employee? he tried to recall. Something about Ruth being already suspicious *enough*? Could there be something going on at the Wickland Gallery that would arouse real suspicion from her?

Raleigh had always doubted that Nigel Wickland would give him an honest fifty-fifty split when the paintings were sold in Europe, and he had intended to deal with that when the time came. He decided to visit the gallery tomorrow whether Nigel Wickland liked it or not.

TWENTY-THREE

Jonas Claymore did not like the bunk, the food, or his cellmate in the Hollywood Station jail, where he spent the night. The cellmate was a Latino with a vicious-looking scar that ran from the bridge of his nose across his jaw to his throat. He was fully inked out with gang tatts, and he snored so noisily that Jonas couldn't have slept even if he hadn't been jonesing.

Jonas had tried to reach Megan on the phone an hour after he was booked, but she did not answer his cell. He wasn't sure if they'd impounded his car or left it locked in the strip-mall parking lot as he had begged them to do, but either way the cell might still be in the car. The disloyal bitch had probably bailed the second she'd seen the cops pull into the lot. She could've run into Pablo's and warned him, but no, all she'd thought of was herself. She didn't care that he was in a place where a guy looked up his ass like a plumber inspecting a drainpipe. Jonas decided then to just give her a few Franklins when he saw her next and kick her out of his apartment along with her fucking cat.

The next morning Jonas learned that he'd be taken by sheriff's deputies to arraignment at Division 30 of the Criminal Courts Building downtown on Temple Street, but he would have to spend another night in the Hollywood jail while the paperwork was being done. He was outraged.

*   *   *

Megan Burke's night had been slightly better than Jonas Claymore's. The perks she'd bought from Wilbur had helped her get a few hours' sleep all curled up with Cuddles, who seemed overjoyed to be sleeping on the bed with his mistress in the place that Jonas previously claimed. In the morning the calico cat crawled up on the pillow and purred happily while Megan stroked her, and they stayed like that until Megan decided that Cuddles needed her breakfast.

She knew there'd be hell to pay when Jonas got out of jail, so she made several calls and was told that his bail would be set later, or he might be given an OR release before day's end. She was told to call back in the afternoon for further information. Instead, she began calling motels with ads that said pets were welcome.

Megan packed what clothes were worth packing along with enough cat food for a few days, and by 1 P.M., a Sikh taxi driver was helping her carry her suitcase, a carrier containing Cuddles, and two large objects wrapped in mover's blankets. Those he had to strap to the luggage rack. She took the Sikh's cell phone number and promised him a $100 tip if he would pick her up whenever she called him and take her and her possessions to a destination in Beverly Hills and then to LAX. She said to be sure to bring the same taxi with the luggage rack for the bundles.

Before Megan left Jonas Claymore's apartment for the last time, she wrote a note and left it on the kitchen table. It said, "You told me there would be an 80–20 split and that the 80% was for the brains. I agree. Here is your 20%, less the $500 that I gave you last night." She left $1,900 on the kitchen table beside the note, along with her apartment key and his cell phone.

Hollywood Nate woke earlier than usual that day, probably because he had the Wickland Gallery on his mind. He phoned and Ruth answered.

He said, "This is Officer Weiss at Hollywood Division, LAPD. I had occasion to question someone in a Wickland Gallery cargo van the night before last, and we need to know if your van was stolen."

Ruth said, "Oh, that must've been Mr. Wickland's nephew. He borrowed it and left it in east Hollywood. We had to pick it up yesterday morning."

"That explains it," Nate said. "Is his name Jonas Claymore?"

"Reginald something," Ruth said. "He's a bit of a black sheep, according to Mr. Wickland. Is he in trouble?"

"He was arrested for possession of a controlled substance," Nate said. "For some reason he's denying ever being in the van. We're not sure why. It's possible that he was using it to do drug deals or for some other illegal activity."

"I'm not surprised," Ruth said. "That may explain why he just abandoned the van on the street the way he did. Mr. Wickland's gone to the bank. I'll tell him when he gets back, but I don't think he's going to drive over there and bail him out."

"Okay, thanks," Nate said. "At least I know now that he didn't steal the van from you."

When Nate got to work, he told all of the midwatch officers who knew about the Wickland Gallery van what he'd learned.

"I figured it was nothing," Georgie Adams said. "Just some little ass-wipe taking advantage of his uncle."

Nigel had to endure an in-person meeting to convince the bank manager that neither a bunco artist nor an extortionist was victimizing him, and that he had a good and legitmate reason for needing such a large amount of cash. He was told that he could pick up the $100,000 the next afternoon after 1 P.M. That withdrawal had wiped out Nigel's savings account and put his commercial account in grave jeopardy. He planned to call his European art auctioneer to find out if he could get a wire transfer of some advance money as soon as the paintings were received over there.

When he got back, Ruth said, "The LAPD called. Your nephew got himself arrested for drug possession. You can call Officer Weiss at Hollywood Station if you're interested."

"What?"

"Yes, it appears that he was stopped in our van on the evening you loaned it to him and now they have him on a drug charge."

"Did they give his name?"

Ruth smiled quizzically and said, "Don't you know your own nephew's name?"

Nigel said, "He might have used an alias."

"You said that his name is Reginald, but they have him under the name of Jonas Claymore."

"That's him," Nigel said. "He's using his father's name. Always in trouble, that boy." He entered his office and closed the door behind him.

Forty minutes later his cell phone rang.

"It's Valerie," Megan said. She was in her motel room, lying on the bed with Cuddles, who seemed excited by their new surroundings.

"I'll have it tomorrow, sometime after two P.M.," Nigel said.

"Why not today?"

"You can't walk into a bank and draw out that kind of money unless you're superrich. That money is all I have. I'm penniless now."

"You'll be okay when you sell the paintings," Megan said. "They're very valuable, according to Mr. Dibble."

"Yes, dear Mr. Dibble." Then he said, "Is your partner still in the dark about our bonus arrangement?"

"He's very much in the dark," Megan said. "He believes the paintings are yours and he doesn't even know the name Sammy Brueger. He's a brain-dead addict, to tell you the truth."

"Will he be accompanying you here tomorrow when you bring the paintings?"

"Of course not."

"Just wondering," Nigel said, trying to decide how he could use the information he'd just learned from Ruth. Her crime partner was in jail. Would she be alone? Was violence still an option? Could he possibly eliminate both of the thieves?

"But I *will* have protection," Megan said as though telepathic. "There *will* be someone delivering me and the paintings and waiting for me outside. You'll be able to see him."

"My dear girl," Nigel said. "I am not a dangerous man. You have nothing to fear."

"I'm going to be with a gentleman in a turban," Megan said, "who looks like he could easily cut the throat of anyone who tried to hurt me. But first he would call the police immediately if I didn't walk out of your gallery wearing a happy face."

Raleigh Dibble couldn't bear it any longer. He pulled the Brueger Mercedes out of the garage and drove to Beverly Hills late that afternoon. Another day was almost over, and still no call from Nigel Wickland. His suspicion that Nigel was secretly dealing with the thieves was overwhelming now, and his nerves were in tatters. He dressed in his best sport coat over somewhat threadbare gabardine trousers with a white dress shirt and necktie. He arrived at the Wickland Gallery thirty minutes before closing and was met by Ruth, who was turning out the painting lights over some of the more valuable consignment pieces.

"May I help you?" she said.

"I need to see Mr. Wickland," he said. "My name is Raleigh Dibble."

Ruth smiled and said, "Oh, yes, Mr. Dibble, I remember you. Sorry, but Mr. Wickland left early today."

"Really?" Raleigh said. "I talked to him today and he didn't say he was leaving."

Ruth looked at Raleigh and said, "I don't recall taking a call from you today for Mr. Wickland."

"I called him on his cell," Raleigh said, trying a convivial smile. "I'm a personal friend."

Ruth looked doubtful until Raleigh rattled off Nigel's cell phone number. Then she said, "Sorry. It's just that so many people seem to want to talk personally to Mr. Wickland these days."

"I know how it is," Raleigh said. "We're working together on an estate sale for my aunt, and I'm dealing with some of the same people." Then he took a wild shot and said, "I guess the fellow came in yesterday that I've been working with? Or was it today? Anyway, I told the gentleman to come and speak with Nigel personally and bring a couple of the estate's paintings. Did he arrive?"

"Nobody brought any paintings in yesterday or today," Ruth said.

"Oh," Raleigh said, feeling that maybe he had it wrong after all. "Didn't someone come and ask to see Nigel privately?"

"Not a gentleman," Ruth said. "Only a young lady yesterday. I don't know if she was from the estate or not."

"I see," Raleigh said, and now he was sure it was hopeless. Nigel would be furious when he found out that he was pumping this employee for information. He made a last feeble attempt and said apologetically, "I guess it wasn't my client, unless the young lady happened to bring some paintings here with her."

Ruth laughed and said, "Dear me, no. The poor little thing was lucky she could carry her purse let alone any paintings. She was so frail."

Raleigh looked away quickly and felt that sensation again, the blood rushing to his head and ice cubes in the gut. He said, "Was she a very young woman with dark hair?"

"Yes, she was so adorable in her little candy-striped dress," Ruth said. "I guess she's also working with you on this estate sale?"

After a long pause Raleigh said, "Yes, she's the granddaughter of my aunt. Everybody's trying to get in on the money from the family art collection."

"I know what you mean," Ruth said.

"I'll give Nigel a call after I get home," Raleigh said. "Thanks."

Raleigh genuinely feared he might go the way of Marty Brueger as he drove up into the Hollywood Hills. He was almost hyperventilating as he neared home and had to practice normal breathing and tell himself to stay calm. At last he understood all of it. The theft of the van was not a random act at all! It was part of the carefully planned scheme of Nigel Wickland. Valerie, or whatever her name was, and her companion thief were part of Nigel's conspiracy from the beginning. Nigel had induced Raleigh to allow the theft and reproduction of the million-dollar paintings. But for all Raleigh knew, they might be worth $2 million. Or $3 million! And then Nigel had hired a pair of young criminals to help him remove Raleigh from the conspiracy.

Nigel would eventually tell Raleigh that it's a terrible tragedy but the thieves apparently did not intend to ever call him again. It was such a simple but brilliant scheme, and he, Raleigh Dibble, was the dupe. The fall guy. The patsy. The fool. The thing that made it so diabolical was the trick with the van keys. Nigel had banked on Raleigh not looking for the keys, which Nigel said he left in the van. Nigel knew that Raleigh would not search for the keys, not inside a gate-guarded estate. And it had worked beautifully by allowing Nigel to shift the fault for the van theft to Raleigh.

What would Nigel have done if Raleigh had found the keys and brought them into the house? Well, that, too, was explainable. In that eventuality, Nigel's young crime partners probably had a spare key, and Nigel would have covered their escape by claiming that they must've hot-wired the van. But that wouldn't have been quite as neat. That might have thrown up a red flag for Raleigh. No, it had all worked perfectly, just the way Nigel had planned it.

Raleigh wondered where Nigel had found frail little Valerie. So vulnerable, so delicate, so young, so ruthless! Raleigh remembered how she'd kissed his cheek before she'd departed and asked if he'd like to meet at a bistro, and how that gesture had touched his heart. When Raleigh pulled into the Bruegers' five-car garage, tears were streaming down his cheeks.

Raleigh let himself into the foyer, turned off the burglar alarm, and recalled that Leona Brueger had informed him that because of the burglaries in the Hollywood Hills, she now kept a handgun in her bedroom. He was going to find that gun. He was going to visit Nigel Wickland tomorrow, and the backstabbing sissy was going to bring those paintings back. Those paintings were returning home where they belonged, one way or the other.

Raleigh searched the master bedroom for more than an hour before he found the gun in a hatbox in the closet. It was a nickel-plated, snub-nosed .38 caliber revolver, and it was loaded.

Nigel returned to the Wickland Gallery at closing time, and Ruth said, "Oh, Nigel, you're back. I thought you had left for the day. There was a Mr. Dibble here insisting to see you. When I tried to find out what it was all about, he was vague and said something about an estate sale you're working on."

Nigel scratched his chin, trying to stay composed, and said, "Dibble? Would it be Raleigh Dibble?"

"Yes, that's him," Ruth said.

"He's a fool," Nigel said. "He completely overestimates the value of everything. Did he say if he was coming back?"

"No," Ruth said, "but he seemed eager to know if anyone had come here in the last few days with some paintings for you. Of course I told him no."

So that was it! Raleigh suspected that the thief had brought the paintings and been paid, and that he was being double-crossed! Nigel said casually to Ruth, "Yes, the estate sale. I didn't mention it to you because it's all part of his inflated personal appraisal of art that he knows nothing about. He's not worth a moment of my time."

"He claimed he was a personal friend," Ruth said. "He knew your cell number."

This was getting uncomfortable and Nigel wanted to end it. "He asked for my mobile number when we spoke, and in a weak moment I gave it to him. A personal friend? Never."

With that, Nigel entered his office and debated whether or not to phone and chastise Raleigh for coming and grilling Ruth because of his own uncontrollable paranoia. But he decided to let it be. Raleigh would eventually have to accept that the thieves must have disposed of the paintings themselves. What else could he think?

Because her employer had ended the discussion abruptly, Ruth hadn't bothered to mention all of her conversation with Raleigh Dibble. She thought about telling him of Raleigh Dibble's peculiar interest when she'd casually mentioned the only visitor who *had* insisted on seeing Nigel yesterday—the girl in the candy-striped dress. She decided to forget about it. After all, Nigel said the man and his estate sale was of no interest to him.

It was not a night of a Hollywood moon, but if it had been, the pizza might have gone to 6-X-46. During the first hour of their watch, Della Ravelle and Britney Small got a call to a popular bar and grill on north Vermont Avenue, where a drunk was causing a disturbance.

It was one of the older chop houses with the red imitation leather and walnut paneling that previous generations loved so much. A sixty-something hostess with a retro bouffant hairdo, wearing an inappropriate sheath dress with spaghetti straps, was standing at a tall table in the foyer taking reservations.

She put her hand over the mouthpiece of the phone when the cops entered, and said, "In the bar."

Britney started in until Della grabbed her arm and said, "Wait a minute. Let's first find out what we're walking into."

When the hostess finished taking the dinner reservation, Della said, "What's the disturbance all about?"

The hostess said, "There's a crazy man in there, buying two drinks at a time and pouring every other one into a vase."

"That's it?" Della said. "That's the disturbance?"

"He's frightening customers," the hostess said. "Several people left the bar because of him. And he's disturbing the bartender."

"Is he ranting and raving and talking gibberish or something like that?" Della asked.

"No," the hostess said. "But he seems to be talking to himself."

"Quietly?" Della asked. "There's no law against that."

"Maybe not, but it's scary," the hostess said.

"Okay," Della said. "Let's have a look, partner." When they were walking to the bar, Della whispered to Britney, "Remember, we don't hassle loony tunes if they're peaceful. This is fucking Hollywood."

Their eyes had to adjust when they got inside the barroom. It was one of those very dark, formerly elegant barrooms, where after a martini or two, the aging patrons could appear to each other the way they used to be and not the way they currently were. They saw that the hostess was right. He'd scared everyone away. He was seated on a stool at the far end of an old mahogany bar complete with a dented but shiny brass rail several inches from the floor.

The bartender looked at the cops and moved his eyes toward the lone customer, who had two bucket glasses in front of him. He was not old, but he was older than Della. She figured him for about fifty. He was losing his hair but it was mostly dark with only sprinkles of gray. He was getting a soft roll around his middle that his yellow golf shirt didn't hide, but Della thought he wasn't a bad-looking guy. In fact, he reminded her in some ways of her second husband, even to the arching heavy eyebrows. He looked to be talking softly to himself and he appeared boozy enough that he should not drive home.

Della said sotto to Britney. "You're contact, I'm cover. Go for it."

Britney walked up behind the man and said, "Evening, sir."

He didn't turn around, but said, "Evening."

"What're you doing, sir?" Britney asked.

"Having a drink," he said.

It was so dark in the bar that she couldn't clearly see the object on his lap, so she said, "Why don't you put that vase up on the bar. It makes police officers nervous when people have strange items in their hands. You can understand that, can't you?"

He picked it up carefully with both hands and put it on the bar, saying, "It isn't a vase. It's an urn."

"An urn?"

"Yes," he said, and for the first time turned on the stool and looked at Britney.

"Have you been pouring drinks into it?" she asked.

"Yes, a few. I don't think it's against the law, is it?"

Britney turned to look at Della and said, "Not that I know of, sir, but it's scaring the customers because it's so . . . unusual. Would you please tell me why you're pouring drinks into the urn and talking to yourself?"

"I'm not talking to myself," he said. "I'm talking to my dad. He's in there."

"I see," Britney said. "That urn contains your dad's ashes?"

"Yes," he said. "Digby G. Randolph was a great father and a wonderful man. This was just about his favorite restaurant. He asked me to come here from time to time and have a drink for him."

"But you had the idea to give a drink *to* him, is that what you're saying?"

"Exactly. I'm buying a few drinks for my dad."

"And when you're talking, you're not talking to yourself?"

"I'm talking to my dad. I know he can hear me."

Britney turned toward Della and then back to the son of Digby G. Randolph and said, "Are you driving tonight?"

"No," he said, "I came by taxi. I live in a condo at Sunset and Genesee."

"Okay, Mr. Randolph," Britney said. "I think you've had enough to drink tonight. The bartender thinks so, too. I'm going to ask the hostess to call you a cab, and then you and your dad can finish that last drink and go home, okay? And the next time you come here, I'd like you and your dad to take the dark corner table. Just put him on the chair beside you and whisper softly, and I don't think anyone will bother you. Do not belly-up to the bar with your dad anymore, okay?"

"I'll do what you say, Officer," the son of Digby G. Randolph said, "but Dad so liked to stand at the bar with his foot on the rail."

"I understand that, sir," Britney said. "But he had feet then. I'd like you to do it my way from now on."

"I will accede to your request, Officer," said the son of Digby G. Randolph, opening the lid of the urn and giving the last of the Jack Daniel's to his dad.

There was a reunion that night in unit 6-X-66. Hollywood Nate got Snuffy Salcedo back, complete with a bandage across his nose and a plastic noseguard. It made him look to Nate the movie buff like Lee Marvin with his false nose in *Cat Ballou.*

"Glad to be back?" Nate asked.

Snuffy said, "Yeah, my mother gets to kicking my ass after I been laying around the house too long, wounded warrior or not. She thinks idleness invites the devil."

Hollywood Nate was being extra solicitous and was doing the driving. "Let's not do anything heroic tonight," Snuffy said. "I'd like to just sit back and be the scribe. I don't wanna bump the beak before it's healed."

"Is it gonna look better when the bandage comes off?" Nate asked.

"It can't look worse than it's looked all my life," Snuffy said.

* * *

"Dude, I didn't think you were ever coming back," Flotsam said to Jetsam, on duty together in unit 6-X-32 for the first time since the battle at Goth House.

"Bro, I learned a few things about neck injuries," Jetsam said. "I learned you don't wanna have one. They hurt."

Flotsam had insisted on driving so that Jetsam didn't have to do too much craning at intersections. In fact, he was so solicitous that Jetsam finally said, "Bro, I ain't an invalid."

"I missed my li'l pard," Flotsam said. "Of course, Hollywood Nate's a cool dude, but he don't know shit about the beach and briny. After a while I couldn't think of what to talk about."

The surfer cops had taken a crime report just after dark from a Gallup, New Mexico, tourist who had had her purse picked while she was taking photos of the marble-and-brass stars on the Hollywood Boulevard Walk of Fame. They drove to the station to get a DR number on the report as required, and to have it signed by a supervisor, but they didn't find Sergeant Murillo in the sergeant's room. The troops, especially the surfer cops, always tried to avoid the nitpicking watch commander.

Jetsam said to Flotsam, "I hate taking our report to the kinda guy that would wear a ring on his index finger and make us call him 'His Excellency' if he had his way."

Flotsam said, "If he's in there, let's hold the report till later and get Murillo to sign it."

But at that moment Lieutenant O'Reilly wasn't in his office and Sergeant Murillo was, so Flotsam and Jetsam thought it was safe to enter.

"What's the air like?" Sergeant Murillo asked, meaning the airwaves.

"Quiet," Jetsam said. "A few calls going out to south-end units, and a prowler call in the Hollywood Hills that turned out to be a raccoon."

Much to the surfer cops' consternation, the watch commander

swept into the room just then, but not with his usual look of intensity and purpose. He was actually smiling. In fact, he was unable to contain his excitement.

He said to Sergeant Murillo, "The captain's finished with the citizens meeting at the Community Relations Office and he wants me to join him for code seven at El Cholo."

"I'm surprised he still has an appetite," Sergeant Murillo said, trying to concentrate on the report that the surfer cops had handed to him.

"Yeah," Flotsam agreed. "There ain't been a rational citizen walk into the Hollywood Crows Office since Hitler was still hanging wallpaper."

Ignoring both surfer cops, Lieutenant O'Reilly said to Sergeant Murillo, "The captain said he loves the green corn tamales at El Cholo. Tell me, are green tamales different from regular tamales?"

Sergeant Murillo looked up from the report and said, deadpan, "How would I know, Lieutenant?"

The young watch commander, who was nothing if not politically correct, was disconcerted by the sergeant's unexpected reply and said, "I just...well, I assumed..."

"That I'm Mexican?" Sergeant Murillo said.

"Well, your name and you...you look Hispanic, sort of, and I thought you would know Hispanic food."

"What's a Hispanic look like? And what in the world is Hispanic food?" Sergeant Murillo said, and now the surfer cops were grinning like hyenas, watching the lieutenant squirm and sputter.

"Damn, Murillo, you know what I mean," the watch commander said, genuinely angry that his sergeant was showing him up like this in front of two officers, especially these two.

Jetsam only made things worse when he said artlessly to the watch commander, "The sarge is just hacking on you, sir. He does that to us all the time. One time he pretended he was giving us serious roll call training and he goes, 'Listen up. Orders from the bureau commander. Officers are forbidden to wear any off-duty clothing that reveals body ink portraying one of our female senators doing fellatio on the president of the United States.'" Jetsam chuckled and said, "He keeps our morale up with funny stuff like that."

Lieutenant O'Reilly stared icily at Jetsam for a long moment and said, "Yes, I'm certain you would find something like that amusing."

Sergeant Murillo winked at the surfer cops and said to the watch commander, "Okay, Lieutenant, I confess, I'm Mexican. Or at least my grandparents are. And I can promise you that El Cholo's green tamales will make the captain as happy as a drunken mariachi on Cinco de Mayo. You can order yourself a margarita manqué, and by the end of the meal you two will be real *compadres*."

Lieutenant O'Reilly noticed that the surfer cops were smiling fondly at their smart-ass sergeant, and it made the lieutenant angrier. He redirected his pique toward Flotsam, saying, "Don't any of the sergeants around this station ever tell you people that gelled-up surfer hairstyles are unfit for police officers?"

Flotsam looked down at the watch commander, whose nose almost touched the tall cop's badge number, and he stopped smiling.

Jetsam again tried a show of goodwill and said, "Actually, sir, only the barneys wear gel or hairspray on the beach. The real kahunas go au naturel, so to speak."

That made the lieutenant turn on Jetsam and say, "I also think the so-called sun streaks in your hair look like highlighting. It's vaguely effeminate for male police officers to highlight their hair. Didn't Sergeant Murillo ever mention that to you?"

Neither surfer cop was smiling now, and both were shooting hate beams at the watch commander, when Sergeant Murillo stood up and said to them, "Okay, we're through here. You can go back to work."

Flotsam and Jetsam were grim and silent when they strode across the parking lot to their shop. After they were in the car,

Flotsam said, "Dude, I think we should drop by Yerevan Tow Service. I got an idea."

Jetsam, who was angrily alliterative, said, "I hope it's a real brain bleacher, bro, cuz I got, like, the image of that slithering snarky slime-sucker stuck in my cerebrum. Feel me?"

"I feel ya, dude," Flotsam said.

Yerevan Tow Service was known to many of the cops at Hollywood Station as a kind of outlaw one-man tow service that picked up scraps that LAPD's official tow garages left behind or couldn't handle. Sarkis, the owner, was a happy-go-lucky Armenian, always eager to impound any vehicles at the scene of traffic collisions or radio calls, which he picked up on his police scanner.

He usually had some of his wife's stuffed grape leaves in his tow truck, and on a couple of occasions he shared them with the surfer cops. And one night he was rewarded for his generosity. On that occasion, 6-X-32 had stopped Sarkis while he was in his private car, driving home from a bar in Little Armenia, absolutely hammered.

As soon as Flotsam and Jetsam saw whom they'd stopped, Flotsam said to Sarkis, "Dude, when you get your swill on, try to remember, it's not a sprint, it's a marathon."

They locked up Sarkis's five-year-old Lincoln and drove him home in their black-and-white. Sarkis tried to invite them into his house for some leftover shish kebab, but Jetsam said to him, "We gotta get back to our beat, bro, but we got your marker. Someday we may need to collect on it."

And now was the time. Sarkis was working late at his tow garage and was happy to see his LAPD friends. He was good at bodywork and had been reassembling a damaged Ford pickup with junkyard parts. After hugs and greetings, he listened intently to what Flotsam and Jetsam had to say about a major problem at Hollywood Station.

Thirty minutes before Lieutenant O'Reilly left his office to join the captain at El Cholo, 6-X-32 received a confidential cell phone message from one of the desk officers at Hollywood Station. It concerned the approximate arrival time for the watch commander's code 7 rendezvous with the station captain.

Lieutenant O'Reilly had a marvelous time at El Cholo that evening, going well over the allotted time for his code 7 meal break. He told the captain of the many things wrong with the personnel at Hollywood Station. He was especially critical of the midwatch troops, who worked from 5:15 P.M. until 4 A.M. four days a week. He admitted that the officers liked the four-ten shift, but he had many reasons for why the watch hours were inefficient. He said that he wished they could go back to the old eight-hour-and-forty-five-minute work shift five days a week, because efficiency trumped morale. And he told the captain how he wished he had more authority when it came to overtime being granted. He had a strong belief that many officers were padding the books with phony "greenies," as they called the OT slips, and he was planning to put a stop to it. He said that he was working on ways to make supervisors — and he mentioned Sergeant Murillo by name — more responsive to orders and roll call training from the bureau level and less attuned to all of the petty gripes and special requests from the officers on his watch, especially certain officers who flouted good discipline.

All in all, he was wrecking the captain's dinner of green corn tamales, and his boss wished it were possible to get drunk on virgin margaritas so this eager beaver could pass out on the table or something.

After their meal break, Lieutenant O'Reilly thanked the captain excessively for buying him the tamales and they said their good-byes outside El Cholo's front entrance. And then Lieutenant O'Reilly walked to his car, which he'd had to park on Eleventh Street just east of Western Avenue because of the crowded restaurant parking lot. He had his keys in his hand, preparing to unlock the door, when he saw that he couldn't.

The front door on the driver's side was gone. He stopped and stared at the inside of his car in disbelief, only to discover that the door on the passenger side was also missing. The bolts and hinges on each side had been attacked and the doors...were...gone.

Lieutenant O'Reilly put in a code 2 call for a patrol unit to assist, and the first to arrive was 6-X-32. The surfer cops bailed out and ran to their watch commander with gusto.

"Your doors ain't here, Lieutenant!" Flotsam cried. "What happened?"

"How the hell would I know what happened?" Lieutenant O'Reilly said. "I can't believe this!"

"Those car strippers stop at nothing!" Jetsam cried. "Musta been those rotten little Eighteenth Streeters."

Two other midwatch units arrived very fast, and Snuffy Salcedo got out of the car and started snapping photos of the watch commander's car with his camera phone.

"Stop that!" Lieutenant O'Reilly yelled at him. "Broadcast a code four. We've got enough people here. I don't want anyone else seeing this goddamn travesty."

While Hollywood Nate was broadcasting a code 4, indicating that there was sufficient help at the scene, Lieutenant O'Reilly began searching the street and sidewalk with his flashlight, looking for evidence of the vandals' identity. He knew that this was no ordinary crime of malicious mischief, and he suspected that slackers from Hollywood Station had done this to humilate him. The midwatch cops at the scene were fascinated, watching the way Lieutenant O'Reilly circled the wounded police vehicle like a predator wary of dangerous prey. His eyes were bulging and his face looked like a tomato about to explode.

Flotsam said sotto to Snuffy Salcedo, "Dude, I think the lieutenant's gone to dizzyland. This here outrage should not go unpunished."

Jetsam said sotto to Snuffy Salcedo, "Bro, these are perilous times we live in. Nobody's safe no more."

Snuffy Salcedo listened to the surfer cops and whispered something to Hollywood Nate, something he'd asked before. "Are you telling me these two don't rehearse this shit?"

"Maybe some of it," Nate conceded in a whisper of his own. "They're sort of the Gilbert and Sullivan of Hollywood Station. They write and sometimes star in their little asphalt operettas."

"This looks to me like somebody's idea of a prank!" Lieutenant O'Reilly said after his search for evidence turned up nothing. "I want this unit taken to the parking lot and dusted for prints. I'm going to get to the bottom of this."

"Let's glove up, partner," Flotsam said, taking latex gloves from his pocket.

"You won't need to," Lieutenant O'Reilly said to Jetsam. "I want you to drive me to the station right this minute."

"Roger that, sir," Jetsam said.

"And you drive my unit in," Lieutenant O'Reilly said to Flotsam, handing him the keys. "Book anything you find in my car that even remotely might be evidence. A matchstick, a chewing gum wrapper, anything. I want the bastards that did this, and I'm going to get them."

"I'm on it, sir," Flotsam said. "I'll do a diligent search for clues. We sure wouldn't want the doors to turn up at a swap meet or maybe in an *L.A. Times* story."

Jetsam opened the passenger door on 6-X-32's shop for the watch commander to get in, but Lieutenant O'Reilly paused and showed all present a grimace of a smile. He probably thought it showed self-confidence and was intimidating, but Hollywood Nate thought it looked like the other contenders' smiles on the night they lost the Oscar to Kate Winslet.

When Jetsam got behind the wheel, he said, "If this does happen to get in the news, don't let it embarrass you, Lieutenant. It's not your fault. This is fucking Hollywood."

Flotsam enjoyed driving a car with no front doors, and he

decided to take Hollywood Boulevard so that he could cruise past Grauman's Chinese Theatre and give the tourists a show. When he was stopped for traffic directly in front of Grauman's forecourt, a clutch of tourists with cameras ran to the curb and started snapping photos of the doorless police car.

Flotsam waved and yelled, "Tough town! Last week somebody stole my front fenders!"

TWENTY-FOUR

THIS WAS THE day of reckoning as far as Raleigh Dibble was concerned. He did everything he could to make time pass faster. He dusted and vacuumed the master suite for Leona Brueger's return and even washed her windows. That involved some precarious labor on a tall stepladder. He drove his own car to the markets where his employer had charge accounts and made sure that there was enough fresh produce, chicken, and fish to provide meals for several days in case she was too tired to dine out.

When he was finished with chores, he called Cedars-Sinai and received a report on Marty Brueger. His condition was not as serious as had been thought, and it was hoped that the old man could soon be moved to a managed-care facility. Raleigh was living in such a state of fear for his own plight that he hadn't had time to pity Marty Brueger. But now Raleigh thought that if Marty Brueger was moved to a less-structured facility, he would take the poor old geezer some of his favorite Irish whiskey. It pleased him to be concerned with someone else for a change.

When Raleigh was finished with everything he could think of to do, he found himself wondering if he would even be there to prepare a homecoming meal for her or if he would be in jail. Or would he be dead? He sat in his bedroom and stared at Leona Brueger's nickel-plated revolver. One thing he knew for sure, for the first time he was capable of violence, at least as far as Nigel Wickland was concerned. Nobody in his life had ever harmed him so grievously. Regardless of the consequences, he was not going to let that arrogant son of a bitch get away with it. He knew exactly what he was going to do.

Raleigh planned on going to the Wickland Gallery at 4 P.M., but not to enter. He could watch the gallery entrance from the coffee shop across the street to know if Nigel left. Just before the gallery's closing time of 5 P.M., Raleigh was going to enter, demand to see Nigel, and strongly suggest to him that he send Ruth home because a private talk was essential and unavoidable. And of course Nigel would be angry that Raleigh had come, but when they were alone, the anger would turn into something else. Mr. Nigel Wickland, the master schemer and manipulator, was going to experience a bit of what Raleigh Dibble had been living with ever since he'd been insane enough to join the gallery owner's plot. Nigel Wickland was going to experience fear! Every time Raleigh looked at the nickel-plated revolver lying on his bed, it made his palms sweat.

At 1 P.M., Megan Burke made the call to Arjan, the Sikh taxi driver to whom she had promised the $100 tip. She had packed her bag, leaving space for a thousand hundred-dollar bills. She had no idea how big a package that would be, but there was plenty of room in her suitcase, since she had so few clothes left after her year of riding the ox in Hollywood.

She was surprised that she did not feel worse than she did. The joint pain from her opioid withdrawal was still severe, but the diarrhea had abated and she wasn't vomiting as much. She looked in her pill container and saw that she had enough medication to get her home to Oregon, and from there it would be a few hours of hugs and kisses with her mother and brother and then she'd go directly into rehab.

She had spent the morning talking and crying with her mother on the phone, after which her mother phoned several Oregon rehab facilities until she found one close to home that would permit Megan to bring Cuddles with her to the ninety-day treatment program. Megan's mother told her that she would go to the bank and see if she could take out a second mortgage to cover the $25,000 cost, but Megan told her not to worry about it, because she had won a big prize in the California lottery and she was paying for her own rehab.

The last thing Megan said to her astonished mother was that there would be $75,000 left from the prize money after taxes. She insisted that her mom take it all, along with profound apologies for having been such a miserable daughter.

Before they hung up, her mother said to Megan, "Honey, you could never be anything but a wonderful, loving daughter. I can't wait to have you home. The only mistake you ever made in your life was going to Hollywood, California."

Megan went to the bathroom to dry her tears and touch up her makeup and then called Nigel Wickland on his cell number. When he answered, she said, "I'll be there at two o'clock. Are you ready for me?"

"Yes," he said. "I've given my assistant the afternoon off. I'll be here alone."

"I won't be alone," she said.

"I don't doubt that," Nigel said, ending the conversation.

When Jonas Claymore arrived in court, he looked for Megan, but she wasn't there. He was growing very concerned for his money. Thinking about it made him uncontrollably jittery. When he'd had his fill of waiting, he jumped up and told a bailiff that he demanded to speak to a public defender. He also demanded an own-recognizance release. He said he'd never been arrested before except once for DUI, so he deserved to be OR'ed as soon as possible. He said he wanted immediate access to counsel, any counsel. He said he'd even settle for one that advertises on bus benches and takes his orders from sleazy bail bondsmen.

The bailiff told Jonas if he was smart, he'd zip his lips.

Jonas Claymore was still sitting with other in-custody defendants when court convened after lunch. He had been able to speak with a harried public defender, who had verified that Jonas had only one arrest on his rap sheet, for DUI, and he agreed to represent Jonas and ask for an own-recognizance release. The judge, who was just as harried as the public defender, and who was looking at a roomful of miscreants and their friends and families, granted the OR release. Jonas was set free and his property was returned, which included a cheap wristwatch and a wallet containing the only hundred-dollar bill he had left. He used that money to call a taxi to take him to his car in the parking lot at Pablo's Taco Shop, where he paid the driver and looked around in vain for someone he knew who might have some ox.

All the way to the apartment he thought of what he was going to say to Megan Burke, who had left him rotting in that filthy jail with smelly savages who'd terrified him. She hadn't tried to post bail, she hadn't come to his arraignment, and she hadn't done shit to help him, despite all he had done for her during the year they'd been together. He had shared his life and everything he owned with that cunt! He had never laid an angry hand on her, but he thought that just might change when he got home. It would all depend on what she had to say for herself.

When he got home, he found out what she had to say for herself. It was on the note. And beside the note were his cell phone, her key, and $1,900. He read the note three times, his rage mounting. Her clothes and bag were gone and so was her cat.

He snatched the money off the table, put it in his pocket, and phoned Wilbur. He was jonesing bad and needed something to smooth him out so he could think. So he could do what he had to do. The bitch had robbed him and he was going to find her if he had to check every motel in Hollywood. He'd get her when she went to Pablo's to score, or maybe when she called Wilbur for some ox. He'd slip Wilbur a President Grant to tip him off as to where she was staying with his fucking money.

When Jonas looked behind the sofa, he was shocked. The paintings were gone! She had even stolen his paintings. His outrage turned to fury. He felt like he might keel over in a faint. He wished she'd left her cat there so he could kill it.

There was only one thing she could have done with them. She must've kept her schoolgirl promise and returned them to the gallery owner. And now she was out there spending Jonas's money. She'd probably already spent a few grand on ox and was holed up somewhere chasing dragons with some other stupid bastard who was dumb enough to take her in. Well, somebody was going to pay for how he'd been screwed. She'd pay dearly if and when he found her. But until then he wasn't taking this like some screwed-over pussy. He was going out and getting what was coming to him.

Wilbur didn't answer, so he got in his car and drove to the cybercafé, where he saw a guy named Beatle who he used to buy crystal meth from, back before Megan, back when he was a tweaker. Beatle used to run a chop shop and would do anything for meth. He was now so strung out, he'd kill you for your liver if he could find a buyer for it. He could slam a gram and think nothing of it.

Jonas gave Beatle a pair of Jacksons, and Beatle showed teeth like jagged licorice drops, and he said, "Dude, you bought yourself a meth run on my shit pipe. Follow me to my crib."

They went to his nearby rat hole of an apartment, and Jonas smoked crystal meth once again. It was nothing like smoking ox, but it was better than nothing. He remembered how he used to love it, but now he hated it. After riding the ox, meth seemed like nothing but a lowlife drug smelling like cat piss. Nowadays he was way better than this. Still, it beat jonesing, so he smoked a lot of it. And when he was finished, he found that it made him feel agitated. It made him feel paranoid. It made him feel wild!

When he was about to leave Beatle's apartment, the tweaker showed him eyes as empty as a haunted house and said, "Don't trip, potato chip."

It was just after 2 P.M. when Megan and her Sikh taxi driver walked from his parked taxi to the front door of the Wickland Gallery. Megan was wearing a long-sleeved red jersey, jeans, and tennis shoes, and was carrying a tattered suitcase in one hand and in the other hand an airline-approved cat carrier with Cuddles inside it. The tall, bearded Sikh wore a cobalt-blue turban, a guayabera shirt, khakis, and sandals, and carried the two blanket-wrapped paintings, one under each arm.

Megan opened the door and saw Nigel Wickland waiting at Ruth's desk in the main room of the gallery. He was as elegant as ever in a double-breasted navy pinstripe, a white button-down shirt, and a rose-colored silk necktie. He looked very tense, and there was even a tic working the corner of his left eye.

Nigel stood and said to the Sikh, "You can lean those items against the wall."

The Sikh looked at Megan, who nodded to him. Only then did the taxi driver comply. Then she handed the Sikh the cat carrier and said, "Arjan, please wait just outside the door with Cuddles. I'll be in here no more than fifteen minutes."

The Sikh nodded again and left the gallery, taking Cuddles with him. Nigel could see him through the gallery window, standing on the pavement with the pet carrier firmly in his grasp.

Nigel gave Megan a lopsided smile and said, "Yes, I see that you are well protected. But you have nothing to fear from me. Not anymore. In many ways you have done me a favor."

"By eliminating your partner?"

311

He didn't respond to that but said, "Let's go back to my office to complete our business."

Nigel picked up a wrapped painting in each hand, and Megan followed him to his office, and this time she did not feel frightened when he closed the door.

"Have a seat," he said, indicating a client chair in front of his desk.

She sat and put her suitcase flat on the floor and opened it. He looked at the suitcase and said, "I'm afraid I can't fill up a bag that big, but I have your entire bonus as requested. Although first I'd like to examine my merchandise."

He opened a door from his office that led to a storage room with a large sliding door leading from there to the alley. The cargo van was parked inside the storage room, and there were gallery supplies on shelves and benches. Nigel Wickland entered and turned on a light over one of the benches. He cut the duct tape and unwrapped the largest bundle. He lifted the painting and held it under the light, inspecting it closely. Megan stood in the doorway of the storage room and watched him.

"Ah, yes," he said. "*The Woman by the Water.* Isn't she lovely?" He carefully rewrapped the painting and then unwrapped the second one, holding it under the light, and nodded with a smile on his face.

"Satisfied?" Megan said.

Nigel said, "I am, indeed."

He rewrapped *Flowers on the Hillside* and opened the side door of the van, putting both bundled paintings inside on the floor. Then he closed the door of the van and said, "Now let's complete our business before your turbaned friend comes in here and dispatches me with his dagger."

They went back to Nigel's desk, where he opened a deep bottom drawer and removed a shipping carton without a lid. He placed it on his desk and said, "Go ahead and count it. I already have."

Megan picked up a packet of hundred-dollar bills, her heart beating in her ears, and counted. When she got to fifty, she stopped and fanned through the rest of the packet. Then she fanned through each of the other packets without counting. It was too staggering an amount of money. She said, "It looks okay. I trust you, Mr. Wickland."

Nigel emitted a burst of nervous laughter at that, and even Megan had to giggle. Then she put each packet into her large suitcase among a jumble of underwear, jeans, two books, T-shirts, and tank tops. When she was finished, she closed and locked the suitcase with a small luggage key.

"Yes, that should get through an airport baggage scanner with no problem," Nigel said. "I'll bet you'll be waiting anxiously for it to come down the carousel when you reach your destination, wherever that is."

Megan smiled without comment. Then she simply picked up the suitcase, opened the door of his office, and walked across the display room of the gallery to the Wilshire Boulevard door.

Before she opened it, Nigel called to her, saying, "Have a good life, Valerie. Your ambition has been for me a blessing in disguise."

She didn't respond but wiggled her fingers at him in a final farewell. When she got outside, the Sikh took her suitcase, and she carried the pet carrier to the taxi for the ride to LAX. Megan Burke was so overjoyed that she decided to increase Arjan's tip to $200.

And on that ride to the airport, with her hand inside the pet carrier stroking her cat, Megan Burke tried to take with her something positive from her two years away from home. But the addiction that had resulted in her physical, emotional, and moral decline had obliterated all positives. And then she thought, no, there was one gift that Hollywood, California, had given her. It came when she had walked into the animal rescue facility fourteen months ago. Hollywood had given her Cuddles the calico cat.

TWENTY-FIVE

RALEIGH DIBBLE HAD taken the longest shower of his life. He never wanted to leave the hot water. When he did, he went to the bathroom sink and shaved with a new blade and did as good a job as he could in combing his thinning hair. He laid out his best sport shirt and newest chinos. He even brushed the lint from his best blazer and ran a cloth over his old loafers. He'd seen movies of men who were facing momentous events in their lives who took such care, sometimes before putting a gun to their heads and pulling the trigger.

By 4 P.M., he was across the street from the Wickland Gallery, having first ascertained that the lights were on inside and the gallery was open for business.

Jonas Claymore was on a meth ride that he hadn't been on in more than a year. He was driving in frenzy from east Hollywood to Beverly Hills through rush-hour traffic. His central nervous system had come unwired and his hands were out of control. He kept touching the instruments in the VW bug. He'd make sure the headlights were not on and the emergency brake was not on and the radio controls were working and the heater switch was off. Every time he finished he'd do it all over again. His hands didn't belong to him anymore. They just kept fiddling and fretting in perpetual motion.

He knew how much he needed some ox to get himself under

control, but there was no time to waste. He fantasized that Megan Burke might be there when he arrived. He would deal with her if he found her there. Oh yes, he would. They were laughing at him, Megan and that gallery guy who had *his* paintings. She'd stolen them from him. They'd been his to dispose of as he chose, but she'd clowned him. Now they were both laughing at him.

He had to remind himself to slow down and obey the traffic laws. He couldn't afford to get stopped by the cops again. It was bizarre, but everyone he saw on the streets looked like an undercover cop, and they all seemed to be watching him. But they couldn't stop him from doing what he had to do. Nobody could.

Jonas only wished he'd had time to talk to Wilbur to see if he could sell him a burner. He'd never had one before, but he was sure he'd handle one okay. Maybe a pistol like all the cops carried on *CSI*. But he hadn't had time to strap up. All he had was the large carving knife that was riding inside his waistband, the handle of it digging into his sunken belly. It would be enough because he was starting to feel invincible.

Five minutes before its scheduled closing, Raleigh Dibble crossed Wilshire Boulevard and entered the Wickland Gallery. He didn't see the woman at her desk, so he walked back to Nigel's office just as Nigel was coming out of the little restroom.

"Surprise," Raleigh said, and sat in the client chair, trying to stay cool.

Nigel frowned and said, "I didn't hear you come in. What're you doing here? You should know better than to come here again."

"Oh, your assistant told you I was here the other day?"

"Yes."

"Why didn't you call me to complain about that, Nigel?"

Nigel sat on the corner of his desk and said, "What good would that have done? I've tried everything in my power to persuade you to be patient until the thieves contact us. What more can I do?"

"I've forgotten your employee's name," Raleigh said.

"Ruth is her name. You look tense, Raleigh. Can I get you a cup of coffee? Tea, perhaps?"

Raleigh said, "Did Ruth tell you what we talked about when I came looking for you yesterday?"

"Yes, she said you inquired whether a man came here asking to talk to me personally."

"Did you understand why I asked that?"

"Of course," Nigel said. "You think that I'm doing business with the man who phoned me and that I'm concealing it from you."

"Yes, that's right," Raleigh said, thinking, Calm. Stay calm.

"Well, it's silly, Raleigh," Nigel said. "We may never hear from them at all, and if that's the case, I'm the only one who's out any expenses."

"There's nothing to worry about, then?" Raleigh said.

"Nothing," Nigel said. "Leona will never notice what we did, and I will proceed with assisting her to crate and store the replicated pictures when the time comes."

"I see," Raleigh said. "Then it was just a big swing and a miss, our whole caper?"

"In your baseball terms? Yes, that's what it was. I'm sorry for you and I'm sorry for me. I spent money on this plan, if you'll remember."

"Yes, I certainly do remember," Raleigh said. "More money than I knew about."

"What's that supposed to mean?"

Raleigh's demeanor changed and he said, "I'm referring to the money you paid your accomplices to screw me after you used me up."

"The pressure's become too much for you," Nigel said, standing up from his perch on the corner of his desk and walking around to his desk chair.

"I don't think so," Raleigh said. "I know that you hired two people from the get-go to pull that bogus theft of your van so that you could cut me right out of the picture. After I helped you switch the paintings, I was taken right out of it, as neat as you please."

"Jesus wept!" Nigel said incredulously, looking at the door to the storage room, which was ajar. "Is that what you really think? That I hired a couple of blokes to pretend to steal my van so that I could cut you out of the arrangement?"

"That's what I think," Raleigh said.

"On my word as a gentleman," Nigel said, "my van was stolen by unknown persons. Full stop. End of story."

"You're no gentleman, you son of a bitch," Raleigh said, smoldering now.

"Get out, Raleigh," Nigel said. "You're making a fool of yourself."

Raleigh watched Nigel's face very closely when he said, "And how about the girl in the candy-striped dress?"

"The what?" Nigel said instantly.

He was good, Raleigh thought. He didn't flinch. But the tic at the corner of his eye began working overtime. "Valerie, if that's her name."

Nigel felt truly gob smacked. How did Raleigh know that Valerie had come here? He said, "Please explain yourself, Raleigh. You're not making sense."

"You're a conniving bastard, aren't you?" Raleigh said. "Me, I'm just a dumb old ex-con who's a servant for rich people and makes their meals and wipes their asses, just like you said. But now I realize that I was actually pretty content with my lot in life until I met you. Now that I see what you are."

"This is going nowhere," Nigel said. "Whatever I tell you won't matter. You're simply overwhelmed by paranoid thoughts. Believe me, I wish as much as you do that we'd never met, but if wishes were fishes, as they say."

"Tell me about the girl in the candy-striped dress," Raleigh said.

"Tell me about darling, adorable little Valerie. Why did she come to see me? That's the only thing that puzzles me. What was that all about? Was she doing a little work on her own as a private agent? Maybe she wanted to see what other art was in the house so she and her thieving partner could steal more from Leona Brueger? I can't figure out that part of it. Why did she come to the Brueger house? Tell me that much, if you know."

Nigel Wickland was more exhausted than he'd been when they'd done the switch and watched it all implode with the stealing of the van. He was more exhausted than he'd been anytime in the past several days when he'd worried that the police would come to his gallery to say that they'd caught a man with his van and some blanket-wrapped paintings that he would need to explain. He was drained. Raleigh Dibble had most of it wrong but enough of it right. He had let himself be trapped by a fool.

Then it came to him. "Ruth," Nigel said. "Ruth mentioned the girl in the candy-striped dress to you, didn't she?"

"You kept her a secret from me," Raleigh said.

"Bloody hell," Nigel said. "Yes, I have kept some things from you, but for good reason, trust me."

"I'm all ears," Raleigh said, "like a cornfield in summer. Enlighten me, Nigel."

"They truly stole the van," Nigel said. "A man I've never seen and the girl we both know as Valerie. Will you at least believe that much?"

"Go on," Raleigh said.

"She's a smart girl, infinitely smarter than her crime partner, whom I've never met. She saw the Brueger name and address on the framer's tag that's stapled to the stretcher bars, and she figured out that something was wrong with my claim that the paintings belong to me. She went to you on her own to try to work it out, and I guess she charmed you into inviting her into the house, where you generously showed her around. And she saw *The Woman by the Water* and *Flowers on the Hillside*. All because you showed the goddamn paintings to her, Raleigh. You caused all this. It's all your fault, not mine!"

"I've never stopped wondering about the generosity of the thieves," Raleigh said. "You, know, the way they gave back your van as a show of good faith?"

"They're not master criminals, those two," Nigel said. "They're addled drug addicts who got extremely lucky. You saw Valerie. Couldn't you see that she's physically unwell?"

"And they took your twelve thousand and gave you back the paintings as promised, right along with your van, didn't they?"

"Good lord!" Nigel said. "No, I haven't paid them anything yet because I haven't heard any more from them since Valerie came here and blackmailed me. All because you invited her into the fucking house."

"And did she tell you how much more money she wanted not to break it all down for the police or for Mrs. Brueger?"

"No!" Nigel said. "I've been waiting to hear from them. I decided that your nerves were so frazzled you couldn't take another shock like this, so that's why I wasn't going to tell you until I received their demand. Don't you understand?"

"You were protecting me. That's kind of you," Raleigh said.

"I was protecting both of us. Believe me, this has become so convoluted I don't know where I am half the time. I knew that you couldn't possibly deal with more stress. Of that much I was certain."

"So all we can do is wait to receive the new instructions from Valerie or her partner, is that it, Nigel?"

"That's about it," Nigel said. "We must wait."

"That's not about it," Raleigh said. "I have another plan in mind."

The buzzer sounded in the office, indicating that someone had entered the gallery door on Wilshire Boulevard.

"Oh, Christ!" Nigel said. "I should've locked up. Will you excuse me for a moment?"

Nigel got up and left the office, and when he entered the display room, he turned and said, "Raleigh, if you want coffee, it's on the table by the restroom door. Help yourself."

Jonas Claymore, who was standing in the middle of the display room, heard what Nigel said and realized that the gallery owner was not alone.

It was hard for Nigel to repress a sneer of disgust when he saw the gangling, disheveled young man in a hooded gray sweatshirt looking at him with a crazed expression. Nigel thought that the Beverly Hills police should do a better job in keeping panhandlers from harassing the business owners along Wilshire Boulevard.

"I'm afraid we're closed," Nigel said to Jonas. "I'll be locking the door as soon as my last customer leaves."

Without a word, Jonas scowled, turned, and slouched across the display room to the door with Nigel following after him. When Jonas stepped out onto Wilshire Boulevard, the gallery owner locked the door behind him, pulled a blind over the glass door, and placed a "Closed" sign in the display window.

Okay, you prissy asshole, Jonas thought. We'll play, but it's my move. He walked around to the alley and saw that the gallery had a large sliding door big enough to accommodate a van. There were two parking spaces in the alley, one of them containing a red BMW roadster. Yeah, that's his, Jonas thought. A fag car.

He hurried to his VW bug, moved it to the end of the alley, and sat there watching the rear door of the gallery, thinking he'd trade three Franklins for just half an ox at this moment. An elderly woman left the door of the jewelry store behind him to empty a trash container in a Dumpster. Jonas eyed her in his rearview mirror and she looked to him like an undercover cop.

When Nigel Wickland had finished locking up and turning out

the lights, he returned to his office and found himself looking at the muzzle of a gun.

Raleigh was standing by the door to the storage room, and he said, "Let's you and me have a look in here, Nigel. If the paintings aren't here, we'll take a ride to your condo and look for them there."

And at last Raleigh Dibble saw something that he had longed to see ever since the entire misadventure had begun. He saw something that he knew too well from his own experience. He saw real fear in the face of Nigel Wickland.

"What're you playing at?" Nigel said, and Raleigh was pleased to see that the tic at the corner of Nigel's eye had intensified.

"I'm not playing," Raleigh said. "Not anymore."

"Please, Raleigh!" Nigel said.

"You're looking at a desperate, angry man," Raleigh said. "I believe that I'll spend many years in prison if I don't put this thing right, and that's what I'm going to do tonight, one way or the other."

"You won't use that," Nigel said. "You can't!"

"I will certainly kill you, Nigel," Raleigh said, "if you don't walk into that storage room right now. And then I might kill myself. Don't test me."

Nigel didn't just walk, he skated. He seemed to glide along the floor with his hands held in front of him palms up, as though to ward off any bullet that Raleigh might fire. When he stepped into the storage room, he switched on the light.

"You see," he said, "there's nothing here but store supplies..."

"How about your van," Raleigh said.

"Go ahead and search," Nigel said. "This is ridiculous."

Raleigh said, "Get me a flashlight. It's too dark in here."

"On the workbench," Nigel said. "But I'd like you to put the gun away."

Raleigh saw the toolbox, the one that Nigel had had the day

they removed the paintings from their frames and installed the replicas in their places. The small flashlight was in the top tray. Raleigh took it out and said, "Turn around, Nigel, with your hands held high."

"What're you going to do?" Nigel said, sounding like he might weep. Sounding the way he did on the night that the thieves stole the van.

"Just be very still," Raleigh said, shining the beam into darkened crannies and inside cabinets and even up to the exposed beams.

"Satisfied?" Nigel said. "Can we stop this charade now?"

"Not yet," Raleigh said.

When Nigel heard the door to the van open, he said, "For god's sake, Raleigh!"

"Do not move a hair," Raleigh said. Then he shined his beam inside the van and saw the familiar blanketed bundles.

"Raleigh...," Nigel said, unable to immediately come up with more than that. "Raleigh, Raleigh..."

"Do I need to have you take these out and open them?"

Nigel turned his face and spoke over his shoulder, saying, "I swear to you that I didn't know anything until the girl Valerie marched in here today with the paintings. I gave her the twelve thousand and she marched out again."

"And you were going to tell me about it when you got around to it, weren't you?"

"Can I put my hands down?"

"No, but you can turn around and face me."

Nigel turned, hands still held high, and said, "I couldn't tell you! All you've been talking about lately is how much you've regretted what we've done. You wanted to return the paintings to the house. I was afraid you would do it. I wasn't going to tell you about this until I shipped them to Europe and made the deal. Then I was going to surprise you with your share of a million dollars. I swear it's the truth, Raleigh!"

"You're amazing," Raleigh said. "You're an utterly amazing liar and four-flusher."

Nigel then began wheezing and reached frantically for his inhaler, but Raleigh said, "Move those Joan Crawford hands very slowly, Nigel."

Nigel said, "I…I…can't…can't catch my breath!"

"Slowly," Raleigh said, and Nigel complied, taking two puffs from the canister and inhaling deeply.

When his breathing improved, he said, "We can still make this work, Raleigh. There's no real harm done. You can't turn back now. Let me do what I was going to do. Half a million, Raleigh. Tax-free!"

"Very carefully, toss me the van keys," Raleigh said.

Nigel took his key ring from his pocket and tossed it ten feet across the storage room to the floor. Raleigh picked it up, returned the flashlight to the toolbox, carried the toolbox to the van, and put it behind the passenger seat.

"Get in the van behind the wheel," Raleigh said.

"This is madness," Nigel said. "Madness!"

"Get in!"

Nigel scurried to the van and got in the driver's seat.

"How do you open the sliding door?" Raleigh asked.

Nigel's voice was nearly inaudible when he said, "I have a remote here in the van."

Raleigh sat in the passenger seat and said, "Open the door."

Nigel pressed a remote clipped to the visor, and the door slid open.

"Drive," Raleigh said. "I think you know where."

"Madness!" Nigel Wickland said.

Jonas Claymore started his engine the minute the storage room door slid open. He saw the cargo van drive out and the door slide shut again. Darkness was arriving sooner now that Los Angeles was experiencing its version of autumn weather. It was too dark for

Jonas to see if the gallery owner was alone in the van. The other man in the office could have gone out the front door, for all he knew. Alone or not, the gallery owner would be coming back for his little red car, but Jonas opted to tail him rather than just to sit there. There might even be a better place to confront the sissy and make him give Jonas what was coming to him. And anyway, the crystal had made Jonas feel too supercharged to wait.

Jonas had to control himself as he drove in the early nighttime traffic. He didn't figure that the gallery owner would be looking for a tail, so he could get close, but in the heavy traffic he couldn't get close enough to see if the man was alone in the van.

He almost lost the van on Sunset Boulevard when it turned north on Fairfax. He picked it up again going east on Hollywood Boulevard but lost it for a moment when it made a left turn on Sierra Bonita. He picked it up again when it was eastbound on Franklin, and he lost the van completely when he was stopped by a traffic light on Outpost Drive. Jonas sat meth-crazed in his VW bug, and he banged on the steering wheel and kept his other hand on the horn, screaming out the window at the cars, at the traffic light, and at life in general.

A man next to him in a new Lexus lowered the window and said, "What's wrong with you, buddy?"

Jonas pulled the kitchen knife from his waistband, waved it, and said, "Nothing if I could cut your fucking eyes out, you rich cocksucker!"

The Lexus sped away and Jonas turned onto Outpost Drive, moving northbound aimlessly until a thought occurred to him. If he kept on going to Mulholland and veered left, he'd be climbing high into the Hollywood Hills on his way toward Woodrow Wilson Drive. Could the van be going back there? Back to the big house where all this had started in the first place? Where his betrayal had begun?

* * *

Raleigh Dibble made Nigel Wickland remove the bundles from the van at gunpoint while he carried the toolbox into Casa Brueger. Once inside, Raleigh turned on the foyer and corridor lights, and he sat on the carved antique chair with the needlepoint seat cushion, and said, "Go to work, genius."

Nigel sighed, removed his suit coat, opened his collar, loosened his tie, and took down the framed replica of *The Woman by the Water.* He unwrapped the original painting and worked silently, trying not to think about the fact that he'd given away $112,000 of his own money to be right back where he'd started days ago. He was a ruined man now. He saw no way to save his business, not with both his savings and commercial accounts looted. The only silver lining was that there was no more fear of going to prison. But to Nigel Wickland at this moment, prison didn't seem as terrifying as facing old age penniless.

When he removed the replica, he tossed it onto the mover's blanket and replaced the original painting in its frame. Then he removed the framed replica of *Flowers on the Hillside* and did the same. It was slow and tedious because he loved and respected the Impressionist pieces too much to do anything less than his best for them. He felt a sudden sentimental wish that someone who appreciated them as much as he did might possess them someday.

When Nigel was nearly finished, he said, "Could you at least get me another of those Vichy waters?"

Raleigh said, "It was tap water, you supercilious snob. You can have all you want when you're done."

Jonas Claymore had let out a howl of triumph the moment he'd seen the van in the Brueger driveway. He couldn't imagine why the man had come back to the house unless he was making another attempt at selling them the two paintings now that Megan had returned them for 12K. *His* 12K. Gone!

Jonas was getting itchy now. The meth was producing all sorts of side effects that he hadn't felt before, at least not to this extent. His whole body was twitching. He felt like his teeth were twitching. It was all he could do to stand there peeking through the junipers again and not run down and kick in the door and put the knife at the throat of that art dealer who'd double-crossed him with Megan. He could only hope the fucker knew where Megan was holed up. He would make him talk, oh, yes.

Jonas took a piss on the junipers and then passed the time fantasizing about climbing into the window of wherever Megan was staying and cutting her tits off. But they were so small it would be no big loss to her.

"Can you please put the gun away now?" Nigel said when he had both worthless replicas loosely wrapped in the mover's blankets.

Raleigh tucked the gun in his pocket and picked up the toolbox, saying, "You carry the replicas. Maybe you can get a few bucks for them somewhere. They're almost as beautiful as the originals. You might try craigslist."

"I couldn't get enough to pay for the lab work we did," Nigel said. "I'll just use them as remembrances of things past. When I'm residing on skid row."

"You'll be all right, Nigel," Raleigh said. "An English gentleman of your quality can easily get a job doing what I do. I can see you as a domestic servant for a rich old man who needs someone cultured to wipe his ass."

Raleigh Dibble walked outside with Nigel Wickland, who tossed the blanketed replicas onto the floor of the van. "I won't ask you for a ride back to my car, Nigel," Raleigh said. "I'll taxi down and pick it up tomorrow. I think we've seen enough of each other."

Nigel said, "Perhaps I'll have to see you again if Leona still plans to use me to supervise the storage of her artwork. But I certainly hope not."

Raleigh said, "Good-bye, Nigel. Sorry how things have turned out for you. I guess you'll just have to face old age as irrelevant as the rest of us."

Nothing else was said. Raleigh watched the van drive away over the fake cobblestone driveway for the last time. He turned and entered the house, not seeing the one taillight of the little VW bug following the van, and winking at him just as before.

When Raleigh Dibble fell into bed, he knew he'd be able to sleep soundly at last. He didn't have great prospects for a successful future, but he thought that perhaps he'd get a good reference from Leona Brueger before she sold the house and moved away. He thought it would be wonderful if the new buyers of this house needed a butler chef with his skills. He wanted to stay in this house. He liked it here with or without all the artwork.

He was lying in bed with the window open watching moonbeams fluttering across the wall of his bedroom, and he was content. Before drifting off to sleep, he thought of the fragile, charming tulip of a girl with alabaster skin who had kissed his cheek. She was so wistful, so delightfully young. Raleigh Dibble would always remember her as the girl in the candy-striped dress.

TWENTY-SIX

HE DIDN'T NEED to take the trouble to stay behind the cargo van. Jonas knew where it was going and he wanted to be there before the van arrived. He drove so fast that he didn't make the yellow and blew through a red light on Sunset Boulevard. He looked around frantically for a black-and-white but saw none. When he reached Beverly Hills, he pulled onto the side street next to the Wickland Gallery and ran into the alley, relieved to see that he had not been wrong about the red BMW Roadster. It belonged to the fairy art dealer, he was sure of it. The man would be back.

He squeezed his bony body behind the Dumpster in the alley, but since the container was full of trash, he couldn't budge it, and he had trouble folding his tall frame so that his head was not protruding. It was miserable there, and he was still flashing on paranoid thoughts. His discomfort made him ever more furious at what this sissy and Megan had conspired to do to him. He was bent over in an angular squat, listening to all the nighttime traffic on Wilshire Boulevard, when he heard the van enter through the alley. Jonas took the knife from under his sweatshirt, pulled up his hoodie, and got ready to attack.

Nigel thought he'd need to sleep around the clock to recover from this horror. He touched the remote-control button and the door slid open. He drove the van into the storage room, turned off the headlights, and pushed the button to close the door. When he stepped out of the van, the interior van lights stayed on briefly, and he used the light to open the side door and remove the blanketed replicas. He tossed them contemptuously onto the workbench. And then he felt the knife at his throat.

Jonas Claymore, who was even taller than Nigel, grabbed him from behind by the collar of his suit coat and pressed his cheek to Nigel's, saying, "Don't fucking twitch."

"Oh, my god!" Nigel said. "Oh, my lord!"

"Right now I'm your lord," Jonas said. "And you better do what your lord says."

"Anything!" Nigel said, his hands in the air just as before. "Anything!"

"Turn on the lights in here."

"The switch is by the door to my office," Nigel said.

"Move over there real slow," Jonas said.

Nigel could smell the hooded man's body odor. It was foul. He moved awkwardly to the light switch, like a dog whose master had him by the collar, and he switched on the lights.

"Where's my paintings?" Jonas said.

The voice! Yes, it was the thief who'd called him with his demand for a reward. Nigel said, "Sir, please release me and take away the knife so we can talk."

Jonas tightened his grip on Nigel's collar and stayed behind him, saying, "We're gonna talk, but first, where's my paintings?"

"Sir," Nigel said. "I truly don't know what you're talking about."

Jonas said, "I'm talking about cutting your head off like a fucking Eye-raqi dune coon, that's what I'm talking about."

It was too much. Too much terror for one night. It was so unbelievable, he felt like screaming himself awake. But he didn't scream. He peed. Jonas saw it running from under the cuff of Nigel's trousers onto the concrete floor of the storage room.

"You fucking dick-drip," Jonas said. "You pissed your pants."

Nigel Wickland hadn't heard him. The sweat poured from him and he was sobbing, his body heaving so hard against the knife that the blade broke the skin and his throat burned. He managed to say, "Don't hurt me. I'll do anything. I'll give you anything!"

Jonas moved Nigel sideways until they were standing beside the workbench. And he said, "Pull the cloth off those paintings."

Nigel reached over and gave a yank on the mover's blankets, and Jonas stood looking at *The Woman by the Water.* "My paintings!" he bellowed.

"Oh, no!" Nigel said. "Dear god, this can't be happening!"

"Get in there and turn on the light," Jonas said, shoving Nigel forward from the storage room into the office.

"May I sit at my desk?" Nigel said, and he concentrated on one thing: the pistol in his middle drawer. But the drawer was locked!

Jonas said, "Sit!"

Nigel recognized the hooded young man now. He was the panhandler who had come into the gallery just before he and Raleigh left in the van for the Brueger house.

Jonas was feeling omnipotent. He was in total control. He was powerful. He kept moving the blade of the knife twelve inches from Nigel's face, and he enjoyed the naked terror he saw there.

Nigel reached up and ran his fingers across the burn on his throat. He saw the bright blood on his fingers and said, "Sir, I'm hurt."

"You ain't hurt," Jonas said. "Yet."

Nigel's wheezing sounded like radio static, and he said, "Sir, I'm asthmatic. Please let me use my inhaler. I can't breathe."

"Go ahead, but take care," Jonas said.

Nigel drew the inhaler from his pocket, took two puffs, and held his breath.

Jonas looked at him and said, "Hurry the fuck up or it'll be your last breath."

When he could breathe again, Nigel said, "I paid the young

woman the twelve-thousand-dollar reward you wanted. I did everything you asked me to do. Why are you here now? Why am I being treated like this?"

"You and that cunt scammed me," Jonas said. "You made a special deal that I didn't know about. She gave you the paintings behind my back. Did she give you a blow job, too?" Then Jonas said, "On second thought, you wouldn't want one from a girl, would you?"

"Sir," Nigel said. "She did not give me my . . . I mean *your* paintings. Those pictures in the storage room are replicas. They're not the originals."

"Listen, butt-lust," Jonas said. "Don't talk to me like I'm straight-up stupid. I got eyes. Those're my paintings on the workbench. And if you wanna keep *your* eyes, talk to me like I got some brains in my head."

Nigel was weeping now and he cried out, "Dear god! Why won't anyone believe me?"

"Stop your bitch-bawling and talk to me while you still can," Jonas said.

Now Nigel didn't know what to say. How could he be logical with an obviously doped-out maniac? Everything he said would be rejected as a lie. He decided to say what the thief wanted him to say.

"Here's what happened," Nigel said. "Your friend Valerie came here—"

"Megan."

"Right, Megan," Nigel said. "She came here a second time. She said you sent her to give me back my . . . *your* paintings to complete our deal. How was I to know she didn't tell you about it? I assumed you were waiting for her in the car or something. Sir, I did everything you wanted."

"How do I know you didn't give her more money the second time?" Jonas said. "I know those paintings're worth way more than you said."

"They're not, sir," Nigel said. "I haven't been able to sell them."

"Have you tried lately?" Jonas said, eyes narrowing.

"No, I just keep them in my van in case a client seems like a prospect."

"You lie!" Jonas said. "You took them back to that same house tonight. I tailed you, you fucking rump ranger. You got something going with that house and these paintings. They're worth a whole lot, ain't they?"

The sweat had soaked clear through Nigel's shirt. He could only stare at the knife blade floating in front of his face. This gaunt, hooded specter with the menacing eyes would surely begin slashing him if he didn't say the right thing. He said, "Sir, that client wanted to see them again, but he said the same thing as last time, that they're not good enough. But I have an idea. May I share it with you?"

"Go ahead," Jonas said.

"Why don't you just take them with you? I'd be pleased if you would. If perhaps you could sell them and make a few dollars, more power to you. Would you do that, please? Just take the paintings and go. My heart can't withstand this kind of tension. I'm not a well man. I have asthma and a heart murmur."

Jonas said, "You got no shame in your game. So, okay, maybe I'll call your bluff. Maybe I will take my paintings back. But you're still gonna come up with something for all you and that bitch put me through. Now where's Megan at?"

It took Nigel a moment, but he could think of nothing to say except the truth: "I don't know. She didn't say where she was going."

"I think she did," Jonas said. "Your twitchy eye tells me you're lying. And I think she got more money outta you. But me? I got shit for all I went through. You and that cunt thought you could jist hoop my flow and kick me to the curb, didn't ya?"

Nigel opened the expansion band on his wristwatch, tossed it on the desk, and said, "Here, this is a Rolex. Take it. And I've got about a hundred dollars in my wallet. May I get it for you?"

"Yeah, get it," Jonas said.

Nigel reached into his pocket and removed his wallet, tossing it onto the desk next to the Rolex.

Jonas put the wallet and the watch in the pocket of his jeans and said, "The paintings're worth a lotta money, ain't they?"

Nigel sighed and paused and finally said, "Yes."

"I knew you didn't wanna give them back to me. How much're they worth?"

"Thirty thousand, maybe more," Nigel said. "You can get that much from any art dealer in L.A. Take them with you and go. Please go."

"Now we're finally getting at the truth," Jonas said. "So let's have all of it, you fucking pole climber. Where did Megan say she was going to?"

And that did it. Nigel Wickland decided that he was at the end of this night's terrible journey. There was nowhere else to verbally run and hide. He concluded that drug-crazed paranoia trumps logic and lie and everything in between. So he summoned courage born of despair and said, "I've got about three hundred dollars in the petty cash drawer. You can have that, too. May I get it?"

"Get it," Jonas said.

"The drawer's locked," Nigel said.

"Get the key," Jonas said.

Nigel opened a papier-mâché box on his desk, removed a desk key, and unlocked the middle drawer with hands so sweaty he almost dropped the key. Then he opened the drawer and said, "Here it is."

Jonas didn't see the Smith & Wesson 9-millimeter pistol until it was halfway out of the drawer. Then he took a wild swing with the knife and cut Nigel across the mouth, opening up a grotesque smile from the corner of his mouth to his ear. Then a flash and explosion blinded and deafened Jonas for a moment. Nigel had fired a round next to Jonas's face that missed by inches. Jonas dropped the knife and fell onto Nigel's lap, grappling for the gun.

The desk chair overturned and both bodies hit the floor, Nigel screaming and Jonas screaming, as each had hold of the pistol. Then Nigel closed his bloody mouth over his assailant's ear and bit down, grinding the gristle, and Jonas screamed louder than ever. Then it was a test of strength as four hands tried to wrest the pistol free.

Drugs had reduced Jonas's strength by half, but he was much younger, so the struggle was even. They moaned and grunted and growled and occasionally sobbed as they lay face-to-face on the floor. Then, for a brief second when the gun muzzle was pointed up toward the face of Nigel Wickland, Jonas Claymore got a finger through the trigger guard.

The explosion inches from his head made Jonas's ears ring, and the blowback from the muzzle blast hit him in the face. The smell of cordite penetrated his brain, and the 9-millimeter slug penetrated the brain of Nigel Wickland after first passing through his twitching left eye, and that ended the struggle.

Jonas looked at the art dealer in horror, at the macabre bloody smile and the mangled, oozing orbit that would never twitch again, and at the skull fragment lying on the floor beside Nigel's head. He got to his feet, so weak he almost collapsed. Then he turned and ran to the storage room in panic, looking for a button to open the siding door so he could escape. He couldn't find it and then realized that, since the door had opened when the van pulled up to it, there must be a remote control inside the vehicle.

He opened the van door and saw the remote button and was about to push it and run to his car, when a single thought knifed through the panic. The paintings in the blankets, his paintings, were worth $30,000 anywhere! Nigel Wickland had said so. But he couldn't carry them in his VW, so he ran to the body, keeping his eyes averted as he rummaged through the dead man's pockets until he found the key ring. He picked up the bloody knife and the pistol, both of which bore his fingerprints, and he ran back to the store-room, opening the passenger door of the van and throwing the weapons onto the passenger seat.

Then he covered the pictures in the mover's blankets and placed both of them on the floor in the cargo section. He closed the door and, getting behind the wheel, pressed the button on the remote device attached to the visor. He felt a burst of elation when the stor-age room door slid open.

"I'm gonna make it!" Jonas said aloud, and he drove out of the storage room into the alley and headed toward the safety of his apartment in Thai Town.

TWENTY-SEVEN

Six-x-thirty-two was cruising westbound on Sunset Boulevard when Jetsam said, "While I was off, I got thinking about the Wedgie Bandit. You know the apartments by Ivar and Franklin? The white building with all the palm trees in front?"

"Yeah, I think I know which one you're talking about."

"I got thinking that the Wedgie Bandit lives in that building. That's why he strikes more in the vicinity of the library. He don't have to run so far to get home. I worked out a plan."

"What's that?"

"The next time we hear any kind of call about a four-fifteen man anywhere near the library, we haul ass straight for that apartment building. If anything jumps off, we're ready. I'm about the only copper at Hollywood Station who can ID him."

"You can ID the back of him," Flotsam reminded his partner. "He left you in the dust when he shifted to his fourth gear."

"The doofus can run," Jetsam had to admit. "But next time I'm gonna catch him. Losing that guy feels like a stain on my career. I gotta make it right."

"Okay, dude," Flotsam said. Six-X-Thirty-two is gonna be the unit to catch the Wedgie Bandit. If we do, you think the sarge will buy us a pizza?"

*   *   *

Viv Daley said to Georgie Adams, who was the driver in 6-X-76, "Don't rock the boat, Gypsy. I ate the world's hottest curry last night and my stomach's still reeling from the abuse. That's the last time I date a Thai guy in Thai Town."

Georgie Adams said, "Most Thai guys are no taller than me, sis. Didn't you two look funny together?"

"No, I got to enjoy the top of his head after looking at it all night. He had bad hair plugs, and pretty soon I started counting the hairs in each plug when I didn't know what he was talking about. He has a really strong accent, but he's rich and it was a lot nicer than my last date, with a class-action lawyer who pops up on Channel Five every other day with an offer to make you rich. But no more dinners in the Thai guy's 'hood."

"Why would you date a trial lawyer that advertises on TV?"

"We all kiss a frog at least once in our lives."

"Frogs, yes, cobras, no," Georgie said.

She turned the rearview mirror to check her lipstick and Georgie said, "Why do you always have to do that when I'm driving in heavy traffic?"

"You're getting very territorial for a Gypsy boy, aren't you?" Viv said.

Georgie was silent for a moment and then said, "Well, if you're dating short people with bad hair plugs, not to mention slithery trial lawyers, maybe you oughtta do something semiworthwhile for a change and go with me to the track next week. I got a few hundred bucks burning a hole in my checking account."

Viv turned to Georgie with a hint of a smile and finally said, "Okay, it's a date, if you promise to look in your crystal ball like a good Gypsy and pick a couple of winners for us."

A horny businessman on his way home to West L.A. from downtown almost sideswiped 6-X-46. His problem was that he was ogling the streetwalkers who emerged after dark on the east Sunset Boulevard track. Two of the hookers were black and one was white, and they were dressed for duty in tank tops, short skirts or shorts, and leggings or nosebleed stilettos.

"This one's for momma at home with the kiddies," Della Ravelle said to Britney Small when she turned on the red-and-blues and honked him to the curb.

To explain his erratic driving he said to Della, "I'm sorry, Officer. Something blew in my eye."

After she'd written the citation and he was gone, Della said to Britney, "It's another kind of blowing he's interested in. We mighta saved him from a flaming STD, which would be hard to explain to the little missus."

Britney said, "Have you noticed how quiet things have been all week? Hardly any code-three calls."

"That's okay for an old lady like me," Della said. "But I know what follows quiet times. Remember where you work, kiddo."

Britney giggled and said, "Right, I almost forgot. This is fucking Hollywood."

Jonas Claymore was coming down fast from the methamphetamine frenzy, but there was still plenty of residue paranoia. He was in the number-one eastbound lane on Hollywood Boulevard, passing Grauman's Chinese Theatre, and he looked over at Barney the Dinosaur, who was talking to the Incredible Hulk, and both street characters seemed to be looking at him.

Narks! he thought. They're undercover cops. Then he saw Spider-Man say something to Darth Vader, and he was sure they were pointing at him. They were all fucking narks. He suddenly got so terrified he began panting. They wanted him for murder! They wanted to execute him! There were two cars in front of him stopped by heavy traffic at Hollywood and Highland, even though the traffic light was green.

Jonas looked toward Grauman's again. Now Batman was looking at him. Then a second Batman walked to the curb, and he was
looking also. And pointing. They were all narks! Jonas Claymore
pulled the van out into the westbound lane right at the oncoming
traffic and sidewiped the rear fender of a Prius that had swerved
just in time to avoid a head-on crash. Jonas kept driving eastbound
and just failed to make the yellow light, and when the Wickland
Gallery van roared into the busy intersecion, all north and south-
bound traffic had to screech to a stop, causing two whiplashing
rear-enders and lots of horns blowing and a huge traffic snarl. But
Jonas Claymore was past the famous intersection, and the stream
of traffic had thinned, and there were no more narks dressed as
Street Characters staring and pointing at him. He was heading
home. He had escaped them all.

Six-X-Thirty-two was waiting to turn right onto Hollywood Boulevard from Vine Street when the Wickland Gallery van drove past,
heading eastbound.

"Whoa!" Flotsam said. "That's the van that Nate and me checked
out the first night you were off."

Jetsam said, "What was wrong with it?"

"Turns out nothing," Flotsam said. "The guy driving was a
nephew of the owner, but the way I got it from Nate, he shouldn't
be driving it anymore. Wanna check it out, dude?"

"Go for it, bro," Jetsam said. "Nothing else to do."

Flotsam sped around the traffic until he was behind the van and
then turned on his red-and-blue wigwags and beeped his horn. The
van kept going. Then he flicked the switch and hit the siren.

Jonas Claymore had been seeing so many hallucinatory cops
everywhere he looked that he almost didn't recognize real ones.
Then he heard the yowl of the siren and he looked in his sideview
mirror. Now he was sure of it. They were onto him. They were

stalking him. They were going to kill him! He jammed the pedal to the floor and pulled out into the number-one westbound lane, causing all oncoming traffic to swerve right.

Jetsam keyed the hand mike and said, "Six-X-ray-Thirty-two requesting a clear frequency! We're in pursuit!"

After that, he gave the make, model, and color of the van, including the California license plate number. And then, over the din from the wind rushing through their open windows and the yelps of the siren and the RTO's squawking radio voice repeating the streets and direction of travel that Jetsam was yelling into the mike, Flotsam hollered to his partner: "Tell them it's got Wickland Gallery on the side of the van! I want Nate and Viv and Georgie to know who it is!"

The black-and-white Crown Vic suddenly skidded at Hollywood and Bronson after braking for the driver of a Toyota who they figured had to be deaf. And after the radio car got straightened out, Jetsam yelled into the mike, "Cargo van has Wickland Gallery printed on the side panels!"

When the RTO at Communications Division repeated that information, Hollywood Nate, who was already racing toward the pursuit, said to Snuffy Salcedo, "Hey! That's the van I checked out when you were off getting the nose job. Man, there's something going on with that guy."

Six-X-Seventy-six was one of the many units coming from several directions, all hoping to intercept the pursuit vehicle. The driver, Georgie Adams, said to his partner, Viv Daley, "Yo, sis! I think that's the van our boy Jonas Claymore was driving when Nate and Flotsam jammed him, wasn't it?"

Viv Daley cinched her seatbelt a bit tighter and said, "If it's him, I can't wait to hear his explanation this time. Hit it, Gypsy!"

Six-X-Forty-six, the only midwatch unit that was too far away to be racing toward the pursuit, was driven by Della Ravelle, who said to her rookie partner, "Damn, Britney, we had to get that call way up in thirty-one's district. Those lazy bastards're probably screwing off as usual. I wanted you to get in on your first pursuit. And this sounds like a good one. Damn."

"My luck," Britney Small said with a little sigh of resignation.

Jonas Claymore decided that getting anywhere close to his apartment in Thai Town was hopeless. He looked in his rearview mirror and saw at least three cars with red-and-blue lights flashing. There were too many headlights and too many cops and too much traffic. He couldn't go fast enough to shake them. The yelping siren made it hard to think.

Then he thought of where there wouldn't be so much traffic at this time of evening. An area where he could abandon the van and escape into the brush and hide in the darkness where cops couldn't find him. And lately it was an area that he had come to know. He made a hard, sliding, screeching turn northbound on Gramercy Place and then turned westbound on Franklin Avenue. He was heading for the Hollywood Hills.

Della Ravelle said, "Hey, they're coming our way. Maybe we're not completely out of it after all."

"They'll probably double back and head east again," Britney Small said glumly. "With my luck."

The lead chase car, containing the surfer cops, careened up over the sidewalk on the north side of Franklin Avenue to avoid a bicyclist with no lights who'd darted across the wide street at midblock. When the black-and-white came crashing back down onto the street, the Crown Vic was lurching and nosediving. The tires screamed when Flotsam jumped on the brakes, but then he jammed down on the gas pedal again, and silhouettes rocketed past on both sides and horns blared.

Jetsam groaned and said, "Our shop's shaking like a shuttle entering orbit. I think I just got me another muscle spasm."

"Sorry, dude!" Flotsam said, cranking the wheel hard to the right when the car fishtailed again.

"I'm gonna try to parallel them on Yucca," Hollywood Nate said to Snuffy Salcedo, who once again cinched up his seat belt and replied, "Is this any way to treat an old man with a new nose?"

Georgie Adams was doing his best to stay close to 6-X-32 by riding in their siren draft, but he drifted back a few car lengths when they hit heavy traffic at Cahuenga and even worse traffic at Highland.

Jonas Claymore was beyond reckless now and he simply blew across Highland Avenue heading west with complete disregard for the red light and the traffic moving north and south. He caused three fender benders before he miraculously crossed the busy thoroughfare and kept going west. That slowed Flotsam and Jetsam, who had to weave around the traffic collisions, siren still blaring, and it allowed Georgie Adams and Viv Daley time to catch up.

By then, Lieutenant O'Reilly and Sergeant Murillo were monitoring the chase in the office. The lieutenant was almost apoplectic because of the dangers posed to motorists by this wild pursuit.

"Get on tac! Get on tac!" he yelled to Sergeant Murillo. "There're too many units involved. Tell them to drop off!"

But of course in a pursuit like this, with adrenaline erupting and endorphins exploding, the risen Christ couldn't have made them drop off, and Sergeant Murillo knew it. Still, he issued the order on the tactical frequency, knowing that none of his coppers would listen to a drop-off order at this moment. And they didn't.

When Jonas Claymore made the northbound turn onto Outpost Drive, he felt like cheering. This seemed familiar. This seemed possible. This was the area he'd been casing with that bitch that deserted him. This was Bling Ring country. This was the Hollywood Hills!

Della Ravelle and Britney Small were still driving east on Woodrow Wilson Drive approaching Mulholland Drive when they heard Jetsam yelling into the open mike that the pursuit had turned north on Outpost.

"No shit!" Della Ravelle said, making a hard right turn onto Mulholland.

The Wickland Gallery van careened north on Outpost Drive with three midwatch units behind it. And when 6-X-46 heard Jetsam yelling into the mike that the van was now turning west on Mulholland, Della Ravelle said to her young partner, "They're coming right at us! Unlock the shotgun!"

She turned on her red-and-blues and her high beams to get the Mulholland traffic out of the way of the pursuit that was coming right at them. Jonas Claymore saw those lights in the distance just after he passed the big house where he'd first stolen this van. He was hyperventilating and had trouble filling his lungs, and now with cops behind him and cops ahead of him he considered bailing out, but then thought, No, not here. He was going to bail by the big house where it had all started. Where he had first set eyes on this vehicle that was taking him to his destiny.

He made a sliding, squealing U-ee and was heading back down only a hundred yards away from the cars coming up. And then he lost it. He veered too far right and hit a large steel mailbox in front of a view home and the van went skidding left on a collision course with the first chase car.

Flotsam yelled, "Hang on, partner!" And tried to crank it left to swing around the fishtailing van coming right at them, but their Crown Vic was T-boned and got spun into a 360, crashing into a eucalyptus tree before coming to a steaming stop.

The van had almost rolled, but another eucalyptus saved it from turning over, and Jonas felt the hardest jolt he'd ever felt in his life when the driver's side of the van slammed into that tree, the hubcaps cartwheeling across the asphalt. And then he had to get out. He had only seconds. He crawled across the passenger seat. He could look out and hear yelling. He could see cops running with flashlights. His left hand was on the floor and it found the pistol. He wasn't going down easy, not for murder.

He took the pistol with him and bailed out the door and limped toward the brush, where he thought he'd be safe. Where they'd never find him. Where he'd have time to wait them out and then go home. He had money. If he could just get away from this place. If he could get to a taxi, he could still make it!

But Jonas didn't make it to the thick brush on the hillside. He almost limped right into a small figure with a flashlight. He heard a woman's voice behind the beam of light yelling, "Drop it! Drop it!"

He didn't drop it. He raised the pistol toward the flashlight, toward the voice, and Britney Small fired her Glock from ten feet away.

Jonas Claymore saw the first fireball and that was all. Two of the .40 caliber rounds missed him completely but three slammed into his bony chest and sunken belly. He went down on his back, eyes open, and they never closed again.

There was pandemonium then, with Della Ravelle running to Britney, her shotgun pointed at the supine body of Jonas Claymore. And Viv Daley came running with her shotgun, and Georgie Adams pointed his pistol at the unmoving body.

Hollywood Nate and Snuffy Salcedo helped pry open Flotsam's door. He had blood on his face and on one hand, but he wouldn't get out of the car. He was yelling at them, "Get an RA! Now, god-damnit!" Then he turned to Jetsam, who was moaning in agony, his right foot trapped by mangled metal, and Flotsam said, "Easy, bro! Easy, partner! We'll get you outta here!"

It took both Hollywood Nate and Snuffy to pull and pry at the passenger door of 6-X-32's Crown Vic before they got it open, and when Nate shined his light onto Jetsam's right foot, he yelled to Viv Daley, "Get me a tourniquet or a belt or anything!"

By the time the rescue ambulance arrived, Jetsam was lying on the roadside and was going gray. Kneeling beside him, Flotsam waved away Della, who'd torn open a first-aid kit and wanted to tend to the bleeding contusion at Flotsam's hairline.

He kept saying to his partner, "Easy, bro. Stay with me. Don't go nowhere, bro. Stay here with me. I ain't gonna leave you, so don't you leave me!"

The tall surfer cop insisted on riding in the back of the ambulance when they loaded Jetsam aboard, and he talked to him all the way to Cedars-Sinai, even when the paramedic said that the officer was showing signs of shock and wouldn't understand him. Flotsam remained outside the ER until Hollywood Nate and Snuffy Salcedo came to get him and transport him to Hollywood Station.

Before they were separated and before Force Investigation Division arrived at the station, Della Ravelle took her rookie partner to the women's locker room and said to the shaken young woman, "You have nothing to fear from FID or anybody else, Britney. It was an in-policy shooting, a good shooting."

"Funny thing," the young cop said. "It doesn't seem right to call killing somebody a good shooting. It doesn't feel good. I don't feel good."

"He's dead and you're alive," Della said. "That's good. Very good."

"He was my age," Britney said.

"And you would never have gotten a day older if you hadn't done what you did," Della said. "Now listen to me. After you get interrogated and after they say you can return to duty, you're gonna be treated different. The male cops, particularly the macho OGs, will pat you on the back and praise you and show you some deference. You won't get treated like a rookie anymore."

"Because I killed somebody?" Britney said.

"Because you've proven yourself to them," Della said. "Just go with it and smile politely and you'll find that your job will go better in this man's world we live in. From now on, you won't be a little female boot they make fun of. They'll respect you and even admire you. Like it or not, girl, you're now an authentic and bona fide gunfighter."

* * *

By daybreak, both Hollywood Division and Beverly Hills homicide detectives had worked out what had transpired at Wickland Gallery on Wilshire Boulevard. Their reports said that Jonas Claymore, who had recently been arrested for felony possession of controlled substances, had probably been in a drug-induced state when he'd entered the gallery and caught Nigel Wickland by surprise in a blitz attack, cutting his face with a knife that was found in the wrecked van. There were signs of a life-and-death struggle in which Nigel Wickland apparently managed to get his hands on a Smith & Wesson 9-millimeter pistol registered to him. However, he was overcome in the struggle and was shot dead by the assailant, who then stole the gallery owner's wallet and wristwatch, which were found in Jonas Claymore's pocket after he was shot and killed.

Because an art gallery wasn't the kind of business that would be a normal target for this kind of attack, the detectives made a note that the gallery owner was openly homosexual. They surmised that because Jonas Claymore was a handsome young man, he may have had a past intimate relationship with the victim, a relationship that had soured and turned violent. The fact of the van having been in Jonas Claymore's possession on at least one other occasion when officers of Hollywood Division had questioned him tended to validate the theory of an intimate relationship between victim and assailant.

By the next afternoon, Ruth Langley, the only employee of the Wickland Gallery, told detectives through copious tears that she was led to believe that the young man who had borrowed her employer's van on the prior occasion was his nephew. Nigel Wickland had described him as a kind of black sheep. But the deceased killer's mother, who lived in Encino, denied that they were related to Nigel Wickland. She could offer no explanation for her son's bizarre behavior other than that he had been using drugs heavily and had lately been living with a young woman whose name she did not know. Jonas Claymore's mother suggested that the young woman had no doubt enticed her son into the drug use that led to his death.

Ruth Langley of Wickland Gallery could not account for the poster-board photographs of two Impressionist paintings that were found in the wrecked van. She told detectives that they must have been something that Nigel Wickland had picked up from one of the many art dealers he knew, perhaps to frame and hang in his condominium. She told the detectives that the pictures had no value other than as decorative art and that she would like to have them as mementos of her years working at the Wickland Gallery.

Two days after the murder of Nigel Wickland, Hollywood Nate Weiss went to Cedars-Sinai before reporting for duty at Hollywood Station. The floor nurse told him that the patient's mother and two sisters had just been there, and the patient's father had visited separately. She added that the police partner of the patient was in his room now and that the patient should only have visitors for brief periods of time.

She asked Nate if he was aware that the patient's foot could not be saved, and Nate said that everyone at Hollywood Station knew about it. She said that if he wished, he could join the officer and the patient's partner for a little while but added that the patient would soon need to rest.

Hollywood Nate walked down the corridor and was surprised that his palms were moist. He didn't know what he'd say to Jetsam other than something trite: "You're looking great. Are they treating you okay? Everyone sends their best. Is there anything you need? Anything at all?"

Nate stopped at the door to Jetsam's room to try to think of something better to say and he heard the voices from inside. He decided to listen to them for cues on how he should handle this. Flotsam's voice sounded somber even though his words were meant to be uplifting. Jetsam just sounded feeble.

Flotsam said, "Dude, I talked to the captain, and you don't have to worry about only working the desk when you come back. You'll be working in the field with me just like always."

"With one foot? They might as well retire me," Jetsam said.

"I been talking to people," Flotsam said. "LAPD once had a cop with one hand. He got it blown off by a bomb. He got a cool prosthesis. The gangsters started calling him Captain Hook. He was, like, kinda famous after that. And we had some coppers that got an eye shot out. They stayed on the Job and did good work."

"A cop's gotta be able to walk, bro. A cop's gotta be able to run."

"You'll walk. You'll run. I been talking to people about the kind of prosthetic foot they can give you. It's gonna be better than your old foot, dude. You'll be good to go. You'll see."

"My foot, it hurts bad sometimes, but it ain't there. They call it phantom pain."

"I know," Flotsam said.

"I wouldn't mind so much but . . . but I'm a surfer."

"You're a *great* surfer," Flotsam said. "You're way better than me, dude. You're way better than I ever could be. Why, I seen you do chocka backsides that nobody at Malibu could do. You're a crusher. Nothing can stop you."

"I don't wanna lay on the beach like a stranded seal and just watch," Jetsam said. "I wouldn't wanna do that."

"That ain't gonna happen," Flotsam said. "Sure, maybe at first we gotta take it easy. I'm gonna take you to Malibu every day if you wanna go, and we'll let the ocean heal you. The ocean is a great healer. And soon as you're ready, we're gonna get you that new foot. They can make you a prothesis that'll grip that board like Elmer's Glue."

"What'll I do at the beach till it heals, bro?"

"We'll bodysurf or boogie board."

"I ain't no booger, bro. Can you see me, like, sponging-in on a real kahuna and getting in his way like some snarky squid?"

"Dude, the boogie board would be temporary till we heal," Flotsam said. "Till we get our new foot."

"I guess the Wedgie Bandit's safe now, bro," Jetsam said.

Flotsam said, "Trust me. Real soon it's gonna be us two kahunas ripping like always. And we'll get that Wedgie Bandit, you and me. Don't cry, dude."

"You'e the one that's crying, bro," Jetsam said. "In case you didn't notice."

Hollywood Nate turned then and walked back down the corridor past the nurse's station, heading for the exit.

The floor nurse said, "Aren't you going in?"

"Not today," said Hollywood Nate. "Not today."

TWENTY-EIGHT

THE SECOND YEAR of the Obama presidency saw big changes at the Los Angeles Police Department. The Eastern chief had resigned and moved back to New York to take a top job with the private security firm that had been overseeing the federal consent decree under which the LAPD had suffered for so many years. Some said that his connection to that security firm had been a conflict of interests, but the fact was, he was gone for good.

The new chief was not an outsider, far from it. He was second-generation LAPD. His father had been a deputy chief. His son and daughter were both LAPD officers, and his wife was retired from the L.A. Sheriff's Department. Even his sister was a retired cop. They didn't come more insider than this one. He inherited the tough job of being chief in the great recession that had just about bankrupted the state of California, and the city of Los Angeles right along with it. There had to be lots of maneuvering of personnel, including sending a large number of officers from the elite Metropolitan Division back to patrol.

But there was at least one officer going from patrol back to Metro. One quiet evening on patrol, Snuffy Salcedo said to Hollywood Nate, "I went downtown and talked to a few people and I'm gonna be taken back as a security aide to the new chief."

"Is it my deodorant?" Nate said. "What brought this about?"

"Don't get me wrong, partner," Snuffy said. "I've really enjoyed working here at Hollywood Station, and it hasn't been too awful having you as a partner."

"I'll put that in my diary," Nate said.

Snuffy said, "But I think for the next few years, till I pull the pin and say adios, I should take it easy. And the new chief ain't nothing like Mister. So I see myself driving for him for three more years and then I'll retire and spend the rest of my life cutting grass and trimming trees like a typical Mexican gardener, except it'll be my grass and my trees."

"Was it stuff like the rumble at Goth House that made you wanna leave Hollywood?" Nate asked.

"Naw," Snuffy said. "It was fun tuning up Rolf Thunder, sort of. I even got a new and better nose out of it. It's just that patrol needs people who have real thick skin. Young people. So they can look at stuff like that baby in Little Armenia and go home and say, That's not my tragedy. That's somebody else's tragedy. That has nothing to do with me. When you get old like me, the skin thins out and bleeds."

"Who's gonna bring me homemade enchiladas then?" Nate said. "Tell me that."

"You'll find some other Mexican whose mother can cook," Snuffy said.

Nate said, "On this sad occasion I'd like to devote a few minutes to my own future. Would you mind if I stop by a house in the Hollywood Hills? I gotta see a director about making me a star."

"Anything you wanna do," Snuffy Salcedo said. "I'm just a short-timer along for the ride."

Nate drove up Mulholland Drive to the vicinity of the crash that had cost Jetsam his foot and Jonas Claymore his life. He stopped at the gate of a particularly large estate and pressed the button.

A man's voice answered and Nate said, "This is Officer Nate Weiss. I'd like to see Mr. Ressler if he's there."

The male voice spoke to someone and came back, saying, "Come in."

Nate and Snuffy Salcedo entered the gate, driving over the faux-cobblestone driveway, then circled around the fountain and parked next to the front door.

"Just be a minute," Nate said and got out.

"Take your time," Snuffy said. "I'll have a siesta."

Raleigh Dibble opened the door and said, "Good to see you again, Officer Weiss. Mrs. Brueger is in the great room."

Nate found her in silk pajamas and a matching peignoir, sitting on a lounge with a glass of wine beside her and a copy of *Cosmopolitan* in her lap. The music coming from surrounding speakers was Duke Ellington's "In a Sentimental Mood," one of Nate's favorite background melodies for any movie that promised glamour and sophistication.

"My, my, Nathan," she said. "You're even more handsome in uniform."

"Evening, Mrs. Brueger," Nate said.

She said, "It's Leona, remember? Can Raleigh get you anything to drink? Coffee, maybe?"

"No, thanks," Nate said. "My partner's waiting."

"Bring him in," Leona Brueger said. "Or her."

"Can't stay but a minute," Nate said. "The reason I'm here is that I've called Mr. Ressler half a dozen times in the last few months and only hooked up with him once. He said he'd be starting to prep his movie in February, but here it is March and I haven't heard anything. He hasn't returned my calls lately. You said you might be able to help me get this job and, well, here I am. Hopes and dreams, remember?"

Leona took another sip of wine and said, "Oh, Nathan, I'm so glad I'm not an actor. The truth of it is, after we got back from Europe, things went from bad to worse for poor Rudy. His investors pulled the plug on him and the project died, but he doesn't want to admit it to anyone. That's probably why he's dodging your calls. He's scratching and clawing and trying to stay afloat, but the fact of the matter is, his career is circling the drain. He's drifting into irrelevancy, and in Hollywood that's Hell's last circle. A living death. I'm sure you know that the irrelevant are Hollywood's zombies."

Nate was silent for a moment and said, "I see."

"Aren't you used to it yet, Nathan?" Leona Brueger asked. "The rejection?"

"I should be," Nate said.

The phone buzzed and Nate heard Raleigh Dibble answer it in the butler's pantry, and then Raleigh entered the great room.

He said, "Mr. Brueger needs his heating pad and perhaps a back rub. I'll be in the cottage, Mrs. Brueger."

"Fine, Raleigh," Leona said.

After Raleigh was gone, she said to Nate, "My brother-in-law had a stroke last year but he's doing pretty well for a codger his age. I think he'd be dead without Raleigh. I can't imagine a more dedicated caregiver, not to mention that he's a fine butler and a divine chef. I'm so lucky to have him. I'll never let him go."

"Give my regards to Mr. Ressler, please," Nate said and turned to leave.

"Oh, he's gone the way of all second-raters," Leona said boozily. "He was only going to marry me for my money, which was okay with me until his limited charm ran out in Tuscany. I've decided not to move to Napa. I'll just drink wine and forget about making it. I think this house in the Hollywood Hills is a good place to grow old in. What do you think, Nathan?"

"It's a beautiful home," Nate said.

"Money is an answer," she said. "How soothing money is when we can't attain our real dreams. Thousands of failed actors will never know that because they'll never see enough of it."

"That sounds like me you're talking about," Nate said. "If I was a method actor, I'd think of a grapefruit or something else I hate and start crying now."

"Why don't you visit me from time to time, Nathan?" she said. "Who knows? I might meet another director. Maybe even a first-rate director who could actually promote you. Maybe I can help you keep your dream alive. Would you like that?"

He was silent for a moment and remembered what this fire-proof aging woman had said to him when they'd first met: that in Hollywood everything is for sale if you know how to shop. Then Nate said, "Somehow I don't think I'm ever gonna see my name on the curb at one of the studios. Thank you anyway,...Mrs. Brueger. I gotta get back to my beat now."

Leona Brueger gave him a long look, and then with a sigh of resignation and sadness she said, "Bye-bye, gorgeous."

Snuffy Salcedo was gone from Hollywood Station on the next transfer. And Hollywood Nate found himself teamed with Flotsam again during the new deployment period.

On their first night together in early March, Nate said, "How's your partner?"

Flotsam said, "Dude, my li'l pard's not only ready to come back to the Job, he's ready to try out his new foot at Malibu. I am totally amped. We been going to the beach for months and I think he's ready to go for it. I know for sure he's ready to do police work, but surfing, that's another story. But if anybody can do it, he can."

At 8 P.M., a call was given to 6-X-46 to see the woman at a souvenir shop on Hollywood Boulevard. It seemed that the Wedgie Bandit was back. He'd slipped into the store with a clutch of customers, and when an attractive young woman was bent over a shelf examining some Hollywood memorabilia, he sidled up behind her, grabbed her underwear, and gave her a world-class wedgie.

Nate said to Flotsam, "Hey, I've had some thoughts about the Wedgie Bandit and where he lives in relation to the library. You know that apartment building on Franklin near Ivar? The white one? Let's just post up over there and see who we find running home in a hurry."

Hollywood Nate was heading for Franklin Avenue when Flotsam said, "Dude, the Wedgie Bandit's a series offender. He likes to do a few jobs at one time. Maybe we should check the subway station. There's lotsa potential victims down there."

"I like my idea," Nate said. "Let's first check out the apartment building on Franklin."

Flotsam said, "Maybe he headed for Grauman's. All those tourists looking at Batman and Spider-Man? They'd never notice that little freakazoid sneaking up behind them."

The urgency in the surfer cop's voice puzzled Nate for a moment, but then he remembered the hospital conversation and he got it. Nate said, "Maybe you're right. My idea is dumb. Let's cruise on over to Grauman's Chinese Theatre. The Wedgie Bandit's probably there right now going after big game. Maybe the Green Lantern or even Darth Vader if he can get under Darth's cape."

Flotsam grinned in relief when Nate turned away from the apartment building on Franklin Avenue and headed west. He said gratefully, "Dude, until my li'l pard gets back, I gotta teach you some vocabulary so we can, like, communicate as equals, okay? Now to start with, a fibro is a surfboard."

"Fibro," Nate said. "Got it."

"Getting tubed is when you're inside the wave, right? So it might apply to certain things in life."

"Roger that," Nate said. "Getting tubed."

"A goat-boater is one of those donks that kayaks into our surf. So that's a pushy dude."

Nate said, "Never goat-boat the kahunas. How am I doing?"

"You're boglius, dude," Flotsam said. "That means you are one coolaphonic copper and it is rad to be sharing your shop for a while."

Nate said wistfully, "And I guess being a coolaphonic copper is even better than being a movie star the way you see things."

"That is rightous, dude. So, are you, like, finally coming around to that conclusion in your own life? Has the old acting bug been sorta swatted?"

"No way," said Nate. "It's just been on hiatus. I'm still determined to grow old and die in the Motion Picture and Television Country House. You can come see me when I'm there and feed me Jell-O shots. Just check my diaper if you bring fastidious people with you, and pour some premium vodka in my sippy cup when the nurses aren't looking."

"Whatever happened to your movie connection up in the Hollywood Hills? Where we dropped the business card on the butler that time?"

"Didn't work out," Hollywood Nate said. "I've seen *Sunset Boulevard* too many times."

"What's that supposed to mean?"

"Joe Gillis always ends up facedown in the swimming pool."

"He shoulda went to the beach," Flotsam said, "where they got lifeguards."

"Speaking of old movies," Nate said, "we'd better head for Grauman's Chinese Theatre right this minute before we're too late."

"Go for it," Flotsam said. "It'd be way wack and totally bleak if little kids witnessed the dude giving a humungous wedgie to Batman."

"And can you even imagine the shock and awe on the Walk of Fame," Hollywood Nate added, "if that fiend had the gall to give a wedgie to, let's say, Marilyn Monroe? Oh, the horror! Would it be scenery chewing to drive there code three?"

ABOUT THE AUTHOR

JOSEPH WAMBAUGH, a former LAPD detective sergeant, is the bestselling author of nineteen prior works of fiction and nonfiction, including *The Choirboys* and *The Onion Field*. In 2004, he was named Grand Master by the Mystery Writers of America. He lives in Southern California.